P9-CFB-202

THE MERRY RECLUSE

Also by Caroline Knapp

Drinking: A Love Story

Pack of Two: The Intricate Bond Between People and Dogs

Alice K's Guide to Life: One Woman's Quest for Survival, Sanity, and the Perfect New Shoes

Appetites: Why Women Want

THE MERRY RECLUSE

A LIFE IN ESSAYS

CAROLINE KNAPP

COUNTERPOINT
A MEMBER OF THE PERSEUS BOOKS GROUP
NEW YORK

Copyright © 2004 by Caroline Knapp

Published by Counterpoint
A Member of the Perseus Books Group

All rights reserved. Printed in the United States of America. No part of this book may be reproduced in any manner whatsoever without written permission except in the case of brief quotations embodied in critical articles and reviews. For information, address Counterpoint, 387 Park Avenue South, New York, NY 10016.

Set in 11-point Goudy

Counterpoint books are available at special discounts for bulk purchases in the United States by corporations, institutions, and other organizations. For more information, please contact the Special Markets Department at the Perseus Books Group, 11 Cambridge Center, Cambridge MA 02142, or call (617) 252-5298, (800) 255-1514, or e-mail special.markets@perseusbooks.com.

Library of Congress Cataloging-in-Publication Data

Knapp, Caroline, d. 2002
The merry recluse : a life in essays / by Caroline Knapp.
p. cm.
ISBN 1-58243-313-5 (alk. paper)
1. Knapp, Caroline, d. 2002. 2. Journalists—United States—Bibliography. I. Title.
PN4874.K575A3 2004
070.92—dc22

2003028184

04 05 06 / 10 9 8 7 6 5 4 3 2 1

CONTENTS

IN HERE, 219

Reflections

THE MERRY RECLUSE, 269

Solitude, Shyness, Loneliness

INTRODUCTION

THE MERRY RECLUSE?

The truth is, we had some debate about the aptness of this title, centered on whether it accurately reflected the weight and seriousness of Caroline Knapp's talent and intelligence. Indeed, the work for which Caroline has been most widely known has been nothing if not serious: In "Appetites: Why Women Want," she explored, via her own harrowing experience with anorexia, the way culture controls women's bodies. In "Pack of Two," she examined the complexity of our attachment to our pets, and in "Drinking, A Love Story," she fearlessly faced sobering truths about her addiction to alcohol.

As her longtime friend and former editor, I'm delighted that this collection—and its title essay—will show readers an often overlooked but essential facet of Caroline's work, and thereby give a richer, more detailed picture of her, as a writer and a woman.

To understand what I mean, a little deconstruction is in order. "The Merry Recluse" is a snappy and provocative title, created by Caroline for what she hoped would become a series of columns about her ongoing attempt to balance the life of solitude she preferred with the more public life her writing demanded. In fact, I think the term "Merry Recluse" portrays exactly how she and many writers live in order to do our work: a reclusiveness that can border on the pathological, although at the same time it feels absolutely necessary. This reclusiveness isn't about shutting out life, only the demands that can sometimes obscure our scrutiny, reflection and—especially for Caroline—our delight in the world around us.

Caroline was always precise in the words she chose. That's why this collection is not called "The Jolly Recluse" or "The Happy Recluse." The word "merry" suggests something a little less goofy than "jolly," and slightly less innocent than "happy"; to me, it suggests the kind of knowing amusement that perfectly embodies Caroline's view of the world.

The pieces collected here span a career, and are a great illustration of Caroline's view of the world. Although her career was cut short when she died in 2002, she left behind a body of work extraordinary not only for its quantity but for its breadth. In four books, a large body of freelance work, and a weekly column she wrote for nearly ten years, she explored love and friendship, grief and loss, cars and purses, men and women, ambivalence and passion, solitude and intimacy. She had a rare talent, in her life and in her writing, for marrying her demons to her angels, resulting in work that was deeply felt, compassionate, and insightful.

She was also wickedly funny.

Take her peeves. Almost twice a year for ten years, she devoted her *Boston Phoenix* column to itemizing the annoyances of life. Here's a small sampling:

> Here are some things that bug me these days.
>
> • *Boundary violations within the food industry*. Have you noticed this? Life Savers now makes their own version of popscicles. Certs makes fruit-flavored breath mints. Snickers and Mars bars have branched into ice cream. I don't like this. Certs should not be dabbling in fruit: it seems against the laws of nature somehow and I find it unsettling.
>
> • *Drag queens*. Sorry; sick of hearing about 'em, sick of reading about 'em, just generally sick of 'em.
>
> • *People who think I'm interested in their dreams*.
>
> • *Watching other people eat corn-on-the-cob*. Corn-on-the-cob is one of the most truly disgusting foods to watch other people eat—the kernels get stuck in their teeth, and they get butter all over their chins, and they become totally focussed on the cob, and every time corn-on-the-cob makes an appearance at a dinner table, you have to endure an

interminable conversation about whether or not it's best to eat it in horizontal rows or in circles. I think corn-on-the-cob ought to be reclassified as a controlled substance, to be eaten in private.

• *Hurricane names*. Hurricanes should have strong, fast, powerful names, like Hera or Athena. But Bertha? Agnes? Why so ugly?

• *Errands*. Don't you feel sometimes as though life is simply the stuff that happens during the few small spaces when you're not doing errands? This occurred to me the other day: here I am, going to the store to get milk for the 892nd time, and stopping at the bank to get cash for the 934th time, and driving to the drugstore to get shampoo and toilet paper and cotton balls for the 756th time, and when you toss in trips to the post office and the hardware store and the grocery store and the shoe-repair guy and the gas station and the coffee store, your entire life feels like one giant errand. This is why I have become such a devotee of catalogue shopping, although that creates its own set of annoyances. To wit:

• *Returning stuff you get from catalogues*. It is disappointing enough to order something from a catalogue and have it fail on you (wrong size, wrong color, bad fabric), but then you have to repackage the whole thing, schlep it to the post office, and pay to have it shipped back, which not only adds insult to injury but also involves an errand. Feh. I think the catalogue companies should make a deal with UPS, in which the UPS man delivers the catalogue package, waits patiently by the door while you go try stuff on, and then simply hauls away what you decide you don't want. Much more effective.

Keep the material, change the venue to a stage and the writer to a stand-up comedian, and you wouldn't be too far off. Of course, the idea of Caroline as a stand-up comic, as shy as she was, cannot be imagined. But she had everything else a great comic needs: a keen eye for life's absurdities, an intolerance for fools, and a pitch-perfect delivery. And I've never known anyone who could utter "feh" with the same combination of relish and disgust.

In Boston, where the talent pool is deep with writers, being an editor can be easy work. It was never easier than when I was a *Boston Phoenix* editor looking for a columnist and met Caroline in

1987. Soon after, we launched her column, which we called "Out There." The column became a mix of reported pieces, and more personal explorations of her life.

Though I was her editor for a relatively brief time, I was a friend for far longer. In some ways, my friendship with Caroline was the least complicated relationship I've known, in part because our friendship was grounded in our work. When I moved from Boston to Philadelphia, we communicated almost daily, usually via e-mail, that friend to all recluses, sharing work as well as details of our life; for both of us, the distinction was not always clear.

Reviewing and collecting this work of hers, then, is a return to familiar ground for me, although reading it with fresh eyes, I'm struck with how relevant, moving, and hilarious it is.

I'm also struck with how strongly this collection stands as a testament to a writer's evolution. Readers familiar with Caroline's books will recognize the origins of much of that work here, in her earlier columns. Although we've presented this work thematically rather than strictly chronologically, it's easy to witness a writer's increasing maturity and growing sophistication.

This collection also shows the evolution of a human, one intensely engaged in finding her truth. As Caroline knew, it's the nature of truth to be constantly shifting, eluding our full grasp. It usually reveals itself to us only in parts, and then, rarely kindly. Caroline sought her truth relentlessly, almost from the time she began her writing career, until the very end. As a result, for many people, she made the path to their own truth a little brighter.

And, at least for me, a little merrier.

Sandra Shea
December 2003

WITH

Friendship, Family,
Love, Lucille

ON BEING A TWIN

RIGHT BEFORE MY twin sister and I were born, the doctor listened for heartbeats and only heard one. "There's just one baby in there," he assured my mother, who was certain she felt more than one set of limbs kicking around. "Just one," he repeated. "Trust me."

Rebecca was delivered first, a six-pound baby girl. The doctor held her up with a flourish, prounounced our mother finished, and left the room. Mom lay there for a while longer, sure there was a second baby, moaning with more contractions, but the nurse didn't believe her, either. "It's just your body expelling the placenta," she said. "Like little aftershocks." A few minutes later, while the nurse's back was turned, my head crowned. When she turned around, the nurse screamed and nearly fainted.

My sister and I grew up on that story; over time, it would acquire the quality of a myth: we were synchronized, so close as to be indistinguishable. We were twins, and that made our relationship special.

With 35 years as a twin behind me, I still see kernels of truth in that logic: Rebecca and I do share a rare sort of bond, a depth of kinship that's nearly impossible to duplicate in other relationships. In our closest moments, we do all the things you might expect of twins: we communicate in a kind of emotional shorthand, often finishing each other's sentences, conveying volumes in the simplest gestures—a raised eyebrow here for irony, a wry smile there for understanding. A few times a year, I'll pick up the phone to call her and find her on the line, having called me at precisely the same moment. I'll hear dead air on the line for a second, then say, "Becca?" She'll say, "Caroline?" And then we'll both marvel at our timing. Our hearts, you might say, are still in synch.

At the same time, the myth of our perfect closeness is also just that: a myth, a fantasy that's deeply seductive but also difficult to live up to. Twinship, after all, begs a question about identity, one that all close sisters probably struggle with to some extent: if you can't hear the beat of your own heart, who are you?

We aren't identical, which I've always considered a mercy. As well as being older (by a life-defining seven minutes; she's always been considered my "big sister"), Rebecca is taller (two inches), heavier (15 pounds), and darker. If you saw us on the street, you'd think "sisters," though not necessarily "twins," and we've both found that fact helpful, as though it's kept us from feeling too merged. The idea of looking at a sibling and seeing your own image reflected back has always seemed eerie to me, a little too close for comfort.

Being a fraternal twin is close enough. You grow up fielding the same question over and over—adults lean over and ask, "Which one are *you*?"—and after a while you can't help wondering the same thing: well, which one *am* I? Separating, learning to define ourselves independently of one another, has been difficult and complex, a delicate dance of individuation that my sister and I have choreographed carefully, often unconsciously, over many years. Without being quite aware of it, we learned to stake out different territory from an early age, to divide up an invisible set of pies: the talent pie, the temperament pie, the lifestyle pie. Our agreements were always tacit, the terms clear only in retrospect: you be this, I'll be that; you excel here, I'll excel there. As a kid, she was good at math and science; I did better in English. She was the athletic one; I was the bookworm. She was assertive, a bit of a loner; I was shy, a conformist.

In high school, we began to wear such differences, and quite literally. Rebecca chose earthy, understated, vaguely preppy clothing: khaki pants and wool sweaters and hiking boots, not a trace of makeup. I followed the fashions of times much more self-consciously, wearing hip-hugging jeans and lots of eyeliner, plucking my eyebrows into thin lines, growing talon-length fingernails. These were our uniforms of autonomy, ways of announcing to the outside world that we were, in fact, two very distinct individuals. Sometimes the strategy worked, sometimes it didn't. Rebecca and I are continually astonished by the number of people who come up to us, look from one to the other, and say, "So. Are you two identical?" Mostly, we just groan quietly at that question, but on occasion we'll get fed up with it and shoot back with a response we developed during college. "We used to be . . . ," one of us will say, pausing for effect. "*Until the accident.*" A lot of outsiders seem to cling to the idea that twins are actually the same person, clones instead of mere siblings. Our retort may not disabuse them of that notion, but it usually shuts them up.

As Rebecca and I entered early adulthood, our dance of individuation became more complex, extending beyond matters of taste and style. We've chosen utterly different paths: I am single; she's married and has a child; I'm a city-dwelling writer; she's a suburban doctor; I'm a two-pack-a-day smoker/die-hard coffee drinker/recovering alcoholic; her drug of choice is tea. Herb tea. And an occasional cup of Postum. In ways, these differences feel oddly deliberate, as though we've both worked hard to keep ourselves distinct, to prevent the threads of our lives from becoming too entangled. *You stay in your territory*, we seem to say to one another, *and I'll stay in mine*.

And yet we've never strayed too far from one another, either, never quite lost sight of each other's emotional whereabouts. That's part of the dance, too: maintain distance but don't sacrifice availability, don't surrender the connecting threads entirely. That effort is reflected most dramatically in the fact that we are almost never in crisis at the same time. If you plotted our lives on a graph, you'd see the lines marking our respective victories and failures peaking and falling at opposite points: during my last major relationship failure, she got married; during her last major bout of professional self-doubt crisis, I wrote a book. We seem to do this with strong emotions, too. Two years ago, in the aftermath of our mother's death, we literally, if unconsciously, took turns grieving: she'd call me in tears when I was feeling strong; I'd go to pieces almost as soon as she put herself back together. There's an uncanny rhythm to these shifts, as though we literally hand off emotions to one another, pass the baton of depression and chaos back and forth, back and forth. You be strong, I'll be weak. You take care of me this year; I'll take care of you next year.

I think such transitions stem from the degree of sharing that's inherent to being a twin: when you grow up dividing up so many key things—womb space, birthday cakes, parental affection—you become acutely tuned to the relative availability of resources, to potential limits. You grow up understanding, deep inside, that there might not be enough time for both of you, or enough attention, or enough room in the world. So you develop an odd instinct for timing, a way of stepping up to the plate when you sense it's your turn to succeed or fail or fall apart, of retreating to the dugout when you sense it's hers.

Although I took it for granted for years, I've acquired a deep appreciation for that aspect of our relationship, the sense of moving in tandem, the way we seem to travel through our lives in relation to one another, one stepping forward then waiting for the other to catch up. But that kind of intimacy also comes at a cost. For one thing, we've both had a difficult time tolerating imperfection in other relationships. I tend to want every friendship to feel as deeply connected as my friendship with her, every romantic partner to grasp the ebbs and flows of my inner life as instinctively as she does. I am very hard on boyfriends: *What? You haven't learned to read my mind? To hell with you!*

And then there's that business of the myth: the two hearts beating as one; the soulmate. Any dance—whether between friends, lovers, colleagues, or twins—is subject to false moves; even the best-trained partner slips from time to time. My disappointment threshold, low with most people, is abysmal with Rebecca: if she's too busy to talk to me on the phone, if she's late for a scheduled dinner, if I sense her availability to me beginning to waver, I feel a flash of rage I almost never experience with anybody else: *You're not here for* ME*? How dare you!* On a deeper level, I think we both have difficulty accepting the times when we're out of step, when one of us moves forward too quickly, or dominates the stage, or somehow leaves the other behind. I was furious at her—irrationally but viscerally—when she got married, as though she'd literally traded me in for a new partner. I was deeply confused when she had a child, as though her new status as "mother" somehow negated her status as "twin." Times like that have been painful, forcing me to look at the extent to which I've defined myself as a sibling instead of a self, measured my worth against her accomplishments instead of mine, listened to the beat of her heart and not my own.

Mercifully, though, the dance changes, as it must between all siblings. As we've both grown, made separate mistakes, learned to feel comfortable in our own individual skin, our repertoire has expanded: we've incorporated steps of autonomy, learned to tolerate dips of disappointment, practiced acceptance of each other's differences. Today, we talk on the phone four or five times a week, she from her sprawling country home, me from my little nest in the city. I hear her baby cry in the background; she hears me flip on my computer, or strike a match to light a cigarette. The background music we live by is utterly different; it even clashes at times. But still, when I hear her voice, when we talk about what matters in our lives, or simply make each other laugh, I think we're both moved by the same fundamental chords. They're old and familiar and deeply reassuring: the chords of shared history, scoring a waltz of closeness.

New Woman magazine
December 1995

THE CORD THAT BINDS

THE BEST FRIEND and I were gabbing on the phone the other day, full girl-style, no topic too trivial or too deep: five minutes kvetching about Ally McBeal (juvenile, mysoginistic); two minutes on hair (hers, pouffing; mine, flat); a more significant chunk on existential despair, which covered several key bases (men, therapy, real estate). I could hear the best friend pause occasionally to quiet her dog, who barks wildly every time another dog passes by the house; if she'd listened closely, she could have heard a quiet clicking coming from my end of the line, a soft, periodic click-*click*; click, *click*: while we talked, I was calmly clipping my toenails.

As we all know by now, Monica Lewinsky heard a different kind of clicking: a periodic double-click in the background during her sometimes banal, sometimes anguished dialogues with Linda Tripp. She actually comments on this in the transcripts of their conversations. "I heard it again," she says. "What *is* that?" Linda blows her off, changes the subject, says, "Wait a minute—I've gotta get the dog off the couch."

Of all the appalling aspects of the Tripp-Lewinsky relationship (and there are too many to count), this one got to me the most. Linda Tripp can rationalize until the cows come home about self-protection, about the art of covering your ass in Washington, about Beltway friendships, but in my mind, she broke the sacred trust of the telephone, one of the most hallowed, enduring, and cementing tools of intimacy between women.

I grew up as witness to the telephone friendship. My mother, a very reserved woman who tended to shy away from face-to-face interactions, experienced the bulk of her intimate contact over the phone. In the afternoons, she'd retire to her bedroom and lie back, receiver tucked between ear and shoulder, gaze fixed on the ceiling. She'd gab and gab. If I passed by the room, I'd hear giggles and snippets of conversation, some of it Lewinsky-Tripp-esque on the banality scale (recipes, jokes, shopping), some of it undoubtedly much deeper. She talked to her sister this way three, four times a week, their conversations often lasting an hour or more; she maintained friendships with women that she might not see in person more than once or twice a year; the phone was her lifeline, her primary source of information, of gossip and support and cameraderie.

I rarely overheard my mother discuss anything specific over the years, but I did learn that there was something almost precious about the telephone, that it offered a rare blend of intimacy and distance, paved the way for a particularly rich kind of contact. As it is for most girls, the lesson was sealed for me as a teenager, over God knows how many hours of phone calls with girlfriends. We had an old rotary wall phone on the second floor of our house, in a hallway just outside the bathroom; I used to stretch the cord into the bathroom as far as it would go and sit on the floor with my back to the door, gazing up at nothing the way my mother did, yakking and yakking. Hours and hours on that bathroom floor, topics spanning the full adolescent spectrum, algebra to zits.

Today, the subject matter may differ but the effect is the same. There is something so deeply satisfying about a long gab on the phone with a woman friend, something almost analytic in the combination of invisibility and presence it offers, something very freeing about being simultaneously solitary and in direct contact. The big difference between phone contact and in-person contact, I suppose, has to do with safety: there's the safety of your own space; there's the comfort of a known voice on the other line; there's relief from the more complicated rules of face-to-face dialogue, which demand attention to subtler cues, like eye contact and body language. That degree of safety both focuses conversation and opens it up, allows it to flow from the banal to the profound with remarkable ease.

You can hear this in the Tripp-Lewinsky transcripts—talk shifts (literally) from Bloomingdale's to blow jobs in a heartbeat—and I can't imagine a woman who doesn't appreciate the dynamic, who doesn't indulge in it, who doesn't recognize it as something that sets us apart from men. Guys (at least the ones I know) just don't talk like that; the ability to gab unself-consciously on the phone is one of the great hallmarks of women's friendships, a sign that the relationship has shifted onto new territory, that it's acquired a degree of ease and trust and investment that's absent among mere acquaintances.

All of which makes Linda Tripp's tape-recording particularly horrifying. The transcripts are easy to make fun of: the dialogue is often boring and inconsequential, the subject matter (Linda's new haircut, Monica's "beautiful, beautiful rad new red sweater") can be painfully superficial and self-absorbed; together, they sound like the kind of women who give women a bad name—one obsessed with a bad relationship, the other cooing hollow words of support ("Oh, Monica, Monica, Monica, Monica"). But if you read the whole, nearly interminable thing, if you forget for a minute that "the Creep" in question happens to be the leader of the Free World, what you're left with is a truly grotesque act of betrayal. Taking for granted an established degree of intimacy and confidence, one woman reaches out to touch somebody; the friend she touches is carrying a grenade.

One of the great myths of female friendship is the idea that women will be be fully supportive and nurturing of one another 100 percent of the time. Nice idea, but not always true. We worry that even the closest of friends may break confidences, let us down, fail us on the empathy front; we've all been victims of grade-school friendship triangles; we've all felt betrayed or dumped when a best friend develops a closer relationship with someone new, or when a new man enters the picture and she vanishes into the land of early infatuation. What women don't tend to worry about are truly overt acts of betrayal, ones that are unambiguous, Iago-like. Those are the kind men tend to execute: power plays that may be ruthless and horrific, but are at least somewhat clean, if only because they're devoid of the implied intimacy that exists between women.

That's what makes the Tripp-Lewinsky transcripts seem so perverse: you can hear Linda Tripp cultivate that sense of intimacy; you can hear her draw Monica into that telephonic safety zone, that deep, easy, gabby place where trust feels like a given. And then—click!—you can hear her bludgeon it. Just imagine. Imagine how you'd feel if you discovered your own unguarded and intimate musings were in fact on tape, excerpts available as front-page breakfast reading from coast to coast. So say what you will about Monica Lewinsky's naïveté and stupidity and self-delusion. As the year draws to a close and I count my blessings, chief among them is that I don't have a friend like Linda Tripp.

Boston Phoenix
December 1998

BREAKING AWAY

AS OF THIS WEEK, I am hopeless. Or, more precisely, Hopeless. My friend Hope, whom I've known for just over a year, has moved to California, and her departure has raised questions for me about friendships: what it takes to form them, and why we either hold on to them over the years or let them go.

Like a lot of people in my social world these days, Hope started out as a dog acquaintance, in the category of circumstantial friend. We met at a dog group, our animals befriended each other long before we did, and when the group disbanded, we found a new park and took to getting together most evenings after work. We'd sit on a picnic table while the pups wrestled and romped and for the most part we talked dog: training stories; anecdotes about this cute behavior or that destructive one; assorted tales of woe and attachment. We passed most of last fall this way, often joined by fellow dog-owners, and then we suffered through a long, fierce winter together, huddled on that same bench each evening for as long as we could bear it. I suppose that's when the friendship began to move out of the circumstantial category and into something bigger, in the gradual and elusive way that such things happen. We were the diehard dog-owners, partners in canine devotion, and we'd sit out there alone almost every evening from 5 to 6:30, shivering on that bench while the dogs raced around; I suppose we developed a sense of shared struggle, the same way medical students or colleagues in a difficult workplace do. We might freeze our butts off, but by God the dogs would get a good workout.

Winter became spring and then summer; our evening get-togethers became easier as the weather warmed, and at some barely-conscious and indefinable point, we crossed a kind of friendship line. Conversation had broadened, shifting from matters canine to matters of the heart. A body of knowledge had been amassed: from daily reports on our respective days, Hope came to know about me and my work and my assorted struggles with men and intimacy and depression and I came to know about her and hers. By midsummer, the evening meeting had come to be as much about our friendship as the one between the dogs, as much an excuse for us to get together and talk as it was for them to get together and play. I'm not the sort of person who admits very readily to needing others, or who forms easy attachments. In June, Hope's work took her to Alaska for three weeks and I fell into a mild depression; it took me two of those three weeks to acknowledge to myself how much I missed her, how important a ritual our daily meetings had become.

And yet our friendship has never extended beyond the dog park—Hope and I have never had a meal together, never gone shopping together, never gone to a movie or passed an evening together without the dogs, and it's this rootedness in time and place—5 o'clock at the dog park—that makes me wonder both about the future of our bond and about friendship more generally. Will we stay in touch once she's moved 3,000 miles away? Once the insistent motivations of daily life are removed—in our case, exercising our dogs—what happens to such a bond?

I have become much more ruthless about friendships as I've gotten older, much more willing to cut cords when a relationship stops working, much quicker to separate the good from the mediocre, the functional from the damaged. Ten years ago, or even five, I had a much higher tolerance for unsatisfying friendships than I do now, in part because I had a less well-developed understanding of how hard it is to cultivate and maintain a friendship and in part because I tended to see any failures in a bond as my fault. If I left a lunch or a dinner with a friend feeling disconnected or compromised, I'd figure I'd done something wrong, somehow failed to make contact in the right way. So I'd hang on to friendships far longer than I should have, keep subjecting myself to the same disconnected encounters, pounding the square pegs of failing friendships into the same round holes. Today, I have better radar and a far lower threshold for dissatisfaction. If it doesn't work—if a prospective friend turns out to be too different from me, our values and sensibilities and needs and goals too far afield—he or she gets scratched off the list. I'm not always terribly direct about making those determinations (I tend to employ gradual distancing-strategies, like failing to return phone calls) but I'm a lot clearer about my own criteria for friendship than I used to be, and also a bit more cynical. Friendships can be so hard and so transient: it's enormously difficult to find a soulmate, and making a commitment to one—fostering it, seeing it through rough patches, tolerating the inevitable disappointments—requires sizable investments of both time and emotional resources.

My cynicism is both an asset and a liability, and it explains why I watch Hope's departure with a bittersweet tenderness, as though it's a real good-bye. I've been here before, after all, watched old friends and colleagues exit my world amidst heartfelt promises to stay in touch, and then watched the bond slowly dissolve, all the best intentions notwithstanding. Write to me! Promise you'll call! Come visit! People say these things, and often mean them, but time passes and the demands of daily life encroach, and the letters go unwritten, the calls aren't made, the visits are unscheduled. I suspect that Hope and I will exchange periodic e-mails, perhaps even a call or two, but once she's landed on the opposite coast and settled into a new life, we'll essentially let go.

This isn't necessarily a bad thing, although I observe it with considerable sadness. Knowing when to say good-bye to a friendship is as important in its own way as knowing when to hang on, and I suspect I'll place Hope in a small but precious category of relationships that worked, and worked quite beautifully, in their own place and time. A handful of former colleagues are in that category—people who battled alongside me at work, whom I respected and admired and then lost once we both marched off the battlefield. So are friends I made at rehab, people with whom I shared an experience so distinct and so particular to context that the bonds vanished almost as soon as we walked away from the hospital grounds. Perhaps Hope and I will surprise each other, stay in touch for years, watch the friendship shift into another small and precious category of relationships that don't require daily contact or geographic proximity in order to survive. But I don't think we've known each other long enough, or built up enough of a shared history, to make that a realistic possibility. Hope, friend of circumstance, then friend of the heart, will become friend of the past, someone I will remember well and with utter fondness.

Boston Phoenix
November 1997

GIRL CRUSHES

PSSSSST. WANNA HEAR a secret?

I have a huge crush right now, on S.

I *adore* S. S. is sophisticated and worldly and striking, the kind of person you never tire of watching. S. has thick, dark hair, an intense gaze, a charismatic smile, the kind that seems reserved especially for you. S. is also older than I am, and (in my view) wiser, funnier, *superior*. So I get a little case of the jitters whenever we talk, feel a little shy and self-conscious. My heart flutters. I feel like a kid.

In all, I suppose, this is a garden-variety crush. A basic, everyday case of infatuation. Except in this situation, there's a twist.

S. is a woman. I don't want to sleep with her—S. and I are both unambiguously heterosexual and my feelings for her are decidedly nonphysical—but I have a major crush on her all the same.

This is a girl crush, big time.

Do you have girl crushes? Do you know what I mean? Are there women in your life you quietly worship, whose attention you secretly covet? Do you find yourself watching such women the way you might watch a man you're attracted to, paying attention to every detail of her dress and manner, hanging on her every word, wanting to be *just like her*? If so, welcome to the club.

A girl crush is in many ways a nonsexual counterpart to the kind of crush you get on a guy. It's a dizzying, infatuation-based brand of that love most of us experience at some point—as young girls with our babysitters, as teenagers with teachers or coaches, as adult women with our bosses or peers. And whether or not we define them as crushes, almost all of us seem to have them.

Most of us probably worry about them, too. We develop these giddy, awe-struck feelings toward someone—toward a *woman*—and we feel a little baffled or disarmed, as though the intensity of our feelings is inappropriate, or even shameful. A crush on a girl? What gives?

Well, set the anxiety aside. Girl crushes are natural, healthy, and safe. They don't mean you're crazy, and they probably don't signal any latent lesbian impulses, either. In fact, one of the things that distinguishes them from guy crushes is their essential lack of eroticism: you may feel nervous or charged up by the object of your infatuation, but chances are you don't want to sleep with her.

What you *can* do with the object of your crush is learn something. Girl crushes can be enormously instructive. They can help us develop standards and ideals, help us articuate our deepest wishes by shedding light on the sides of ourselves we find lacking or incomplete. Psychologists Luise Eichenbaum and Susie Orbach touch on this phenomenon in their book *Between Women: Love, Envy, and Competition in Women's Friendships*. When we're attracted to another women, they note, it's often because we see a part of ourselves that's either "unformed or dormant"; the women we feel drawn to help "shape and legitimize our own desires." That's precisely what happens when I look at S. (okay, her name is Susan): I see in her a model of professional competence and personal flair, a combination of femininity and confidence I long to develop myself but haven't quite nailed down. In this sense, girl crushes are quite literally fantastic: they help us dream about the people we want to be.

Beyond that, girl crushes also speak to a particularly elusive aspect of female friendship, to the particularly sensual (though not necessarily sexual) way women look at and admire one other. Girl crushes are about aesthetics: they're about the kind of admiration a woman feels when she sees someone she knows put together an amazing outfit, or whip up an incredible meal. They're about appreciation, shared values, and connection.

In a word, girl crushes are about female love.

Here's a textbook case: Several years ago, Patricia, who's 41 and happily involved in a relationship with a man, joined a women's reading group and was drawn instantly to one of the members, a tall, striking woman named Anne. Anne seemed "incredibly together" to Patricia: she was funny, wise, graceful, beautifully dressed. The two struck up a friendship within weeks of meeting and Patricia describes feeling "all giddy around her for a long time—really thrilled to be in her company." They laughed at the same things, discovered they shared the same favorite movies and plays, began to have long, intimate phone conversations nearly every day. Patricia's admiration felt bottomless: Anne was the kind of woman who could whip up a fabulous meal with whatever ingredients she had on hand, she lived in a beautifully decorated apartment, worked at an interesting job. "I was in awe of her," Patricia says. The giddy feelings persisted. "In a lot of ways, it was more exciting to be with her than it was to be with my boyfriend," she says. "I'd get dressed with that kind of self-consciousness you have when you're going out on a first date: 'Ooooh, I want to look nice for *Anne.*' It was really *fun.*"

Bingo: a girl crush.

"A crush is about really wanting to be liked by someone who's better than you—or who you perceive as better than you," says Karen, 37, who had a major crush on a woman named Amy during her late 20s. Karen met Amy during a very fragile time in her own life: Karen was deeply insecure, socially awkward, isolated; Amy was confident and extroverted, and shortly after they met, she literally took Karen under her wing. "She took me shopping. She helped me buy clothes," Karen recalls. "She helped me put on makeup. She did my hair. I would have done *anything* for her." But the crush extended beyond gratitude. "Amy was larger than life, she was Jackie O.," says Karen. "She was the kind of person who walked into a room and everyone wanted her attention. She just exuded this energy." Being singled out by such a charismatic figure made Karen feel special in a way she simply hadn't before. "It was like a prize: 'Someone like *that* wants to be *my friend*?!' That's like a drug. It's a big hit."

It's the kind of hit most of us look for in other women all our lives. In ways, a woman's crush history is like the emotional equivalent of a long salad bar, with her infatuations representing bins of desired attributes: a little confidence here, a dash of physical beauty there, a particular way with words or humor or makeup there. My current crush, on Susan, was preceded by a huge crush on a former boss, Sandy, who was (and still is) a tall, strong, sensual woman with fabulous taste and great shoes. Before that, it was a college friend named Judy, who was extroverted and self-assured in a way I longed to be but wasn't. And before that, a friend's older sister, Julie, who wore greenish-gray eyeshadow, smoked Virginia Slims cigarettes, and seemed (at least at the time) to epitomize cool. In each instance, I can look back and see myself grazing at that salad bar, trying to fill up my own underlying hungers: I wanted Sandy's sensuality, Judy's energy, Julie's élan. I wanted, at least in some sense, to *be* those people, to take the parts of them I worshipped and incorporate them into my own lesser being.

That brand of hero-worship seems to come particularly naturally to females. In some ways, the smitten feeling we develop toward each other speaks to a yearning that most of us carry around in our hearts—a wish for the kind of profound identification we felt in our very first relationship with a woman, our mothers. Psychologists Eichenbaum and Orbach believe that a woman's early relationship with her mother plays a central role in the way she forms female friendships in later life. The mother-daughter bond, they argue, is a deeply complicated, fused phenomenon, based on a mutual need for a kind of psychological merging. Boundaries between mother and daughter are blurred; both develop a hypersensitivity to the other's needs and state of mind. As she begins to separate from her mother, the daughter seeks a sense of self through that same feeling: profound connection with other women. "Without connection," they say, "a feminine identity is at risk. Attachment and concern for others becomes her guide."

Girl crushes, which are so often directed toward women we perceive as superior—older, wiser, more sophisticated—are one manifestation of that drive to connect, to merge with another woman, and, through that process, to take on her coveted attributes. In her book *Just Friends: The Role of Friendship in Our Lives*, sociologist Lillian Rubin writes that "Friends help to affirm new roles undertaken, parts of self not formerly met." That seems to be particularly true with crushes: the women we admire help us experiment with those "un-met" parts of self, as though seeing in action the qualities we long to develop in ourselves—her confidence, her style, her humor—gives us permission to emulate them, try them on for size. That's why there's often an element of mimickry to crushes, why you typically find yourself adopting certain of her mannerisms, incorporating little bits of her vocabulary into your own, buying clothes that remind you of her taste. Crushes are an extension of the way we've been taught to learn: first through our mothers, then through other women.

On rare occasions, they extend beyond that—and get out of control. My friend Maggie tells of an acquaintance, Debbie, who had what she calls a "scary crush" on a mutual friend named Lucy. Lucy was eminently crush-worthy—a striking woman with a beautiful son, a gorgeous husband, and a particular flair for cooking—and Maggie harbored characteristically crushlike feelings toward her herself: she quietly admired the qualities Lucy seemed to represent, and over time the two have become good friends. That wasn't so with Debbie, whose crush spilled over some elusive boundary and began to border on obsessive. "Debbie called Lucy every day, even though they weren't really good friends," Maggie says. "She started dressing like Lucy. Lucy would have on some really beautiful olive cardigan, and Debbie would show up the next day in an identical olive cardigan, wearing it exactly the same way."

When a crush gets creepy like that, it's mutated into something different: obsessionality, loss of boundaries. For the most part, that doesn't happen: crushes are about admiriation, not over-identification; the fantasies they generate are about *being like*, as opposed to *turning into*, another person.

That seems to be true despite one's sexual orientation. Rachel, 33, is gay, and says there's a distinct difference between her girl crushes and her more sexual, lesbian interests. "If I see a woman I'm really attracted to, I know it. There's that knock-me-off-my-socks, *Whoa!* feeling. But the crush thing is different: it's a warm feeling. It's exciting, but it's nonsexual." Rachel contemplates this for a moment, then describes a recent meeting with her friend Sarah, on whom she's had a crush for years. "She came into the kitchen, and we hadn't seen each other for a few weeks, and we hugged and did all that 'Oh! You cut your hair!' 'Oh! I love that sweater!' stuff. And my friend John, who was there, looked up and said, 'God, you guys are such *girls*!' and we busted up laughing. There was such warmth to that. It wasn't at all sexual, but it was really *sensual*. I think that's the difference. A love interest is sexual but a crush is sensual."

Unfortunately, that distinction seems to be lost on a lot of people. One of my earliest crushes was on a girl from my third-grade class named Lauren. I can't remember much about her now except that she was beautiful, with dark, shiny hair, and she had all kinds of *things* I wanted: toys, patent-leather shoes, a bed with a canopy. The crush was classic: I looked up to her, felt shy in her presence, wanted to look and dress and act just like her. One afternoon, for reasons I can't quite recall, we ended up in Lauren's bedroom playing with dolls under the covers of her bed: location aside, the episode was completely nonsexual. I remember feeling cozy and warm and accepted by Lauren, as though she'd singled me out, invited me to join her in a very special, intimate place, under that fabulous canopy. After 30 minutes or so, Lauren's mother came into the room and discovered us under the covers. Again, I don't recall precisely what happened but I remember that her mother was angry and seemed shocked: she ordered us out of the bed, scolded us, somehow made it clear that two little girls didn't belong together in the same bed. I remember feeling ashamed and not knowing quite why. My crush on Lauren remained intact, but after that I had the sense that there was something wrong with it, that her mother had somehow gauged the intensity of my feelings and disapproved.

No doubt, she *had* disapproved. After all, we live in a society that's generally edgy about sexuality and particularly edgy about homosexuality. Women are taught to reserve their most intense feelings for men, and to do otherwise is to behave inappropriately at best, shamefully at worst. Irish sociologist Pat O'Connor, one of the few academics who've studied women's friendships in depth, writes about this in her book *Friendships Between Women*, noting that our culture has "a strong tendency to trivialize and derogate friendships between women—seeing them as culturally 'suspect,' as in some sense lesbian and hence 'sick.'"

This, it's worth pointing out, is a relatively new phenomenon. If I'd been born 100 years earlier, no one would have blinked twice at my little romp under the covers with a childhood friend; in fact, it would have been *condoned*, rather than condemned. In the 19th century, and in centuries before, friendships between women were unabashedly sensual, characterized by what looks today like decidedly romantic behavior: cuddling on the divan; strolling arm-in-arm together outdoors; openly expressing deep affection, both physically and verbally. Just pick up a Jane Austen novel, or leaf through poet Emily Dickenson's passionate letters to Sue Gilbert, the woman who became her sister-in-law. The language you hear between women from that era sounds exactly like that of heterosexual love, full of pledges to be faithful, promises to stay in each other's thoughts, loving declarations. For a wide variety of reasons (among them, widespread acceptance of Freudian theory, which suggested that deep bonds between women were somehow neurotic and perverse, to increasing economic independence among women, which made their closeness, with its suggestion of even greater automomy from men, threatening), that attitude shifted around the turn of the century. We still can and do love each other deeply (according to the 1987 Hite Report, the overwhelming majority of both married and single women have their deepest emotional relationship with a woman), but we're no longer supposed to show it.

Which strikes me as rather sad. A good crush, after all, can be exciting, *joyful*; it should be cause for celebration, not shame. Think of them as a less visible, 20th-century counterpart to the kind of love women expressed so freely in an earlier era. They're about seeing what's beautiful and admirable and special in another woman and then revelling in those traits. They're about falling in love with details, the way you do when you stand in awe before a painting.

What's wonderful about a crush is that over time you get to hold on to those details, make them your own. Today, for example, my taste in shoes is still very Sandy-inspired (I'll see a a little low-heeled, suede number and think, 'Ooooh, a Sandy shoe'). I've also stolen certain of Susan's speech habits, like a particular way of saying, "Terr-*if*-ic" when I'm really excited about something. There's comfort in hijacking a part of someone you admire like that: every time I wear a Sandy shoe, or say the word *terrific* in Susan's way, I feel like I've dropped into a slightly new persona, one that feels more stylish and interesting than my own.

But perhaps, in the end, it has *become* my own. We mimic what we admire and, if the fit is right, we begin to incorporate that quality into our own beings. Today I can see that Sandy didn't actually "teach" me how to buy shoes; rather, something about our friendship helped crystallize my own nascent sense of style. Patricia feels the same way about Anne, the woman from her reading group. Patricia was attracted to Anne's intelligence, her way with words, her insight, and she says her intense, crushlike feelings began to subside as she realized that she didn't just covet those qualities; she also *shared* them. "Anne helped bring out those things in me," she says. The crush diminished as Patricia began to see that the two women were, in fact, on equal footing.

Even when a crush has a less-than-perfect ending, it's usually because you've gained something, cemented a piece of knowledge about yourself along the way. My crush on Julie, the personification of cool, began to wane as I noticed how nasty and mean-spirited she could be to my then-best friend: in fading away, the crush unearthed a small jewel of self-awareness: I learned that I valued kindness in others.

And if the admiration remains, even after the crush has ebbed? That's even better. Today, the early excitement Patricia felt with Anne has mellowed into something she describes as "warmer and safer"—in other words, into feelings of friendship: "Anne is a really close friend now," she says. "I'm not as infatuated with her, but I still really love her a lot." So some of us get new directions in personal style out of crushes: new shoes, a new word, new tastes in books or movies. And some of get something richer: a lasting friend.

New Woman magazine
1996

WHEN YOU JUST WANT TO BE LOVED

(AND LOVED AND LOVED AND LOVED)

More.

I want more.

I want to be held all night while I sleep and kissed mere seconds after I open my eyes in the morning. I want loving glances over coffee, and 50 hugs a day, and flowers and phone calls and tender notes in the daily mail. I want to feel that he can read my mind, that he knows what I want before I do, that we are so in synch he can finish my sentences. I want the best sex: fluid and easy and laced with passion. I want lofty conversation and constant laughter and the kind of joy most women only dream about.

In short, I want to be loved.

And loved and loved and *loved.*

Here's the question: Do you think I'm asking for too much?

And here's the answer: Yes.

And then again, no. Not at all. Absolutely not.

Dreams, after all, are important, and the wish for that particular kind of love is clearly a dream of the most powerful sort. It has to do with wanting romantic perfection, with a yearning for ideal love, with a longing for connectedness so pure and complete it would eradicate even the wispiest memory of loneliness and disappointment.

Those fantasies exist to one degree or another in every human soul, male and female, and I value them. In fact, I cling to them, in part because it's taken me years to accept that they're valid. For the vast majority of my adult life—and in the vast majority of my romantic relationships—I've operated under the assumption, common to so many women, that at heart I want too much, that my expectations far exceed my options, that I'm destined to be let down and dissatisfied. I've also tended to gravitate toward men who, consciously or not, have reinforced that perception, who have been incapable of living up to the dream, who've emerged as inherently limited in their capacity for giving. It's the age-old recipe for frustration in love: take one potent fantasy, add one damaged or limited man, and stir.

And yet the fantasies persist. Perfect love. Perfect closeness. Fusion and automony and sexuality and friendship all rolled into one. The difference today is that I'm a little more conscious of what lies behind the dream, of how it serves both to motivate and undermine me, of what it says about the nature of women's needs.

The scene: I am sitting in a café with my friend Eliza, who is staring dejectedly into her cup of coffee. She looks like she's about to cry but is clearly struggling not to. "Half the time," she says, looking up at last, "I feel like John doesn't even *like* me." John is her boyfriend of the past seven years and I've been dubious about him from the very start. He's bright and handsome and capable of being quite charming, but I've never had the sense that he fully appreciates the things about Eliza that I do. Or, for that matter, that *she* does. Eliza, for example, is a wonderful cook; John is lukewarm about food, sees it as little more than physical fuel. Eliza is a passionate gardener; John considers gardening an idle hobby, a frivolous pursuit. More important, Eliza is a warm, giving woman who yearns for intimacy while John is a more witholding, distanced sort, the kind of man who tends to flee if he feels her getting too close. Not coincidentally (in my view, at any rate), every time Eliza talks about moving in together, John takes off somewhere, decides to go camping for the weekend or develops a sudden need to visit an old friend on the other side of the continent.

At the moment, Eliza and John are contemplating a separation, a decision they've danced around for the past year or so. Eliza's dilemma: she knows she wants more out of the relationship but at heart she's not certain she *deserves* it. "I keep feeling like there's something wrong with me for not being more accepting of what I have," she says. "So what if we don't share every single interest or hobby? So what if we're not always in synch?" She pauses, then adds, "No one man is going to meet every single one of my needs. Right?"

Right. And, in a way, beside the point. When Eliza talks about her relationship with John, she describes more than a sense of occasional disappointment or mismatched interests. What comes through is a feeling that she's simply not valued by him in a way she clearly wants and needs to be, that he doesn't make her feel special. When I hear her talk, I get the image of a plant that badly needs water, a flower that's been poorly tended to and cannot properly blossom.

I spent seven years involved with a man who reminded me a lot of John: edgy about intimacy and commitment, distant a great deal of the time, and clearly (at least in retrospect) ambivalent about me. We were a terrible match in many ways: I loved to sleep all curled up with him; he liked to stick to his side of the bed, plenty of physical space between us. I felt strongly about spending weekend time together; he liked to use weekends to go off on his own. I wanted to be taken care of; he perceived that wish as excessively needy and it made him nervous. As our time together went on, I felt increasingly frustrated and angry, and yet I hung in there. And hung in there. And (inevitably, perhaps) a terrible vicious cycle developed: the more distant he became, the clingier I felt; the clingier I felt, the more distant he became.

Did I want too much? At the time, I thought so. Like Eliza, I harbored a deep suspicion that my frustration in the relationship was somehow my fault, that I'd be more content if I managed to change somehow, to turn myself into someone who needed or wanted less. It took me years—*years*—to break that particular train of thought, in large part because it took me that long to understand that my needs were valid, that the level of closeness and love I yearned for was natural and good and not a sign of weakness, that my dissatisfaction came from the fact that I honestly wasn't getting what I needed.

Women are so good at being chameleons: we're so accustomed to molding ourselves into whatever shape our partners want us to be, we so instinctively assign greater importance to his needs and desires than to our own, and we're so quick to accept blame for any failure in a relationship that frustrated dreams are almost inevitable: nine times out of 10, our own yearnings are simply lost in the romantic shuffle. I try to tell this to Eliza: "You *deserve* to feel loved. You should *listen* to the part of yourself that isn't feeling sufficiently appreciated or special. It's *okay* to want more." She looks at me, an uncertain expression in her eyes. You can tell she's not sure: her own needs feel excessive to her; the dream feels out of reach.

Of course, Eliza may be right: the dream in many ways *is* out of reach, unrealistic and inherently unattainable.

Another scene: I am with Michael, who is the polar opposite of his edgy, intimacy-fearing predecessor. We are at the kitchen table drinking coffee, which Michael has prepared for me, and he is telling me a joke, making me laugh. Michael is loving and sweet and emotionally generous. He loves to sleep all curled up with me. He not only wants to spend his weekends with me, he arranges his schedule so that he can. He is a steadfast caretaker, with an intuitive sense for what I need so precise that he often anticipates my wants before I can even name them. "He's the perfect boyfriend," my friend Sandy says, and there's very little evidence to suggest that she's not absolutely right. Michael loves me—and loves and loves and loves me.

So what's wrong with this picture? Nothing, except that at heart—or at least at times—I *still* feel dissatisfied, still feel something gnawing at a corner of my soul, an emptiness that cries out for more. In my worst moments, I sit there at the kitchen table with Michael and tick through my list of disappointments: he's not *quite* intellectual enough, he's not *quite* assertive enough, he's not quite X, Y, or Z enough. In short, this man may make me feel valued and loved but hey: he's not quite *perfect*. And I want perfect.

My struggle with Michael, my chronic bouts of ambivalence and dissatisfaction, suggest that there's a downside to the dream, a downside to all that yearning. In my most lucid moments, I am aware that my persistent sensation of wanting more has more to do with me than it does with any real failing on the relationship's part, or on Michael's. There's an element of narcissism to it, a wish to be at the center of someone else's universe, even a trace of vanity. I still cling to a vision of love that's shaped more by Hollywood than it is by reality: I want to be Katherine Hepburn to his Spencer Tracy, Meryl Streep to his Clint Eastwood. This is the same operating fantasy that leads me to other sources of dissatisfaction in my life: I want Michelle Pfeiffer's cheek bones, not my own. I want Rita Hayworth's legs and hair. I want someone else's life, someone else's personality, someone else's relationship.

I'm also aware that these feelings of want often stem from a deep, internal source, one that has little to do with Michael or the reality of the relationship. There's a hunger behind the need, an abiding fear of being without, a compulsion to latch on to something (or more to the point, some*one*) in order to assuage some deep discomfort. This is what my friend Eliza alluded to when she said that no one man could meet every single one of her needs: she's right. Most of us understand on some level that we want more than is realistically available to us, that our dreams of romantic perfection have to do with the fantasy that someone will come along and do a lot of our dirty work for us: meet needs we need to meet ourselves, give us the qualities we feel lacking in ourselves, fill up all the empty spaces that, at heart, simply go along with being human.

And yet, the dream remains powerful. In part, I suspect that the yearning for romantic perfection is culturally determined or, at least, culturally reinforced. The search for a fix, for a ready solution to what ails, has become a uniquely 20th-century undertaking, an ingrained part of consumer culture, as prevalent as the nearest diet workshop or plastic surgeon. In some ways, my wish for Michael to do and be everything for me—to be my perfect soulmate, to meet every last one of my needs—is an ideal expression of that particular brand of searching, an example of the way so many of us are taught to confront deep yearnings: *Fill up the emptiness. Find something outside yourself that will eradicate any and all feelings of loneliness and inadequacy and dissatisfaction*. Our society has become marvellously adept at presenting easy—or seemingly easy—solutions to that impulse: find the right diet, the right wardrobe, the right career, the right *man*.

The qualities I find lacking in Michael, in other words, are often the qualities I find lacking in myself. If he's not perfect—if *we're* not perfect—then it stands to reason that I'm not perfect.

So what's an ordinary dream-hungry, 20th-century woman to do? What *is* enough? How can you tell if your wish to be loved is excessive and unrealistic or normal and healthy?

Those are tough questions and, as usual, the answers tend to exist on elusive, internal levels. When I look at a woman like Eliza (and I know lots of women in similar straits), I tend to evoke the language of self-worth: she probably won't find the level of satisfaction she craves until she feels she deserves it, until she can look at herself in the mirror and truly believe that she's *lovable*. When you just want to be loved—and loved and loved—it often means that you don't really experience love from within, that you don't feel sufficiently valuable in your own right, that you need it—probably in excessive doses—from the outside, from someone else.

At the same time, I'm aware that love itself, both for the self and from others, has limits. I know that when I'm feeling truly comfortable in my own skin—confident, capable of taking care of myself, worthy—I tend to need less from Michael, tend to feel that gnawing hunger less acutely. And, by the same token, I know that when I'm in needier and more insecure states, the longing will intensify. I understand that feeling loved—truly loved—involves a kind of balance, that it stems in equal measure from him and from me, that love is a dynamic feeling which rises and wanes, that tides of doubt and disappointment and ambiguity are inevitable and part of love's natural flow.

I don't relish this awareness: I resent it, I fight it frequently, and I have a terribly hard time surrendering my fairy-tale fantasy, my belief, ingrained since girlhood, that a perfect man will come along and sweep me off into a future that's clear and bright and utterly lacking in ambivalence. But in the end I'm only human. I want to be loved, you see—and loved and loved and loved.

CONFESSIONS OF A CONTROL FREAK

I WANT ONE . . . *But I'm not sure . . . But I have to have one someday . . . But it seems inconceivable . . . But if I don't, I'll miss out on something huge . . . But my life seems so incompatible with what it takes . . . But not to have one seems so selfish . . . But pregnant? Me?*

And so churn the wheels of ambivalence, round and round and round, a cycle of yeses, nos, wishes, fears, assumptions, realities, and miscellaneous conflicts that get amplified immeasurably this time of year, when the holidays put me face-to-face with a growing cadre of little ones: nieces, nephews, the children of friends and relatives.

Until quite recently, this, the question of kids, occupied a low place on my internal priority list—and happily so. I've had time on my side (I'm 32), work on my mind, and relationships at the forefront of my struggles. In the midst of all that, kids have seemed little more than a distant assumption, something I've always figured I'd do but didn't feel particularly compelled to think about. You know the logic: it'll happen when it happens. When the time is right, when the right man comes along, when the ticking of the biological clock gets louder.

But as time passes, as I see friends and relatives enter into the murky, messy, and (it seems to me) overwhelming business of child-rearing, that line of thinking seems increasingly less realistic. At the very least, I'm less certain that children are something that just land in your life at the end of some preconceived series of events. After all, aren't people a little more self-directed than that? *I* tend to be. Looking back, I can say with a fair degree of certainty that every time I've really wanted something in my life, I've gone after it furiously, whether it's landing a job or preserving a relationship. Accordingly, to impose such an arbitrary line of thought on the question of kids, to sit back and say, "Oh, it'll just happen," seems a bit like a cop-out. Isn't there more to it than that?

Indeed. There's a lot more to it. And when I think about what I'm really like, when I try to imagine what kind of mother I'd make, my earlier assumptions start to fly out the window and I'm left instead with questions: Am I capable of entering into that kind of relationship, of taking on that sort of responsibility? Am I too selfish? Too stuck in my ways? Too conflicted about questions like dependence?

For the first time, I've started looking at babies and small children without thinking, "Well, one of these days." Now the quesiton that comes up is, "Could I really do it? Ever?"

For years, I've assumed that something was just wrong with my biological clock. That perhaps I didn't have one. Or, more likely, that by dint of various other preoccupations (career, men), mine was simply on hold.

It's not that I don't like children. When I see my two-year-old niece, a small dynamo of a human named Roxanne, I turn into a veritable bundle of maternal feeling: I want to grab her and hug her and kiss her tiny face and hands; I can spend hours playing the kinds of endlessly repetitive games that two-year-olds play (I chase her in a circle 30 times, she chases me in a circle 30 times); and when I see her do something particularly childlike and endearing—curling up in her bed for a nap, clutching her father by the leg in a shy moment—my heart just melts. *She's captivating*, I think. *I want one*.

But that feeling can be surprisingly short-lived. I see a fair amount of this child—once or twice a month, if I can—but at best, that adds up to a mere 24 days a year. And the other 341 days? I spend them in the office, in my apartment, in restaurants and movie theaters and the homes of my (primarily) single or childless friends. And in those settings, maternal rushes don't exist. I don't think about it. The clock, such as it is, falls silent.

Those settings, moreover, represent a life I've struggled hard to feel comfortable with—they're the places I've learned (and not without difficulty) to feel at home in. Whether you're a woman with a biological clock or a man without one, I think the business of becoming an independent, self-reliant individual in 20th-century America is a difficult—and largely solitary—process. And the skills I've picked up over the years seem, in several important respects, almost antithetical to the business of becoming a mother. I have become a highly organized person, with a fairly compartmentalized life: work occupies me from this time of day to that time of day; friends take up *x* number of nights per week and family *y* number of nights; I do *x*, *y*, and *z* to soothe myself, and *a*, *b*, and *c* to have fun. I exercise a set number of hours each week, spend a set number of hours by myself. And when that schedule gets interrupted or interfered with? Well, suffice it to say that tolerating ambiguity and disorder is not my forte.

All of which confuses the question of kids tremendously. There's a growing discrepancy between the person I thought I'd be as an "adult" (someone deeply and successfully involved in relationships, with a man as well as with children) and the person I actually am (someone more passive and self-protective than that). And though I certainly don't rule out the possibility of future change and growth, I do know this: I've learned more over the past decade about keeping people at a safe distance than I've learned about bonding; more about tolerating independence than about fostering interdependence; more about living alone than about living with others; and—to be frank—more about quelling fears of involvement than about confronting them.

And where, I have to ask, would children fit into the mind-set I've developed? Could I really give up all my self-protective habits and routines, my highly cultivated independence, to enter into a relationship that requires such levels of flexibility (not to mention dependence and responsibility and God knows how many other characteristics I'm not sure I have)?

I watch my brother and sister-in-law dealing with Roxanne and their new baby, a three-month-old son named David. I see how devoted they are as parents, but I also see how drastically their lives have changed. How exhausted they can be, how frustrated they can get. How pulled they are between the demands of job and family. I see a level of chaos—in day-to-day life, in the screams of infants, in their toy-strewn, cluttered house—that I'm not always sure I could tolerate.

As time goes by, having children seems less like a certainty and more like an act that would require fundamental changes in the ways I organize my life, in the ways I've come to define myself.

These are not pleasant things to write about—or to think about, for that matter. I read over these words and wonder what's wrong with me, wonder where to place the blame. Am I a selfish person? Am I the dysfunctional product of a dysfunctional society, a world that neither values nor supports the lives of families? I also wonder how much fear lurks beneath the surface, beneath my rather rigid urban professional existence: *am I really that afraid of intimacy?*

Moreover, the pressure to have children—to create a family—can be profound, whether it comes from images and ideals you grew up with, from parents who'd like you to "settle down," or from those moments when you realize that independence and self-protection often come at a high price—loneliness. It can be most unsettling to see yourself as a woman who simply won't have kids.

And indeed, that's not something I'm either willing or able to do. I still hope for some sort of change—the "right" this or that, perhaps, or the sudden shift of an internal clock, something that will kick my drive to reproduce into gear. I still cling to the freedom offered by my comparative youth—I may not have decades ahead of me, but I do have a good number of reproductive years. At the same time, though, it frightens me to realize that having children is not only a choice I'm free to make (as opposed to a culturally imposed mandate) but a choice I could conceivably find myself unable to make.

A few Sundays ago, at the end of a visit to my brother's family, I tucked my niece into bed for a nap. She looked up with big round eyes and asked me not to leave, her little voice saying, "Don't go!"

I looked down at her and thought what a brave thing it must be to have a child, to set aside your own needs and fears, to surrender your self-absorption to something so vulnerable as a child. It makes the challenges of my brother's life seem extraordinarily real, and mine seem superficial.

As I left her room, she said it again, "Don't go!" And I felt a little twinge of pain, not because I was leaving but because she made me wonder: could I ever stay?

BOSTON PHOENIX
DECEMBER 1991

LETTER TO ZOE

Dear Small One,

You sneezed the first time I looked at you. Very strange—not having had much contact with babies before you, I found it alarming. You were the most miniature thing I'd ever seen, like a tiny replica of a human being, with fingernails so small and perfectly formed they looked like they'd been imagined. I remember I stood there in the hospital, peering over you all swaddled in your crib, and suddenly your little face wrinkled up and you sneezed—a tiny "ch!" I jumped back, as though I'd caused an allergic reaction. From then on, every time you've sneezed when I've been in the room, I've figured it's my fault.

I mention this only because it seems to say something about how much power I've imbued you with, and how much influence someone as tiny as you can exert, all without knowing it. As I write this, you are only two-and-a-half years old, too young to remember much of anything that happens between the two of us, least of all your tiny sneeze back on Day One. My role in your life is necessarily limited—I'm probably a bit of a mystery to you, in fact: your mother's sister, an occasional voice on the phone, a periodic presence in your house, bearing gifts. But you occupy a very special role in my life nonetheless, one that I imagine other aunts and uncles my age experience, too. After all, being an aunt or uncle—particularly an unmarried, childless one—is a strange thing these days, a deeply gratifying and yet oddly frustrating phenomenon. A lot of people I know (men as well as women) find themselves in similar circumstances: single; uncertain whether we'll have children of our own; simultaneously fascinated and terrified by the prospect; and (perhaps accordingly) deeply attached to the nearest thing, our nieces and nephews. Deeply attached, in other words, to small ones like you.

Hence this letter. One of these days, when you're old enough not just to read but to understand certain things about attachment, I'd like you to have a sense of how much meaning you've held, how important your tiny being is, and will continue to be. Perhaps because I didn't spend much time with them, I grew up figuring I was of minimal, or at least secondary, importance to my aunts and uncles. In fact, I have learned through you that nieces and nephews evoke very powerful feelings, and a very particular sort of love.

❧

You were born under rather extraordinary circumstances, which has always given your existence a particularly precious quality. Your maternal grandfather—my father—died just weeks after you were conceived. Your mother, who'd been trying to have a child for years, found out she was pregnant with you the very day he fell into a coma, three days before his death. He was very sick by that point, and rarely lucid, but when she told him the news on the phone that day, he was just clear enough to comprehend, and just verbal enough to choke out a single word: de-light-ed. The whole family spent the next three days gathered around the dining room table in a vigil, waiting for him to die. We spent hours talking about what your name should be—hours—and I think the fact of your conception kept us sane those three days, the promise of a new existence. Your parents settled on the name Zoe, which means life.

At the very moment you were born, I was at a bar across the street from my office in Boston, slugging down a glass of Scotch. Back then, this seemed like a pretty apt metaphor for the difference between your mother and me: she was off being productive in the most literal sense while I was getting drunk. I joked about that in a caustic, embittered way for a long time but I also quit drinking about two years later, and I think one of the motivations behind that decision had to do with the memory of that feeling, the sense it gave me that my life was stagnating in a bar while other people's lives moved forward. When you were two or three months old, I came over to visit and spent some time sitting on the sofa holding you while you slept. The feeling was astonishing—how warm and tiny and solid you felt, how life itself seemed embodied in that bundle of blankets—and it made me ache. You were four months old when my mother died, your maternal grandmother. We all wanted to hold you in the days before and after her death, to feel the future in you, to ache in that same way.

Now you are bigger: verbal, mobile, equipped with your own tiny personality. You're my twin sister's child, so perhaps I'll always feel like there's a tiny piece of me somewhere inside you; I look for those seeds of commonality and am charmed every time I see a glimpse of something familiar—you seem, for example, to be well on your way to developing a fascination with shoes, a passion I feed with great diligence. (Those little red corduroy slip-ons with the white polka dots? I bought 'em. Same with the black velvet high tops.)

In small ways like that, I suppose you, like lots of nieces and nephews, are the perfect repository for my own fantasies about children and child-rearing, a tiny being with whom I can test out some of my own maternal feelings, tentative though they may be. I am continually struck by my wish to rescue you, even though you don't need rescuing. A few months ago, your mother told me that you'd woken up in your crib at 3 a.m. crying. When she went to check on you, you sat up and wailed, "I want to sleep in a real bed." Bingo! Four days later, you had a brand-new solid oak bunk bed and two new sets of sheets. Power Aunt saves the day. I harbor dozens of narcissitic ideas about how our relationship will unfold as you grow, about future perfection, about how you'll look reverently at me when you're 10 or 15 or 20 and say, "Gee, no matter how bad things were at home, I could always count on you." Perhaps it will not surprise you to learn that I spent an inordinate amount of time when you were two trying to teach you to point at me and say, "Role Model." Shameless, I know, but it worked.

It's odd for a person like me, who doesn't have kids of her own and doesn't spend much time around them, to feel such a range of potent feelings around someone as tiny as you. Kids used to scare me a bit—I saw them for the most part as little unformed psyches, just waiting to be irrevocably damaged—but I feel less of that fear around you—or, at least, the fear has given way to other, more powerful emotions. A few weeks ago, I came over with a small gift, a bee knapsack, black and yellow with wings on it. You put it on and you marched around in it, and times like that you look so cute I have to physically restrain myself from scooping you up and hugging you to death. I stare at you sometimes like I'm watching a fire, mesmerized by your tiny presence, your perfect child's skin, your two-year-old saunter. I spent most of my life assuming you had to earn the affection of others, that being loved required passing tests and jumping through intellectual hoops and proving yourself worthy. It's amazing to me to see, in you, that it's possible to be loved, and deeply so, simply because you exist. That is your gift to me, as precious to me as you are.

Boston Phoenix
August 1995

GRACE NOTES

AN ODE TO BEST FRIENDS

I TURNED 40 THIS YEAR. Big milestone, much ado. The boyfriend sprung for a fancy dinner, the relatives sent cards, the phone rang, e-mails popped up on the computer from pals and colleagues. And amidst it all, one rather startling surprise: the most gratifying part of the day involved not gifts or romance or family, but a quiet walk with my best friend, Grace. We ambled along with our two dogs, we talked about work and men and shoes and TV, we laughed.

Grace and I met almost four years ago, at a time when both of us were quietly reassessing our places in the world. Both of us were single, both crazy in love with our dogs, and both secretly wondering if we should be living with men and kids instead of puppies. We developed a Saturday afternoon ritual of walking our dogs in the woods where we stumbled upon acres of common ground: similar relationships with our fathers, similar addictive tendencies, shared tastes for everything from Levi's 501 jeans to junk TV. We'd even shopped for clothes at the same stores for years and possessed nearly identical wardrobes. "I have that vest!" Grace squealed one day, early in our relationship, when I showed up in a black fleece number identical to one of hers. "Of course you do," I said. "We have the same life."

Sounds familiar, right? We women have a gift for closeness. So why was this friendship so wonderfully surprising to me? Contrary to conventional wisdom, sustaining a close, trusting friendship can be a dicey business for women—at least in my experience. This may be true by definition: institutionalized relationships like marriage and family are bolstered by social supports. Friendships, on the other hand, are subject to few rules, few measurable standards of success or failure. When things get rocky with a girlfriend, you don't cruise the Yellow Pages for a Friendship Counselor. When a friend lets you down or goes through a major life change that makes you feel left behind (marriage, babies, moving cross-country), family members don't urge you to "work" on the relationship. Friendship bonds can be very real and vital but they're also among our most transient ties, and so a certain degree of attrition is natural and predictable: people change, they go their own ways.

An added burden: women are also notorious for shying away from conflict. I have tossed more female friendships than I care to count into the great relational dumping bins of transience and unresolved conflict. Some vanished from my orbit six years ago, when I quit drinking: the friendships were forged on a shared taste for long, liquid, confessional dinners; without wine, it turned out we had a lot less to talk about. Friendships based on common struggles—say, with work or men or weight—can wither away just as easily. When Lauren, a former office mate-turned-soul mate, left the company where we'd met, the bond dissipated within months: no office politics to dish about, no enemy boss to agonize over, no more social glue.

This isn't necessarily a bad thing—some friendships *should* end (the drinking pals are cases in point), and others simply don't build up enough history or affection to weather personal changes or shifts in circumstance. But others die much more needless deaths: from jealousy or insecurity or a reluctance to navigate stormy seas. After a girlfriend of many years compared breaking up with a not-so-great boyfriend to the death of my parents, I remember thinking, *You know, I'm just not going to call her anymore*. I didn't quite keep that promise, but I filed the comparison away in my mental archive of empathic failures, never addressed my feelings with her, backed off instead.

Directness can seem so dangerous that the first run-in Grace and I had terrified both of us. She's a painter—brilliant and creative and abstract—and I'd never said anything about her work, in part because

I know little about abstract art and didn't want to expose my ignorance, and in part because Grace is so accomplished and confident about her work I figured (wrongly) that she didn't need any shoring up from me. When she finally broached the subject, her voice shook: "I need to talk to you about something." The edginess in her voice signaled that we were about to enter difficult terrain, and my heart started pounding. She blurted it out: "We've known each other for months and I have no idea what you think of my work." I rushed to express horror: "Oh my God! I'm so sorry!" And then, after a few stammering moments in which we both acknowledged how daunting the territory felt, we proceeded to have a long, complicated, earnest talk about work and self-esteem and competitiveness and need. We both felt shy around each other for days, and many months had to pass before we could acknowledge just how much courage that conversation required, how frightened each of us was of alienating the other, how difficult we both found it to talk about what we needed from each other.

But why? Why can choppy waters—an inevitable feature of any close relationship—be so monumentally hard for women to navigate? Sometimes, when one of us has her back up about something, Grace and I talk about "the male blow-off valve," a reference to the blithe, no-big-deal style of male conflict-resolution. Exhibit A: Several summers ago, Grace and I spent a weekend together in New Hampshire, accompanied by a mutual friend named Tom, who's a real guy's guy. Our first morning, Tom borrowed Grace's sports watch when he went out for a run and promptly lost it. Grace blew up at him briefly ("Oh, you idiot, I *knew* you'd lose it!"); he huffed back ("C'mon, it's no big deal, I'll buy you a new one"); one $20 Timex later, the incident was forgotten.

But throw two women into a similar situation (or, at least, throw the two of us in), and you get Exhibit B: Not long ago, Grace borrowed a pair of my favorite gold hoops and lost one at a party. This was an accident, and certainly not an unforgivable offense, but it set off a little storm between the two of us that extended far beyond the tangible matter of a missing earring: a girl storm, full of dark undercurrents. I was miffed (I loved those earrings); she was miffed at me for being miffed (it was an *accident*, after all); I was miffed at her for being miffed back (didn't I have a right to express my irritation?); she was miffed at *that* (she'd spent an hour searching for the earring, scouring the sidewalks, didn't that count for anything?), and so it went, the ante on miffedness going up and up. Two days and a boatload of processing later, it turned out we'd had a fight not about earrings at all but about anger (our mutual anxiety about inciting or expressing it), and about responsibility (her projected fear that she's slothful at heart and that the incident would prove it to me), and about trust and boundaries and . . . well, you get the idea.

What's striking to me about run-ins like these is how threatening they can feel, as though expressing even mild irritation or slight differences of opinion can have catastrophic consequences. I suspect there's something remniscent of mother-love at work between women: the kind of closeness and warmth and affection between girlfriends can not only approximate that initital, vital bond; it can actually seem to eclipse it, with a friendship holding out the promise of a more egalitarian and perhaps richer intimacy than the kind we had with our mothers. So when a great new friendship comes along, it flips some internal switch marked SUPERMOM (in its truest sense), igniting a longing for feelings we either once had and lost or never had to begin with: a fantasy of complete trust and openness, unwavering loyalty and affection, emotional synchronicity. Talk about inflated expectations: there's precious little room in that picture for even garden-variety failures (say, a lost earring).

But something else is at work, too. Somewhere, etched in a corner of the female psychic circuitry, there must be some ancient memory of our primate ancestory, of a time when females turned to each other for strength. Scientists have noted that the powerful female alliances you see in primate groups afford the females a degree of freedom and autonomy that, among humans, faded once women became economically dependent upon men. Out of that central shift may have sprung the deep reservoirs of ambivalence and complex feeling that women often harbor toward one another: our old, primal sources of strength are gone, leaving us in competition with one another for men and male-dominated resources, but leaving us, too, with a hard-wired respect for the power of intimacy between women.

That mixed stew of competition and primal love seems key to me. I often feel darkly competitive with Grace; a sensation comes upon me in a stealthy, edgy way that feels inappropriate and mean-spirited and wrong. On bad days (i.e., insecure days) I'll think: she's prettier than me, she's more talented, more articulate, more this or more that, and I'm bothered not so much by the fact that I harbor these feelings (I suspect they're human) but by their fierceness and irrational intensity. Who's keeping score here? And what's the battle about?

I understand that some of my discomfort is socially supported. Women in our culture are poorly schooled at competition: unlike boys, who are trained from the earliest ages to compete—in the schoolyard, on the ballfield, in the classroom—we're trained to be cooperative and accommodating, to submerge such "unfeminine" feelings as aggression and selfishness in the name of keeping peace. But female envy and drive still exist under the surface, no doubt as enduring as our belief in the power of intimacy. No wonder our friendships can have a life-or-death quality, that the bonds can feel like air, the conflicts like fire and gasoline. And no wonder that it's hard to hang in there with a woman friend, hard to tolerate this range of dark and conflicted feeling, hard to even understand why the stakes can feel so high.

The reality, of course, is that the stakes *are* high—that's the price of opening your heart to someone else—and that real intimacy requires hard work. I've always known that a successful relationship with a man takes energy and commitment and honesty, but it's taken me a surprisingly long time to apply the same principle to friendships. Nor, I suspect, am I alone. It can take eons for a woman, no matter how smart or strong she may be, to disabuse herself of the notion that relationships with men are the "important" ones, that friendships are mere adjuncts, that romantic love is what injects meaning into life, fills emptiness, validates existence.

The truth is, love *can* have that effect, but it can come in surprising packages. I've found it in my work, in my dog, and (in part because I've accepted that even the greatest romance won't fix my life or make it perfect) in a boyfriend. Just as important, I've found it in Grace, who has shed new light for me on the nature of true connection. The friendship is by no means perfect—we can, and do, drive each other nuts. But when one of us is genuinely disappointed or hurt by the other, we do our best to thrash things out. "We go good places in this friendship," Grace said to me not long after the earring incident. I nodded. Closeness can be scary and difficult, but ultimately it's the stuff of comfort and depth, the path toward feeling valued and known and a little bit more at home in the world.

So the great gift at 40 was not just the quiet birthday amble with Grace and the dogs; it was the appreciation of how much hard-won trust underlies the bond; it was the sense of cement between us; it was the wonderfully warm and freeing sensation of two grown women walking through the world, together.

SIREN MAGAZINE, 2000

HOW TO HAVE A DOG'S LIFE

HAVE YOU EVER CONSIDERED, or are you currently considering, acquiring a canine companion? If so, understand in advance that your life will change dramatically. When asking you to contemplate life with a dog, most experts ask you to consider a fairly standard set of questions about leisure time and household space: how many hours a day might the dog be left alone; do you have a yard where the dog can play; are you willing to train the dog; and so on. The experts also outline a fairly predictable set of general expectations: you'll need certain equipment for the dog (dish, leash), and you'll need to walk the dog, and here and there you'll have to take it to the vet. These are all important questions and factors, but acquiring a dog is actually a far more complex matter. This is what you are likely to go through.

1. You idealize.

This happens before you get the dog. You have a charming set of images about man's best friend. Dogs are wonderful, obedient, intuitive creatures, correct? You will acquire one for yourself, and occasionally you will walk it and feed it, but for the most part you will go about your business as before while the dog sits quietly by your side and gazes lovingly into your eyes.

2. You have a quick reality-check.

You acquire the dog. In the car on the way home from the animal shelter, the dog sits quietly by your side and gazes lovingly into your eyes. You beam with pride at your fine judgment and wise decision. Ten minutes later, you open the door to your boyfriend's apartment, shout "Look what I got!" and watch as the new pup trots up to the boyfriend and defecates on the rug. In shame, you hustle the pup over to your own home, where she promptly urinates all over the kitchen floor. Reality sinks in: this is all going to be a little more complicated than you thought.

3. *You lose your life.*

Once upon a time, you were a busy, active, articulate young professional who spent the bulk of her time engaged in serious activities: working, reading, discussing important matters with friends and co-workers. Suddenly, within the course of three days, you become a frenzied, confused person who spends the bulk of her time standing in a stooped position with her arms dangling by her sides ready to swoop the urinating, defacating puppy up off the floor and outside. Your vocabulary has degenerated with amazing speed and now appears to consist of only two or three key words and phrases. "Yes!" "No!" "Drop it!" "No . . . no . . . no! outside! outside!" Stoop-and-swoop, stoop-and-swoop: this is what your life has become.

4. *You fall in love.*

So, who minds a little stooping and scooping? By day two or three, you are so enchanted with the new pup you can hardly stand it. Everything she does is cute: her paws and ears and sharp little teeth are cute, the way she curls in a circle on the farthest corner of the sofa is cute, even the way she squats to pee is cute. You worry you might literally cuddle her to death and you periodically forget your boyfriend's name ("Who?"). At first, the pup slept in a crate. Then on the floor by your bed. Now she's on, and in, the bed. Your side. You are so smitten that you find yourself doing things like standing in the kitchen boiling her a chicken for dinner. Free-range chicken, from Bread & Circus. (Notably, you have a fight with your boyfriend about this: you haven't cooked him dinner in three years.) You suddenly appreciate why people join bereavement groups when their dogs die: you're already worrying about how you'll handle your dog's demise and she isn't even four months old yet.

5. *You freak out.*

This phase immediately follows. You wake up at 3 a.m. on the second or third day with your dog and you think, Oh my God, what have I gotten myself into?! This helpless, alien creature is totally dependent upon you and you feel completely inadequate to the task of caring for it. You worry about your inability to anticipate its needs. You worry about your basic character, your capacity for giving and nurturance. You worry about failing the dog in some fundamental way, scarring it for life. You feel completely sandbagged by these feelings—no one told you a tiny pup could generate such a flood of emotion and self-doubt and intensity—and you worry that you're in way over your head.

As the pup develops, other anxieties follow. You begin to act like the mother of a toddler. You take the dog to the park and find yourself worrying about her social skills: will she get along with the other dogs? Does she have the right toys? You become way over-identified with the dog: if she refuses to obey a simple command (sit; heel; stop trying to follow the pizza-delivery guy out to his car), you take it as a sign of personal failure. If she rests her head sweetly on your boyfriend's knee instead of yours, you feel betrayed and paranoid: you haven't bonded with her sufficiently; you're not good enough for her; she hates you. You realize you've got way more emotions than you anticipated tied up in this tiny creature and you find yourself actually discussing your relationship with the dog in therapy. You ponder the irony: at $125 per hour, this is vastly more expensive than the dog was.

6. *You become obnoxious.*

As the dog's social skills improve, yours deteriorate. You realize you are having conversations about such topics as canine stool color and consistency with total strangers at the park, often at great length. You stand on street corners and enthuse loudly, wildly, as your dog pees in public. You begin to bore your friends with lengthy descriptions of the latest incredibly cute thing the pup did, and finally, you exact a promise from your family: if they ever—ever—find that you've added the dog's name to your answering machine message, they will take you out and shoot you.

7. Your social world changes.

You develop a new set of acquaintances, many of whom meet each morning at the same park to walk their dogs: the dogs romp and play; the humans stand in a clump and oooh and aaaah like mothers at a sandbox. The dogs in this particular group have names like Max, Marty, Murray, Rita, Sadie, Frannie, and Lucille. You all stand around discussing the animals, sounding as though you're talking about a group of old Jewish people in the Catskills.

8. You develop canine empathy.

Five or six weeks pass and you begin to settle in. The pup is house-trained (mostly), the two of you have established a set of routines, and you are through the most acute phases of adjustment. You notice at this point that you have begun to think like a dog, probably because you have read nothing but tomes on dog psychology for the last month. You now consider the pup a member of your pack and you are confident about your role as the leader, or alpha wolf. You understand that your pup thinks of you as the head of the pack, and you empathize with her interpretation of the world around her. Thus, when you return from your morning foray to the bakery to purchase breakfast, you blaze into the house with a flourish and announce proudly to the dog that you've been out hunting and killing scones. The dog looks excited by this, so later, when the guy from Bertucci's comes to deliver a large pepperoni pie, you emerge from the front hall with the box and inform the dog that your alpha wolf skills are so sophisticated and acute that a pizza has actually come and died at your front door. The dog wags her tail; your heart swells with pride.

Later that night, you're actually engaged in something non-canine related (reading, watching TV), when you look up and notice: sitting across the room, the dog is gazing lovingly into your eyes. You gaze lovingly back. Then you stop for an instant and relish the moment: this is it; this is the combined result of all that love, all that anxiety, all that work. This is joy, the purest sort.

Boston Phoenix
October 1995

LUCILLE VERSUS STUMPY

THE (REAL) TRUTH ABOUT CATS AND DOGS

A FEW QUESTIONS:

Anyone out there ever heard of a search-and-rescue cat?

How about a seeing-eye cat? Or a seizure-disorder cat? Ever seen a cat saving its family from a flood? Fending off a burglar? Pulling a sled? I thought not.

I ask these questions for a reason. Late this summer, Ron Rosenbaum, an otherwise highly talented and intelligent journalist, wrote a column for the *New York Observer* called "Stumpy Versus Lucille: The Great Pet Debate," a wry little treatise on the superiority of cats to dogs, specifically the superiority of his cat (Stumpy) to my dog (Lucille).

Hah! I say. Hah! and Harumph! and Feh!

Rosenbaum believes that dog owners such as myself are deluded: we love our dogs, and we choose to believe that our dogs love us back, and in fact all our dogs are doing is sucking up, fawning and whimpering over us because we feed and shelter them. It's all, in a word, about Ken-L-Ration. "The 'love' of a dog," he writes, "means nothing. Zero. Dogs are the slavering sycophants, the slobbering indiscriminate flatterers, the bootlickers, the pathetic transparent brown-nosers of the domestic animal kingdom." He says dogs "fake orgasms of affection." He calls dogs "an easy lay emotionally." He is . . . dead wrong.

Herewith, with every bit as much bias as Rosenbaum exhibits in his column, the real truth about cats and dogs.

1. All animals are suck-ups when it comes to food, not just dogs.

Pre-Lucille, a small neighborhood tiger cat used to sneak into my house whenever he found the patio door ajar. I'd find him in the kitchen and as soon as he saw me, he'd start rubbing up against my shins, purring, gazing up at me—the feline version, in other words, of pathetic, transparent brown-nosing: the animal was gunning for a bowl of milk. Rosenbaum suggests that dogs will suck up to anyone—serial killers, child molesters, mass murderers (Hitler's German shepherd dogs, he notes, sucked up to the Fuhrer)—and he uses this argument both to denigrate dog owners (as deluded) and to elevate felines (as dignified). Specious, specious, specious! No cat worth its salt would walk away from an ax murderer if he or she had an ample supply of tunafish. Himmel, I might add, kept cats.

2. The canine "suck-up," unlike the feline suck-up, extends far beyond gastronomy.

When it comes to meting out affection, Lucille is an extremely discriminating dog. A small handful of close friends who have known her since puppyhood get what we refer to as The Greeting on sight—paroxysms of joy, tail wagging furiously, a frantic leaping about that is wholly unrelated to the presence or prospect of food. Other people (secondary acquaintances) get a cursory sniff or two, perhaps a wag if they (or I) seem to send out sufficiently good vibes; total strangers are routinely ignored, often disdained. True, some dogs appear to grovel more than others, and will leap up in shameless delight on anyone—the Fed Ex guy, your mother, Hitler—but Rosenbaum is confusing the canine social nature with the canine food drive. Dogs are pack animals, conditioned over 14,000 years of domesticity to orient their instincts and capacity for attachment toward humans. The fact that cats are aloof and disdainful by comparison doesn't mean they're more discerning or intellectually superior or equipped with higher self-esteem; it simply means they have poor social skills.

3. *The best cats don't act like cats.*

When people talk about having "a really great cat" they invariably describe behaviors that imply high intelligence and responsiveness to humans. The cat is cuddly and affectionate. The cat seems to "know" them, to sense and respond to their mood shifts. The cat follows them around the house, or accompanies them on walks, or comes on command. Ron Rosenbaum describes his own cat, Stumpy, an orange cat who was found abandoned in Brooklyn, half his tail missing, in precisely such terms: Stumpy, for instance, has a way with "the ladies," winking at them, and engaging them in a kind of cat-chatter; he patrols the apartment, keeping an eye on his master, taking his supervisory role very seriously; he even wags his little stump of a tail. Get it? Like all great cats, Stumpy acts like a dog.

4. *The worst cats are scary, strange, and sadistic.*

Okay, I'll be blunt. Cats are weird. They leap up onto high places and sit there, swishing their tails. The females make horrifying noises when they're in heat. On the grooming-and-fastidiousness front, they are like four-legged poster children for OCD. Cats are also mean, at least to dogs. Fred, a big orange cat in my neighborhood, used to sit on a fence post outside my house and torture Lucille. He'd leap up there if he heard her ambling around on the patio and stare at her, a mean-spirited, slitty-eyed, evil stare that she found completely unnerving. Why did he do this? Because he was scary, strange, and sadistic.

5. *Cats require the use of a cat box.*

Plastic box, kitty litter, inside the house. Enough said.

6. *Cats are narcissistic.*

Their needs come before ours. They don't understand the word "No." They carry themselves with that aloof, arrogant sense of perpetual entitlement, they will jump up and insinuate themselves wherever they please—on your lap, on your newspaper, on your computer keyboard—and they really couldn't care less how their behavior affects the people in their lives. I've had boyfriends like this; who needs such behavior in a housepet?

7. *Dogs are like human children; cats are like human children with autism.*

Dogs bond with us. Dogs interact with us, they read and respond to our moods and body language. Dogs, in a word, live in relation to us. Cats, on the other hand, live apart from us: behind those blank stares, they occupy a mysterious world very much of their own, and while this is not necessarily a bad thing, it makes cats most suitable for people who are not particularly interested in a mututally involving or high-maintenance relationship with an animal. At heart, the traits that Rosenbaum finds distasteful in dogs—their sociability, their capacity for attachment—are the very qualities that make living with them both hugely challenging and hugely rewarding. And they're the traits that are missing, for good or ill, in cats.

6. *Cats do not, as a rule, make valuable contributions to society.*

Border collies tend to flocks of sheep. Labs and German shepherds and golden retrievers assist the blind and deaf. Dogs warm hearts in nursing homes and hospitals, they track down criminals, they dig survivors out of collapsed buildings and save them from avalanches, they offer prison inmates lessons in compassion and nurturance.

Cats? Well, let's just say this: you don't see a lot of cats working in law enforcement.

I rest my case.

Boston Phoenix
October 1998

MY CANINE, MYSELF

THE WOMAN WHO runs my dog's day-care center says that Lucille and I are "a little too attached." She says it's "a little unhealthy."

Read that paragraph a few times and then answer a question: have I gone totally off the deep end?

I think so. I think this dog thing has gotten just a tad out of control. Lucille, it seems, picks up on the anxiety I experience when I drop her off at day care every Wednesday. Seems I communicate to her that something bad is about to happen, something ominous is in the air, and this makes her a little edgy: she has a hard time relaxing after I leave, settling in with the other dogs. "She's so tuned in to you," the day-care woman says. "You have to do a better job at communicating that day care is fun!"

Oy vey. This news upsets me. It upsets me to see the look of vague terror in Lucille's eyes when I head toward the door without her (her tail curls under and she looks at me like I'm sending her off to the lions), and it upsets me to hear that I'm contributing to the poor little thing's distress, and most of all, it upsets me that I've gotten this enmeshed—this profoundly involved—in yet another relationship.

Is there no middle ground for some of us? Is there no safe place, no natural harmony between intimacy and distance? Am I so inept at maintaining boundaries that I can't even protect a dog—a dog!—from the debilitating jaws of codependence? Pathetic, ain't it?

Well, yes and no. If I truly thought the dog was as enmeshed and over-involved as I am, it would be pathetic indeed, and I'd be too ashamed of myself to write about it. I've seen dogs who can't leave their owners' sides, who cower and fret when strangers enter a room, who don't "play well" with other dogs, and that's not Lucille. She may feel an edgy pang or two when I leave her with strangers, but she's actually an exceptionally confident and social animal and her anxiety isn't really the issue here. Mine is. Simply put, it embarrasses me that I'm this attached to the dog. It embarrasses me that I drive to the day-care center with my teeth clenched, and that both she and the day-care owner pick up on this. It embarrasses me that this little, 40-pound fuzz-ball has become such a central part of my life, that she occupies so much brain space.

Such a small animal, so many things to worry about. She sits and stares at me and I get edgy: what is she thinking? Is she lonely? Bored? Am I boring her? I eat in front of her and she gets that devastated dog look: you're not going to share that with me? I feel guilty, and try not to look her in the eye. I worry about her mental health, her physical health, her social life (which happens to be better than mine is), and her phobia about highway driving (which is significant; she once sat in my lap all the way from Newton to Fairfield, Connecticut, a three-hour trip during which she would not budge). I am hyperaware of the creature: her diet, her bowels, whether her toenails need trimming, how she's sleeping, how she's playing, how she feels. Sometimes this is exhausting.

"Take a vacation! You need a vacation!" My friend Sandy has been hounding me about this for months, not because she thinks I'm exhausted by the dog but because she thinks I need to get away. She wants me to get on a plane and fly somewhere far away, some place hot and sunny where I can loll on the beach and relax. I hear this and it sounds nice in theory, but the honest, embarrassing truth is that I don't want to be away from the dog that long; she'd be fine, but I'm not sure I would: I'd miss her too much. In the spring, I have to go on a four-city book tour to promote a book I've written. My anxiety about this is considerable—I loathe public speaking and public appearances of any kind—but the fear of exposure pales in comparison to the anxiety I feel around leaving the dog. Four days? Four days without the dog? Anxious little voices start whirring in my brain—she'll forget about me; she'll get mad at me—and it makes me crazy. I hear that Amy Tan gets to bring her dog with her on book tours; it's apparently in her contract. This is motivation enough for me to become a writer of Amy Tan's stature: I don't really care about long book tours and huge levels of visibility, but I very much like the idea of being important enough to write Lucille into my travel plans.

"Has your world narrowed since you got the dog?" A friend asked me this after I confided that I don't do a lot of the things I used to do since I've gotten her, don't go to movies as much, or shopping, or out to dinner, not because I no longer enjoy those things but because my anxiety about leaving the dog behind is sufficiently potent to prevent me. I thought about that question for a long time before I answered it. "It's narrowed in ways," I said, "but it's also opened up in ways. It's a trade-off."

That trade-off is both practical and emotional: on the former level, it means fewer movies and more hikes in the woods, fewer dinners at restaurants and more at-home entertaining. Those are simple exchanges, common to anyone who decides to share life with another species. On the emotional level, it's more complicated. In a way, the level of attachment I feel can be (and, by some readers, probably is) seen as narrowing, constricting: it affects the decisions I make and the degree of freedom I allow myself. I know I worry way too much about the dog's "feelings," that I project mountains of my own stuff onto her—fear of abandonment, feelings of inadequacy, an abiding wish to be special that needs to be constantly reinforced. This feels neurotic at times (it no doubt is), and, yes, neuroses tend to narrow one's focus.

And at the same time, I understand that those very feelings—the fears, the wishes—are the stuff of any important relationship: it's the stuff we're capable of projecting upon people as well as pets, the stuff we need to wade through in order to grow. In that sense, by bringing all those murky feelings to the fore, the dog has helped open my life, helped bring me a little closer to my own soul.

In January, I had her spayed, a daylong affair that involved dropping her off at the vet in the morning and picking her up, still woozy with anesthesia, late in the afternoon. Driving home, the poor dog was completely out of it, shivering, droopy-eyed, unsteady on her feet. I pulled into my driveway, helped her out of the backseat, then watched her pick her way across the snow toward the front steps. She looked ancient and half-crippled, and I immediately (and needlessly, neurotically) projected 10 or 15 years into the future, to a time when she'd be old and arthritic and I'd have to face losing her. I got all weepy, picturing that, and for many days afterward I couldn't get the image out of my head. It made me think about how painful it can be to love deeply, and about how strenuously I've worked, for most of my adult life, to avoid the risks that come with that level of feeling. I adore the dog; accordingly, I'm terrified that something bad might happen to her, that the level of joy she brings might one day be matched by a comparably high level of pain.

This is not a novel insight; it's just one I haven't allowed myself to get too close to in a long time. And in that sense, I welcome whatever complicated, dark, neurotic feelings she evokes: a dog can give you the chance to explore, in a relatively safe but genuine way, what it means to be truly attached.

Boston Phoenix
March 1996

DOG GROUP

A NEIGHBORHOOD FOR THE '90S

SIX O'CLOCK IN the evening. A quiet stretch of grass. Sharp summer light. A small group of humans grouped around a picnic table. And—the main attraction—a pack of dogs, tearing around in various stages of racing, romping, wrestling.

This is part of my new daily routine, an informally organized dog group that congregates at a grassy Harvard courtyard every night from 6 to 7 p.m. If you're an observer of dogs, you see groups like this everywhere—by the banks of the Charles River in the early morning, at schoolyards, at city parks, at open expanses like the Fresh Pond reservoir. And if you frequent one of them, you come to understand that they serve as far more than places for the animals to let off their canine steam. They're for human groups, too, places where people who otherwise might have little in common unite over a mutual concern, where attributes like generosity and kindness replace the workaday ethics of competition and stress, and where that increasingly rare commodity—a sense of community—is allowed to flourish.

Welcome to the neighborhood, '90s-style.

My real neighborhood, the one where my house is actually located, functions like most urban neighborhoods these days, which is to say not at all. People come and go privately: they may wave hello, stop periodically to exchange pleasantries or tidbits of information, but they rarely engage in the kind of communal activity that seemed to characterize an earlier age. This may be less true for some of my neighbors, who've lived in the area for decades, but it's certainly true for me: I don't spend a lot of time, for example, leaning over the fence to chat with the woman next door in her garden. I don't invite the neighbors over to my house for barbecues, or get invited to theirs. Truth be told, I don't actually know most of my neighbors' *names*, and when I need something—a power tool, a cup of sugar—I hop in my car, drive to a store, and buy it.

For the most part, this has been fine, a fact of urban life, something I've barely even questioned. True, it may speak to some of the downfalls of urban living: to our increasing isolation from one another, to the wariness with which we tend to greet strangers, to the somewhat remote manner of New Englanders. But most of the time, I've see my distance from my own neighborhood as unremarkable and easy to explain: my house is my retreat, a place I can indulge my needs for solitude and privacy, and for the most part I haven't felt any compelling need to extend my sense of belonging beyond my own front door.

But the dog group has shifted my view somewhat. I've been taking my dog there regularly for the past few months now and have been finding myself anticipating it with a kind of quiet enthusiasm, a sense of social glee that's unusual for me. I look up at my clock in the late afternoons and think: Ooooh, five o'clock—only an hour until dog group. If the day is particularly stressful, I find myself longing for it: Dog group; wish I were at dog group. This is a neighborhoody feeling, something I've never experienced around my own geographic home, and something I'm realizing now I've missed.

Part of my daily enthusiasm, of course, comes from the fact that I work at home, in solitude—the six o'clock ritual has come to represent a scheduled slice of human contact, which can be a vast relief if you've been at home all day staring at a computer screen. And part of the appeal comes from the simple pleasure of watching dogs at play, something I never tire of. But the anticipation also has to do with the group itself, which is both relatively anonymous and strangely intimate and, in turn, offers a special sort of comfort. Beyond the fact that we all have dogs (and are all fairly obsessed with them), I know very little about the dozen-odd other dog owners: don't really know what they do for a living, where they live, what their personal lives are like. For months, I didn't know anybody's name, and would refer to different members by their dogs' names—that's Berkley's owner, for example, or Martha's owner. The group, moreover, is totally lacking in the kinds of rules or rituals that characterize more structured social clubs and organizations: there are no dues or fees, no process to go through in order to join. People just show up if and when they feel like it: no strings or expectations, no pressure to stay or to return. And yet despite all that—or perhaps because of it—a remarkable sense of connection has cropped up in that little park, a sense of mutual regard and commonality, something that feels like safety.

Dog owners, perhaps, are a breed unto themselves. We're all nuts about our animals and I think that shared obsession is central to the sense of connection: it joins us in the manner of new mothers or medical students, linking us with the kind of deeply felt experience that renders other sorts of similarities—age, background, career—unimportant. All I need to know about those other people is that they're dog people, and that's pretty much all they need to know about me. *She's got a nice dog; she takes good care of her dog:* simple sentences, but they speak volumes about deeper values, the same way I imagine saying "she's got a nice garden" might in other neighborhoods.

The focus on that shared value—dogs—also gives the group a particular and rare feeling of ease. Our talk is eminently simple: we trade training tips and anecdotes about pet care (the dog-group equivalent of trading cups of sugar and power tools); we sit back and watch the dogs in silence; our worries are reduced to tiny things: is one of the dogs digging where it shouldn't be? Is there enough fresh water for the animals?

Contact with other humans is rarely so simple, so easy. In most areas of our lives—at work, in social circles, with our families—interractions can be fraught with edges of judgment, strains of anxiety, flashes of self-consciousness. This has been particularly true for me over the last two months, which has been an exceptionally public period in my life. In mid-May, a memoir I wrote about my lifelong history with addiction was released and I've been in the middle of a publicity maelstrom ever since: at last count, I'd been interviewed 54 times, been dragged through more than a dozen TV appearances, had my face plastered in newspapers from Boston to San Diego. The whole thing makes me acutely self-conscious, and the dog group has taken on even greater importance in the midst of it. It's a sanctuary, in much the same way my home has always been, but it's a less isolated one, and considerably less lonely. No one at dog group gives a hoot about whether I've written a book, or what it's about, or how it's selling in the bookstores; no one judges my work or the personal history behind it; my past is irrelevant. There's a wonderful freedom in that: it gives me a daily chance to slide back into normal life, to focus on nothing but the present, to engage with other people around something considerably more joyful.

My dog, Lucille, turned one last month, a Thursday in June. I mentioned her upcoming birthday to a couple of people at dog group early that week and then showed up on the day in question with a pocketful of extra treats, my version of a dog birthday party. The group's version was better. One person brought a cake and box of Milk Bones. Another brought a tray of brownies with a one-year candle in it. People whose names I barely know brought presents for Lucille: homemade liver biscuits; rubber balls; chew toys; a foot-long rawhide bone. The evening was still and gray and lovely; the dogs raced around with particular vigor, as though they understood the occasion was special; I was astonished. In many ways, these people are all relative strangers and the outpouring of spontaneous generosity and enthusiasm moved me beyond words: it was the sort of experience that restores your faith in human nature, that underscores the importance of simple pleasures, that makes you feel at home in the world, as I suppose any good neighborhood would.

BOSTON PHOENIX
JULY 1996

NO DOGS ALLOWED

THE GUY AT THE computer repair shop sees me coming through the door. He rushes over. "No!" he says. "You can't bring that in here! Leave it outside."

The "it" in question is my dog.

Hours later, I arrive at a local park just as two women are entering, a couple of kids in tow. I ask, "Do you mind if I bring my dog in here?" She looks at me like I'm poison. "Our children are playing in here," she huffs. Then she glares at me, like I've just threatened to dump toxic waste on the grass.

No dogs. A small group of dog owners and I used to meet in the mornings at a Radcliffe quadrangle to let the dogs play: got kicked out. We moved to a little park near Harvard, then another one: got kicked out of both. We get tickets. We get protests and hostile stares. We get yelled at. "Get your dog under control!" I heard a man scream this at Fresh Pond a few weeks ago, one of the few places where dogs are allowed to run off-leash. I turned around and saw that my dog, an eminently gentle creature, was sniffing his shoe.

This is the bane of my existence: contempt for canines.

In a perfect world, dogs would be welcome everywhere: I'd take Lucille with me to the movies, to dinner at Rialto, to my therapy appointments at the Mass General. Alas, there is a perfect world, but it's thousands of miles away and they don't speak English. France is heaven for dog lovers, the cultural attitude toward dogs so different from ours it might as well be a different planet. On a trip through Brittany some years ago, I went to a three-star restaurant with a small group that included a couple and their dog, a five-year-old Shar-pei named Ruby. Not only was Ruby allowed into the establishment, but the waiter promptly asked if he could bring her anything special from the kitchen. Ruby lay quietly by the table while we dined; the wait staff gingerly stepped around her while they served us. Like I said, dog heaven.

A certain graciousness toward canines is creeping gradually into parts of the United States, home to some 55 million dog-owners, but Boston hasn't quite caught on. In California these days, perhaps the most dog-friendly state in the nation, you can find hotels with bone-shaped beds and special doggy room-service menus; in Chicago, you can take your dog to a ballgame at Commiskey Park on specially designated Dog Days ($12 for humans; canines are allowed in for free); in New York, shoppers can take their dogs to Bloomingdale's while the more spiritually inclined can trot them into the Church of the Holy Trinity on the Upper East Side (early service only). But here, this new spirit of openness toward dogs exists at only a few select spots (to name two, Videosmith hands out Milk Bones to dogs, and the Brookline Booksmith welcomes canines openly). More often than not, when I try to bring Lucille into a public place, I get responses like the one from the guy at the computer repair shop: no way, don't even think about it, leave that filthy creature outside. Public parks aren't much more accommodating. In Cambridge, I can count the number of parks where dogs are allowed to run off-leash on two fingers.

This both saddens and annoys me. "People don't understand. These dogs are our children." A woman at one of my since-disbanded dog groups said this right around the time we'd been banished from a Harvard-area park. I'm not sure I'd phrase it quite that way, but I agree with the sentiment. Good dog-owners (and I won't pretend that all dog-owners are good ones) care deeply about their dogs, as deeply in our own way as parents care about their children, and we're often baffled by the extent to which our concern and affection are disregarded. Just try substituting the word "child" for "dog" in some of the above scenarios and you'll get a sense of how I feel. Imagine asking a mother to tether her two-year-old to a street post while she runs into the store to do an errand. Imagine getting huffy with a mom for asking to let her kid play in a park. Imagine screaming at her to control her child when the kid's doing nothing more menacing than exploring its environment. That's how I experience such episodes, like little bullets of contempt: your dog doesn't count; your feelings about your dog don't count; you are too low on the social totem pole to even warrant consideration.

In fact, my wish to provide my dog with a good life, to let her run in open spaces and play with other dogs and accompany me as I go through my day, is as real and as genuine as a mother's wish to provide her child with quality time. It's also, to my mind, as valid. Dog owners—particularly female dog owners—tend to get pathologized for harboring deep attachments to their animals: we get accused of treating dogs as surrogate kids, of sublimating our "real" (translation: appropriate and culturally sanctioned) wishes for children into dogs, of indulging in rampant anthropomorphism. If anything, I think the opposite is true: no single being has taught me more about my lack of interest in having children than Lucille has and I'm quite clear on the fact that she is a dog, a member of a different species and not a little fur-cloaked substitute baby. I revel in the fact that she's a dog, revel in her otherness, revel in the way this alien creature so ably satisfies my need to nurture, and this makes the anti-dog sentiment I come across that much more irksome. The feelings she generates—love, admiration, marvel, protectiveness, a desire to provide—would be applauded were they directed toward a human child; because she's an animal, they're discounted, shooed away, perceived as weird or neurotic, even yelled at.

For the past year, a dog-owning friend and I have been meeting regularly at a tiny, nearly abandoned, postage-stamp-size park in Cambridge to let the dogs play. No one ever goes there after five o'clock; the park is in an out-of-the-way location, hidden behind a wall, and we've considered it a small, undiscovered sanctuary. We go out of our way to keep it clean—litter blows in and we pick it up; we patrol the grass religiously, wielding our blue plastic *New York Times* bags, pooper-scooper-of-choice for the Cambridge dog-owner; in the spring, we planted grass seed, then watched the little space grow lush and green over the summer. A month or two ago, signs sprung up: All dogs must be on leash. Then a groundskeeper came around, telling us there'd been complaints from people who worked in the adjoining building: dog feces on the grass. Our dogs wrestled happily on the grass nearby, content and oblivious, and our hearts sank: banished again.

Boston Phoenix
October 1997

BEST OF BREED: THE MIX

I LIKE TO TELL PEOPLE she is a Sicilian goat hound. (*Very rare breed, only a handful in this country.*) I wax eloquent about her conformation. (*Compact but diminutive: excellent for chasing goats across scraggy landscapes.*) I even make wistful noises about showing her. (*Too bad the goat hound isn't recognized by the American Kennel Club—she'd be a real contender for Best of Breed.*)

In fact, Lucille doesn't need the formal honor: to my mind, she already is Best of Breed—a classic representative of the generic American mongrel.

Of course, most of the 140-odd purebreds currently recognized by the AKC are, in essense, mixes, developed over the centuries by blending particular lines of dogs in order to highlight specific traits. Take the Tibetan and Old English mastiffs, add a dash of greyhound—you get the Great Dane, circa 1500, designed to track wild boar. Blend the setter, the water spaniel, and the curly-coated retriever: there's the golden retriever, created in the early 1800s by hunters who wanted a bird dog that was agile both on land and in water.

This process, known as selective breeding, clearly has served humans (we developed dozens of hardworking, highly skilled breeds), but dogs themselves haven't always fared so well. Particularly in this century, as our culture has come to regard dogs primarily as pets, not as working partners, breeding has become an increasingly aesthetically driven process, emphasizing form over function. The result: generations of over-bred dogs; a steep rise in inherited genetic disorders among purebreds; increasingly exaggerated (and damaging) physical characteristics—the German shepherd's low-slung hips, the bulldog's broader and more deep-set nose, the Irish setter's narrowed head and muzzle. Pleasing to the eye? Maybe. Good for the dog? A few phrases spring to mind: Hip dysplasia. Respiratory ailments. Nervous temperaments.

Give me a genetic hodgepodge; give me the mongrel. My dog might not have the sleek, muscular beauty of a German shorthaired pointer, but I defy you to find a purebred pointer as calm and focused as she. She doesn't have a collie's grace or silky coat, but she's not prone to skin conditions, epilepsy, or eye disorders, either. (A syndrome called collie eye anomoly, which can cause blindness, afflicts 90 percent of today's collies.)

With a mix, you can get the best of everything we've developed in the dog over the last 1,000 years—a border collie mellowed with a dash of Lab, say, or a blend of terriers that comes up calm. You also get a quality of mystery, something I've come to cherish in the mix. What is *in* Lucille? What drives her? Breeding can define canine behavior in such particular ways—the terrier will dig, the sled dog will pull—but motive is an endless puzzle with a mix. What accounts for Lucille's stubborn streak? Her aversion to games of fetch? Her fascination with miniature schnauzers? Mixed-breeds are physical and temperamental enigmas, unique as snowflakes.

Beauty has its benefits—there's nothing quite like the sight of a purebred Rhodesian ridgeback loping across a meadow, nothing like the sharp blue of a Siberian husky's eye—but so too, does wonder.

New York Times
November 1998

WITHOUT

Grief, Loss, Sobriety

THE GRACE PERIOD

REFLECTIONS ON FAMILY LOVE, LOSS, AND GUILT

HAVE YOU GONE HOME for a visit lately and noticed that one of your parents is looking a little older than he or she used to, a little more fragile?

Have certain thoughts flitted across your mind—*shit, what if my father died and my mother was left all alone?* Or, *what if my mother died before my father: how would he ever take care of himself?*

Have you experienced that familiar little stab of family guilt: worry that you haven't been a good enough son or daughter? Or worry that you *won't* be a good enough son or daughter if one of them gets sick?

Yes on all counts?

Then join the club. You have come to the end of the parental grace period.

The parental grace period is a small window of freedom, in which you are too old to be dominated by your parents but too young to really worry about them.

The onset usually takes place at about age 17, when you leave home for the first time and begin thinking of yourself as an independent human being who no longer has to worry about parental rules or curfews or expectations. During this period, you think of your parents in simple, one-dimensional terms: they're your folks. They cook you dinner and maybe do your laundry when you come home to visit. They raise their eyebrows at you when, sheepishly, you bring up your "little cash-flow problem." But basically, they're just *there*, as they always have been and (you presume) always will be—a pretty low-maintenance couple who essentially take care of themselves and give you the freedom to do the same.

This grace period, however, is usually fairly short—10, 15 years max in most cases, sometimes even less.

And when it ends, it frightens you. It keeps you awake at night sometimes, and it often causes you to sit around with friends, shuddering and saying things like, "I can't stand the idea of one of them dying before the other. It makes me crazy."

All of this represents a significant shift in perspective. After all, your parents are the ones who worried about *you* all these years, and you're probably not used to reciprocating quite the same kind of concern. They—not you—are the grown-ups here, right? It can be nearly impossible to imagine any reversal in those roles, and the prospect of it causes all sorts of assumptions to crumble. *Oh my God,* you start to think, *my parents are real human beings, and that means they're vulnerable, and that means they might actually experience such horrors as grief and loneliness and physical pain, and . . .* argh!

Scary stuff.

~

The fear is understandable: it's nearly impossible to think about a parent's mortality without thinking about your own fears of loss, your own fears of that horrid word "orphaned."

But what is the guilt about? When friends of mine talk about the prospect of seeing their parents vulnerable (or sad, or lonely, or in pain), almost all of them get looks of horror on their faces, as if they've just been caught committing a crime.

Some of this probably comes from a certain selfish impulse: the thought of an ailing parent means the thought of a potentially needy parent, and that's not a simple concept for this, the most pampered generation in history. After all, we're used to thinking about the future in terms of what we'd like for ourselves, not in terms of what we might need to do for others.

Accordingly, when we realize that an ill or widowed parent doesn't necessarily fit neatly into our plans, we feel lousy. "I'd probably insist that my mother move up here and live with us," a friend told me not long ago, talking about what she'd do if her father died and her mother were left alone. "But I wouldn't *want* her to." She wasn't being cruel, saying that, just realistic: she and her mother aren't very close, and she understands what kind of strain her mother's presence would create.

But even those of us who are close to our parents feel those twinges of guilt. My father died last spring after an 11-month illness, and when he first became ill the previous year, I felt them in spades. Hearing the diagnosis, one of my first and clearest thoughts was, *If I don't show him how much I love him before he dies, I will spend the rest of my life feeling guilty.*

That awareness actually proved helpful: I spent a lot of time with my father during his illness, and I was able to take some comfort, when he died, in knowing that he did feel I loved him. But the guilt was illuminating all the same. It's a potent force: part love, part obligation, and part regret about what we haven't been able to say, or show, to others in the past.

Today, I've transferred a big chunk of that same feeling to my mother, who's technically a widow (I prefer the term "single mom"). She is one of the strongest, most stoic and forward-looking people I know, but I still cringe when I think of her alone in the house. I call her relentlessly. I worry: is she okay? feeling sad? keeping her spirits up? And I feel enormously guilty: I should be doing more for her, I should be actively improving her life, whatever that means.

It's taken a long time to realize that some of this is plain old concern, that for some of us, guilt and love are instinctively intertwined.

It's also taken a long time to realize that this is life. We all grow up with the myth (and it *is* a myth) that things in life get easier as we get older, not harder, and there are few things like the sight of an aging parent to make you realize how untrue that is. Losses mount as you get older. Challenges become larger and more daunting. Mistakes become more irrevocable.

And maybe that's what's so frightening about contemplating our parents' mortality. When the parental grace period ends, so does one of the last phases of innocence. They *won't* always be there. Life *won't* become simpler.

Boston Phoenix
November 1992

GRIEF STAGES

LETTING GO OF A LOVED ONE (BIT BY BIT)

On Christmas morning this year, I happened to walk into my mother's bedroom, where my sister was changing her newborn baby, Zoe.

I stopped and watched. The baby, only 18 days old, was lying on the floor on a changing mat, uncovered and cold and unhappy. Tiny tears welled in her eyes, and her little arms and legs—all skinny and exposed—kicked out in the air. She broke my heart. I'd never seen the baby naked before and the sight of her, so needy and dependent, overwhelmed me. How tiny and fragile she was! How utterly helpless!

The news that my sister was pregnant with this baby was one of the last things my father heard last spring before he died, so she's had special significance to the family from the start.

My father had been just lucid enough at the time to understand the news, and to choke out the word "delighted" in response. The following day, he lapsed into a coma. And three days later, in the same room where the baby now lay, he died.

Loss—acceptance of a loss—is something that creeps up on you gradually, takes you by surprise in unexpected moments. In the months since my father died, people have warned me about certain dates and occasions—I'd feel grief-stricken on his birthday, at Thanksgiving, at Christmas. The implication has been that these are watershed events, moments that force you to look up from the daily grind, take pause, and fully recognize someone's absence.

Well, yes and no. For the most part, I've gone through all three of those occasions feeling very little—or, at least, much less than I would have expected.

My father died of a brain tumor in April, and his birthday, which fell in late June, came and went too quickly to react to: in the beginning, the fact of a death still feels like an abstraction, something you're barely able to absorb. I spent his birthday with friends, taking note of the date periodically but not thinking about it in too much detail.

I remembered the previous November, when we'd hauled him in his wheelchair out to the car, driven him to an aunt's house where we traditionally spend the day, and hauled the wheelchair into the house. He was so sick and debilitated at that time he could barely feel himself, and the memory of him sitting there in his wheelchair—hunched over, bloated from medication, able to participate in only the most vague and peripheral manner—was so awful that I just felt glad it was over.

Well, not exactly glad, but lighter somehow, less burdened. My father's illness was disfiguring and cruel and horrible to watch. I think that when someone you love dies from something like that, a lot of the grief process gets diverted into a weird cycle of memory and relief: every once in a while, you recall the horror and you just feel thankful, for everyone, that it's over. There's not necessarily a sense of finality in that; you just shudder at the images and then, instinctively, try to shut them out.

I expected I'd feel the same thing during the holidays this year: abstract relief. I remembered the year before, handing him presents as we were all hunkered around the tree. The rest of the family was making a brave attempt to act like this was a "normal" Christmas day—exchanging gifts, taking pictures—but my father had just sat there, clutching whatever gift got handed to him on his lap, too physically helpless to open them and too out of it really to notice.

It couldn't be any worse than last year, I'd told friends, and in a sense I was right. As Christmases go, this one was pretty low-key, pretty uneventful, certainly devoid of visual horror.

Then again, loss is something that creeps up on you. In some ways, I think I've gone through the eight months since my father died assuming on some level that he's still around—on an extended vacation, perhaps, or off recuperating somewhere. Some of this feeling has been manifested in a vague preoccupation I've had with my father's ashes, which currently sit in a brass box in his study. I've wanted to bring the ashes to my apartment, to tend to them in some sense, and I suspect that wish has been related to the lingering feeling that he's still here, still watching over me, still aware of what and how I'm doing.

But in fact, he's not. And I suppose that's the feeling that washed over me when I stood and watched my sister changing her newborn baby on Christmas. Same room, entirely different drama. A place of grief nine months earlier, joy and new beginnings now. So I guess the sight of the baby said something about continuity: his helplessness had given way to hers. We took care of him, we'll take care of her. He is gone, but she is here.

My sister changed the baby, swaddled her up, and calmed her crying. I went upstairs and wept: for the little baby with her life stretched out before her, and for my dad, who, I finally felt, was gone.

BOSTON PHOENIX
JANUARY 1993

MID-MOURNING

REFLECTIONS ON THE LONG ROAD TO RECOVERY

THE OTHER DAY, I forgot my phone number.

Lately, I've been having a great deal of trouble remembering which comes first in the alphabet, *n* or *m*.

And last night, I looked down, noticed I was wearing a pair of off-white shorts and a light green shirt, and I thought: *Oh, how appropriate: I'm dressed like a giant Prozac.*

I think I'm losing my grip.

Grief makes you nuts after a while, it really does. My mother died in April, one year and 11 days after my father died, so I have gone through much of this summer in a crazed state. Foggy. Disoriented. Unable to concentrate. And panicky, very panicky from time to time.

"How are you doing? Is it getting any easier?" People ask me things like this and nine times out of 10, I don't know how to respond.

"Lousy."

"Horrible."

"No. It's worse. *Worse*."

These are the things I'd like to say, but most people don't want to hear them. Which is one of the first things you learn when someone close to you dies—people *don't* want to talk about it. Our culture does a horrible job—an abysmal job—of dealing with death. Three days of bereavement leave: standard. After that, about six weeks of gentle treatment, during which people deal with you gingerly and don't expect too much. And then your public grieving allowance runs out: it begins to feel inappropriate to sit at your desk in a daze, or to come out of the ladies' room with red eyes three times a day, and you feel compelled to act normally again, to feel normal.

I hate it. Sometimes I want to stop people on the street and say, "My parents are dead. My *parents*. Do you understand?" So much has to be suppressed, choked back. "I'm really depressed." I said that to a male colleague a few weeks ago, and he looked at me blankly and said, "Why?" There was a note of genuine surprise in his voice. Depressed? *Why?*—and I wanted to strangle him.

Grief is accompanied by many small indignities—that's another thing you learn. The other day, going through the mail at my parents' house, I opened a letter addressed to my dad, who died slowly and horribly of a brain tumor. It was a chain letter, informing him that if he didn't send out seven copies of the letter to seven friends within seven days, he'd have bad luck. Bad luck. You look at things like that and you just roll your eyes and hope you can muster up enough black humor to appreciate the irony.

I notice this happening with my mom's death, too. After a few months, after the enormity of the loss begins to ease a bit and you aren't conscious of it every single waking moment, the small things become the worst part. We still haven't unpacked the bag we brought to the hospital the last time my mother was admitted, and now it's sitting there at the foot of her bed, right where we put it the day we brought her home to die. Every time I have to walk through that room, I look at the bag and shudder. Everything becomes a symbol of what happened: *There's the bag; she died. There's her container of tea in the kitchen; she died. There's her knitting bag, her checkbook, a grocery list she made in March; she died.*

It's exhausting. Sometimes I understand that I will look back on this period and think, God, I was tired, but right now I'm sort of used to it. Chronic fatigue born of too many intense feelings, too many 5 a.m. nightmares (she's alive; she's dead; we're back in the hospital; she's dying; she's not), too many *tasks*. Her bills. Her estate. Phone calls to the lawyer and the accountant. Lists of things that need to get done. Water her plants. Get an inspection sticker for her car. Call the guy who cuts the grass.

I don't know if all this maintenance, all this tending to the details of the life she left behind, is a form of denial, a form of distraction, or a reality—tasks you simply have to do. But it's so tiring that sometimes I feel like I could fall down and sleep for a hundred years.

Do I sound as if I feel sorry for myself? Well, I do. I can't help it. I feel sorry and angry and cloudy-headed and even though there are plenty of respites from the feelings, moments when life feels calmer and more manageable, I can't escape the understanding that it will all return. That something will trigger the sense of loss all over again, that I'll be sitting there and it will sweep over me—*she's gone; he's gone; they're both gone*—and I will feel so alone in the world I'll think I can't bear it.

Those bad times are a bit fewer and farther between these days (it's true; time does help), and when they hit, I'm a bit better at getting through them. I call my sister, or my mother's sister. I think about the handful of my mother's friends who've been so solicitous and kind, the surrogate moms. I think about my uncle, who phones and checks up on me and calls me "sweetie," like my parents used to.

But sometimes you just lose it. A week ago, I came across a letter my mother had written to me when I was in college, during a particularly bad time in my life. She was being her supportive, empathic self, describing her own lonely college days, her own sense of being insecure and ill-formed in her 20s. The letter was so sweet, so *maternal*, and it made me think about all the times over the years that I've felt lost or depressed or hopeless and I've called my mother. It made me think about her voice in the night, about the depth and constancy of her understanding. It made me think about how much I *miss* her.

I sat there and clutched the envelope and cried and cried, a kind of weeping that's so intense it physically hurts.

It can be a relief to cry, but it doesn't really ease the pain. The worst of it, you understand, is that the only person who could really make me feel better in those moments, the only person I really want to turn to, is my mom.

BOSTON PHOENIX
SEPTEMBER 1993

A MOTHER'S WORK

TALES OF STARS AND SPIRIT; LESSONS IN LOSS

A FAVORITE MEMORY of my mother:

I am about eight or nine years old, at my family's summer house on Martha's Vineyard. A friend of my dad's is there for the weekend, with plans to take us all out blue-fishing on his enormous boat the next morning. I am secretly petrified of boats, and I lie in bed that night imagining terrible things: the boat pitching and tossing, the boat capsizing. My heart pounds.

Finally, late in the night, I get up, slip into my mother's room, and wake her up.

"I think I'm sick," I lie, meekly. "I think I'm too sick to go on Bob's boat."

I don't remember her expression, but my mom must have understood. She reassured me, and told me it was fine: I could stay at home with her while the others fished. Then she took me outside and we sat on the deck, looking up at the sky for what seemed like hours. She pointed out constellations and told me the names of stars. She explained the Milky Way. When I went off to bed again, I felt safe.

That memory has been circling in the back of my mind for days.

My mother, who was a painter, died last April, and I've spent the bulk of the past few weekends weeding through the work she left behind, preparing for a visit from an appraiser hired to value the paintings for estate-tax purposes.

This has been a huge task; my mother's career spanned more than 40 years. In 1948, when good Jewish girls from Brookline were not encouraged to pursue serious artistic careers, she went off to Paris, spent a year at the École des Beaux-Arts, and returned to study at the Museum of Fine Arts School, in Boston. Over the years, her work (she worked first in oils, moving into collage in the mid 1970s) appeared in four solo shows and 20 group shows, and became part of the permanent collections of 11 corporations and museums. In January of 1992, a little more than a year before her death, one of her paintings was accepted as part of the permanent collection at the MFA.

For the appraisal, each piece had to be catalogued, documented, accounted for: which works came from which period, which ones were shown, which ones sold. There are well over 300 paintings and collages, about 150 of them still in the house. There are hundreds of slides, a lengthy notebook recording every piece, every transaction. There is a whole life embodied in her work, and it's been a remarkable process to walk through it: a way to understand her more intimately, a new way to experience her loss.

Stars were a recurring theme in my mother's work (hence the recurring memory). Stars, moons, water, and sky. She wasn't a religious person, but she was deeply spiritual in her own way, and that's reflected in her art, in an ongoing preoccupation with the natural and eternal worlds. Abstract representations of canyons, pueblos, and mesas. Altars, shrines, and talismans. Series of works depicting magic carpets and house blessings, sandcastles and cliffs and gardens. There is a remarkable serenity to nearly every piece: a deep understanding of color and form, a profound feel for balance.

My mother and I talked a lot over the years about the creative process, about her painting and my writing, but I don't think I fully appreciated her work while she was alive. My mom was a private, somewhat self-effacing person, and she rarely, if ever, called attention to herself or her work. Sometimes, she'd talk about a particular piece she'd finished, or she'd bring me into her studio to show me something. I would generally look, and nod, and say, "That's beautiful." I always meant it—her work *is* beautiful—but I rarely went much deeper: rarely asked her what the work meant, what it represented, how she felt about it.

I'm not sure why I kept my distance (I was a "word" person, not a visual person; I was more deeply entangled in my father's life than in my mother's), but I regret having done so: I missed a lot, missed sharing large chunks of her life with her.

But it was all there, laid out on canvas and on paper, as it is still: her inner life, her spirit, her struggles. There are series of collages with names like "Duet," "Trio," and "Concerto"—*ah, yes*, you think, weeding through, *there's her passion for music*. There are works that speak volumes about how moved she was by the land and sky: collages based on trips she took to Chaco Canyon, in New Mexico, and to Japan; paintings based on the water and harbors around Martha's Vineyard; a whole series of works called "Star Charts."

There are more haunting pieces, as well. My sister, a physician, is certain that two in particular are about my mother's health, something she was loath to worry about openly. The first, from 1987, shows a set of coppery circles on a shadowy blue and black background; the second, from 1989, shows four mysteriously illuminated spots. Both bear an eerie resemblance to a bone scan that, in 1989, would show tumors on her skull and spine, the first metastasis of the breast cancer that had been diagnosed in 1981.

It's the struggles like that, the personal difficulties underlining certain periods, that make my heart ache today. Her collages in the years just preceding her recurrence suggest a consistent urgency about time and mortality, with titles like "Calendar," "Shrine," and "Altar." The scanlike collage from '87 is called "Game of Chance." Other years are notable for what they lack: her notebook, in which she scrupulously recorded each piece, is blank from May 1991 to May 1992, the year she spent taking care of my father, who was dying from a brain tumor.

❧

The day before the appraisal, my cousin and I took all the work we'd identified from the house and lined it up, chronologically, in the living and dining rooms. At one end stood a self-portrait she'd done in art school, in the early 1950s; at the other end, my mother's four last collages, a series of "Magic Carpets" inspired by a trip she'd taken to Morocco just six months before her death and just weeks after tumors in her liver had been discovered.

I stood and looked at those last pieces. They represent some of her best work: beautifully balanced, full of vivid blues with flashes of silver, the most vibrant reds, magical shapes. She produced them between January of 1993, three months into chemotherapy, and March, three weeks before her death.

My mother's hair had fallen out by the beginning of that period; she was chronically weak, she had almost no appetite. We talked a lot during that time about her art—not specific paintings or collages, but about the impetus, the tremendous frustration she felt at not being able to produce. She'd talk about standing in her studio for half an hour, then having to sit, or lie, down. Sometimes, days would pass when she couldn't work at all, and she hated that. Still, she finished the first three "Magic Carpets," and almost—almost—completed the fourth.

The night before my mother died, she lay in bed in her room, some 12 hours away from a coma. She was barely speaking at all by then, and hadn't eaten anything more substantial than ice chips for nearly two days. She was in intense physical pain. But at one point, with my brother and I on either side of her, she opened her eyes and said, "I just want to finish that painting. Damn it, I just want to get up and *do* it."

During the weeks spent poring over her work, organizing and cataloguing, I had struggled not to feel too much. But at that moment—looking at that last collage, recalling those last words—I felt a pang of sadness and regret so strong I wanted to burst. She was only 65. She had so much more to do. We had so much more to learn about each other.

Mercifully, there are positive memories, too, better times evoked by that body of work. That night, for the first time in years, I remembered the incident on the Vineyard, sitting with my mother under the stars.

BOSTON PHOENIX
JANUARY 1994

DETAIL WORK

NOTES ON DISMANTLING A FAMILY'S PAST

HERE IT IS, THE inevitable house column: about dismantling my parents' house, sifting through 38 years' worth of family stuff, completing yet another loss ritual.

Ugh. I've been dreading this one—both the task and the act of writing about it.

In the last three years, as regular readers of this column may recall, I've written a lot about loss: about my father's death (April 1992) and my mother's death (April 1993); about the first Christmas my brother and sister and I spent without parents (December 1993), and about burying my dad's ashes (May 1993), and about burying my mom's ashes (May 1994), and about the long, circuitous process of accepting and moving on. Of healing.

Writing those pieces has been an important part of that process: there's always been something helpful to me about the act of recording events, about setting down, in print, the details of what happened and how it felt. It's a little like pressing flowers into a book, or saving mementos in a special box—if you preserve the details, you can move forward, fill your life with other things without worrying too much about leaving the memories behind.

But dismantling the house—that's another story. That process is about eradicating details, stuffing them in boxes, literally carting them off to the dump. It hurts in a whole different way, and I hate it.

Details—almost four decades of them. We grew up in that house, my brother and sister and I, so every inch of it was familiar.

It also hadn't changed much over the years—my parents weren't much into redecorating, so most of the stuff in it had been there, in the same place, for years. In the living room: the same long wooden coffee table, and the same Oriental rug, and the same collections of Colette and Dickens and Henry James in the bookcases. In the dining room: the same oak table we ate at from childhood on, and the same old china cabinet with the same old broken doors that fell off their hinges every single time you opened them. And in the kitchen: the same equipment hanging on pegboards, and the same stove, from 1958, and the same squares of linoleum we once crawled across as babies.

"It's overwhelming." I think that's all we could say for the first month after we sold the house, last May. "Completely overwhelming." My parents—my mother especially—were pack rats, too, so every odd inch of the place was jammed with stuff, attic to basement. *Stuff*. We'd just stand there, staring at a file cabinet jammed with documents and financial records, or into a closet crammed with old clothes and old stuffed animals and old linens and books, and we'd say, "What are we going to do with all this *stuff*?"

Dreck and treasure, treasure and dreck: a vintage photograph of my father's family, all lined up on horseback in descending order of height, stuffed in a milk crate with a bunch of outdated Medicare receipts; my mother's wedding dress, boxed in the attic beside a carton of somebody's ancient highschool notebooks; an entire carton of love letters from my dad to my mom sitting there in the basement next to a shelf of turpentine and old paint.

Where do you even begin with all that stuff? What do you toss? What do you save?

The hardest things to sort through, of course, turn out to be the things with only the most oblique and personal meanings: you stumble upon a cookie tin filled with beach glass from Martha's Vineyard and it evokes a precious and specific memory—my mother, inching down the shoreline in her terry-cloth beach robe, hunting for specimens on the sand—but do you actually save it? And if not, can you bear to throw it away? Each small discovery and decision is accompanied by a burst of conflicted feeling—the warmth of memory, the pang of loss, the confusion about having to let go—and you just struggle to keep sifting through.

Anyone want this? You're holding a pair of mittens that Mom knitted in 1969 from a special Norwegian pattern. Or a platter that held the turkey every Christmas for 30-plus years. Or something as simple as a juice glass or a mug, something you know you drank from as a child.

And in the end, a lot of it simply has to go. There's no other way. *No. Chuck it. It'll just sit in someone else's basement.*

We saved what feels like a vast amount—important stuff like valued pieces of furniture and china and the family silver; smaller stuff like letters and pictures and folders of art we made as kids. But we got rid of so much more. In the end, we tossed that beach glass into a garbage bag, tin and all, and hauled it out to the curb.

ꕤ

We sold the house in May and emptied it by mid July. Cleared and sorted and dragged stuff out. Gave this to the homeless, that to the Salvation Army. Filled a 22-foot dumpster to the brim with junk and had it hauled away, packed scores of boxes, picked through every last cupboard and closet and drawer. My mother was a painter, and dismantling her studio was probably the worst part: a vivid physical reminder of a life cut short. She'd worked there until the very end; her drawing table and brushes and paints were still set up the way they'd always been; the room was littered with small works in progress, sketches and notes, bits of material for collage, heaps of colored paper. I hated seeing that room empty, bare. It seemed cruel and unnatural, and I couldn't stand to look at it for more than a minute.

So the house is empty now. Or, rather, it's being filled with someone else's stuff. The last time I went in there, about a week after the closing, the new owners had started renovating parts of the kitchen, which abutted my mom's studio. There was a doorway between the two rooms, and over the years, when we were kids, my mother would periodically line us up against the door frame and measure us, recording our height with a pencil line. It was a little ritual of hers, a way of charting our growth over the years, and I have fond memories of standing there and looking at the lines, seeing how little we used to be and how tall we'd gotten over time.

From what I could gather, slipping into the house that last time, the new owners had torn down the wall between the two rooms. The door frame, with its record of change, was gone.

BOSTON PHOENIX
AUGUST 1994

GRIEVING LESSONS

NOTES ON ENTANGLEMENT, A POWERFUL TEACHER

YOU KNOW HOW sometimes you talk to your mother on the phone and she says something that seems repetitive or critical or inane and you have to suppress the urge to scream?

You know that particular kind of mom-related guilt you feel when you know you should call or visit her but you really, really don't feel like it?

You know how sometimes you regress the instant you walk through her front door, how you turn within seconds into the angry, sulking, sullen adolescent you used to be?

I miss all that.

It's been just over a year and a half since my mom died, and it's surprising to me how the more negative stuff has crept into the process of grieving—the annoying stuff, the wrenching stuff, the complicated parts of the mother-daughter equation. Sounds kind of silly, or bizarre, but I miss being able to gnash my teeth about mom from time to time. I miss being able to gripe about her, or to roll my eyes with exasperation because I think she's fussing too much or talking too much or not paying enough attention. I hear other women snipe about their mothers all the time—"Oh, she's driving me crazy!"—and my heart kind of sinks.

My mother didn't drive me crazy very often, but I find myself feeling curiously wistful when I think about the times she did. I guess I miss the entanglement, which is so often at the heart of mother-daughter relationships. There's so much to be learned from the feelings behind it.

My mom carped when she got anxious. That was her way. She'd carp when she ordered something from a catalogue and it didn't come on time. She'd carp when she went grocery shopping and discovered some outrageous new price on milk or paper towels. She'd carp when repairmen didn't show up when they said they would. Detail-carping.

It used to drive me nuts. You'd call on the phone to say hi, and she'd start talking about some window shades she'd ordered, and how they arrived six weeks late, and how she'd opened them up and they were *ecru* instead of *eggshell*, so she had to send them all the way back and then wait another six weeks for the eggshell ones, and—well, five minutes later my jaw would hurt from clenching. I'd sit there on the phone and quietly steam, far more annoyed than I had a right to be. And then I'd weasel my way out of the conversation ("Yeah, well, gee, Mom, too bad about the shades—gotta fly!"), and then I'd hang up the phone and feel that particular brand of mother-guilt settle in my gut, the kind that tells you you're bad and ungrateful, a selfish, intolerant daughter with warped priorities.

Right now, of course, I'd give anything to hear my mother rant about shades or paper-towel prices or errant repairmen. Just five minutes of her voice—I'd take it. And right now, the thought of those phone calls fills me with a terrible regret: at my impatience, at feeling annoyed even once with someone I miss so much now. It makes me long to go back and be kinder on the phone, to respond in ways that convey appreciation instead of irritation.

But I think the longing also goes much deeper. In retrospect, I find that the more difficult moments with my mom, the more wrenching or guilt-provoking ones, were often the ones that taught me the most.

In truth, for example, those phone calls were rich with code, with underlying messages, the stuff of mother-daughter dynamics. I know today that my mom carped about externals because she was too private and too proud to carp, particularly to her daughter, about the deeper sources of her anxiety: about her health, about her own abiding sadness, about her own fears and regrets. On some level, I must have heard an undercurrent of that anxiety in her voice, and I suspect that the painful stabs of annoyance and guilt I'd feel in response had to do with my own sense of impotence and confusion in the face of her distress: my own discomfort with it; my frustration at feeling compelled to help her and not knowing how; my wish (perhaps childish) for the anxiety to subside, for everything to be *okay*.

Her fears, my fears, our whole quiet, entangled way of reacting to each other—so much stirred up in a single five-minute phone call! And I guess that's what I miss: the depth of those ties, and the power of the feelings they evoke.

Looking back, I can see evidence of those ties, of those hidden tugs between us, in just about every little thing that seemed to bug me.

Like my mom's kitchen, which used to drive me crazy. I'd walk in there and see stuff everywhere—counters cluttered with old jars and half-full bags of potato chips, dishes everywhere—and I'd have an almost visceral reaction to the mess. Teeth-gnashing; tension; *how does she live in this mess?* But my mom's aversion to housecleaning isn't really what got to me at all; it's what that sight brought up for me—namely, my own persistent fears of chaos and disorder, feelings bred in childhood that linger into the present. Her action; my reaction.

I think it's true that anger at others very often reflects anger at ourselves, discomfort with who we are: it's clear to me now, for example, that as a teenager I'd get annoyed with my mother's shyness because I shared it (and found it painful). Or I'd feel a stab of disdain if I sensed she wasn't standing up to my dad, because I struggled (and so often failed) to stand up to him, too.

I guess it's rare to feel that deeply identified with another person. And I guess that's why a mom is capable of pushing so many buttons—the lines between the person she is, the person you are, and the people you want each other to be are often so crossed and muddied and overlapped.

But if that's what makes mother-daughter relationships so entangled, it's also what makes them so rich. A mom, after all, is like an internal road map or a mirror; your relationship with her reflects a lifetime of lessons learned, of paths followed and then settled upon or abandoned. It's hard to make any decision as a woman—about a career or a relationship, about where to live or how to dress or what sorts of friends to have, about *who to be*—without measuring it, on some level, against the decisions your mom made, without gauging how her struggles helped shape or limit her, strengthen or weaken her.

I turn 35 in a few weeks, and have years of big decisions ahead of me. I still feel like I need that mirror, that map, those aggravating phone calls. I don't feel nearly old enough to be going it alone, with just my memories.

BOSTON PHOENIX
OCTOBER 1994

CLEARING UP

GRIEF IN SOBRIETY: CONFRONTING LOSS ONCE MORE, WITH FEELING

THE DREAMS START coming this time of year, in April, like clockwork. In one, my mother calls me on the phone and I realize she isn't dead at all; she's simply been away on a long trip. In another, my father appears at my front door with flowers, sorry about causing so much grief, assuring me that it was needless—See? I'm right here—and that it won't happen again.

I wake up from these the way I always do: relieved to tears at first, then confused, then oddly chastened, embarrassed that my mind still plays these tricks on me, a little stunned that I still harbor such potent feelings about my parents' deaths. Then my instincts snap into action and I look for relief from the feelings. Almost always—even if it's 6 a.m., even if it's a Monday morning and I have a full day of work ahead—I want a drink.

Drinking. I miss it.

I drank through both my parents' deaths, which took place in 1992 (my dad) and 1993 (my mom); it was the only way I knew how to handle it.

My mother died on a Sunday. She'd been at the hospital for four days and on the final day, Saturday, it became clear she wouldn't survive. So we decided to bring her home, to let her die in her own bed. My brother and sister and aunt went with my mother in the ambulance. I took my own car, stopping on the way home at a liquor store near our house, where I picked up a fifth of Dewar's and hid it in my purse. I drank most of it that night, slipping upstairs or into the bathroom with the purse tucked under my arm.

I drank through my father's death the year before. Drank the night he died, the night after he died, the night of his funeral, and every night after that for a long, long time. The drinking had a wonderfully paradoxical effect, loosening me up enough so I could cry but also numbing the pain so I didn't have to cry too hard, or for too long.

Same with my mom's death. She died on April 18, and that spring and summer I got into the habit of curling up in a chair at the kitchen table almost every night, a bottle of white wine and the telephone as my armor against grief. I'd call her close friends, or her sister, or my own sister, and I'd mourn into the phone, drunk and weepy and maudlin. It seemed to work at the time. In any event, the wine helped me talk, and it replaced the panicky, disoriented feelings of grief with something that felt like a kind of comfort, and it got me to sleep at night, a deep, dark dreamless sleep.

I had my last drink on February 19, 1994, and haven't had another one since. A few months after I quit, I explained it this way to a friend: "I had all these *things* coming up—a book coming out, a 35th birthday, the anniversary of my parents' deaths. I had all these milestones ahead, and I didn't want to go through them drunk."

Which, I suspect, I would have. I drank for many years before my parents' deaths, and I always drank (and often too much) through the important parts—graduations, weddings, and funerals; first sexual encounters, fights, and break-ups; good times, bad times, powerful times. Drinking works—it's a wonderfully effective tool for bolstering confidence, easing fear and pain, managing strong emotions—but if you do it long and hard enough, you begin to understand that it stifles and impedes in equal measure. Confidence acquired through alcohol is ultimately artificial; pain addressed through liquor ebbs temporarily, then washes back up again, as raw as it was beforehand. Drinking mutes strong emotions—anger, grief, anxiety—but only for a little while.

One of my mother's favorite sayings was, "Life is not a dress rehearsal," and I thought about that a lot in the months before I quit. When you drink enough, when you consistently rely on alcohol to get you through the tough spots, everything in life begins to take on the abstracted quality of practice: the summer after her death, mourning into the telephone night after night, I was practicing grief instead of really doing the work. Pain diluted is simply not the same as pain confronted. Same with the liquor-confidence equation, or the liquor-anxiety equation. Sophistication acquired from a martini at a cocktail party is simply not the same as sophistication acquired from within, from the hard work of meeting anxiety face-to-face.

Sometimes I look back and think my whole adult life has been underlined with a feeling of waiting—waiting for something to happen, waiting for circumstances to change, waiting for the right man or the right job or the right shoes-and-clothes-and-haircut to swoop down from above and *change* me, to infuse me from the outside in with a feeling of well-being and validation and peace of mind.

It didn't occur to me until well after I'd quit drinking that alcohol played a large role in maintaining that holding pattern, in shielding me from the painful steps involved in moving forward.

Drinking works: it soothes, eases, calms, lightens. But it doesn't help you grow up.

So the anniversaries roll around again, and this time they hurt in a different way. There's a clarity to the feelings, a sharpness that seems both more painful and more pure. It's a little like looking at the world through new glasses, long after you've gotten used to seeing it slightly out of focus. You look up one day and see the edges of things, the nuances: *Oh*, you think. *That's how it is*.

Last week was the three-year anniversary of my father's death; next week will be the two-year anniversary of my mother's. I used to feel sorry for myself when concrete reminders of their absences came up: morbid and withdrawn, bumping up against the edges of sadness. This time, facing them soberly, I feel sad—and also brave.

Grief and clarity; once more, with feeling.

Boston Phoenix
April 1995

FOOD AS ENEMY

THE ANATOMY OF AN EATING DISORDER

From the summer of 1982 through the winter of 1985, I ate the same thing almost every day: a plain sesame bagel for breakfast, a Dannon coffee-flavored yogurt for lunch, an apple and a one-inch cube of cheddar cheese for dinner. Nothing more.

Once in a while—with long, painful deliberation—I varied the diet. I'd substitute 10 Wheat Thins for half the apple at night, or I'd have a vanilla yogurt for lunch instead of a coffee one. On even rarer occasions, I had a bad day: those happened if I became overwhelmed by longing, or if I found myself in social situations where I really couldn't avoid eating, or if I absolutely couldn't stand it anymore. And then I would give in and eat, and eat, and eat, and eat—until I felt sick or crazy or both. But that didn't happen very often. For the most part, I had good days: a plain sesame bagel for breakfast (80 calories), a Dannon coffee-flavored yogurt for lunch (200 calories), an apple and a one-inch cube of cheddar cheese for dinner (150 calories). And nothing else.

Nothing else mattered—just food and my weight—and the effort to control them superseded everything. I lost friends because of it. I lied about it. Feelings—of love, sexuality, passion, rage, whatever—became no more than alien concepts, things that other people felt. Starving was my only goal.

The technical term for this affliction is anorexia nervosa. But in everyday language, it's an addiction—as powerful as alcoholism and in some cases as lethal. Conservative estimates are that one out of every 100 young women are case-book anorexics. Scores more, however, fall into anorexic behavior on a regular basis.

ꕥ

At the time, I was working for a Providence paper, my first journalism job. I was young, shy, scared, lonely, and, probably most of all, angry. I didn't know what else to do, so I starved myself.

Like any addiction, starving is a coping mechanism. It is self-protective. When I was starting, all I could think about was food: what I'd eat next, when I'd eat it, how I'd eat it, and whether it would be too much or not enough. And because all I could think about was food, I didn't have room to think about anything else: not the past, not the future, not men or friends or world events, and certainly not things like the fact that I was young, shy, scared, lonely, and angry.

Starving also gave me a sense of power. On good days—the days I stuck to my regimen—I used to test my will by walking home from work down a street full of food stores and restaurants. I passed a restaurant where I could see trays of pastries through a glass window. I passed a gourmet-food shop, a Dunkin' Donuts, a candy store, an outdoor café, a bakery. I could smell the honey glaze on doughnuts. I could smell French fries, teriyaki chicken wings, and homemade oatmeal bread. It gave me a tremendous sense of control. There I was in the midst of all that food and I could resist the craving to eat, no matter how hungry I was. I was strong, different.

On good days, I also felt superior. I would look at people on the street—shoppers carrying bags of food, couples eating at the café—and I felt detached from them. Above them. They were giving in to appetites I had transcended, impulses I had conquered. At a time when I felt essentially worthless, starving was the one thing I could say I was good at.

ꕥ

I was very, very good at it. My normal weight is about 120 pounds. By the end of 1984, I weighed 85. I have a photograph of myself finishing a six-mile road race that fall. In the picture, my knees are wider than my thighs.

ꕥ

A little background on "typical" anorexics: About 90 percent are women. Most come from well-educated, affluent families that emphasize achievement. Most are young, 12 to 25 years old. And from what I can gather, most are excessively driven, perfectionistic people with abysmal self-perceptions, people who derive what little esteem they have from pleasing others.

I grew up in an upper-middle-class family, went to a private prep school, then an Ivy League college. I was pretty, popular, got straight A's, and won lots of academic prizes, none of which ever meant much because I tended to see anything good that happened to me as the product of something external—a fluke, warped judgment on the part of others, "luck." Inside, I was pretty certain I was flawed.

I wasn't ever fat, though. Growing up, I rarely gave much thought to what I ate, and until I created one, I never had a weight problem.

Then I lost some weight during college, almost by accident. I didn't consciously diet—I didn't think about food or obsess about it. It was a rough time, I felt depressed and stressed out, and I just remember not eating much in response.

I also remember that people noticed. Girls said, "Oooooh! You're so thin!" And "How do you *do* it?" And I think that planted a seed: becoming very thin was a way of standing out.

I ate less and I lost more weight. It was easy. I'd go to a bar near campus with friends, and I'd watch them dive into bowls of buttered popcorn. I wouldn't eat the popcorn—not even a kernel—and I felt very disciplined by comparison. Not eating made me feel strong.

Then, for a long time—and like a lot of women—I was just plain weird about food. After college, a boyfriend I'd been living with moved to California and I was living by myself for the first time. I hated my job and I was lonely. Sometimes I was very rigid with my diet. Other times I ate for comfort: cookies, huge salads full of meats and cheese, tuna melts, salt-laden soups. My weight fluctuated a lot, and my hunger signals started to get screwed up—I couldn't tell when the hunger was the real, physical kind and when it was a more manic, frantic kind, the signal of some other kind of emptiness. For the first time, I started to understand what was going on with women I'd see at dinners and parties, women who seemed excessively preoccupied with food and diets and weight, women who expressed an almost palpable anxiety as they reached for a second slice of cake or an hors d'oeuvre and said, in voices a little too loud, "Oh, I really shouldn't." For the first time, my self-esteem started to get hopelessly tied up with the feel of my stomach and my thighs and I started to worry about being fat.

Early in the summer of 1982, the boyfriend who had moved to LA came back to visit. He had planned to spend the summer with me, but something came up and he ended up going to Europe with a friend instead. I didn't really feel it, but I guess I was furious. The day he left, I walked him to the train, then went back to my office. As I was walking along, I knew somewhere inside that I was going to starve myself until he came home. It wasn't so much a conscious decision as a response: he has done this thing to me and this is how I am going to react. By the time he got back from Europe, I had lost 15 pounds.

At some point in any addiction, a behavior stops being something you use to control your feelings and turns into something that controls you instead. I probably crossed that line that summer. Whatever I was trying to starve away—loneliness, uncertainty, anger—gradually became less important than the starving itself. It started to influence the decisions I made and the ways I spent my time: I started refusing invitations to go to dinner with friends because that would mean eating. I started calculating calories, and then eating fewer and fewer and fewer in order to protect myself against the times I did eat—a weird sort of "just to be on the safe side" mentality. I started eating privately, and eating only specific things, and then I started looking forward to those times, and then I started building elaborate rituals around them to make them more important.

And at some point, I crossed way over that line and there was no turning back. Normal eating came to mean guilt, failure. It ceased to be an option. So I clamped down, stopped eating altogether, or tried to.

And in the process, I stopped having people in my life—and the risks associated with them—too. Trying to keep food at a distance was a metaphor for trying to keep other things at a distance: people, feelings, vulnerability.

❧

This was how a typical good day started: I would get up at six o'clock and buy my sesame bagel, a cup of coffee, and a *Providence Journal-Bulletin* on the way to work. I always got there by seven, a full hour and a half before anyone else came in. I would set the bagel on a little plastic plate that I kept in my desk, as if it were a gem. Then I would read through the front section of the newspaper, every word. And then I would eat the bagel, with the deliberation and intensity of someone performing surgery. Actually, that hour and a half was my favorite, most reliable time of day. The solitude was consistent, the ritual perfect and precise. I would tear off tiny bites of the bagel, each timed to a different section of the newspaper. A bite for each editorial on the Op/Ed page, a bite for the comic page, and so on, until it was gone. Then I would press the sesame seeds that had fallen off the bagel and onto the plate into my index finger and I would eat those. This became such a familiar pattern, and the familiarity was so comforting, that I wondered if I'd ever be able to give it up. Or want to.

No one at work knew I did this, even though the paper I worked for was small and quite collegial. Actually, that may not be completely true. I imagine lots of people suspected something was wrong, but I wouldn't let them close enough to do anything.

I kept them at bay mostly by lying, by creating illusions of normalcy and contact. I'd lie about spending time with friends in order to hide how isolated I was. I'd lie about some huge breakfast I'd eaten—French toast or bacon and eggs—in order to establish in their minds that yes, I was an ordinary, functioning human being who ate regular meals. I told them that big lunches made me sleepy, that I just liked yogurt. And even though they said things to me—"You're so *skinny*!" "You must eat like a *bird*!"—I got good at deflecting concern. "Birds actually eat twice their weight every day," I'd say. "Did you know that?" End of subject.

Going home was harder. I lived with two friends during this time, and hiding it from them took almost as much energy as actually starving. I was anxious all the time. I would walk home at night praying that my roommates—whom I genuinely liked—would be out. If they were, I could just shut myself up in my room. If they were home, I had to act. I would make a point of keeping my bedroom door open, not wanting to expose this wish, this need, for isolation. If they were eating dinner, I would make a point of joining them in the kitchen for at least 20 minutes. Then I'd perch up on the counter, a safe distance away, and listen to their various sagas, trying to feign genuine interest. "A raise? *Great!*" "You did! *Terrific!*"

Ignoring their meals was the hardest part. "Oh, no thanks," I'd say, lightly, when the offer came. "I grabbed a sandwich on my way home from work." Then I'd watch as they ate. It amazed me how casually they treated food. One of my roommates used to recline in her chair after dinner and smoke a cigarette. Almost invariably, she'd leave some of the food on her plate untouched, and while she smoked she'd push the uneaten portion around the plate with her fork—taking a bite of chicken, for example, and making little swirling patterns in the leftover sauce. I found that sight, the lack of reverence for food, astonishing.

Because all I could think about was food. When I was alone, I read food magazines and cookbooks the way other people read porn. Wednesday was one of my favorite days because the paper's food section came out. I still have a collection of recipes I copied down during that time, painstakingly, on index cards: they're all for breads, cakes, chocolate desserts, things with the richest fillings. Things I longed for and wouldn't let myself have.

Which is part of what the behavior was all about: food itself became a terrible, powerful symbol—of how much I wanted on the one hand, and how terrified I was that I'd never get enough on the other. Controlling food became a way of both expressing that conflict and denying it. At the time, I was furious at the important people in my life—at the boyfriend I felt had abandoned me; at my parents, whom I saw as passive and remote; at my sister, who had moved away—but

I couldn't express the anger so I wore it instead: see what you've turned me into, see how desperate and unhappy I am? I was terrified of people, of being disappointed; on a deeper level, I was terrified of appetites in general—emotional and sexual, as well as physical. So I resolved to suppress them instead, squelch them, will them away. If you don't have any needs, they can't go unmet.

One night I came home and found my roommates in the kitchen with a friend. They were sitting at the table drinking beer, sending out for Chinese food, and they were all laughing. I felt incredibly wistful for a second, watching them there. It was such a relaxed, normal picture, and I was so far removed from it.

But it didn't matter. The rule was not to give in, not to give in, not to give in. It was the way I organized my life, the way I defined myself. So I went out running instead.

I remember how it felt, to run. My whole body ached. I felt all drawn and tight, as if my ribs and the bones in my knees were literally pressing against my skin. I was also exhausted. At one point, I tripped and just caught myself from falling on the pavement. I still have an image of how that looked and felt—three great, awkward, loping steps, arms outstretched and groping for balance; eyes wild. I panicked, and for a second I saw myself as wildly out of control, flailing in the dark, alone. I pulled myself together and kept running, but in that one moment, I realized how much I wanted to be there in the kitchen, eating Chinese food and drinking beer with my friends.

But I didn't join them. I came back, pretended I had stomach cramps (sometimes it was a headache), and disappeared into my room. On a ledge outside my window, for just that kind of situation, I kept a baggie with the cube of cheese and the apple in it. That way, I could retrieve and eat my food in secret.

Times like that I knew how lonely I was, and how fucked up my life was, but I couldn't do anything about it.

About once every two or three weeks, something would come up—a party at work, someone's birthday, a family visit—and I would eat. I planned for those times with a vengeance, cutting out the cube of cheese at night for days beforehand, calculating calories, imagining what would be served and how much I'd let myself eat. I often cooked, too, making something I'd fantasized about from my recipe file.

In a way (and on some level I knew it was a bizarre way), those were the events I saved up for, week by week. A buildup of pressure, followed by a release, an unleashing. But the release was horrifying—a terrifying reminder of powerlessness, of the fact that underneath it all, my appetite was really much greater than my capacity for denial.

I remember making a dinner for friends one New Year's Eve. I spent all morning shopping—five different stores—and all day cooking. I bought the best bread, I made fettuccine with chicken, garlic, and three kinds of cheese. I made a chocolate-glazed hazelnut torte filled with buttercream. When we finally sat down to eat, I was so focused on the meal, so overwhelmed by it, I barely remember speaking.

Times like that, I tried to mask my preoccupation by imitating the others: ignoring the bread basket until they passed it around, taking seconds only after they took more too. But once I gave in, I was insatiable. And later, after everyone had gone home or to bed, I always did the same thing. That night, I stole back into the kitchen and knelt by the refrigerator-door light. My stomach aching, I ate two more pieces of bread, another plate of pasta, and two hunks of cake. It was like making up for lost time. Or hoarding up for the next long stretch, like a squirrel.

I loathed myself after episodes like that. I would go to bed aching and humiliated, my head reeling. When I woke up, the first thing I'd think about would be my stomach and face: bloated. And I would lie there, terrified that the bloat was eking its way into the rest of my body, into my thighs and chest and arms, that it was creeping in, undermining all that work, destroying my very identity. And my resolve would grow even more fierce: I will not eat. Today will be a good day. I will not eat.

Sometimes, in a small back corner of my mind, I would also acknowledge that the pain was more than merely physical: I was absolutely unable to manage my life. And I was furious, at least on some level. There I'd been, racing around the kitchen, a 90-pound waif cooking a 9,000-calorie meal. And no one had stopped me.

~

I finally told my parents sometime in early 1984. I had gone home for a weekend and I was probably at the lowest weight I ever hit, about 84 pounds. It was a Saturday, early in the spring. I had been home for hours and they hadn't said anything about the way I looked. At one point, my mother was drinking tea in the kitchen and I peeled off my sweater, ostensibly because I was cold and wanted to put on something heavier. Underneath, I was wearing a camisole. I wanted my mother to see how the bones in my chest stuck out, how skeletal my arms were. I wanted her to see how sick I was. I may be remembering it wrong, but I don't think she said anything.

I drank a lot of wine that night and I finally started to cry and told them: I am having a problem and I don't know what to do about it; I think I am anorexic. All I remember is their eyes: concerned, a little scared, but mostly helpless. They couldn't identify with it, and I couldn't explain it.

People don't understand what this is about, even—or maybe especially—when it happens to someone close. About a week later, I got a note from my mother in the mail. It said, "EAT."

~

Once, a Sunday in May, my roommates were away and I had the house to myself. It was the first warm day of the season and all the trees outside were budding. I stayed inside all day, the shades drawn because I didn't want to see the spring, all that growth. Late in the afternoon, I went for a walk around the Brown University campus. Students were all over the place, sunburned, lounging on the grass, playing frisbee. I watched a couple in khaki shorts and white T-shirts walk past, holding hands. I felt so alien and so alone I couldn't stand it. I went home and sat in the living room and looked out the window at an apple tree that was blossoming. The disparity between my life and other people's lives seemed so great I wanted to lie down and die.

But most of the time, I denied it all. I was cold all the time, even on warm days, and I denied that. I had dizzy spells, I'd stand up and lose my vision, and I denied that. I didn't menstruate for two and a half years, and I denied that. I was 23, 24, then 25 years old and I had virtually no close friends, only the most superficial social life, certainly no sex life—and I denied that, too. I could live with the isolation. I could live with the profound boredom of thinking about nothing but my weight. But I could not live with losing control. I got used to being depressed.

❧

I thought of the good days as "concave days." My hip bones would jut out a full inch on either side and I could run my hand across my stomach and follow the curve inward. When I took a deep breath and sucked in my stomach, I could see my whole rib cage. I found that extremely relieving.

At night, I often took a bath before my dinner. As I settled down in the water, I would examine my legs and arms and shoulders. I would ring the top of each thigh in my hands to make sure my thumb and index finger could meet around them. I'd run a finger against the bones that stuck out on my chest, press my forefinger along my collar bone on either side, examine the points of bone that ran up under the skin on my shoulders.

I never actually thought of myself as "thin" or "fat." On good days, I just felt angular. And even though my stomach throbbed, pulling inward in little aches, the sharp, angular feeling was a comfort. It meant I'd made it. I'd won.

❧

This is how I ate dinner: At 10 minutes to nine, I would reach out to the ledge outside my window, pull out the baggie, and bring it to my bed. From my desk drawer, I'd get out a small china saucer and a knife, and then I'd settle down in front of the TV. I never ate before nine o'clock—any earlier would have meant exchanging anticipation for an unbearable longing for morning; it was easier to eat late, knowing I could just fall asleep afterward.

At nine I would start to slice the apple: first into quarters, then into eighths, then 16ths. I lined these slices around the saucer, forming a perfect circle, then moved to the cube of cheese. With the same precision, I sliced it into 16 slivers, paper-thin almost, and placed a sliver on each piece of apple. Then, one by one, I cut each slice of apple and cheese in half and took it to my mouth. I ate each fragment in exactly the same way, nibbling the corner of the fruit first, forming it into the same shape as the square of cheese, then eating the apple and cheese together, edge by edge, until nothing remained but a tiny square center, saved for last.

I ate slowly enough for each fragment to last four minutes. The ritual lasted two hours.

When it was over, I would wash the saucer and knife, put them back in my drawer and get into bed. And then I would lie there in the dark, thinking about the bagel I'd eat in the morning, and hoping that the next day would be a good day, too.

A woman I know who's recovered from an eating disorder once told me, "At some point, I just decided: I'd rather be fat than crazy." At some point, the damage you've wrought—on your life, your happiness, your relationships—simply becomes too clear. At some point, usually after you've been in therapy for years and made all the intellectual connections about what the behavior means and what you're trying to accomplish with it, you begin to accept that it isn't working, it just isn't working. And at some point, the obsession becomes so thoroughly, deeply, profoundly boring that you simply have no choice: you just can't do it anymore; you have to find other ways to cope.

Today, my weight stable and the bulk of this behind me, I see women everywhere who have not learned to cope. I see them at the beach in the summer, legs like sticks on the sand. I see them running along the banks of the Charles River, their faces gaunt and grim as those of prisoners. I want to stop them in their tracks and shake them. I want to say: "I know where you are, I know what you're doing, and believe me, it doesn't work." But I know they have to see that by themselves. And I know some of them never will.

I didn't start to recover until I left Providence, in the fall of 1984, and moved to Boston. That, at least, was a symbolic move, physically leaving the place where it all started. Another important move was to find the right kind of help. For me, that meant a shrink who didn't feel sorry for me and who described therapy as a "joint venture," something I would have some say in.

But there are no guaranteed ways to change. You just do. I stopped starving in the smallest ways: eating one and a half bagels in the morning instead of one because I simply couldn't stand to be so hungry; introducing cream cheese. In 1985 I stopped weighing myself altogether (and I haven't weighed myself since). In 1986 I took up sculling on the Charles River, a difficult and demanding sport that gave me something to master besides my own appetite. Later that year, I joined a support group for women with eating disorders. Each step teaches you something: slowly, you learn that relinquishing rigidity does not mean losing control; you learn that there are other, more sustaining ways of feeling strong; you learn that involvement with other people may feel burdensome and risky, but that it's a hell of a lot better than being alone.

Which are tough lessons. The process of giving up all that sharp angularity means giving up a range of other things: a blanket of protection, a deeply ingrained, safe, familiar lifestyle, a way of defining yourself. For a long time, I simply didn't trust myself around food: could I sit in front of a plate of cookies and not eat *all* of them? For a long time, I just felt conflicted and hopelessly confused: I'd refuse a dinner invitation and not know if it was because I was afraid of eating, afraid of interaction, or because I genuinely wanted to be alone. And for a long time, even when I knew exactly what I was doing with food, exactly where the impulses to starve or binge came from, there were terrible middle-points when I simply didn't have access to any other responses.

But managing food is like managing life. Factor in some time, some self-knowledge, some courage, and a lot of support—slowly, you learn how to cope. You learn how to feed yourself, in all senses of the word.

These days, I have good days, bad days, mediocre days, and—probably best—days when I don't think about what kind of day it's been at all. I can't remember the last time I used food to make a decision. I can't remember the last time I went hungry for more than a couple of hours. Which doesn't mean I never worry about food or weight. I'm still highly conscious of both, and I still wonder if I'll ever be completely "normal" about food—but then again, if normal means self-accepting, I'm not convinced that any woman in this culture is completely "normal."

I am convinced of something else, though: recovering is almost as hard as starving—but not quite. About a year ago, on the heels of a disastrous relationship, I wrote something down in a notebook about how useful starving had been, how well it had shielded me from things like disappointment and anger and loss. Then I crossed it out and I wrote, "This is hard, but it's not as hard as starving. It's not as hard as starving."

For anyone who struggles with an eating disorder or knows someone who is, that's an important fact to keep in mind. Anyone who has the strength to starve has the strength to change.

Boston Phoenix
February 1989

GETTING BETTER

MEASURING GROWTH IN APPROACH, NOT IN POUNDS

"DO YOU EVER really get over something like anorexia?"

A friend asks me this at a restaurant. I shrug and say, "Oh, sure." And then I return to my menu. I stare at it, obsess and calculate. *Should I be a loathsome, self-indulgent slob and have the bacon cheeseburger and a heap of fries, or should I be a good girl and order the puny Greek salad, dressing on the side?*

So there. The easy answer is yes: of course it's possible to "get over" something like anorexia. And the real answer is no: not really, not completely.

I've been thinking about this question a lot lately, perhaps because I'm coming up on an important anniversary: 10 years ago this month, I started therapy with an eating-disorder specialist, thus beginning in earnest the long and slow recovery, such as it is, from anorexia. Ten years ago, I showed up in his office wearing black boots, a matchstick-size pair of black jeans, and a gray sweater, my colors at the time. I weighed about 95 pounds, which was 12 pounds more than I weighed at my very lowest, and I felt fat.

Today? Hmmm. I saw the therapist this morning. I was wearing black boots, a pair of black leggings (slightly bigger than matchstick size, but not much), and a *cream* colored sweater. I now weigh about 108 pounds, another 13 pounds of improvement, and I feel fat only intermittently.

So: cream instead of gray, 25 pounds, and a slight loosening of my definition of "fat." Is that recovery? It may not sound like much, but in many ways, yes: that's exactly what it is. Gradual and slight. Two steps forward and one step back. Minuscule changes, one ounce at a time, that begin to look and feel like substantive changes only after you've amassed enough of them.

❧

Once or twice a year, I get together for coffee with my friend Joan, whom I met in a support group for women with eating disorders about five years ago. She's since moved to Texas with her husband, but she comes back to visit when she can. And she always calls me. There is always a moment of strange, mutual inspection when we meet: we size each other up, quite literally, mentally marking weight gain or loss, subtly checking to see if we can feel each other's ribs or shoulder blades through our sweaters when we hug. I last saw her a few months ago, and when she called to tell me she was coming to Boston she said she wasn't doing too well. I asked her what that meant, and she summed it up in three words: "Eighty-four pounds." I weighed 83 pounds at my very worst—and I automatically dreaded seeing her. *Stuck,* I thought. *Starving, obsession, counting every calorie. She must be a mess.*

And yet it's not so simple. Joan looked tired and thin, fragile as a bird. She did a lot of food-rationalizing, trying to convince me that the milk in the cappuccino she drinks every morning really does represent a lot of calories. She talked about setting time aside every afternoon at three o'clock to go to a coffee shop and eat a muffin, a ritual that sounds mildly comforting until you realize that that's *it,* the only thing she allows herself to eat all day. But those were only the externals, the thin, tired face and the food rituals. Joan also talked about looking for meaning in her work. She talked about standing up to her husband. She told stories that had to do with learning to set limits, learning to delegate responsibility, learning to be gentler with herself. And I think *that's* recovery: momentum in some areas, backsliding in others; improvement here, stagnation there. It's not something you can measure strictly in pounds.

❧

Anorexia tugs at you. I think it's always there, the same way a drink is always there for an alcoholic, tempting and seductive. The pull is strongest when I am weak, when I feel confused or distraught or out of control, when I've strayed too far from the rituals I've developed to replace my rigidity around food, when I'm uncertain about my own value. Then, it beckons, a safe haven. I starved myself for a thousand reasons—to feel in control at a time when I felt I had no control; to numb anger and anxiety; to wear pain instead of expressing it; to feel invisible and (paradoxically) to stand out, to be absolutely expert at this one thing, being thin. And sometimes it's inevitable: I want to go back there. Anorexia is self-limiting and lonely and painfully monotonous. But it's also enormously self-protective. A hard wall of bone and angles to hide behind.

The trick, over time, is to find other ways to protect yourself, other ways to answer the impulses that beckon and tug. This is what makes recovery monotonous, too: You have to work hard at it, practice the same little exercises over and over and over, pound the same stuff into your own head: *Eat enough*—get too hungry and you will obsess about food. *Exercise enough*—get too lazy or (heaven forbid) flabby and you will obsess about being fat. *Rest enough, communicate with friends enough, be nice to yourself enough*—get too tired, isolated, or angry and you'll be that much more vulnerable to the old pulls, the old ways.

Sometimes, when friends ask about the recovery question, I fall back on cultural images: Kate Moss, waifs, bathing-suit ads. What woman *does* feel normal about food and body image in the face of all that? Can it be possible, really, to "get over" something like anorexia when you are deluged so relentlessly with those ideals of slenderness? I still think those are powerful forces that very few women are immune to, and I strongly resent the messages they send: *You'd be happier if you looked like this. Your life would be better if you were skinny.*

But reinforcing as they may be, the messages provide only the background music. The real music is in our own heads, every day, and it circles around in confusing ways. Do I exercise today or not? If I don't exercise, will I feel okay or slothful? And if I feel slothful, is that a sign that I'm being obsessive, too hard on myself? Likewise with the damn menu dilemma. If I order the puny Greek salad will I feel virtuous or deprived? If I feel deprived, will I overcompensate by eating 17 cookies when I get home? And, if I overcompensate, will I . . .

Those aren't just anorexic questions; they're human questions, with particular relevance for women. I suspect most of us go through some version of those mind games on a fairly regular basis, whether or not we've had eating disorders. And in the midst of it, I suspect we're all struggling with much bigger questions. Do I feel all the things I need to feel in order to make reasonable choices about food? Good about myself, and safe in the world? Capable of seeking comfort when I need it? Worthy of being fed?

The answers aren't usually clear; they can shift from day to day and from month to month.

That day in the restaurant, when my friend asked me the question about recovery, I compromised: the Greek salad and, on the side, the heap of fries. After we ordered, I let the matter go. Together, we had a nice, comforting evening.

Boston Phoenix
January 1995

ON LONELINESS

A SUNDAY MORNING. Sunlight streams through the window, a bird trills, and time stretches before me, an unstructured, obligation-free day. For lots of people, this is joy, the light of leisure at the end of the workaday tunnel.

For me, it is a terrifying thing. I wake on such days full of disquiet, aware of a vague longing, a nameless anxiety that scratches on some internal door, a sense of ache. I lie in bed and stare at the ceiling.

I think: I am lonely.

There are many brands of loneliness—there's the loneliness of disconnection, which hits when you find yourself standing at a party with no one to talk to; there's the loneliness of yearning, which comes when you miss someone you love; there's the loneliness of isolation, the product of too many consecutive hours or days without human contact. But the kind of loneliness I know best is the Sunday-morning variety, a form that seems to bubble up from deep inside, often without warning or good cause. When it hits, it feels big and permanent and insurmountable. If you could shop for loneliness in the grocery store, you'd see the Sunday brand packaged in a huge box, with a label: warning—industrial strength.

I have had a long, intimate relationship with this particular form: sometimes I think I was born with it, born with a particularly acute sense of myself as apart from the world, as somehow different or lacking. I can remember sitting in my bedroom on a spring day as a child, watching leaves rustle against the windowpane, aware of a feeling I was far too young to name: it was a sense of absence, I think, a belief that the world bustled on outside that window without me, that I was unable or perhaps unwilling to join in. It's not that I didn't have friends—I always had, and still have, many friends—but the loneliness of my experience tends to be immune from reality, from circumstance or logic: it lives within me, a small, persistent demon that stirs in my quietest moments, during unplanned evenings, on Sunday mornings. It is a sense of void.

This is more than a sad feeling; it's a scary feeling. To me, loneliness has always seemed a baby step away from depression, and I react to it warily, the way you might react to a snake or a spider: the fear is that if I allow a bout of loneliness to persist for too long—six hours, a day, several days—it will fester and grow, mutate into a paralyzing despair. Get too lonely and you won't get out, you'll fall into the abyss. For this reason, I've spent much of my adult life trying to outrun the feeling, busying myself, filling up the schedule, holding on to bad relationships. I've tried drinking loneliness away, exercising and shopping it away, scouring it away in fits of housecleaning. I've also had some success with all of these strategies, particularly the one involving bad men: there's nothing quite so distracting as an obsessive love affair, and if a sour romance makes you lonely—well, at least you can blame the feeling on someone else.

But no amount of obsessing (or drinking or shopping or vacuuming) can eradicate the feeling completely; loneliness always returns, and I've come to think of it less as an enemy than as an acquaintance, a presence I need to respect, if not entirely welcome. I had one of those lonely Sundays not long ago, a bright day in late September. Nothing dramatic set it off—no major breakup, no upheaval in my work or personal life—but I woke up with that familiar ache, an emptiness laced with panic. There's always an acute self-consciousness to the way I experience loneliness, a sense that I'm watching myself from some other part of the room, listening to a running commentary: Here I am, making coffee. Here I am, washing a dish. Here I am, alone in my house. I suppose this is what's so scary about the feeling—that internal video looks so empty and bleak—and this is why my instinctive reaction is to run. But that particular day, I resisted the temptation to race out and buy six pairs of new shoes and instead I sat down on my sofa and thought.

The emptiness, for me, comes from inside: it has to do with not knowing what it is I need in order to feel contented or secure, safe in my own skin. If I listen closely, that running commentary in my head asks big, scary questions: Who is this person, making coffee and washing a dish? What gives her pleasure in life, joy and delight? What might turn a frightening, empty stretch of time into a comforting, satisfied stretch of time?

Those are difficult questions, and in trying to outrun loneliness, I've shied away from the opportunity to answer them. Mind you, a periodic dose of distraction isn't always a bad thing—I, for one, can heartily attest to the healing power of new shoes—but dodging the bigger questions always backfires in the end: when I race around blowing money on things I don't need, all I usually do is reinforce my sense of myself as essentially incompetent, unable to do something as basic as plan a simple Sunday. So that day, I sat for a bit, then dragged myself up off the sofa and attacked a project: I made and hung a pair of curtains I'd been meaning to make for months. It was a simple pleasure, a job undertaken for its own sake, but it reminded me of several things: that I do have resources to combat despair; that I am capable of occupying my own time, tending to my own soul; that when it strikes, loneliness may actually have something to teach us. The day passed from there, a solitary Sunday but not, in the end, a lonely one.

Boston Phoenix
September 1997

LESSONS IN LOSS

ONE NIGHT NOT long ago, I spent some time sitting in my living room with my dog, listening to a taped recording of my dead father's voice. This sounds like a rather morbid undertaking, evoking a voice from the grave, but it actually proved to be a minor lesson in acceptance: acceptance of a loss, acceptance of the person who left you, acceptance of the person you've become without them.

My father died of a brain tumor five years ago. He was a psychoanalyst, a man of stunning intellect, and he'd just started work on a book at the time his illness was diagnosed. The brain tumor devastated that project—he could barely hold a pen in his right hand, his thought processes were gradually becoming more scattered—but, at least in the first months of his illness, it did not interfere with his drive, and he refused to surrender his commitment to work, long the most sustaining force of his life. So I came up with the idea of tape-recording conversations with him: I'd ask him questions about the book, he'd essentially dictate the work to me, and at some point we'd amass enough transcribed material to constitute a manuscript. The experiment lasted one night—one 18-minute session—and this is the tape I listened to.

I'd not heard it since my father's death, and I'm not exactly sure what compelled me to root around in search of it that night, pop it into the tape recorder, and listen: some instinct that the timing was right, I suppose, or some wish to conjure him up, in memory if not in presence. Whatever the motive, I expected listening to it to be first and foremost an exercise in grief, and in some respects I was right: there was a great deal of sadness condensed into those 18 minutes. The brain tumor had caused my father's voice to grow quavery and strained and he sounded like a very old man on the tape, far more fragile than I recalled him. His intellect was failing him, as well, and you could hear him struggling with the reality of his impairment, his awareness of it. He'd lose his train of thought, or he'd forget a word, or he'd be unable to articulate a concept he'd once been able to toss off as easily as the alphabet, and you'd hear him pause and try to collect himself. Then you'd hear him say, "Dammit . . . *dammit.*" My father was the smartest man I've ever known, and he was losing his mind in the most literal sense, and he knew it. This is why we aborted the experiment: I think we both understood, without acknowledging it, that the tape did less to capture his ideas than it did to record his deterioration.

But the tape captured something else, too: me and my dad and what I've come to understand as our strange, intense, disjointed attachment. He and I had the kind of relationship that can keep you in therapy for a decade or more, and listening to our conversation gave me the sensation of time-travel, as though I'd journeyed back a long distance and spent 18 minutes as an observer, eavesdropping on an ancient relationship. I adored my father and I lived partly in awe of him and partly in terror, I so coveted his approval. He was part God to me and part mad scientist, a man of omnipotence and brilliance and distraction whom I could reach only periodically and, then, only imperfectly. Connection with him came in tiny flashes, little bursts, as though he'd descend from the cloud of his own ideas for brief visits, train all that insight and acuity on me for the smallest while—10 minutes, 18 minutes—and then be gone again, vanished. During the course of his illness, I came to understand more clearly the source of his emotional absences—my father waged long and largely private battles with depression and drink and darkness, forces that drove him to disappear into work and caused him to appear preoccupied and remote—but as children will do, I grew up assuming that I was somehow responsible for the flaws in our connection, that his distance was a product of his disappointment in me, of my essential unworthiness in relation to him.

All of this came back to me as I listened to the tape: the power of my father's intellect; his absorption in theory; my sense of invisibility in the face of it. I heard him talk about an image that had come up years ago in a session with an analytic patient—a tiny fragment from a single hour, and something my father had spent 20 years pondering and mulling over and strugging to understand—and I remembered my own feeling of diminishment in relation to his work, the feeling that I'd never be as important, or have as much to offer, as his patients. I heard the self-consciousness in my own voice as I asked him questions—a tightness, a voice straining for a tone of nonchalance, echoes of inadequacy. I heard my father preoccupied with his work, I heard myself preoccupied with my father.

And yet as I sat there listening, I also felt something that surprised me: a degree of serenity that eluded me when he was living, a kind of acceptance. If I'd listened to this dialogue two years earlier, or three or four, I think my primary reaction would have been anger, fury woven into the fabric of grief. I would have heard that self-consciousness in my voice and I would have felt rage at him for evoking fear instead of confidence; I would have heard him—intellectualizing, preoccupied, head-in-the-clouds—and I would have felt that long history of frustration bubble up, the impossibility of loving such an unreachable man. I likely would have stormed into my own therapist's office the next day and railed about it: how *difficult* he was, how hard it was to feel valued and connected in his presence.

But five years after his death, all that felt tempered somehow, less visceral and automatic, less necessary. I sat and petted my dog and thought. We quietly rage against our parents for so long: against the people they are and the people they're not and the people we wish they were, against the disappointments and disconnections, against the complicated ways they've shaped us. Letting go of that struggle is the most elusive undertaking, something that requires a delicate blend of self-awareness and maturity and time, and I don't know quite how or why it happens, how or why complexity of feeling toward a parent loses its most painful edges. But I listened to his voice and I thought about the distance I'd come since his death, the small rivers of tears that have carried me from the night we made that tape to the night I finally played it. I was in my own home, a place that feels like a sanctuary to me; and I was with my dog, who I love in a fearless, unrestrained way that feels enormously corrective to me because it's so different from the way I was able to love my dad; and I was nearly four years sober. That's a lot of work, a great distance to travel. And from that distance, the past looked softer, less agonizing, more human. I remembered sitting with my father at the dining room table that night, making the tape, him in his wheelchair, me clutching a glass of wine like a lifeline. I thought about our mutual awkwardness, and about the way we both struggled in spite of it, struggled in our imperfect and stilted way to be there for each other through his illness. I thought about lost opportunities and missed connections and regrets, but mostly I felt a kind of calm. I thought: *We tried; in the end, we both did the best we could.* There was sorrow in that sentiment, but there was also something else, a degree of peace.

Boston Phoenix
February 1998

LIVING WITHOUT ALCOHOL

FEBRUARY 20, 1997: I had my last drink three years ago today, which is just long enough to teach you this about life without alcohol:

It gets easier and easier to have a life that doesn't include drinking.

And it gets harder and harder to have a life.

This isn't as paradoxical or weird as it sounds. It *does* get easier to have a life that doesn't include drinking: you just do it. You stop going to bars, you hide your cork-screw in the back of a kitchen drawer, you make friends with other people who don't drink, and once you've adjusted to the shock of the lifestyle changes, you wake up one day and realize that you've created a whole world that simply doesn't involve drinking. No popping corks on New Year's Eve, no wine lists at restaurants, no trips down the liquor aisle at Bread & Circus. Such changes can seem massive and alien and terrifying at first, but for the most part they're external shifts, accommodations of habit and structure eased and made familiar by the passage of time.

The hard part, the having-a-life part, has to do with what goes on internally, with the questions and choices and feelings that present themselves when they're not perpetually blunted and obscured by alcohol. This is the big stuff, the stuff that has you staring at the ceiling at 3 a.m. What kind of person am I, really? How do I truly want to spend my time? What kind of a life am I capable of, cut out for? What sustains me, motivates me, satisfies me? These are the sorts of issues of self that most people (at least most thinking people) start addressing in their 20s, and it can be very disconcerting indeed to wake up at the age of 37 and realize you've never really raised the questions, let alone begun to answer them. How to have a life without being drunk all the time: figuring that out is a lot harder than it sounds—and a whole lot harder than I expected.

Active drinkers are masters of the art of titration. How much to drink, when to drink, what rate to drink at, which substances to combine drinking with, which to avoid while drinking, what blend of coffee and food and Advil to get us out of bed the following morning: we learn all that, over many years of practice, lots of trial and error. We titrate substances in order to manage emotion: two drinks after work to relieve stress, another two or four or six to maintain the buzz, a couple before bed so we'll crash, another few when we wake up at 4 a.m. and can't get back to sleep. The hard work of sobriety—the hard work of living, I suppose—involves titrating actions rather than substances in order to achieve the same effects. What to do to manage fear and anxiety and sleepless nights, rather than what to drink; what to do to foster feelings of well-being and safety and meaning; what kinds of relationships to engage in, what kinds of hobbies, what kinds of physical and psychic nourishment. This involves another form of trial and error, one based on acting rather than consuming, and it's a good bit tricker.

At an AA meeting I went to not long ago, people talked about what they missed about drinking. Some people talked about the simple relief of it, others the way it obliterated self-consciousness and inhibition, others the freedom it gave them to lose control. Me, I sat there and thought: I miss being relieved of the responsibility of having to create a life. When I drank, drinking was life in many ways. I used alcohol to lubricate relationships, and to blunt boredom and disappointment and anger and fear. I used it to organize my time, to give my world structure; the question was never, What should I do tonight, or tomorrow or next year? It was, Where should I do it? Where should I drink, how much, and with whom?

Take all that away and life becomes a giant blank screen, backlit by anxiety. "I feel really precarious." I heard someone say that at a recent AA meeting, too. She didn't mean she felt at risk of a relapse; she meant she felt unformed, as though everything in her life was somehow up for grabs. She said, "I could end up married with five kids, or I could move to Europe, or I could become a heroin addict, or—who knows?" I sat there and nodded. You spend years and years drinking, and then you spend a few years learning how not to drink, and then you look up and think: What now? Marriage? Kids? New city? New career? Who knows, indeed?

Those, of course, are all big life questions which can't be answered without some basic information. And here, on my three-year anniversary, I am still collecting data, still struggling to answer the most elemental questions of self: How do I like to spend free evenings and weekends? What's the right mix of solitude and companionship for me? How much to I want to be touched or loved or depended upon? What do I really hunger for? What's fun to me, what's soothing, what's engaging?

Trial and error; data collection: this is painstaking and hard. Seven hundred walks with my dog through the Middlesex Fells and I've discovered: okay, I like this, this feels good, being out in the woods with the dog. Nine hundred failed battles with my sewing machine and I can say: okay, I don't like this, I don't have the patience for sewing, it makes me feel incompetent. These sound like such tiny discoveries (and they are), but they're also the sorts of lessons you can't learn when you're drinking all the time and they're the small building blocks on which a secure sense of self is built. I am this sort of person, these are my needs, these are my particular strengths and weaknesses.

The man I've been involved with for a long time would like to live together, get married, share a life. I keep resisting. I keep saying, "But I'm only 14!" I'm half-kidding when I say this, but there's also a hard kernel of truth to it. People in drinking-and-recovery circles often say that in some important respects you stop growing when you start drinking alcoholically. The drink stunts you, prevents you from walking through the kinds of fearful life experiences that bring you from point A to point B on the maturity-and-confidence scales and teach you who you are. I started drinking in earnest at around age 16, so three years into recovery, I'm actually a little older than 14—

about 19, 20 tops. But I'm still young, or still feel that way: too young to know what kind of life I want for myself, let alone make decisions about sharing it; still too new to the world to know how to shape it.

It's not surprising to me that so many people relapse after a year or two, once the fog lifts and the hard work ahead is revealed. Quitting drinking is a little like emerging from a train wreck: you get up, dazed and disoriented, and you wander around for a long time, stunned and deeply grateful that you survived. And then the mind clears, the sense of trauma ebbs away, and you find yourself standing there gaping at the debris. Who am I now, now that I'm off that particular train? What direction to go in next? And how to get there? It's a scary time and I have to remind myself, often, that it's an important one, too: full of uncertainty, yes, but also full of possibility.

BOSTON PHOENIX
FEBRUARY 1997

A LETTER TO MY FATHER

Dear Dad,

I got drunk the night you died. I also got drunk the night of your funeral, and the next night, and every night after that for one year, 10 months, and 13 days.

This is stuff we never talked about, at least not directly: your drinking, my drinking, our drinking, the way they all got tangled up together, in such subtle and seductive ways. So I thought I'd bring it up. I suspect that you—a psychiatrist, an *analyst*, both in and out of the family—would have a special appreciation for what this means, what it means to broach a secret like this. On the surface, it all looks so unseemly: The daughter of an analyst, an alcoholic. A young woman, an attractive young woman with a future, an alcoholic. Doesn't sit well, does it? Doesn't *feel* right. But you knew a lot about how surfaces deceived, how turmoil could bubble and roil beneath even the loveliest facades, and how complicated this business is, living and trying to love people and coping with difficult feelings.

I don't remember my first drink, but I suspect I had it with you. I suspect we were sitting in the living room, where you and mom had cocktails every evening, and I suspect it was a martini. Maybe just a sip—gin and vermouth and a tiny kiss of sake, the recipe you perfected over years. Maybe a few sips, enough to give me that tingly feeling at the back of my head, that slow sensation of warmth in my chest, the onset of ease. I can't say this for sure, but I suspect I loved that first sip, those first early experiences with liquor, in much the same way I loved you; the attraction was powerful and mysterious, full of promise.

Does that sound too sexual? Possibly. But perhaps that's not too far off the mark. I've come to see drinking as a relationship, a multidimensional relationship, as full and rich and sensual and complex as the kind you have with the key people in your life, as the kind I had with you. I loved drinking, for a long time. I loved it so much I could have died for it, literally. But you died first and in many ways, I guess that spared me. On some key level, you see, I couldn't give up drinking until I'd given up you.

We drank the same way, you and I, and for many of the same reasons. I guess that's not surprising: I learned how to drink from you, from watching you. I saw you come in after work and mix up the pitcher of martinis, and I saw how the tension began to drain out of you after you drank the first one, and I could tell on some level that the sharp feelings you held so privately were dulled and made manageable by the alcohol. There was always such an edge of sadness to you—I couldn't ever say why, but I could see it in your eyes, in the way you'd stop sometimes and look out across the room past all of us, your eyebrows knit just slightly, a quiet depth in your expression, a sense of searching and wanting. You seemed sad and preoccupied and remote, and you reminded me of the way I felt inside. I know that look. I know it eased when you drank, I could see your face soften, and I know that later, when I began to drink with regularity, I experienced the same phenomenon. It's like feeling that something in the way you relate to the world is about 10 degrees off, just out of focus, and the drink makes it right again, brings you into balance inside.

You probably didn't know much about my drinking, did you? That's okay: not many people did. That's the thing about alcoholism: it's so very subtle and insidious, so gradual in the way it takes hold of your soul. And liquor is such a marvellously seductive substance. I still, today, have images of myself loving a glass of dry white wine in an elegant bar. I can shut my eyes and put myself right there: sitting in the Ritz, say, with a cool glass of Fumé Blanc and a cigarette, feeling like something out of a movie from the '40s. Elegant and collected, my shyness dissipating a bit more with every sip, my self-consciousness diluted and replaced with a feeling of courage. I loved the language of liquor—a *splash*, a *twist*. I loved the sounds of it—the gentle clink of ice in a glass, the satisfying thud of a wine bottle set upon a table. I loved the sense of connectedness and cameraderie it could impart—the group of friends hunkered together over a table after work, out for drinks and a little laughter and a few good war stories. For a long time, my greatest compliment to a new acquaintance was this: *We should get drunk together. Let's go out and get drunk.*

It took me in, utterly.

It's probably no surprise that I loved drinking with you the best. I found you so hard to talk to—all those probing, analytic questions, that edge of sadness in your manner. I felt intimidated by your intelligence and your insight, and I often felt voiceless in your presence, certain that whatever I had to say would be inadequate or dull. The drink could take the edge off that, bring us both down to what felt like a regular plane, a lighter, more even playing field where I imagined other fathers and daughters existed.

Or other men and women. It would be no surprise to you, I suppose, that I transferred both the fears and the strategy to my relationships with other men, to romance. I drank in high school because alcohol was available and because it *worked,* transformed me from a scared, self-conscious kid into someone functional, someone who could talk at parties. I drank in college for the same reasons: it was there and it worked, it eased the shy anxiety I'd felt all my life and gave me a sense that I fit into some larger circle. It was simple mathematics: you drink, you feel disinhibited enough live in the world, to go to a party, kiss a man you barely know, sleep with someone.

Everyone does that, don't they? You did. I did. My friends did. This is one of the things that makes me wish you were still alive, you, the analyst: you were my roadmap to the world, the compass I used to navigate feelings and relationships; if you were still here, maybe you could trace the map back with me, put it under a microscope and find the precise place where I crossed over some elusive line, the precise moment where I veered away from normal drinking and into alcoholism.

But, of course, I know better than that, and I imagine you do, too. There is no precision in alcoholism, no single event that takes a healthy person and makes them sick, no aberrant cell that divides or mutates and alters your future, just like that. There's just a slow and vague *becoming*. You know you're drinking too much and you don't know. You know and you *won't* know. You think you can stop, manage it, control it. Nips of anxiety; shots of denial.

We were a northern family, but the best image I have comes from the south: it's like kudzu, alcoholism is, the gradual and insistent way it creeps over your life, moving so slowly you can't really see it until its hold has begun to choke you, crushing any possibility of growth in its grip.

I got used to drinking. It was my best, most reliable way to cope. I used it to dilute anxiety and quell fear. I used it as a reward at the end of a long day. I used it to lubricate conversation. I used it to make love, because if I didn't drink I couldn't get out of my own head, couldn't loosen up. After a while, I'd used it for so long, and to such great effect, that it got harder and harder to *not* use it. Isn't that what happens with addiction? The vicious circle. My social persona, my sense of sexuality, my sense of myself as an adult had been so deeply welded with the experience of drinking that I couldn't imagine functioning without it. A party without a *drink*? A stressful day of work with no *drink* at the end?

Later, the questions became more all-encompassing and more specific: Food without wine? Sleep without booze? Me without you?

But, no: you wouldn't have seen this, your insight notwithstanding. In part, that's because looking at my drinking would have forced you to look at your own, and I'm not sure you were willing or able to do that. But it's also because I hid it so masterfully, even from you. If we all had dinner together, the whole family, I'd get *quietly* drunk, drunk like a good girl, clearing the wine glasses from the table and taking secret gulps of the ones that hadn't been finished. I'd stay in the kitchen and do the dishes, where it was easy to sidle over to the refrigerator every five or 10 minutes and take a long pull off an open bottle of white wine. I'd nip here and I'd nip there and I might have gotten sloppy now and then—slurred my words or stumbled toward the door—but the flip side of heavy drinking is heavy denial, and all family members take part in that to some extent. *She's depressed.* It was always easy to say that. *Give her a break: she's been very depressed.*

Depressed or not, I'd go home and drink more.

By 1991, when you were diagnosed with the brain tumor, I'd been drinking daily—every night, with precisely one exception—for almost five years. The exception was one night 1989, when I was so deathly hungover and so afraid that my drinking had gotten out of control that I actually called Alcoholics Anonymous from my desk at work and dragged myself to a meeting. The meeting was in downtown Boston on a Friday night, and it was full of low-bottom drunks, old men, and street people. It scared me even more than the drinking, but I did manage to abstain that one night. The next day, I had to fly to Seattle on a freelance assignment; it was tiring and stressful and I used the stress that night to rationalize a couple of nips of Cognac, from the mini-bar in my hotel room.

From that point on, I had rules. Two drinks a day. No more. Just two: one after work and one with dinner. I'd make a point of announcing that decision to someone—usually my sister, who actively worried about my drinking for almost a decade—and I'd swear by it. I'd talk about a woman I once worked for, an alcoholic who drank in a far more obvious and messy manner than I did, and I'd say, *Just two drinks. If I can't stick by that, I'm going to end up like her.*

I stuck to that rule many, many times, but never for more than two or three days at a time.

That's the thing about alcohol: it's *there,* it's just there, tugging at your sleeve, beckoning from the shelves of stores and restaurants, promising relief, pure and simple. You can always find a reason to need relief—a bad day, a difficult relationship, a persistent feeling of discontent—and if you're actively drinking, that relief is so utterly available, so easy to knock back, so terribly consistent. How can you say no? Why should you?

~

Then you got sick. I'd go over to the house every day after work and I'd see you in your wheelchair, your face and legs bloated from the steroid medication, your expression vacant and sad, and I couldn't stand it. I started raiding your liquor cabinet at that point, stealing bottles of booze you probably hadn't touched in years—a bottle of Old Grandad, a bottle of gin so old the cap was crusty—and hiding them in the front-hall bathroom. I'd sit with you for a while—the conversations were strained and difficult—and then I'd go off, steal the bottle from its hiding place, take it outside, and sit on the front stoop, smoking a cigarette and drinking from the bottle. I was always careful not to get too drunk until I got home, just drunk enough to keep me numb, to keep me functioning.

Could you tell? I couldn't. I really couldn't. The summer after you died, my boyfriend caught me slugging warm gin from the bottle in his kitchen. It was nighttime and I was on the phone and I wanted something more to drink—something more, *anything* more—and nothing was available except the gin. So I took it out from the cabinet and drank from it and he walked in on me. I still have trouble reconciling that image of myself with the other image, the image of me sitting at that window seat at the Ritz bar with my glass of white wine, elegant and sophisticated. Which was the real me? Could you have known? Like I said, I couldn't see it, I just couldn't.

So you died in April. I drank all spring and I drank all summer. I went to Paris for 10 days in July and I drank my way through every blessed arondissment; the trip is a blur. And then, that October, Mom was diagnosed with liver cancer. I drank more. Drinking as a coping mechanism, as an anesthetic, had been well-established for some time by then, but if there was a line left to cross, I suppose that was it. On the outside, I functioned quite normally: worked, got a contract for my first book, paid my bills, managed. But during that period, the six months while she was dying, it felt like my life was increasingly split in two distinct halves: the daytime half, which operated on automatic pilot and got the job done, and the nighttime half, which disappeared into the enveloping haze of alcohol. Again, you wouldn't have known; no one did. I drank strategically: a drink or two after work with colleagues; a very conservative two beers at

Mom's house so she wouldn't worry or say anything; the rest of the six pack when I got home, plus wine, plus Cognac, plus whatever else felt necessary. I drank until I passed out almost every night; it was the only way I could fathom getting to sleep.

She died on Sunday, April 18, 1993, one year and 11 days after you did. We'd taken her to the hospital a few days earlier and when it became clear that she wasn't going to survive, we took her back to the house so she could die at home. The others went with her in the ambulance. I took my own car and met them at the house. I stopped at a liquor store on my way home, picked up a fifth of Dewar's, and hid it in my purse.

Some things happened over that next summer and fall, things I would have been ashamed to tell you. Rebecca—my *twin*, as close to me as you were—called me at work one morning a few months after mom died. It became clear to both of us after five or 10 minutes that we'd spoken on the phone the night before and I'd been too drunk to remember the conversation. Becca started to cry, realizing that, and she said, "I know you can't help it. I know you can't. But I just can't call you after seven o'clock at night anymore. I never know if you'll be there or not."

A few months later, drunk one night and driving Mom's car, I ran over a curb and blew out the front right tire. I drove for another three blocks before I realized what I'd done, and then I pulled into the driveway of a total stranger and pounded crazily on the door. The stranger helped me call Triple-A and then I passed out in the car waiting for the road guy to show up.

Another night, Thanksgiving weekend, I was out walking after dinner with some friends, and I picked up their two small children, two little girls, and I started running across the street like a madwoman. I was very drunk and I was wearing high heels and I tripped and fell. I was holding one of the girls in my arms, in front of me, and I still think it's a miracle that her head didn't take the fall, that I didn't kill her or cause her a major head injury. Instead, my knee took the fall. I ended up in the emergency room with a gash so deep the nurse could see the bone, and no memory—no memory at all—of getting there.

ॐ

In Alcoholics Anonymous, they call it the gift of desperation. I woke up one morning, December of that year, with a hangover. I thought about you. I thought about the sense of sorrow that had seemed to bind us for so long, the feeling of deep dissatisfaction, of being slightly *off*. I thought about how you'd lived your whole life with that feeling—you'd spent years trying to address it in therapy, trying to excise it with understanding, and one of the things you had to live with when you were dying was the knowledge that you'd never really done that, never found the level of peace you'd so wanted, never really tasted freedom from your own depression. You'd said it yourself that last year—you, the analyst with your special expertise in psychosomatic medicine; you'd talked about all the feelings you'd never come to terms with, the conflicts you'd never resolved, and you described your own tumor—lodged smack in the middle of your brain—as a final metaphor, the only path toward resolution you could find.

Alcohol is such a puzzle. When you're deep into it, it feels like the only solution, the glue that's holding you together. In fact, it is the basis of the problem, the glue that's keeping your feet stuck to the floor. Somehow, that morning, I managed to see that—maybe just in a spark, but the spark grew big enough to move me in a different direction.

The truth is so simple and so hard to see. I loved you, but I didn't want to be you. I loved alcohol but I didn't want to die your death.

Two months later, I quit drinking.

New Woman magazine, 1995

ACAMPROSATE

On my last night of drinking, four-and-a-half years ago, I consumed four beers, two bottles of white wine, and three glasses of Cognac. The next morning, I got up, packed a bag, and drove north, to a rehab clinic in New Hampshire. I chain-smoked the entire way, my whole body shook—one part hangover, two parts terror—and I felt as though I was about to jump off a cliff, a blind leap onto the cold, hard plains of sobriety.

Advocates of a drug called acamprosate, widely available in Europe and poised to hit the U.S. market by the year 2000, claim they might have softened my landing. Acamprosate (which will be sold here under the name Campral) reportedly acts on neurotransmitters in the brain that become overexcited by withdrawal from alcohol; had I had access to it back then, the logic goes, the struggle before me might have been eased: fewer cravings, a reduced appetite for alcohol, a less traumatic entree into sobriety.

Not surprisingly, acamprosate's arrival in the U.S. has generated controversy. Advocates are heralding it as an important new tool to aid recovery, claiming it can help alcoholics avoid relapse, particularly during the early, most vulnerable stages of sobriety. Opponents see that approach as misguided, possibly dangerous: the point of treatment should be to keep alcoholics *off* substances, not to encourage reliance on new ones. Like the ongoing controversy over the use of drugs like Prozac to treat depression, the debate here is really about the nature of alcoholism, which afflicts some 13.7 million Americans: is it a biological illness that should be tackled with medication, or a psychological condition that requires psychodynamic approaches, like therapy and AA? As in the Prozac debate, the truth lies somewhere in the middle. Alcoholism stems from a tangled web of interwoven sources: physical, psychological, social. To approach recovery as a physical process—a matter of fending off cravings—is to regard only one piece of that puzzle; to ignore the physical reality may be just as defeating.

Had someone greeted me at rehab, handed me a prescription, and said, "Here, this will make the next few months much easier," I probably would have found the promise hollow. I understood, even through that early haze of fear, that alcohol had become a central part of my identity, a deeply-ingrained coping mechanism, a way of life I'd cultivated over 20 years. I understood, too, that my wish for alcohol was (and would continue to be) more than merely biological. The physical sensations that characterized my last years of drinking—the cravings that set in daily by 4 o'clock, the morning shakes and hangovers—may have been potent, but ultimately I drank because I was a drinker, because alcohol was my ticket to well-being and relief and connection, my remedy for discomfort and pain. Getting sober isn't just about weathering cravings; it's also about understanding where the cravings come from—what longings and needs and drives fuel the compulsion to drink—and finding new ways to attend to the feelings behind them.

Acamprosate, which is not addictive or mood-altering, might well be helpful if used as one part of a much broader approach to treatment, and, in fairness, that's how its advocates are describing it: no magic bullet, no "cure." In clinical trials in Europe, 50 percent of patients using acamprosate stayed sober for three months, compared to 39 percent of those given a placebo, suggesting that while the drug won't guarantee recovery, it may give alcoholics an edge. I'm all for edges, but I worry that acamprosate's arrival (ushered in as it's likely to be by aggressive sales and marketing teams) will open the doors to wishful thinking and false hope about recovery, playing into our cultural affinity for quick (and cheap) fixes. The patient is drinking too much? Write a scrip. Focus on tangible aspects of the problem (physiology) rather than murky ones (feelings). Rehab can cost up to $450 per day; try a $2 pill first.

With alcoholism, of course, there are no quick fixes. Had acamprosate been available to me four years ago, it might have made that drive to rehab a tiny bit more tolerable. But I doubt it would have gotten me into the car any sooner. And I'm certain that, alone, it wouldn't have kept me on the road these last four years. That journey is long and bumpy, and requires much more equipment.

New York Times
August 1998

THE PROBLEM WITH MODERATION

EVERY EVENING, IN thousands of church basements in hundreds of cities, clusters of us sit in rows of metal folding chairs and listen to a fellow alcoholic tell his or her story. The details always vary: some of us are rich, some poor; some were at the peak of our careers when we first hit AA, some homeless and unemployable; some of us looked shiny and bright on the outside, some were in tatters. But for all the external differences, the central narrative in these stories is the same, identical threads of desperation and grace woven through each. Perhaps you woke up in a hospital, unable to remember the final moments before your car careened off the road. Perhaps you lost your job, or your spouse, or your kids. Perhaps (and this is just as common) nothing at all earth-shattering occurred—there was no tangible turning point, no financial ruin, no injury or loss of life—but you woke up one morning and could no longer bear your own life, the corroded sense of self and dignity and hope that had come to define it.

In the common parlance, these moments are known as "hitting bottom," and they are exquisitely agonizing affairs, portraits in anguish: the jig is up, all systems failed, it's over. You peer into the future and realize that your relationship with alcohol—which feels like your lifeblood, as vital as air, your primary drive and need and love—has got to end.

With rare exceptions, these are also intensely private affairs, personal reckonings that take place in the darkest corners of heart and soul. AA members may understand them intimately—we are fluent in the language of despair and denial and damage, we know how scary it is to lose control over drinking and how unfathomable the prospect of living without it can be—but even we tend to see only the tail end of the process: the drinker who's just surrendered, who's shown up at a meeting for the first time, who's trembling through the first week or day or hour of abstinence. The moments prior to that, the days or weeks or years that lead to the end, are generally solitary and dark and internal, a private hell that's largely invisible to the wider world.

Last week, when Audrey Kishline pled guilty to two counts of vehicular homicide, she gave that brand of hell a public face, an alcoholic's hidden agony rendered extraordinarily and grotesquely visible. I first heard word about Kishline, who's made a career out of teaching drinkers to curb their consumption, an hour or so after coming home from an AA meeting. I froze in my kitchen: the news had such an eerie and familiar ring, such an it-could-have-been-me feel, and it made me cringe. This is a classic alcoholic crash-landing, the kind of story that makes you realize how lethal alcoholism is and how precarious sobriety can be.

The irony here, of course, is 150-proof. Kishline, now 43, is the very outspoken founder of Moderation Management, a self-help treatment program that purports to help "problem drinkers" drink responsibly. Challenging most of the central tenets of alcohol treatment in the U.S., her view offered a tantalizing set of possibilities: alcohol abusers, she suggested, could be taught to cut down on their drinking without resorting to total abstinence; recovering alcoholics might be able to return to drinking at moderate (and therefore safe) levels; budding alcoholics might be able to control their consumption before it got out of hand. Kishline, who clearly knew her own way around a liquor store, founded her program in 1993 and published a book—"Moderate Drinking: The New Option for Problem Drinkers"—a year later. An advertisement for the book said: "Based on her own unsatisfactory experience with total abstinence–based programs, Kishline offers inspiraton and a step-by-step program to help individuals avoid the kind of drinking that detrimentally affects their lives."

As she's made painfully clear, moderation did not serve Kishline so well. Last March, at the tail end of a binge drinking episode,

Kishline, who is a housewife and mother, got into her pickup truck, headed the wrong way down an interstate freeway in central Washington, and smashed head-on into a car, killing a 38-year-old electrician named Danny Davis and his daughter, LaSchell, who'd just celebrated her twelfth birthday. According to prosecutors, her blood-alcohol level was three times the legal limit. When she woke up in a hospital trauma unit, Kishline said she could barely remember getting into the truck.

The moral here is fairly clear: moderation for alcoholics is a very dicey idea, and Kishline will no doubt go down in history as the best evidence against her own theory, the woman who single-handedly, spectacularly, caused it to crash and burn. The line between problem drinking and full-fledged alcoholism may be blurry and difficult to discern—certainly it's difficult for the drinker to accept—but once you've passed a certain point in your abuse, moderation simply ceases to be an option, a fact Kishline's critics have long understood. The very concept of moderation is oxymoronic in the world of alcoholism, and in abstinence-based circles like AA, her approach seemed not only deluded but dangerous, a form of codified denial that offered little more than false hope.

The hope, of course, is powerful: most of us—alcoholic and non—want moderation to work; we want there to be an alternative to complete abstinence, which sounds like such a desert of self-abegnation and deprivation. This prospect—no drinking, no alcohol-laced relief, never again—ultimately turns out to be the great benefit of recovery, the gateway to the rediscovered self, but it's terrifying when you're still clinging to booze, and it's what keeps so many of us grasping for other options, desperate to believe that "normal" drinking is a possibility, that we can somehow find a way to turn back the neurological clock and drink in safety. I don't know one recovering alcoholic who didn't struggle to control his or her drinking, who didn't make rules and then break them, who didn't set limits and make promises and deploy strategies to cut back, anything to avoid doing what the true alcoholic is so thoroughly loath to do: learn to live without it. In the years before I quit, I tried drinking only after 8 p.m., I tried limiting myself to two glasses a night (which invariably turned into two glasses the size of buckets), I tried swearing off hard liquor and sticking to wine. The trials rarely lasted for more than a few days and they never worked; the nagging doubt—*I cannot do this, I have a real problem*—festered and grew. This is what makes Kishline's story so classic: alcoholics are by definition failures of moderation, walking case-studies in its impossibility.

Five years ago, Kishline's movement began to gain a certain amount of cachet, with full-spread coverage in *Self* magazine, *Newsweek*, and the *New York Times* (*Self* headlined it a "radical new approach" to alcohol treatment). I was just about a year sober at the time, and still stunned by the vastness of what it meant to live without liquor, and I wrote a not-very-eloquent column about the movement, calling it, among other things, "moronic" and "bullshit." Today, far from feeling smug or vindicated by Kishline's very public fall, I feel humbled, and sobered, very much the way I feel when someone stumbles into an AA meeting after a relapse. This is a hideous story, one whose horror will only be compounded if we fail to learn from it.

And it has plenty to teach. There are obvious lessons about the dangers of moderation as an approach—and they're important, timely ones, particularly in the age of medical cost-containment when insurers and health-care providers are desperate to find quick and measurable fixes for complex and elusive problems. (In a bizarre twist of timing, just days after Kishline's guilty plea, a feud erupted at New York's prestigious Smithers Addiction Treatment and Research Center, the director resigning over the center's decision to steer its program toward the moderation-management approach.)

But there are also lessons in Kishline's story about the profound complexity of alcoholism, and the insidiousness of its grip, and the enormous challenges of treatment. Few of us can know what Kishline's last few years have been like, although we can certainly speculate about the horrors. She'd apparently given up the moderate approach prior to her drinking spree, and had tried unsuccessfully to stay sober through AA. She's publicly reversed her stance on the movement she helped found, stating through her lawyer that Moderation Management involves a lot of "alcoholics covering up their problem." She has talked, also through her lawyer, about the shame and humiliation of relapse, and about her profound remorse at causing the deaths of two innocent people.

You don't have to read too carefully between the lines to see how deeply and tragically alcoholic this narrative is. It's all there: the desperate struggle to find a way to hold on to alcohol; the failure first of moderation and then of denial; the horror—and horrific consequences—of relapse. Kishline will be sentenced on August 11. Prosecutors are seeking a four-and-a-half-year term, although the maximum penalty is life. To one degree or another, she'll do the maximum.

SALON
JULY 2000

LIFE WITHOUT ANESTHESIA

IMAGINE FEAR.

Imagine that you live in a war zone, a dark place where peril lurks behind every corner: snipers on rooftops; mines underfoot. Imagine, next, that you have developed an elaborate system to cope in this place, to protect yourself against the danger. Outside, you disguise yourself, hide beneath a bulletproof vest and a metal helmet. Inside, you huddle in corners, curl up in bed, keep your ears muffled against the sound of gunfire. You have learned to make yourself safe.

Finally, imagine that one day something changes: you wake up and your vest and helmet have vanished. You are dragged outside, forced out of your protective corners and into the sunlight, without your armor. Imagine how raw you feel, and how fearful. Imagine the feeling of exposure.

Can you picture it? This is what it's like to give up an addiction.

When people enter rehab programs for drug or alcohol addictions, they're often given the Good News–Bad News speech. A counsellor or medical director will smile and say, "The good news is, the war's over." *Pause for effect.* "The bad news is, you lost." As a refugee from battles with both anorexia and alcoholism, I'd alter that sentiment somewhat: If you've given up an addiction, the good news is that *one* war is over—you have officially surrendered to a particular battle with drug or alcohol dependence, or with an addictive behavior like anorexia, bulemia, or gambling. The bad news is, another war has just begun: you're just on new territory, fighting without the old weapons, suffering the casualties of daily life without the anesthesia.

Of course, this is a far more hopeful war—your chances of winning are considerably higher than they were against an enemy like alcoholism or an eating disorder; your battle scars are likely to be a lot less visible; your victories will be both more meaningful and more permanent. But it's a battle all the same, waged internally this time, but directed against the same forces that drove you toward addiction in the first place: your fears and rages and insecurities, your hunger for solace and relief, yourself.

A woman I know named Helen struggled for many years with compulsive overeating. She ate the way I drank: to numb out, to occupy herself, to fend off boredom and anxiety. When she finally hit bottom with that behavior, became so desperate and depressed at the way it had overtaken her life, she joined Overeaters Anonymous and gradually began to connect the internal dots, linking the behavior to the emotions that motivated it. Shortly after that, she found herself at a dinner party, seated in a chair with a bowl of M&Ms on one side and a bowl of peanuts on the other. She wanted those M&Ms so badly it was embarrassing: she kept eyeing them, thinking about them, feeling lured by them as though they were drugs. And at some point, it hit her: all that focus on the M&Ms kept her concentration in one place, on what was *outside*, instead of *inside*. "As long as I could think about the M&Ms," Helen says, "as long as all my energy went into thinking about whether I'd eat them, and how many I'd eat, and how I could hide the quantity from the other people in the room, I didn't have to think about myself, about the fact that I was self-conscious and anxious at that party, about the fact that I hated my life, about how unhappy I was inside."

Bingo. Ultimately, Helen resisted the M&Ms and coped in a new way: she excused herself from the party, went home, and addressed the anxiety with a long soak in the tub. She refers to this episode as her "M&M Epiphany" and says it marked the first victory in her own new battle, one that required new equipment, a new set of survival tools.

It would be lovely if you put down an addiction and woke up the next day with a brand-new life, found yourself plopped down in a new place full of clarity and flowers and light, but I doubt that happens very often, if at all. For one thing, giving up an addiction can be an inherently murky process, particularly when the addictive behavior focuses on something as big and unavoidable as food: there's no clear-cut detox or withdrawal period for an eating disorder; as Helen's story illustrates, you have to make many choices about eating every day, each one laden with multiple motives, fears, and concerns. "I'm always asking myself at least 50 questions about food," Helen says. "Am I eating because of a physical hunger or because of a more emotional, compulsive need to *feed* something inside me? Is this wish for a third chocolate-chip cookie normal and healthy or is it self-sabotaging? Will I feel guilty if I eat X, Y, or Z, or will I feel okay?" Recovery from an eating disorder means redefining a relationship with one's substance of choice, rather than abandoning it altogether, and that can be a complicated daily battle, waged in fits and starts.

By contrast, the battle against drugs or alcohol can feel far more tangible—you make only *one* decision, not to use—but the initial stages are also more shocking, like losing a limb or a best friend. In my first weeks out of rehab, I felt like I was wearing a scarlet letter or a sign: ALCOHOLIC! TEN DAYS SOBER! CAN YOU TELL? I had the odd sensation of living in someone else's skin, so that even the most familiar activities felt alien and strange: Here I am, watching television without a drink. Here I am, eating in a restaurant, without a drink. Here I am, struggling to have a conversation over *coffee*. All the feelings I'd struggled to drown away with drink—anxiety, sadness, self-consciousness—would come rising up at such moments, and I'd sit there feeling disarmed in the most literal sense, without my old, familiar weapons against distress.

This realization hit me with particular force one night about two months after I quit drinking, in a restaurant. I'd gone out to dinner with a man I'll call Edward, an old drinking pal from way back and a mildly lecherous guy, the sort of person who tends to stare at inappropriate body parts when he talks to you: your neck, your breasts. For years, while I was drinking, this never bothered me. Edward is a fairly powerful guy, well-known in publishing circles, and I liked being associated with him, the sense it gave me of being accepted into his world. We'd get together once or twice a year, and he'd always spring for dinner at elegant restaurants, places where the waiters always knew him by name, and we'd sit there together and eat and drink: martinis before dinner, expensive red wines with the food, $12 glasses of armagnac in lieu of dessert. Edward would ogle me during these dinners, make lewd comments here and there, but I'd just put up with it, sit there and sip my wine, numbing away any discomfort I might have felt with the drink. But this time, with me sober, he took me to a new place, a swank restaurant lined with banquettes, and he sat right next to me in the banquette instead of across the table, and every time his leg brushed against me, every time he touched my hair or my arm, I had to resist the urge to pick up my fork and plunge it into his hand. I didn't have the nerve to move, or to ask him to move, and I certainly didn't have the guts to stab him in the hand, so I just sat there, ate my food, watched him drink his wine, and felt genuinely ill-at-ease for 93 full minutes. I clocked it. *Here I am, 47 minutes of discomfort; here I am, 53 minutes; 93 minutes.* On his fourth glass of wine, Edward leaned over and said, sloppily, "You are an incredible woman." He was staring at my chest and I could smell the wine on his breath and for the briefest instant I had a feeling of concentrated rage, as though every minute I'd ever sat in a restaurant feeling objectified and powerless and leered at had coalesced into that one moment. I thought: *This is why I drank: to avoid this very feeling.* I thought: *This is life without alcohol: you actually have to experience your own feelings, instead of escaping them through the drink.* We left shortly afterward, but that evening would stay with me for a long time, a mini lesson in how liquor worked for me and how altered life can feel without it.

After you've lived without an addiction for a month or two, that early sense of shock wears off and a lot of people find themselves entering another, brighter stage called a "pink cloud," a euphoric state that's characterized by surges of confidence and relief, a sense of possibilities that stems from the understanding that you've finally *done* something to improve your life. I had that sensation on and off during my first year of sobriety, but it was tempered, and regularly, by moments like the one in that restaurant with Edward. Anxiety looms and you think: *This is why I drank.* Sadness washes up: *This is why I drank.* Rage surfaces, or doubt or self-loathing: *This is why I drank.* Addictions, after all, are enormously self-protective. They're coping mechanisms, antidotes to strong emotion. So it's axiomatic and inevitable: when you put the addiction down, all the emotions you worked so hard to numb and alter come to the fore, sometimes in a torrent that feels overwhelming.

I met a woman named Abby toward the end of my first year of sobriety. She showed up at an AA meeting on her third day without a drink or drug, a fragile woman of 38, and she looked as shell-shocked as a Vietnam vet, blank and vacant and exhausted. Abby had more reasons to seek escape from her own inner life than just about anybody I know: her family history, peppered with tales of alcoholism, suicide, mental illness and incest, reads like a case study in modern American dysfunction. It took Abby about four months just to thaw out, to begin sensing the vague outlines of her pain, and I can remember how horrified she was when she started bumping up against her own feelings.

One night, when she was about five months sober, Abby came over to my house for coffee and she started to cry. She'd never really wept before in sobriety—just wimpered here and there, then clamped down on whatever it was she felt washing up from inside. But that night, Abby connected on some very core level with a feeling she'd carried around for years but kept buried, a sense of herself as deeply unloved and unloveable, and she finally lost it. I'm not sure what triggered that sensation, but I remember that she sat on my sofa and sobbed, panic in her eyes. She looked up at one point and said, "How do people get through these feelings? How do people ever get over them?" I thought about how shut down and inaccessible Abby had seemed when I first met her, and I said, as gently as I could, "Abby: you're doing it right now. *This:* Feeling what's inside. Sharing it with someone else. Understanding that the feelings won't kill you." She nodded and her eyes welled up again, but this time with less pain. Abby was healing.

But healing hurts. The tools of recovery are inherently difficult for the addictive personality to take up, antithetical to the addictive way of life, which tends to be rooted in the conviction that every emotional or spiritual problem has a *physical* solution. That handful of M&Ms will make me feel better, or that drink, or that line of cocaine, or that relationship. *Something*—some external force—will assuage the discomfort within, turn our lives around, fill us with self-esteem. Like my friend Helen, I also suffered from an eating disorder, starving myself into a protective cage of ribs and bone for nearly five years, and I'm often struck by the parallels between anorexia and alcoholism, the way they both served to distract me from my own emotions, the way they respectively starved and washed away feeling. The trick this time around, in sobriety, is to find healthier ways of addressing those same impulses, safer ways of comforting myself, strategies for confronting pain that allow for healing instead of escape. That's not easy. Sometimes it means doing small but unfamiliar things when the discomfort hits—calling a friend, taking a bath, sitting still with a cup of tea. And sometimes it means doing nothing. Last April marked the three-year anniversary of my father's death and the two-year anniversary of my mother's, a tough time in anybody's book. One night, just around the date of my mom's death, I found myself at home alone, an unplanned evening stretching ahead. Sometimes I think I am literally phobic about feelings. I stood there in my living room at one point, and I could sense emotion creeping up on me like an old, familiar enemy, an edge of emptiness and grief tugging at something inside, or rolling toward me like a tank on the battlefield. My response was instinctive and laced with panic: Pick up a weapon and *do* something about this feeling. Run. Flee. *Eradicate* it. It was an utterly addictive response—act, don't feel—and it took all the will I could muster to ride it out the way my friend Abby did that night on my sofa, to wait for the grief to wash over me, to just sit there, and feel it.

In the end, I lit a cigarette, another weapon against strong emotion, and I made myself a cup of tea. The feeling abated, as it always does despite your unshakeable conviction that it won't, and then the feeling passed. And therein lies both the victory and the hope: you learn, through tiny episodes like that, that you can, in fact, learn to live comfortably in your own skin, to walk without crutches, to tolerate your own growing pains. Another moment, gotten through without a drink; another battle won.

If it's painful, life without anesthesia is also enormously freeing. I spent the two weeks before I finally quit drinking in a state of panic and mourning, contemplating life without liquor. I felt like I was giving up the one link I had to peace and solace, my one true friend in the world, and I found myself thinking in short, declarative sentences: *I'll never have fun at a party again. I'll never have an intimate conversation again. I'll never be able to get married: how can you get married without Champagne?* One of the joys of recovery has been understanding, slowly but steadily, that sobriety opens the very doors I thought it would shut: alcohol may have helped me create the *illusion* of experiences like fun and intimacy, but it never generated those feelings authentically. The chemically disinhibited version of me had fun at parties; the chemically altered version of me sat at bars and had long, liquor-laced heart-to-hearts with friends. When I drank, the real me—confident in some ways and fearful in others; strong *and* vulnerable—retreated to some back corner of my mind, protected perhaps but also fundamentally alone. Giving up drinking has been a little like walking out of shadow and into light, or replacing a broken antenna on a TV set: my vision is less obscured; my connections—to others, to the world—seem clearer, crisper.

The clarity is startling at first, as shocking as walking out of a dark movie theater into blinding sunlight. A recovering drug addict I know named Liz says that the first time she went out for coffee with people after a meeting, she felt so exposed she might as well have been naked. A daily pot smoker for 18 years, she'd simply forgotten what it was like to socialize without the haze of marijuana, and she felt as stiff and awkward as a teenager, self-conscious about her words, groping for things to talk about. "It was like literally stepping out from behind a smoke screen," she says. "There was a sense of having absolutely no protection, nothing standing between me and these other people." I know that feeling well: I'd become so accustomed to sipping that first glass and sliding gently into a more relaxed and sociable version of myself that I thought I might die without it at first, get swallowed right up by my own anxiety. But I also know that such feelings abate. You get used to being clean and sober. You realize that you *can* talk to people without drugs or wine, that the intimacy actually feels more real. The armor may be gone, but so is the loneliness.

And so, for that matter, is some of the fear. Life without anesthesia often has the quality of vigorous exercise, as though each repetition of a painful moment, gone through without one's substance of choice, serves to build up an emotional muscle. When you drink away feeling—or starve or eat or gamble or obsess it away—you deprive yourself of the chance to really understand it, to come to grips with fear and self-doubt and rage, to truly battle the emotional land mines that lurk within. Addictions may protect you, but they also stunt growth, prevent you from walking through the kinds of fearful life experiences that bring you from point A to point B on the maturity scale. When you give them up, when you begin to get through those difficult moments, you find yourself flexing muscles you never knew you had. You find yourself growing.

A painful process? Yes. But also a deeply gratifying one. Addictions, after all, may anesthetize you against difficult and painful emotions, but they keep you shielded from more positive feelings, as well. They numb away joy and delight and surprise; they keep you at a distance from true intimacy with others, and real laughter, and genuine insight. When you give up the anesthesia, you give yourself a chance to reclaim the most meaningful aspects of your own humanity. You give yourself, quite simply, a chance to live. Imagine *that*.

New Woman magazine, 1996

OUT THERE

The State of the World

AN OPEN LETTER TO CORPORATE AMERICA

Dear Corporate America,

Given that we are now four full days into the new year, it seems an appropriate time to share with you some of my thoughts about how you might conduct your businesses in these, our tough economic times.

Yes, things are tight out there. Fat expense accounts? Gone. Fifteen-percent raises? Forget it. Unlimited personal use of such offices services as Federal Express and long-distance phone calls? A thing of the past.

As you no doubt know, recessionary times do little for the morale of your many employees. We sit at our desks and fret about pink slips. We hear the gloomy economic forecasts and our thoughts of improved standards of living wither and die. Overworked and underpaid, we toil through the day, then look at the balances in our checkbooks and think, "Oh, shit. We're still not rich." Our little hearts sink.

But there is something that you, corporate America, can do about this. Ways you can improve our lives that don't involve huge expenditures of dough. Small kindnesses that can brighten our days and soothe our souls simply by reflecting your boundless empathy and compassion. For example:

On-site Laundry

You may not be aware of this, but a tremendous amount of productivity in corporate America is lost because employees are sitting at their desks feeling preoccupied with their laundry. They have no clean socks. No clean shirts. Worse, they are so busy knocking themselves out in these, our tight economic times, that they have no spare energy to wash said socks and shirts.

This is bad for everyone. A messily clad employee is an unhappy employee, and those of us who are forced to work side by side with a colleague who hasn't washed his or her socks for a month are none too pleased either. On-site laundry would vastly improve this situation. Think about it. Employees would race to work in the morning, determined to get a free machine before anybody else. They'd throw their stuff in the machine, hustle to their desks, work, work, work, then leap up to nab the first available dryer. Adrenaline would flow, morale would soar, and offices everywhere would emanate with the clean, refreshing scents of Tide and Cheer.

Mandatory Errand Days

Yes, it's true. Fat vacation packages are a thing of the past. We don't expect to have three or four weeks off a year anymore, and even if we did, we still couldn't afford to go anywhere. That doesn't mean, however, that we don't need some spare time for non-recreational purposes. In fact, our time has become so dominated by work that our lives outside of work are on the verge of chaos. We don't have time to get our cars tuned up. We don't have time to take in our dry-cleaning. We don't have time to pay our bills, or get our parking stickers renewed, or have our teeth cleaned, or stock up on groceries and shampoo and coffee and toilet paper and stamps, and in fact, when we get to the office in the morning, we're often absolutely frantic because our last pair of panty hose has run, and we've run out of toothpaste, and we haven't eaten any breakfast because we haven't had time to buy Wheat Chex in a *month,* and, well, you get the idea.

Which is why mandatory errand days make a tremendous amount of sense. Every six or eight weeks, on a rotating basis, each employee in a given company would be asked to draw up a list of the errands in his or her life that need doing. He or she would present said list to his or her supervisor, then be excused from work for the day and expected to accomplish as many of the items on the list as possible. As a special incentive program, employees who ticked off the most items from their lists would receive small errand-related prizes—a dry-cleaning coupon, for example, or a quart of motor oil.

Is this not a fine, fine idea? During the working day, we would all rest much, much easier. And hosts of ancillary businesses (car repair, drugstores, post offices) would flourish.

Mental-health Days

Same principle, but employees wouldn't be allowed to do anything except sit quietly at home on the sofa, watch soap operas in their bathrobes, and eat bonbons. Supervisors would be required to drop by on mental-health days to make sure no one is moving about. Interns, bearing cartons of Chinese food, would be dispatched to employee homes to fluff pillows.

Nap Rooms

Self-explanatory. We're tired. Let us rest from time to time.

Soundproof Designated Personal-phone-call Cubicles

Anyone who works in corporate America knows how hard it is to maintain a personal life when you work upwards of 50 hours a week, and anyone in that situation gets confronted from time to time with that most awkward of inter-office scenarios: attempting to have a fight with your boyfriend/girlfriend/mother/spouse over the phone at work. This is very difficult. You have to lean far forward in your chair and *hiss* into the phone. You have to communicate complicated, delicate thoughts ("I am *not* being selfish!") in whispers. And you have to pray that the embarrassing details of your personal life do not inadvertently wend themselves into the company newsletter.

Soundproof cubicles would give employees the luxury of complete privacy. They could go in, shut the door, and scream at their spouses with abandon. An added benefit: this would free women from the humiliating business of having to hightail it to the ladies' room to have a good, post-fight cry.

Company Errand Boys

Think how much happier your employees would be if they could sit at work knowing that the kindly company errand boy was visiting their apartments to vacuum and take out the trash!

Company Masseurs

Also self-explanatory. Our little necks and shoulders begin to ache when we sit at our desks for hours at a time. Help us out a little.

Miscellany

Are you getting the picture here, corporate America? Are you beginning to realize that we, the folks who slave and toil for you, are actual people with actual lives that are actually running the risk of falling apart? Have a little empathy, all you CEOs and presidents. Take a hint from your old kindergarten teachers. Put cots in our cubicles, and serve us cookies and juice. Let us out for recess now and then. And once in a while, call for a companywide nap, wherein everyone would take out a blanket and rest comfortably on the floor for 30 minutes. Yes, times are tight, but that doesn't mean we can't have a kinder, gentler work place. Does it?

BOSTON PHOENIX
JANUARY 1991

TWELVE STEPS DOWN

HELLO, MY NAME is Caroline and I have some serious problems. I am going to share these problems with you today, not because I am proud of them, or because I think they make for pleasant reading, but because I feel that by publicly acknowledging my problems, I might get a huge, multimillion-dollar book contract and make an enormous pile of dough—oops! What I meant to say was, by publicly acknowledging my problems, I can help the millions of others who undoubtedly are similarly afflicted feel more comfortable coming forward to seek the help they desperately need.

Anyway, brace yourself, because this is not pretty. Are you ready? Here goes.

First of all, I am laundry-impaired.

I know. It's ugly. I don't even know how it happened, although I'm fairly sure it's my mother's fault. But I admit it. I cannot do my laundry. I loathe doing laundry—it incapacitates me. And sometimes—this is very difficult for me to admit—entire months will go by before I even *think about changing my sheets*.

It has taken me years of struggle and hard work (not to mention frantic early-morning searches for the least-dirty pair of socks I can find) to come to terms with this problem, but finally I am recovering. Listen, here's proof.

"I admit I am powerless over my laundry and that my closets have become unmanageable.

"I have come to believe that a Power greater than myself will restore me to sanity (this Power being extremely expensive services that will do my laundry for me, even folding it nicely, though I know I cannot afford such services).

"And I have made a decision to turn my will and my laundry over to the care and direction of the man at my local laundry service, *as I understand Him*."

See?

This, however, is just the beginning. To this day, I am still struggling with an equally devastating refrigerator impairment, which is also my mother's fault. Or maybe it's low self-esteem. I forget. Anyway, millions of other Americans probably carry the secret humiliation of refrigerator impairment with them day after day, and I hope that by coming forward with my own refrigerator disorder, I can help those victims to recognize that it's useless to listen to famous figures talk about their problems, because people don't come to terms with their own problems until they're good and ready—oops! What I meant to say was, I hope that by coming forward with my own problems, I will help others see themselves in me and take heart that they're not alone.

Anyway, this is my problem: I cannot clean out my refrigerator. I simply cannot. I have not yet been able to admit that I am powerless over my refrigerator (although I do know that my vegetable crisper has become unmanageable), but the warning signs are there. Right now, as you sit here reading this, my refrigerator contains: two cartons of milk with expiration dates going back to July; three heads of lettuce that look far too dangerous to touch (see what I mean about the crisper?); and an aluminum-foil-covered bowl containing the remnants of a lemon-chicken dish I made last April for my sister and her husband. (This was the time it turned out they hated chicken and refused to eat the dish, causing me terrific embarrassment and decreasing my already low self-esteem. Horrifying, right?)

Anyway, I have also developed a host of related syndromes: refrigerator-content denial; refrigerator-content phobia; an extremely expensive restaurant addiction; and a very embarrassing tendency, when I do finally get a grip on my life and force myself to clean the damn thing out, to throw away everything in the refrigerator, without exception. Even the bowls.

I don't know if you can stand to hear more, but I honestly feel that it's important to share all this with you, because as we have learned from so many recent public admissions of personal pain and addiction, the more people talk publicly about their problems, the more excruciating and gruesome details we all have to hear about what it's actually like to ingest nail polish and hair spray—oops! What I meant to say was, the more people talk about their problems, the more sympathetic and aware of human frailty we all become. Right?

So, anyway, I also have an extremely painful Automatic Teller Machine Disorder, which manifests itself primarily in obsessive-compulsive Automatic Teller Machine behavior. This obsession causes me to hit the ATM at least six times a week—sometimes more—so that I can get money I do not have out of the bank so that I can go out and buy cases and cases of hair spray and then disclose the details in a book for reasons that totally escape the public—oops! I didn't mean that. Sorry. I don't know what made me say that, but it's probably my mother's fault, because she had such low self-esteem. Or maybe I did. I forget.

Anyway, the Automatic Teller Machine Disorder is very embarrassing, but it's not quite as embarrassing as my Dysfunctional High Heel Syndrome, which hits me every time one of those little rubber protective things from my heels falls off. You suffer from this *too?* Well, seek professional help! Or better yet, write a book about it! After all, those 12-step problems are very costly!

Anyway, every time one of those things falls off my heel, I come down with a huge, debilitating case of Cobbler Phobia and Procrastination Disorder, which prevents me from getting the shoes fixed, and ultimately I end up with horribly worn-down, mangled heels that cause me to skid across slippery floor surfaces like those at the Star Market, thereby publicly humiliating myself and causing my self-esteem to plummet even further. It's truly awful.

And then there is my Bad Sitcom Theme Song Retention Disorder, a poorly understood phenomenon that seems to be caused by some kind of brain imbalance. In any event, huge portions of my brain that should be used for rational, cognitive thought and learning are instead taken up by all the lyrics to all the bad theme songs to all the bad sitcoms I've ever watched. Thus, so many of my brain cells are taken up with the words to theme songs from shows like *Gilligan's Island* and *The Beverly Hillbillies* that there's virtually no room in my brain for things like learning new skills or understanding my obsessive attraction to hair spray—oops!—I meant, understanding myself and the motives behind my obsessive, compulsive, addictive, and impaired behavior.

Anyway, this is probably my mother's fault too, because I remember that when I was a child watching TV she would walk into the room with a hatchet and *come and listen to a story 'bout a man named Jed, poor mountaineer barely kept his family fed with hair spray*—oops! See what I mean?

I'm sorry. I'm really very sorry, but all this public disclosure seems to be making me disoriented. I'm having trouble focusing. Maybe my Public Disclosure of Personal Problems Addiction is getting in the way. Maybe I've been drinking too much hair spray. In any event, I hope this little discussion has been helpful. I hope you've been able to see some of your own vulnerability and pain in my story and that you've emerged with a deeper understanding of the inherent frailty of the human condition. And if you haven't, I won't worry about it too much. After all, I'm pretty sure it's my mother's fault.

BOSTON PHOENIX
SEPTEMBER 1990

FROM ARES TO RIDICULES

GREEK GODS FOR MODERN TIMES

THE ANCIENT GREEKS had the right idea. Instead of developing complex, repressive, war-fostering religions as a way of explaining the world, they came up with the Greek gods. One for each phenomenon, one to explain each source of angst or chaos in the world, and one to correspond to each human wish. Need to understand why we have war? Blame it on Ares, the god of war. Want to fend off a deadly storm or tidal wave? Just offer up a sacrifice to Poseidon, the sea god.

This system makes tremendous sense, but unfortunately many of the ancient Greek gods are ill-suited to modern times. What use would we really have, for example, for Artemis, goddess of hunting? Or Hephaestus, the god responsible for volcanoes?

Clearly we need our own, updated versions of these higher beings, special gods for the '90s who could help us better to understand the world around us, and to combat the confusion and despair that come from not knowing why things are the way they are.

Consider, if you will, the following:

• *Testicles* (rhymes with Hercules), God of Male Chauvinist Pigs. A cruel god. Responsible for male insensitivity, excessive machismo, and such phrases as, "Check out those knockers!" and "Heeeeey, babeeee!" Men worship at the altar of Testicles in special, designated locations, known in some circles as "sports bars." Although women make many, many sacrifices to Testicles, they have not yet figured out how to appease him.

• *Procrastines*, God of Wasted Time. Explains why your bills are unpaid, your work is languishing on your desk, and your apartment is a mess. Do not attempt to appease. This makes Procrastines angry, and he is likely to retaliate by loading you up with extra work or causing your dishwasher to break down. The best way to handle this god is to appeal to *Apologese*, God of Lame Excuses.

• *Infatues*, *Ambivales*, and *Whyareyoulyingtomes*, the three Gods of Relationships. A most complex and mischievous trio. Infatuese overcomes unsuspecting men and women during the first six weeks of a romance, imparting artificial feelings of bliss and ecstasy. This causes said partners to run around and smile insanely, which results in the erosion of protective ego boundaries. At this point, Ambivales takes over, creating wild mood swings, sudden shifts of heart, and an extended dance known as "come here, come here; go away, go away." When Ambivales tires, Whyareyoulyingtomes steps in and creates sufficient tension, doubt, and mistrust to drive the pair apart.

• *Isosceles*, God of Love Triangles. Often picks up where the previous three gods leave off. Generally makes a mess of things; best way to appease is to enter a monastery.

• *Meus* (rhymes with Zeus), Goddess of Cellulite. A most cruel goddess. Causes thighs to bloat and puff to unnatural proportions, creates inexplicable cravings among women for foods with names like "Yo-Yos," and erodes self-esteem in nearly half the human population. Women spend their entire lives sacrificing at the altar of Meus, engaging in such bizarre, self-flagellating activities as Reebok Step-Dancing and the Ritual Drinking of Ultra Slim-Fast.

• *Accessores*, Goddess of Hats, Scarves, and Handbags. A much kinder goddess. Provides women with temporary escape from worship at the altar of Meus.

• *Hermes*, Goddess of Overpriced Hats, Scarves, and Handbags. Accessores' cruel sister. Attempt to avoid her—remember, the Greek Hermes was the conductor of souls to Hades.

• *Permes*, Goddess of Hair Salons. Causes intelligent humans to engage in such bizarre rites as foil wrapping, scrunch drying, and obsessive application of mousse (not to be confused with Meus). A fickle goddess who may be kind of sadistic. When you see a grown woman weeping in the ladies' room over a bad haircut, you know that the cruel hand of Permes has been at work.

• *Herpes*, God of Unfortunate Encounters. Self-explanatory.

• *Hyperbolese*, God of Politics. An exceptionally cruel god. Responsible for rampant mismanagement and inefficiency, as well as global tension, warfare, and chaos. Is known, in some of his more insidious manifestations, to characterize himself as "kinder and gentler." Don't be fooled. People in more-fortunate lands attempt to appease this god by worshipping every four years or so in small booths. This does not appear to work.

• *Ridicules*, God of Republican Politics. Explains why we have the Bush-Quayle ticket.

• *Preposteres*, God of Political Advertising. Explains why we have the mute button.

• *Whathaveyoudoneformelateles*, God of Cruel Bosses. Explains why sometimes you come into work and your employer yells at you for no reason, fails to give you the raise you deserve, and otherwise deprives you of the respect, rewards, and professional success to which you are entitled. Very difficult to appease. Apologes sometimes intervenes during heated exchanges with the God of Cruel Bosses; employees often attempt to offer sacrifices in the form of Ritualistic Brown-Nosing and False Flattery.

• *Raucchus*, God of Bad Parties. Explains why we have fraternities. Impossible to appease, although keg bans help.

• *Telephone* (rhymes with Persephone), God of Utility Companies. Another mischievous god. Accounts for gas leaks, mysterious breakdowns in furnaces and air-conditioning systems, poor phone connections, and rampant bureaucratic inefficiency. Seems to respond solely to large sacrifices of cash.

• *Whataboutmes*, Goddess of Self-Absorption. Causes selfishness, narcissism, and excessive focus on one's own problems. Is responsible for the prevalence of the phrase "But what about *my* needs?" Also explains why we have psychiatrists.

Of course, these are only a handful of the minor gods, and there are many, many others. There's Dermes, god of bad skin, Proctologes, god of assholes, and Syphilles, god of sexually transmitted diseases. There's Legales, god of nightmare attorneys, and Axles, god of bad heavy-metal bands.

Remember though: just as the Ancient Greeks had Zeus, the Big Cheese of gods, we here in modern times have our own overlord, the god whose presence in the world truly explains why life in the '90s is the way it is: angst-ridden and confusing and unfathomably complex. His name?

It's obvious: *Neuroses*.

Boston Phoenix
August 1999

BEYOND BAD HAIR

THIN LIPS, SQUARE BREASTS, AND OTHER HORRORS

I AM HAVING A LARGE day. I am feeling LARGE. Just plain LARGE.

Has this ever happened to you? You're wandering around and all of a sudden, for no apparent reason, you just feel LARGE? Much LARGER than you really are?

This is a girl thing, I think. A distorted body-image thing: in reality I am quite a small person, physically, but some days my mind plays tricks on me and I just feel LARGE.

Major misconception: people think the only thing that plagues women is the occasional bad-hair day. This is not true. Not true! We have bad-hair days, and we have LARGE days, and we have a wide and fascinating variety of other days, too.

Here are some of the bad days that women experience on a regular basis.

• Along with LARGE days, we have EXTRA-LARGE days, JUMBO days, and FAMILY-SIZE days. The FAMILY-SIZE day, as you may suspect, is the worst: imagine the very worst bad-hair day you could have and then expand it into a full-body experience. Eeeeek. Very scary.

• A good number of bad-type days have to do with underwear. This is puzzling, but true. There are your garden-variety I'm-sure-everyone-can-see-my-underwear-through-my-skirt days, and there are my-undies-are-creeping-up-on-me days, and then there is the particularly horrifying experience known as the Yikes!-I've-got-my-underwear-on-inside-out day. These always happen at times when you're supposed to be feeling adult and mature. For instance, you'll be about to sit on an important panel, or lead an important meeting, and you'll go to the bathroom and realize, Yikes! I've got my underwear on inside out, and you'll feel like a loser. Evidence: a friend of mine discovered that she had her underwear on inside out the very day she was signing the closing papers for a *house*—certainly an indication that she was not as grown up as the occasion merited.

• Note: one of the most frustrating things about these bad days is that if you confide in someone about your concern, that person invariably fails to acknowledge your problem, and in fact often looks at you as if you were demented. Which only leads you to believe that you must be crazy as well as deformed. On the underwear front, for example, I sometimes have an is-it-the-bra-I'm-wearing-or-are-my-breasts-really-square? day. This is not something you want to share with a whole lot of people.

• Have you ever had an Ooooops!-I-missed-a-large-patch-of-hair-while-shaving-my-legs day? This is also known as a bad-knee-hair day, and it's quite disturbing.

• Pants (specifically, ill-fitting pants) play a large role in many bad-type days. The other day, for instance, I had a the-right-leg-of-my-pants-feels-a-little-tighter-than-the-left-leg day, which evoked the image of having one very thin thigh and one very fat thigh and made me most uncomfortable. And not long ago, I had a why-are-these-pants-pinching-me-around-the-waist day, which caused me to obsess all day long about whether I'd gained weight, whether I could remember a time when these pants were looser or tighter, whether I was just a little puffy due to various foods I'd eaten or the time of the month, whether I was secretly pregnant (almost no chance of that, but, worrier that I am, it always occurs to me), whether it was the shirt I had tucked in, whether it was the way the waistband was all bunched up around itself, and so on. You see? Bad hair is the least of it.

• Last week, I had an I-suddenly-sense-my-lips-are-too-thin day. I also had a since-when-have-my-pores-been-so-cavernous? day, but not at exactly the same time as the bad-lip day. Whew! Can you imagine what that would have been like? It would have turned into an I-have-to-stay-at-home-and-hide-under-the-bed day, no question.

• When I was a child, my brother and sister used to tease me about the size of my nose. I guess I did have something of a large nose at the time, perhaps even a FAMILY-SIZE nose (my face has grown into it by now), but to this day, the torture of that experience has stayed with me and I occasionally still have an is-it-my-imagination-or-has-my-nose-gotten-a-little-bigger-lately? day. These are awful. When I have one, I have to run into the ladies' room periodically and study my nose from different angles to make sure it isn't expanding.

• Bad-clothing days are ubiquitous. There is the my-skirt-is-definitely-too-short day, and the for-some-reason-this-particular-blouse-makes-my-armpits-sweaty day, and the why-are-these-leggings-bagging-at-the-knees? day. Predictably enough, bad-clothing days often, but not always, coincide with LARGE days.

• Bad-footwear days are less common, except for the periodic I-don't-have-the-right-black-shoes-to-wear day, which is often more of a chronic state than a "day." But one time, I did have a my-feet-look-like-two-dead-flounders-in-these-shoes day, which was scary. I was wearing one of those pairs of pseudo-cowboy boots, the cut-off ones that only go up to your ankle, and I had the dead-flounder-foot feeling all day long, and I never wore those shoes again.

• Another time—and only once—I actually had an are-my-veins-too-visible-through-my-skin? day. I worried about this for about 12 hours. I'm not kidding.

Some random bad days:

The my-eyes-never-quite-opened-all-the-way-this-morning-and-still-haven't day.

The Ack!-I-just-realized-I-have-had-pieces-of-corn-muffin-stuck-in-my-teeth-since-breakfast-and-now-it's-four-o'clock day.

The I'm-sure-my-teeth-are-moving-into-a-new-and-less-flattering-configuration day.

The I'm-sensing-the-development-of-a-large-zit-on-my-forehead day.

The I-know-these-pantyhose-have-a-run-but-I'm-going-to-wear-them-anyway day.

The is-this-freckle-on-my-face-a-cancerous-growth? day. And, of course, the obviously-my-face-is-lopsided day. God, it's hard to be a girl.

BOSTON PHOENIX
AUGUST 1994

NOTES ON DAVE

THE SOCIOLOGY OF DAVID: A MINOR RANT

I SEEM TO HAVE a problem with Daves.

Do you have this problem, too? With maybe one or two exceptions, I don't think I've ever met a guy named Dave whom I ended up liking or trusting, whereas almost everyone I know named David is okay.

Consider.

There was Dave O., the thick-necked Italian thug whose last words to me, whispered softly in the backseat of a car on the night of our graduation from high school, were: "I don't wanna fuckin' see you no more." (It has since been pointed out to me that his phrasing included use of a double negative, indicating that perhaps he *did* want to fuckin' see me some more; I suspect this was not the case.)

There was Dave R., the idiot jock who, within the first three months of our relationship, totaled two cars, got evicted from his apartment, lost his job, and then managed (don't ask) to charm me into letting him stay at my place ("just for a few weeks"). He subsequently arrived in a truck with all his worldly possessions (including a 40-gallon fish tank) and proceeded to rearrange all my furniture. (I almost had to call the police to get rid of him, two months later.)

And there was Dave M., a.k.a. "Mad Dog," a literature student at UMass who (it turned out) had served in a special forces unit of the U.S. Army in El Salvador where, to prove his machismo, he once bit the head off a live snake. (When I broke up with Dave M., in a Japanese restaurant, in Providence, he threw a glass of saki across the room, stormed out, and drove off with my gloves in his car. I never saw him again. Or the gloves.)

See a pattern here?
Daves. Don't like 'em.

❧

Okay: caveats. I am not currently associated with any Daves. I don't have any friends named Dave, no colleagues named Dave, not even a casual acquaintance named Dave. So this isn't a sideways attack on anyone in particular. Also, I am sure there are some good Daves out there. Plenty of good ones. The presence of bad Daves in my history could be a simple case of bad luck.

But I also think there is something to this, something about the way a name (or a nickname) carries certain connotations and behavioral expectations and so can subtly affect self-image and personality. My parents, for example, briefly considered naming me Sophia (pronounced Sof-EYE-a), which naturally would have degenerated into "Sophie," which sounds like "sofa," which sounds fat. I'm convinced to this day that if I'd been named Sophia, I would have ended up with a huge butt.

Same thing with Dave. Say it out loud. *Dave*. There's something a little dumb-sounding about the name Dave. Something truncated and blunt and insensitive, and I think it must have an effect on personality. To this day, I still think that if Dave O. had been a David, he would have tragically broken my heart on graduation night instead of busting up the relationship with a double negative. If Dave R. had been a David, he would have charmed his way into my life *after* he'd gotten a car, a job, and a home of his own.

Plus, I took a Dave poll. Eleven people: "Where do you stand on Daves versus Davids?"

Results: I heard about a reckless party animal named Dave. A menacing college roommate named Dave. Several wretched exboyfriends, all Daves. (Of course, I left out the good Daves, but this is my column, so I'm allowed to.)

David, on the other hand, yielded far more positive results. Three women, happily involved with Davids. Many close male friends: Davids. Me, I have a dear former housemate named David. A cute, blond nephew named David.

Who else? There's David Letterman (who is sometimes called "Dave" but gets away with it because he makes it sound ironic). In literature, there are David Halberstam and David McCaulay. In journalism, Davids Brinkley, Brudnoy, and Broder. In popular culture: David Byrne, David Lynch, David Bowie.

Yes, there's definitely a pattern. David Copperfield. Dwight David Eisenhower. Michelangelo's David. None of these Davids would seem the same if their names were Dave. David, with its final "d," sounds finished and complete, whereas Dave just kind of hangs there in the air, indefinitely. It sounds silly.

Try it.

Dave versus Goliath.

King *Dave*. The Star of *Dave*.

Henry DAVE Thoreau.

Ridiculous.

One of the only bad Davids I can think of is David Koresh, but I'll bet that if his name had been "Dave" Koresh, he wouldn't have had a following in the first place. "Who, me? Hole up in a compound in the middle of Texas because of some guy named 'Dave'? No way."

David, of course, isn't the only name that has this effect, this way of subtly altering the way you expect a person to be. There's a world of difference between the name Edward, which sounds rather regal and stuffy (Edwardian), and the name Eddie, which sounds like a guy on the bus. Huge difference between Charles (aristocratic) and Charlie or Chuck (buddy-buddy). James versus Jimmy, or *Jimbo*? No contest.

But Dave is the primo example. Daves are big lugs, like Dave Schultz, major-league hockey thug with the Philadelphia Flyers. Daves are kinda dumb, like the protagonist in the movie *Dave*, who might have had an entirely different personality if his name had been David. Daves are silly: can you imagine Dave Barry (a very good Dave, by the way) writing under the byline David Barry? Just wouldn't work. He'd have to be a historian.

Worse, if your name is Dave, the only possible nickname is "Davey," which makes you sound like you should be wearing a coonskin cap. Very bad. David, on the other hand, sounds good in just about any language—Italian (DA-veed-ay), for example, and French (Da-VEED).

Here's a true story.

Some years ago, I wrote a column suggesting that, given how much money I'd spent on my shrink over the years, he should name a wing of his house after me (his name is David). In the column, I wrote something snide, something about how he was probably using all that money to build, say, a new sunroom, and about how I imagined strolling into therapy and saying something snippy and disrespectful, like, "So, *Dave*, how's that sunroom going?"

I sent him the column and we talked about it the next week. He didn't seem to mind the snippiness. He didn't mind the little undercurrent of anger. He didn't even comment on the fact that I sort of talked about his home life in the column, which could have been considered an invasion of privacy. No, the main thing I remember is that he sat back, looked a little disgusted, and said, "I don't much care for the name *Dave*."

I trust this man.

I rest my case.

BOSTON PHOENIX
JANUARY 1994

WHAT WOMEN REALLY NEED FROM SCIENCE

SO NOW WOMEN can have babies at the age of 90. Big whoop. Roll out the Pampers and Geritol. Open a Cribs 'n' Canes shop. And thank you, thank you, thank you, modern medicine.

Something is very wrong here. While a teensy-weensy proportion of women over the age of 75 might welcome the opportunity to procreate in their golden years, and while this development might help ease the pressure some women feel as their biological clocks tick away, most of us shudder at the news. Babies when we're 90? Postmenopausal midnight feedings?

This news also seems to indicate a slight problem modern science has with focus. What about the here and now? What about the daily realities women face in our younger years?

Any doctor or research scientist who truly understood the lives of modern women would be looking in an entirely different direction for ways to ease our burdens and make our lives more manageable. Forget about extending our childbearing years. Forget about finding new and medically thrilling ways to complicate our later lives. We need help now! Here, for ambitious doctors everywhere, are a few suggestions.

The Instant Menstrual Cycle

Consider how much simpler life would be if scientists could develop a way to enable women to menstruate in a mere five minutes. No more messy, five- to seven-day bouts of bleeding. No consecutive nights curled on the couch with heating pads to ease the lower back pain. And no more worrying: Will you run out of tampons? Leak?

Bleed on his sheets? The five-minute menstrual cycle would pack all that discomfort and inconvenience into much more manageable form. One huge cramp. One enormous mood swing. A single flood of tears, and then—*wooosh*—a single rush of blood into a single, extremely absorbent tampon. If science can come up with instant coffee, instant breakfast, and instant cameras, instant menstruation couldn't be *that* hard.

Egg-laying Capabilities

Lots and lots of women like the *concept* of having children. They like the idea of taking care of a newborn baby. They welcome all that nurturing and feeding and holding. The concept of pregnancy, on the other hand, is another story. Morning sickness? Huge, swollen bellies? Stretch marks, 36-hour labors, blood, pain, screaming . . . ?

Why not take a hint from our feathered friends? Why not discover a way to take the human equivalent of egg-laying (ovulation), bring it outside the body, and enable women to sit quietly for a few months while their babies grow in shells? It seems such a tidy solution to so many problems. No more worrying about what you eat and drink and do while you're pregnant. No backaches, weird food cravings, or constant urinating. And no more inconvenience.

For the first few months, women could take their eggs anywhere—work, grocery shopping, the movies—carrying them in pockets or purses the way kangaroos carry babies in their pouches. As the eggs got too big to tote around, women could stay home and keep them warm, or put them in little incubators—whatever's easier. And in the final weeks, women would simply stay home quietly and nest. Marketers could jump into the action here and come up with special nesting tools (nesting thrones would be nice). More important, spouses could jump in any time a woman got tired of nesting and keep the egg warm for her.

And think how wonderful it would be to watch that lovingly tended little egg begin to crack open. Think how sweet it would be to stand by with your significant other and watch as the tiny baby hands and feet emerged from the shell. A completely painless answer to the miracle of childbirth.

Anti-abuse Medication for Women

We all know that the number of women in physically or emotionally abusive relationships has reached epidemic proportions in this country. As things now stand, however, there are few truly effective solutions to the problem, and most of those seem to be the stuff of self-help books, preachy tomes that are geared toward women and their alleged "problems with self-esteem." This is problematic on two counts. First, it puts the burden of dealing with abusive relationships squarely on the shoulders of women, implying in turn that if they are being mistreated, then it is somehow their fault.

Second, the self-help approach appears to ignore any possibility that this syndrome could have physiological roots. Some women, after all, seem to have an almost biological need to be mistreated. They flock instinctively to men who manipulate and criticize them, cut them down, and otherwise ensure that their already low self-esteem remains, at best, marginal. Perhaps, like people who suffer from depression or anxiety, they could benefit from psychopharmacology.

Anti-abuse medication would operate under the same principles as Antabuse, the highly effective drug that makes alcoholics violently ill at the first sip of a drink. So. When the man in your life starts taking you for granted, criticizing you in public, or otherwise hacking away at your sense of self, you'd simply pop an anti-abuse pill and lurch into a sudden fit of vomiting. Three or four bouts of this, and, it seems safe to say, your attraction to abusive males would begin to abate, thereby freeing you to pursue happier, healthier romantic partners.

Science could take this one step further, too, by developing a special extra-strength form designed to teach abusive men a thing or two in the process. This form would induce special high-speed projectile vomiting, making abuse extremely unpleasant for both parties.

Miscellaneous Solutions to Myriad Other Problems

The above ideas, of course, are only a start, designed to get research scientists thinking. But there are many, many other areas of a woman's life that need addressing. Just empathize, folks! Use your imaginations! And if you're still stuck, here are a few suggestions:

• Clones, which seem to be the only true solution to the problems faced by working mothers.

• Salt-free Confrontation Aids, which would enable women to stand up for themselves without bursting into tears.

• Anti-gravity Skin Enhancers, which would fend off the threat of midlife sag.

• Good men.

BOSTON PHOENIX
JANUARY 1990

HE SAYS, SHE SAYS

SIX ESSENTIAL SEX DIFFERENCES

WE ALL KNOW THE standard stereotypes: women are emotional, men aren't. Women cry, men don't. Men like sports and politics, women like shopping.

In fact, the true differences between men and women are more subtle and complex than that, and they require a more delicate kind of probing into the male and female psyches to discern. Consider, if you will, the following, just in time for Valentine's Day.

1) The Three Stooges

Yes, men watch the Stooges and women don't. When Larry, Moe, and Curly come on the tube, a man will respond with wild laughter and a set of immediate and highly developed imitations of Stooge-like noises and gestures. Women, on the other hand, respond with a look of total repulsion, rolled eyes, and the phrase, "Turn that thing off! I can't *stand* them!" But has anyone ever asked why this is so? Has anyone ever pondered the deeper meaning of this phenomenon?

On a psychic level, one must assume that it speaks volumes about differences between male and female orientations toward the world. Men have an inbred affinity toward two things that women do not: total stupidity and rampant violence. Watching *The Three Stooges*, in turn, brings a man back to his childhood (by awakening memories of the inane bathroom humor that sent him into hysterics when he was six) and speaks to his darker, more primitive and aggressive side (by inundating him with images of men poking each other in the eyes, smashing each other about the head and shoulders, tweaking each other's noses, and so on). To women, whose primitive sides are more nurturing and maternal, this is about as appealing as professional wrestling.

It should also be noted that this difference accounts for the rise of the modern men's movement, another bizarre and exclusively male phenomenon that (erroneously) has been considered a male counterpart to modern feminism. Wrong, wrong, wrong. The men's movement merely reflects men in their Post-Stooge Era. After all, didn't men start running around in the woods with war paint and tom-toms right around the time that Moe, the last living Stooge, died? Think about it.

2) The Air Guitar

Have you ever—*ever*—seen a woman play air guitar? Of course not. But have you ever wondered why? One representative of the species says it stems from a simple fact: nine out of 10 men (white men, anyway) have absolutely no sense of rhythm, so they take up the air guitar as a way to compensate. This can be tested. Get nine out of 10 women out on a dance floor and, inhibition or self-consciousness notwithstanding, they'll at least be able to move in time with a beat. But men? If you could diagram the average man's dance ability, this is what it would look like:

Music: . . . *beat* . . . *beat* . . . *beat* . . . *beat* . . . *beat* . . .

Movement: . . . um, step . . . um, snap, snap . . . step . . . snap . . . um, step, step . . .

This speaks to an essential but little-known difference between men and women: women are equipped with a special gene that prevents them from doing things that make them look ridiculous in public; men are not.

3) The Cocktail-party Homing Instinct

When men walk into a cocktail party, the first thing they look at is the women. When women walk into a cocktail party, the first thing they look at is the food. In part, this may be because the women have seen all those men dance before, but it also has a deeper meaning. Aside from the aforementioned gene, women are equipped with two things that men do not have: enormous problems with body image and a highly developed sense of danger in the world. Hence, to walk into a cocktail party is to engage in direct contact with the enemy: the bowl of chips in the corner . . . the hunks of rich cheeses on that sideboard over there . . . the cake on the dining-room table. This is why you will see the eyes of women flitting nervously from corner to corner at the onset of a party. Most men think they're scoping out the other women in the room to size up the competition, but they're not. It's the Cheeze Doodles.

4) The Psychic Relationship to the Bathroom

A primary difference. Women like to go *into* the bathroom; men like to go *to* the bathroom. This sounds crass, but it is true. To a woman, the bathroom is a safe haven. The place where you first bond with other girls. Where you first experiment with blue eyeshadow and learn to smoke cigarettes and begin to talk about boys. Later in life, it becomes a key source of privacy, often emerging as the one place a woman feels free to care for and pamper herself. And in offices across the land, it is a veritable sanctuary, the one place women can—and do—go to cry.

Men, on the other hand, have more of a toll-booth mentality when it comes to bathrooms. This is especially true if the bathroom is situated in an office or other public space—they go in, deposit whatever it is they need to deposit, and leave. ASAP. Some men, however, do have a deeper affinity with the bathroom, but theirs is focused almost exclusively in another direction: on their own bodily functions. Don't ask me why this is true, but it is: some men love to go to the bathroom in a way that women simply don't. They take pride in it. If their digestive tracts are working well, it fills them with satisfaction. Sometimes they even boast about it to other men. In any event, this may be one of the few areas in life where women look outward and men look inward (or, as the case may be, downward).

5) The Giving of Directions

Men are literal. Hence, they give directions like this: "Go two-tenths of a mile west on Route 16, then head due south on Route 10 for approximately 3.5 tenths of a mile, and then bear east until you hit a point where the sun is at a 120-degree angle from the horizon at four o'clock, then . . ."

Women, on the other hand, are visual and time-oriented, and their directions sound more like this: "Go down the road about the length of one song on the radio until you see a red house, and then a white house, and then a little picket fence, and then comes this point in the road that kind of zig-zags a little, so you have to pay attention, but when it straightens out, go about as far as it would take to smoke a cigarette, and . . ."

6) Painful Clothing

A man may be just as vain as a woman, but he won't wear anything that hurts. Women wear high heels. With support hose. In the summer. Case closed.

BOSTON PHOENIX
FEBRUARY 1991

DICKING AROUND

NOTES ON WAR CLUBS, MEAT POLES, AND MALE SEXUALITY

SO WHAT IS it with men and their dicks? I really want to know.

The average man has at least 27 names for his dick: weenie, and wang, and tool, and member, and pecker, and war club, and muscle of love, and love gun, and meat pole, and (my personal favorite) one-eyed trouser snake. And on and on and on.

A man I know calls his, simply, "Persuasion." (Gag.) Another calls it his "Résumé."

Why do they do this?

Men also have 47 ways to describe masturbation. Choking the chicken. Flogging the dolphin. Buffing the musket. Bopping the bishop. Slappin' it. Flappin' it. Wackin' it.

Women are so much more discreet about their reproductive anatomy. See? We call it "reproductive anatomy." We are so genteel in our descriptions we're almost prissy. Just listen to 15-year-old girls talk about menstruation.

"I have it," they whisper, looking alarmed as deer.

"Have what?"

"*It*. You know . . . my friend."

Serious nod: "Oh. Your *friend*."

Men would not talk this way. Gloria Steinem once wrote a whole column about what would happen if men menstruated: they'd brag about it. They'd run up to each other in the school yard and say, "Hey, man, I am *on the rag*!" They'd boast about how many tampons they went through in a day.

But despite their apparent love affairs with their dicks, most men are surprisingly reticent about the subject.

"I am not going to talk to you about men and their dicks," says my friend "Ernest" (let's not even pretend this is his real name). "I am not going to get into this. I refuse."

I pour him another glass of wine and wait for him to soften. I say, "A woman has a very hard time saying the word 'cunt.' To women, this sounds crass and grotesque. It makes them visibly uncomfortable. So why is it that men can use a phrase like 'one-eyed trouser snake' and think it's funny?"

"Because it is!"

Then he loosens up a little and segues into a somewhat familiar train of thought about how male genitals are external and female genitals are internal and because of this difference, men have an easier time talking about things sexual in objective, external terms, whereas women are more prone to thinking about them as internal matters.

"Maybe," I say. "But I don't think it's all physiology and hormones."

"Well, if you had this thing hanging there between your legs," he says, "you'd probably have a different attitude about it, too." Then he starts free-associating about what it's like to be a 16-year-old boy sitting there in math class and getting a screaming erection for absolutely no apparent reason and having to stand up at the end of class and . . . well, how it's just pretty hard to be a guy and not be wildly conscious of your sexuality at least 98 percent of the time.

I sit there listening and I notice the presence of an odd feeling. At first I feel defensive, like I want to say, 'Okay, I am sick of hearing about you boys and your hormones and how ridiculously horny you get just sitting there in math class.' But then the feeling evolves into something more like . . . jealousy. No, not penis envy. I have never once in my life had the desire to have several inches of rather unremarkable-looking flesh determine my entire outlook on life and love. I mean something else.

I was jealous because my memory of being 16 years old and sitting in math class is so decidedly less sexual. Back then, I sat there and worried about zits. Or about what I was wearing. Or about why some particular boy I liked hadn't seemed to look at me that day even once. Probably he was too focused on his screaming erection to look at me, but I didn't know about those things back then, so I figured it was my fault: I wasn't interesting enough, or pretty enough.

And that's precisely the point. It would be so much easier to grow up male and to be so in touch with your sexuality and sexual impulses, to have your whole being dominated by that singular wish: to get laid. It's an equation: you have a dick, you want sex. And you are taught from an early age that this is okay, the way it should be.

But when you grow up female, you get a much weirder set of messages: your vagina is *a*) a place that oozes a disgusting bloody substance once a month, and *b*) something dangerous and scary. If you're a man, you're taught to see sex as a goal; if you're a woman, you're taught to avoid it. So of course you don't think about sex—or talk about it—with that male brand of graphic bravado. Your sexuality gets deflected onto all those annoying externals: how you look and what you're wearing and how you behaved every single time a boy came within spitting distance in the cafeteria.

Simply put, when you grow up female, you get saddled with all the burdens of being attractive—and few of the pleasures of being *attracted*.

Beyond that, even if you happen to be attractive naturally, you're not allowed just to sit back, wallow in the attention, and learn to enjoy your sexuality. This may be 1992, but, as a man might say, I'd bet my left nut that boys will still call you a slut if you sleep around.

This is most unfortunate. It's hard enough, as my reticent friend suggested, to have the kind of anatomy that doesn't scream sexual messages at you the way male anatomy seems to. It's hard enough to grow up in a culture that sometimes equates sex with deep, romantic love and sometimes makes them seem mutually exclusive. But when you add a million mixed messages into that stew (be attractive! not too attractive! be sexual! don't sleep around!), it's no wonder that women get all weird when they talk about their own bodies. It's no wonder we come up with 11 different names for stupid, trivial things (lipstick is "lip gloss" is "lip colour" is "lip stain") instead of meaningful, important things. When you're taught that something isn't valuable in its own right, you don't give it a name.

Think about it, all you one-eyed trouser snakes.

BOSTON PHOENIX
MAY 1992

DEATH TO NICENESS

WHY WE NEED THE ALL-GIRL MARINE CORPS

A FRIEND IS OFFERED a tiny, paltry raise that's way out of line given the vast increases in her workload and responsibility that come with it. What does she say? *Thanks*.

A woman is asked to stand up and turn around by her lecherous, loathsome boss. What does she say? *Er, ah, well, okay*.

A man says something haughty and disparaging and unjustified about a female coworker's work. What does she say? *Nothing*.

Obviously, it is time to establish the All-Girl Marine Corps.

I mean it. Up and at 'em, wimmin. No more fooling around. Drills in anger and aggression! Exercises in self-assertiveness! And an end to all this lingering, persistent, paralyzing *wimpishness* in the face of poor treatment.

Aren't you sick of it? Aren't you sick of sitting there feeling hopelessly unable to respond while some bean-counting louse of an authority figure blatantly screws you over? Aren't you sick of hearing yourself respond to an unfair situation by being accommodating and polite? Aren't you sick of being articulate and strong only in retrospect? In your fantasies?

A good friend (I'll call her Betty) calls me on the phone in a classic I've-just-been-walked-all-over rage. Due to a number of circumstances, she's been doing the job of three people for the past four weeks, a situation that's likely to continue for at least another six months. Her supervisor came into her office and talked to her about money. Money is tight. Yes, he knows that two of the people in her office are on leave, ostensibly saving her company a significant chunk of change. Yes, he knows that her workload has increased by about 20 hours per week and her responsibility has skyrocketed. But policies are very rigid right now, and although he really, really admires the work Betty is doing and he really, really tried to fight for more money, all he could come up with was a figure that amounts to something on the order of an extra $12 a week.

"I sat there, and I said, 'Okay,'" she tells me on the phone, and we both want to throw up. "I heard the word come out of my mouth, and I couldn't believe it. There's something in me that feels like, 'Well, they're giving me all this extra responsibility, they're giving me this opportunity, so I should be grateful. I should do it for free!'"

Gag. Shudder. Give us the All-Girl Marine Corps.

How else are we going to learn to stand up for ourselves? We need to be forced, badgered, beaten into it with the same strength and discipline that's compelled us all these years to be sweet and polite and averse to unseemly discussions about things such as money and fair treatment. We need people with bullhorns to stand around and scream at us: *You there! Insist upon a raise! You there—tell that colleague to fuck off. And you! Recognize your value and demand to be compensated commensurately!*

Without the All-Girl Marine Corps, we're helpless. Hopeless. I cannot count the number of times I've sat there, like Betty, and heard some mealy-mouthed, fear-laden, esteem-lacking response come out of my own mouth.

An editor asks me to write a freelance piece for a quarter of what I know my work is worth elsewhere. "Oh, sure, that'll be fine."

A former boss would bark at me unreasonably for the millionth time and I'd just suck it up. And it's not just work. A man indicates he'd like me to behave or present myself in a way that's counter to my true self, and I accommodate: do the pleasing thing, say the pleasing thing, put on whatever hat is expected.

A lot of men I know just don't do this. I can think of five off the top of my head who'd respond to something like a tossed bone of a raise by looking up from their desks and saying, "You have got to be kidding." Maybe they find it painful and nerve-wracking, too, but at least they *do* it. Women? Niceness and accommodation are instincts for women, so deeply ingrained that half the time we don't even know we're acting on them.

"If you had asked me what I felt at that very moment, when the 'okay' came out of my mouth, I don't know if I could tell you," Betty tells me, and I know just what she means. "I felt: inevitability. I'm not going to get what I want, and there's nothing I can do about it, this is just the way things are. But did I feel anger? Rage? Not until hours later."

It's that buried, female anger, that taboo. Sometimes we don't even know how to feel it.

All these years of feminism has helped a bit. A lot of us are better at asserting ourselves in personal relationships (sometimes). The concept that we deserve to be treated with the same respect granted to men seems virtually indisputable these days. So does the idea that the worth of our work equals that of our male counterparts.

But we have a long way to go before those beliefs are sufficiently internalized, before they're ingrained in our souls so firmly that the right words—words such as "No," and "I'm sorry, that's not acceptable"—come out of our mouths naturally. Right now, all too many of us are still saddled with the burdens of niceness, with the lingering—and potent—assumption that it's our job to please, that our value as human beings has more to do with how we act (sweet) than with who we are (complex) and what we do (our jobs).

So let's establish the All-Girl Marine Corps. Let's rise at dawn, swing out of our bunk beds with our self-esteem held high as our heads. Let's cast off our feelings of powerlessness, force ourselves to experience and express anger, learn the joys of telling others exactly how we feel and exactly what we want.

And if that doesn't work, let's borrow another tool from our male counterparts in the service: weapons.

Boston Phoenix
October 1992

HARASSMENT 101

REFLECTIONS ON VALUE AND VULNERABILITY

THE ANNIVERSARY OF the Anita Hill/Clarence Thomas hearings is rolling around again (early October), so we can expect a tiny return in the media to the issue of sexual harassment: a statistic here, a reference there. This year, for some reason, the anniversary coincides with the return of a memory, something I haven't thought about for years.

In the summer of 1981, three days after I graduated from college, one of my professors—my adviser and first real mentor—took me to lunch. He wanted to congratulate me, wish me well, and I was thrilled by the invitation. I'd idolized the man, and I loved occupying this role: prize student.

We went to a small, pretty restaurant a few miles away from campus (he drove), and when we sat down, he ordered us both martinis, a celebratory gesture that made me feel very grown up. We sat and drank the martinis and ate lobster salads and had a long conversation about my future: newspapers I should send my résumé to, people he might be able to introduce me to, letters he could write on my behalf. After lunch, we got into his car, and he put the key in the ignition. Then he just sat there. A moment later—the details are fuzzy—he lurched over and started to kiss me. That, at any rate, is what it must have looked like, a man lurching. To me, sitting there in this foreign Dodge Dart, pinned in place with a seat belt, it felt like a sudden, wet jolt: a face looming toward me, a strange hand on my breast, a strange mouth over mine, and a complete upheaval of whatever rules had defined the relationship.

There are clear differences between this and other examples of sexual harassment—I wasn't employed by the man; I had graduated from college, so in technical terms, the "rules" of the relationship may no longer have applied. But to the extent to which the incident helps shed light on the use and misuse of power and sexuality, it's worth recalling.

Thinking back to that episode, and to the weeks that followed, makes me cringe—remembering how young and scared I was at the time, and how spinelessly I responded.

When it happened, I just kind of froze. I didn't know what to do, so I think I just sat there while he kissed me, and I have only a vague memory of the moments that followed: he smiled at me, started the car, drove me home in a horribly awkward silence. As he dropped me off, he said, "I'd like to see you again." I didn't know what else to say, so I said, "Okay." Then I went inside and just sat there, not knowing what to do or how to feel.

He was in his mid 40s, a tenured professor at an Ivy League college, married, with two teenagers. I had gone to departmental parties at his home, met his family. Three days before the episode in his car, he had stood on the college green with me, my parents, and my boyfriend. I'd just gotten my diploma and he'd come by to shake everybody's hand, to congratulate my parents: "You must be very proud," he said to them. "She's an exceptional student."

The day after the lunch, he called me and asked me to come see him in his office so we could "talk." I agreed; I didn't know what else to do.

I still don't know what I *could* have done, given who and where I was at the time. I remember thinking about that when details of Anita Hill's story first emerged: people kept wondering aloud why she didn't *act* when Clarence Thomas acted inappropriately, why she didn't *say* anything, *do* anything. Simple: it's extremely difficult to react to an overture like that when you're in a position of such vulnerability.

The professor in my case was someone I'd admired tremendously, someone whose counsel I'd sought and valued. He'd praised my work, inspired me to go into journalism. Me? I was just out of school, shy, unsure of myself, overwhelmed with the prospect of being let out into the world, scared. I had a terrible time letting go of my idealization, seeing him as wrong or out-of-line. I also worried that I'd been naive, sitting there drinking martinis with this man and not acknowledging any possible romantic implications. And I worried about whether I'd done something to bring the incident on, sent out some kind of signal of availability.

More likely, I'd sent out other signals: insecurity, a wish to be seen as special, a yearning to be valued by people I held in high esteem. Those feelings are powerful, and I think some people (some men) are equipped with special radar for them; they pick up on precisely that hunger for approval and move in.

The day after he phoned me, we went for a walk near the campus and he talked about how "interesting" he thought I was, about my "fascinating mind." He told me he'd had several other affairs with students in the past, all of them after their graduations, but he said those were rare occasions. "It has to be someone really special," he said. "These situations require too much emotional energy."

At the time, my only response was to remain dumbfounded and passive. He made it quite clear that he wanted us to become "lovers" (his word, and one I have always loathed). I didn't say yes, I didn't say no. I let him kiss me again, then I went home, feeling more confused and uncomfortable than I had before. I didn't tell anyone, because I didn't know what to say.

Grotesque situation, and completely unremarkable: happens all the time. Looking back, I think what bothers me the most is the confusion I must have felt about what it means to be valued. This culture has such difficulty producing girls who feel good about themselves in terms that are not purely physical, who feel intrinsically worthy as whole people, and I see myself back then—21, scared, insecure—as utterly representative of the times. I knew a lot about being pretty (which seemed important), but not much at all about being powerful (which seemed abstract), so intellectual respect and sexual interest from men felt tied up together, inextricably linked. And how do you say "No" in the midst of that sort of confusion? How do you thwart the sexual part and hold on to the respect? How do you establish boundaries if you aren't equipped with those distinctions inside?

I guess I was terrified of the consequences of rejecting this guy's advances: if I'd said no, I'd have lost not only his access to power and connections but also his admiration, on which my sense of intellectual worth, that sense of being seen as special, depended.

So I hung in there, passive as seaweed on the beach, for about three weeks. I went out to lunch with him and got drunk with him and let him kiss me and paw me. It's disgusting to me in retrospect, and shameful, but I honestly didn't know what else to do.

At some point, I guess I got too ashamed and too disgusted—with him, with myself—and I mustered up the courage from someplace and went to see him in his office. I stammered out something about not being able to deal with the situation anymore, about feeling too uncomfortable and too weird. I remember saying I hoped we could still be friends, and I remember that he looked up and said, "Well, if we're not going to become lovers, why should I bother?"

We never spoke again.

❧

The abuse of power is a cruel thing in any circumstances; the abuse of power in sexual terms is especially cruel. I heard several years ago that this professor had died suddenly of a heart attack; I can't say I felt sorry.

Boston Phoenix
September 1994

PATCHWORK

FOUND MYSELF THINKING briefly—fleetingly, really—about quitting smoking the other day. Began to free-associate. Thought: *Quitting smoking's too hard*. Then thought: *But what about the patch? Wouldn't the nicotine patch help?* Then thought: *Hey, why haven't scientists come up with other ways to make use of patch technology?*

Then thought about the following:

• *The Vodka Patch*

Having a little trouble controlling your alcohol intake? Can't seem to stop at "just a few"? Long to sustain that warm, two-drink glow all the time? Perhaps you need the Vodka Patch™. Affixed to the upper arm, the time-released Vodka Patch™ will infuse minute amounts of ethylalcohol into the bloodstream throughout the day, imparting that heady sense of well being and *joie de vivre* morning, noon, and night. Why wait for cocktail hour when you can feel this good at 11 a.m.? Particularly handy for social events with non-drinkers. Also available: The Caribbean-Vacation-Piña-Colada Patch; The Total-Blitz-Keg-Party Patch; and the Wallowing-in-Depression-Full-Bottle-of-Scotch Patch.

• *The Mousse Patch*

New from L'Oréal, a revolutionary technique that activates tiny molecules around the hair follicles to create volume, lift, and shine—

all day long! No more muss and fuss; no more scrunching and pouffing and blow-drying your hair upside down. Simply affix a Mousse Patch™ to the scalp on either side of your head, allow the special activation formula to seep into the outer membranes, and voilà—hair stands up, up, and out; self-esteem soars; friends remark, "You look just like Heather Locklear!" So simple! So quick! So effective!

• *The Vegetable Patch*

You're stressed out, preoccupied, restless, and we know just how it feels. Can't sit still. Can't stop the mind from racing. Can't sleep, can't concentrate, can't even sack out on the sofa and watch TV. That's why you need the Vegetable Patch™. Just slap one on and let our scientifically tested combination of powerful barbituates ease their way into your overstimulated bloodstream. Available in Regular Strength, Extra Strength, and Deep Coma. Our motto: From Bzzzzzzzzz to Zzzzzzzzzz in less than 10 minutes!

• *The Work-Out Patch*

A carefully blended, scientifically proven formula that activates sweat glands, releases endorphins, *and* lets you maintain your sedentary lifestyle. Affix one Work-Out Patch™ to each major set of muscle groups, assume a prone position (recommended time: three times a week; 20 minutes per session), then rise and shower. You'll feel envigorated, refreshed, *healthy*. Works wonderfully in conjunction with the Vegetable Patch (see above).

• *The Atlantic Monthly Patch*

It arrives month after month: a cover story you know you should read. Columns and columns of uninterrupted type: articles and reviews that would make you a better, more informed person if only you had the intellectual energy to tackle them. Month after month it arrives, and month after month it lingers by your bedside, unfinished and guilt-provoking. Until now, that is. Not unlike a computer chip, each individual *Atlantic* Patch™ is imprinted with the entire contents of an issue of this vexing monthly magazine. Affixed to the temple, it will allow you to acquire the *Atlantic* slowly, gently, and constantly, so that by month's end you'll be entirely caught up. No need to set aside an extra four or five hours each week for actual reading; with the *Atlantic* Patch, you can accomplish household chores, errands, even catch up on your sleep while you keep yourself up to date. Also available: The *Sunday New York Times* Patch; the *Economist* Patch, and the *McNeil-Lehrer Report* Patch.

• *The Testosterone Patch*

Trying to muster up the confidence and grit to ask for a raise? Need a little bolstering before a big confrontation with your mother, boyfriend, or boss? Once upon a time, gearing up for life's tougher battles was an unpredictable, scary affair, requiring loads of internal pep talks, visualization techniques, and other nerve-steeling exercises. Not so today. Just slap on the Testosterone Patch™, and feel the power surge from bloodstream to brain.

• *The Frappuccino Patch*

Leaders of corporate America, take note: do you have any idea how much time and money you lose by letting your employees stand in line at today's glitzy coffee shops waiting for the nine people in front of them to order their overpriced, specially brewed caffeinated beverages each day? As the nation's taste for caffeine becomes increasingly sophisticated and elaborate, industry's original answer to this problem—the lowly office coffee machine—has become an outdated solution. That's why the Frappuccino Patch™ should become a staple of today's modern office: simply affix one to each employee's upper arm, steer the worker to his or her cubicle, and watch productivity soar. Not available in decaf.

• *The Highlights of the 1996 Summer Olympics Patch*

For those of us who completely burned out on the coverage within the first week of the Olympics and now feel badly that we missed the 4056th airing of Kerri Strug's heroic vault or the 7892nd airing of Michael Johnson's pre-race beady-eyed glare, help has arrived. Based on similar principles as the *Atlantic* Patch (above), the Highlights of the 1996 Summer Olympics Patch condenses the best of the games into a single microchip, allowing you to relive these and other exciting moments over and over and over. And over and over and over. And over and over and over. Just as NBC intended.

• *The Chicken-Soup Patch*

Too sick to get out of bed and fix yourself a healing bowl of hot soup? A common dilemma—and, now, an unnecessary one. The Chicken-Soup Patch™ lets mom's carefully blended combination of stock and savory vegetables ease its way slowly into the bloodstream, helping you heal from the comfort of your own bed. This, moreover, is only the technological beginning: why should today's busy American have to stop to eat anything? Start your day with the Wheaties Patch, stop at noon and slap on a Sandwich Patch, rush home at the end of the day and replace that one with a wide variety of late-night dinner patches—the Bertucci's Pizza Patch, the Let's-Send-Out-for-Chinese Patch, the Barbecue Patch. Looking for something healthier? Voila: the Cabbage Patch. So much easier than a phone call, so much less unsightly than an IV tube.

BOSTON PHOENIX
AUGUST 1996

LONGING TO BE ITALIAN

MOST PEOPLE, GIVEN a second chance at life, would come back as a rock star, or a brain surgeon, or a Heisman trophy-winner. Me? If I could do it all over again, I'd be Italian.

This is not a frivolous or passing thought. I have longed to be Italian for some time. I love pasta. I love Italian wine. But mostly, I have come to believe that if I were Italian—or at least had an Italian temperament—I wouldn't find the '90s so woefully upsetting.

Take work. Like most of my peers these days, I spend about 50 hours a week at my job and about 40 additional hours worrying about it.

I worry about whether I'm doing a good job, and I worry about where my career is going, and I worry about whether the economy will improve. I worry about being overworked and I worry about being underpaid and I worry about whether I'm satisfied doing what I do.

After work, I go out with friends and I talk about work. When I go home, I do more work or I go to sleep because I'm tired from working.

If I were Italian, I would have a far more manageable attitude toward work. I would go to my job, I would go home, and—*presto!*—that would be that. I would eat large, lavish dinners with friends and family. I would drink wine. I would stay up well past midnight, then sleep until a reasonable hour the next morning. I would believe in my bones that life is something to be lived each day, not just once in a while on Saturday when I can make the time.

There's another reason I long to be Italian: I get shivers just thinking about it. If I were Italian, I would feel free to explode with emotion and fury and rage.

Wouldn't that be great? As it is, being a responsible woman of the '90s, I maintain a very tight rein on my emotions. I deal with them quietly. Secretly. In the privacy of my own home.

This is very non-Italian. And very '90s. These days, there's just no permission to explode with emotion and fury and rage, no place to let loose. We're so worried about losing our jobs that we don't speak up for ourselves at work. We're so worried about saying the right things in social circles that we only talk about safe subjects—like work. And we've grown so fatalistic about relationships that we figure it's just not worth it to explode with emotion and fury and rage at our spouses. So we all walk around looking tired and repressed, and no one says anything provocative.

All this would be different if I were Italian. I would have a fiercely passionate husband, and together we would have a fiercely passionate family of fiercely passionate children, and we would sit there at the dinner table over huge bowls of pasta and scream at one another from dusk to dawn. We'd scream and scream, and then we'd cry and hug and make up in a flood of tears, and everything would be all right.

But perhaps I'm looking in the wrong place. After all, there is one realm in America where you don't have to work so obsessively, where you can be downright vapid and still become a success. There is one realm in America where it's still possible to explode regularly with emotion and fury and rage. There is one realm in America where all this and more is possible.

So maybe that's it. Perhaps I'll go into politics.

WBUR RADIO
BOSTON

WHY WE KEEP STUFF

IF YOU WANT TO UNDERSTAND PEOPLE, TAKE A LOOK AT WHAT THEY HANG ON TO

STUFF, STUFF, I AM surrounded by stuff. Stuff I don't need, stuff I don't use, but stuff I feel compelled to keep. Here in my office, as I write this, I am drowning in a sea of stuff.

There is the stuff of procrastination—piles of letters I should answer, manuscripts I should return, memos I should file away.

There is the stuff of daily business—interoffice communications in one heap here, this form and that form in that heap there, bills in yet another.

But mostly, there is the more generalized stuff, the stuff we all hold on to for inexplicable reasons—the stuff, in other words, of which stuff is made. Old catalogs of stuff I *might* want to order someday. Old magazines I *might* want to read, or reread. Unsolicited freelance articles I *might* want to publish. And even more useless stuff, stuff with no discernible purpose or future value.

On one corner of a shelf hangs a bunch of ribbons, saved over the years from various packages. On another, a pile of old letters from readers that I'll no doubt never open again and never answer. On my desk, a Rolodex crammed with numbers I'll never call (the National Association of Theater Operators? The Detroit office of the National Transportation Union? *Huh?*). In one corner, I even have a pile of envelopes containing transaction slips from the automatic teller machine that date all the way back to February 1988. That's more than three years of bank slips—stuff, pure and simple.

Yet in an odd way, a lot of the stuff has meaning. Granted, the significance of a pile of old ribbons may be minimal, but I think the things that people choose to hang on to, and the ways they hang on to them, are quite telling—small testimonies to the ways people organize their lives on both external and internal levels. Want to understand people a little more clearly? Look through their stuff.

Several years ago, as I was preparing to move out of an apartment I'd lived in for four years, I undertook my first major purge of stuff, which provided an excellent lesson in the nature of the beast. Historically, I've been a relentless pack rat, the sort of person who keeps vast numbers of relics and mementos in vast numbers of boxes around the house—ticket stubs to concerts and movies; store receipts for goods and clothing I'd long ago stopped thinking about returning; letters from people I'd long ago lost track of; even old shoes. But moving out of that particular apartment was a big step—I was leaving a place where I'd lived alone (with plenty of room for stuff) and into a new apartment—and presumably, a new life—with a man (who had much less room for stuff).

Accordingly, the purge was more than a logistical necessity; it also had a certain psychological value. Sure, it made sense to get rid of a lot of it: I didn't really need to hang on to that broken toaster-oven, or that tattered coat I'd stopped wearing years before. I didn't need to save the letter of acceptance from the graduate school I'd long ago decided not to attend. I didn't need the three boxes of back issues of *Gourmet* magazine. But divesting myself of all that stuff meant much more than whittling down my possessions to a manageable degree.

At one point, I remember going through a dresser in which I kept several pairs of jeans that I'd worn during a long and protracted struggle with anorexia. They were tiny jeans in tiny, skeletal sizes, jeans with bad associations, jeans with no place in the life of someone who was trying to launch into a healthier way of living. But I'd held on to them for years and, in doing so, had held on to a set of possibilities: that I might one day need those tiny, cigarette-legged jeans again; that I might one day fit into them; and accordingly, that what I felt to be my "recovery" from anorexia might be tenuous at best, false at worst.

The message hidden away in that dresser drawer had to do with fear, and, needless to say, throwing out the clothes from that earlier time was an enormously healthy move: it was part of an effort to say good-bye to a person I used to be.

And so it is with most of our stuff: the things we keep stored away in our closets and shelves often mirror the things we hold on to inside: fears, memories, dreams, false perceptions. A good deal of that stuff in my office, for example, speaks to an abiding terror of screwing up, a fear that I might actually *need* one of those articles from one of those old magazines, or one of those old phone numbers from the Rolodex, or one of those memos or letters or whatever.

Lurking behind the automatic-teller-machine slips? My relentless fear of finance, and the accompanying conviction that as soon as I toss them all out, the bank will call and inform me that some huge deposit I could once verify has disappeared. Even the pile of ribbons on the shelf reflects some vague anxiety, a (comparatively minor and obsessive) worry—that one of these days, I'll have a present to wrap and (gasp) there'll be no ribbon at hand to tie it up. My mother keeps a huge basket at home filled with nothing but rubber bands, and I'm sure she holds on to it for the same reasons: it speaks to an absolute certainty on her part that the moment she throws them away, she'll find herself in desperate need of an elastic.

We might need it. We might miss it. It might come back in style and we might want to wear it again. If getting rid of stuff is hard, it's because it feels like cutting off options. Or sides of ourselves. Or pieces of our history. And, the actual value of holding on to stuff notwithstanding, those things can be unsettling to give up. The movie and ticket stubs I'd kept stored away for years in my old apartment, for example, reflected good times, happy moments in relationships that I didn't want to forget; the ragged coat was a piece of clothing I'd felt pretty in, a feeling I didn't want to lose; the *Gourmet* magazines held out hopes for my (then sorely lacking) kitchen skills. Even the broken toaster-oven contained a memory—I'd bought it almost a decade earlier, with a man I'd been involved with, during a very happy year we'd lived together.

The trick, I suppose, is to learn to manage stuff, the same way you learn to manage fears and feelings. To throw a little logic into the heaps of stuff. To think a little rationally. Would the world really come crashing down if I tossed out some crucial phone number? Would my personal history really get tossed into the trash along with my mementos? Would I die, or even suffer a mite, without all those ribbons?

No, probably not. But I think I'll keep holding on to those bank slips . . . just in case.

BOSTON PHOENIX
JUNE 1991

TEDDY BEAR II

ON DIGNITY AND THE ELDERLY

THE FRONT-PAGE *New York Times* photo said it all: John Kingery, an 82-year-old Alzheimer's victim, abandoned outside a dog track in Idaho, left with nothing but a bag of diapers. He is sitting in his wheelchair, clutching a teddy bear. He is clad in a sweatshirt inscribed PROUD TO BE AN AMERICAN. He can't remember his own name.

Since that story appeared in the press, I haven't been able to get those phrases out of my head. Eighty-two. Abandoned. Wheelchair. Bag of diapers.

But it's the teddy bear that really gets me. Terminal illness fosters such horrible regression, pressing the strongest among us farther and farther back toward infancy. A man like John Kingery is probably incapable of accomplishing the most basic functions by himself: eating, dressing, going to the bathroom. And there are few things worse than the image of being left alone in that state: helpless and frightened as a baby, clutching a teddy bear.

We do such a shameful job of dealing with the elderly, and Mr. Kingery's case speaks to that as few other cases have: in what sounds like an act of unfathomable desperation, his daughter checked him out of a nursing home and left him at the track, his wheelchair stripped of identification, his clothing labels removed. It's not yet clear what pressures led her to make that decision, but it's become quite clear that the choice was not uncommon. The American College of Emergency Physicians estimates that 70,000 elderly Americans were abandoned last year by family members who, presumably, were at the end of their financial or emotional ropes.

That's a heartbreaking statistic and it's not hard to assign blame for it: There's the rising population of elderly (one in five families now takes care of an aging parent). Spiraling health-care costs. Diseases, like Alzheimer's, that keep elderly patients lingering in dementia for years, in need of round-the-clock care and attention. Small wonder caregivers fall victim to despair, or burnout, or both.

The federal government, moreover, isn't exactly out there easing anyone's burden. Health care for the elderly and support for their caregivers are inadequate for the same, miserable gamut of reasons that keep minority families in cycles of poverty, women in positions of inequity, and people with AIDS in states of perpetual crisis: not enough people are close enough to that kind of desperation to care about it, and fewer still have the sense of moral imperative to *want* to care. Simply put, health care for the elderly is not high on the nation's priority list, and it's not likely to get there until someone like George Bush is faced with the choice of abandoning an ailing parent at a dog track.

But there's also something less tangible at work. What happens on a national level—apathy, inertia, a wish to ignore the elderly rather than help care for them—also takes place on an individual level, even among those of us with half a heart. Horrible as it is to admit, people who are old and sick (and, to a large degree, voiceless) are simply far easier not to think about. Aging can be filled with ugliness, particularly in a culture that worships its own very narrow images of youth and beauty. And at heart, it is so painful and difficult to empathize with the processes of disease and dying—it takes such a leap of imagination to understand what the experience must be like—that it's unlikely we'll start caring about people like John Kingery any time soon.

I hate umbrella words like "ageism," but I'm beginning to take that one as seriously as I take some other "isms," such as sexism and racism.

A few months ago, a colleague of mine lost his grandmother, someone he had loved dearly. When he came into my office to tell me the news, I reacted as everyone else had. I asked two things: first, was it sudden? Second, how old was she? And when he reported her age—82—I nodded, a gesture that inadvertently conveyed a certain level of relief. "Ah," I might as well have said, "at least she was old. At least the death doesn't mean as much."

That's not to say there aren't differences in degrees of tragedy and sadness—there clearly are—but the automatic nature of my reaction seems rather frightening in retrospect. Relief? Because she was old?

When I think about it, I reacted in a similar way to the illness and death of my own grandmother, who passed away several years ago, at the age of 91. She was hospitalized on and off for a long time prior to her death, and I have distinct memories of not wanting to go to see her. It wasn't that I didn't love my grandmother—I did. But the basic impulse to avoid watching—to avoid the sight of her lying in bed looking shriveled and pained, to avoid contact, to avoid conversation—was so potent I practically had to drag myself to the hospital. In her worse moments, I also found the sight of her chilling: her breath was raspy, her skin sallow, her arms achingly thin. Terminal illness has certain particular smells: acridity stands out, and a certain awful sweetness. I remember just not wanting to be there.

I also remember thinking that her private nurse, an angelic woman named Elaine, had a level of courage and compassion in dealing with my grandmother that I'd never match. Elaine talked to her with unwavering dignity. She combed her hair, put hot compresses on her forehead, held her hand. And when my grandmother finally died, she was in her own home, in her own bed, surrounded by her family. Her two daughters—my mother and aunt—sat by either side of the bed and held her hands. Her son stood at the foot of the bed, and her two sons-in-law stood in an outer circle around them. My grandmother was enormously lucky in being able to afford good health care. She was also enormously lucky in having a family that shared a certain critical set of moral convictions about how to deal with the dying, how to offer love and support until the end.

Perhaps this is a naive sentiment—sometimes death is simply more random and ugly than this—but when she finally passed away, she did so in peace and with great dignity, the way all of us should, and too few do.

BOSTON PHOENIX
APRIL 1992

NESTING FEVER

A PLEA FOR THE ARM-CHAIR-OBSESSED

God, grant me the serenity
To accept the furniture I already own,
The courage to change my decor without breaking the bank,
And the wisdom to stay away from Crate & Barrel.

I HAVE TO SAY THIS prayer constantly these days. I have to whisper it under my breath like a mantra. *Don't let me spend, God. Don't let me become obsessed with linens and kitchenware and little lamps and end tables. Help me, God. Keep me sane.*

I am moving, you see. Moving to a new place that's bigger and better and (of course) screaming for new furniture. And if past experience has shown me anything, it's that every transition from one place to the next is accompanied by a major case—a dangerous case—of nesting fever.

Nesting fever. Have you suffered this malady? Do you know what I mean?

Nesting fever manifests itself in a number of highly specific ways. It shows up in the fervid belief that your life will be meaningless and empty unless your towels match the tile on your bathroom floor. It shows up in the tendency to lie awake and obsess deep into the night about the size, shape, status, and ultimate inadequacy of every piece of furniture you've owned for the last 20 years. And it shows up in the unwavering conviction that you simply cannot live—cannot *live!*—without at least $24,000 worth of new rugs, dining-room furniture, armchairs, and knickknacks.

I hate this. I hate becoming the kind of person who actively looks forward to the arrival of the new Williams-Sonoma catalogue. I hate admitting that I have actually learned what a waffle-weave towel is. The other day I sat in a coffee shop with a friend and had an honest-to-goodness conversation about how badly I wanted a set of 250-thread-count Porthault Chaumont sheets. Of course, she's moving, too, so she knew exactly what I meant. And we spent about an hour drooling over such coveted items as jute basket-weave rugs and French escritoire desks and tub valets with built-in book rests.

"Are we nuts?" I asked.

She nodded soberly. "Absolutely."

And she's right. There are homeless people on our streets. There is bloodshed in Bosnia, chaos in Rwanda, and I'm sitting around obsessing about whether I can possibly justify buying that lovely little $475 hand-carved French Empire nightstand I saw advertised in a catalogue. Can I possibly be that shallow? That superficial and materialistic?

The answer: yes.

Gulp.

A consoling friend offers this practical perspective: "I think we go bazoo when we first get a new place because that's the only point at which we really see the place as it is. Once you get used to living somewhere, you cease to see it; you get distracted by other things. It's like the married couple who haven't really looked at each other in years. So I think we've got a subconscious urge to spiff it up before it disappears from our vision altogether."

There's some truth to that, some truth to the way the glaring newness of a home begs for that special, considered first touch. But this is the same woman who spent an hour with me drooling over jute basket-weave rugs and tub valets, so I don't really trust her for a second.

No, the real impulse behind nesting fever (at least in my case) has to do with a much deeper, much more human urge: it has to do with wanting to fix things from the outside in. With wanting to achieve a sense of serenity and completeness through the elegant and well-appointed surface of things. The thinking goes something like this: I may feel like a wreck on the inside, but if I live in an impeccably decorated home with period antiques and French country throws and wrought-iron scroll lamps, I must be okay. Right? I may feel ill-formed and inadequate, but I hold on to the hope that the beauty and comfort of my paisley *matelassé* bedding will rub off on my inner life. Or, at least, reflect well on it.

This is basic human insecurity, no? It's the same impulse that compelled me, just the other day, to spend $38.50 on *lipstick*, three tubes of nearly identical colors. Absurdly, I've been looking for the right shade for most of my adult life, driven by the stupid little voice inside that says, over and over, "Keep looking! Keep looking! If you find it, you'll wear it and you'll be grown-up and sophisticated and conflict-free forever."

Same thing with the new house. *Ah, yes! That $980 pine lingerie chest is really going to make a tangible difference in the quality of my life and self-esteem! Go for it!*

Sigh.

Admitting all this makes me feel a little pathetic, so I'll add this slightly-less-embarrassing twist: I also happen to really *like* home furnishings. A certain thrill comes with the process of creating a new home, of settling into aesthetically pleasing surroundings, of creating a place that feels right. It brings a sense of hope, a feeling that you might finally arrive somewhere you really want to be. So there's an element of basic human optimism at work in nesting fever, too, along with the more insecurity-driven forces of human neuroses.

But I also know myself well enough to understand something else: I am the sort of person who's entirely capable of considering a $400 halogen lamp an "impulse buy." Who can consider linen dishtowels that match my kitchen a necessity as basic to human well-being as air and water. Let loose in Crate & Barrel with a checkbook, I'm a danger to myself and others. And in the end, what I undoubtedly need far more than a $254 mahogany hamper for my bathroom is a support group: Nesting Fever Anonymous (slogan: "One Sofa at a Time"). Or Al-a-Couch. Or better yet: a pair of $254 mahogany handcuffs.

In the meantime, I will continue to pray. *Help me, Lord. Stop me before I spend again.*

Boston Phoenix
May 1994

SLOBLESSNESS

THE ART OF ANAL-RETENTIVE HOME DÉCOR

I WOULD LIKE TO take slob lessons. Can anybody out there help me?

I would like to become the sort of person who drops clothes on the floor and lets them sit there for a long time. Who is capable of ignoring stacks of dishes in the sink for days on end. Who scatters newspapers, magazines, and mail randomly across sofas, chairs, and table tops, and just *doesn't care* what things look like.

Instead, I am a bit of an anal-retentive nightmare.

Did you move that vase? I'm sure you did. I put that vase precisely three-and-one-quarter inches from the edge of that table top and I can tell it's been moved. It's . . . it's . . . wrong!

It's also kind of exhausting, living like that. I creep about at night, inspecting things: TV positioned back to its spot against the wall? Check. Tea cup washed and drying on the rack? Check. Shoes in the closet, coat on its hook, toothbrush in its stupid little toothbrush rack? Check, check, CHECK.

I get on my own nerves, doing this. Pathetic, eh?

Well, yes and no. A part of me gets a tremendous amount of satisfaction out of this aesthetic control-freakishness. I like seeing everything in its place. I like the high gloss of polished surfaces, the symmetry of vases and candlesticks placed just so, the spare look of a clean countertop. If you're a clean freak, you experience that kind of visual order with a deep sort of relief. *Ah, no chaos: everything is where it's supposed to be. You can relax now.*

But I can also see strains of more troublesome impulses in all that order, and that's what bothers me about it. There's a lot of fear in it, and a lot of *rigidity*, and an almost instinctual impulse to fix what's wrong inside by manipulating the externals. I noticed this in particular last June, when I first moved into the place I now live and my anal-retentive impulses became so powerful I could hardly get up off the sofa without fluffing the cushions back into place. I'd walk around the place like a drill sergeant conducting inspection. *Is that Mission chair in the living room at a precise 90-degree angle from the couch? Does it line up exactly with the opposite chair? Are there errant coffee grounds on the counter? Smudges on the kitchen floor? Yes? What?! Quick! Get out the sponge!*

Not a particularly relaxing way to live.

But a telling one, I suppose.

I'd moved into this place during a particularly trying time; my parents had both died within the past two years, and my brother and sister and I were in the process of selling their house, where we'd all grown up. The parental house was pure chaos: 38 years' worth of stuff waiting to be sifted through and thrown out and boxed, decades' worth of emotion lurking in every corner, on every surface. Against that, it wasn't hard to see my own anal-retentive impulses, in my own home, as a fairly powerful response, a defense against what felt like a lot of internal disorder and upheaval. It's a panic-driven need for control, something I recognize in particular from my prior history with anorexia: when everything else around you feels chaotic, you control what you can, something, anything: your caloric intake, your weight, your surroundings. Panic makes us do some pretty strange things.

A close friend, and a comrade in anal-retentive home décor, is about to move in with her boyfriend, someone who's considerably less anxious than she about neatness and order. She's panicked about this a lot in the months leading up to the move: how is she going to deal with that basket of *stuff* in his kitchen, the one that literally overflows with old mail and bills and catalogues? What about all his junk: the boxes that seem to appear in doorways and expand, the clothes strewn on the bedroom floor?

I've come to see her decision to go ahead and move in with him as extraordinarily brave. Her horror about his mess, after all, is a phenomenon of deflection: the anxiety she feels about the external disarray is a metaphor (and a rather perfect one at that) for the fear she feels about loosening up some more complicated internal boundaries, about literally sharing someone else's stuff, in both the physical and emotional senses.

I'm not able to do that yet. I don't seem to have any trouble messing up the home of my own significant other—when I'm at his house, I feel perfectly free to leave dishes in the sink and newspapers scattered on the tables and floor. But when he comes over to my house—my territory, my space—I start to grimace and cringe if he so much as kicks off his shoes. (And if he does, I pick the damn things up and line them neatly against the wall in the front hall.) He makes fun of me about this. "What's next?" he asks. "Plastic covers on the furniture? *Velvet ropes*?" Other times, he gets exasperated. "This is not a museum," he said, shortly after I moved in. "You're supposed to *live* here."

But that's the point; that's exactly what some of us find so hard to do. The anal-retentive personality is usually fine as long as it lives alone, as long as it can indulge those impulses behind its own private boundaries, straighten and scour to its heart's content. Living becomes problematic when it becomes more real, when other human beings come along and factor into the equation the stuff of human involvement which, of course, can be very messy indeed. When someone is in my house, messing up the surface of things, I can feel extraordinarily threatened, as though those surfaces bear a direct relationship to what's inside: clutter my counters and you're cluttering my life; mess with my kitchen and you're messing with my emotions. I know this is irrational thinking—and I struggle with it, struggle to resist the impulse to follow people around with a dustpan and brush—but when it hits, it can be pretty powerful.

Which is why I need a slob coach, a slob mentor, someone who can help me understand that chaos and disorder are a natural part of human life and human involvement, who can help me see that not every one of life's anxieties can be tackled with a sponge and a broom. *Lighten up!* the coach would say. *Celebrate the mess! Take a risk or two, and relinquish all that control!*

Sounds sensible to me, an eminently admirable goal. But in the meantime, I'm stocking up on the Ajax. Just in case.

BOSTON PHOENIX
NOVEMBER 1994

NOTES ON NESTING

REARRANGING THE CONCEPT OF HOME

THE NESTING PROCESS begins when you find yourself looking around your apartment in dread and despair and saying, "Blech."

Any number of factors can trigger this. Perhaps you have never bothered to turn your apartment into a home, viewing it as a way station or a transitory abode. Perhaps you have never felt the need to establish a sense of hominess in your life, to create a place to live that reflects your personality. Perhaps you have been too broke to move beyond cinderblock-and-plywood shelving. Or perhaps something more dramatic has happened: you have lost a critical relationship that helped you define yourself in life, or a parent has died, and such events have forced you to sit up and realize that you are, in fact, on your own in this world, and that life would feel a whole lot safer and more pleasant if you had a place that felt like home.

And so you set off to nest. Here's how it works.

First, you create a budget. This involves balancing your checkbook for the first time in seven months and then realizing, *Oh, shit! I barely have enough money for coffee filters, how can I possibly justify going out to buy things for my apartment?* Banish this unhealthy thought from your consciousness immediately; it is self-defeating and counter to the nesting process.

Besides, successful nesting depends not on financial considerations but rather on a deep level of self-understanding and an awareness of your true needs. If you know in your heart, for example, that the $950 overstuffed armchair you saw in the Bloomingdale's catalogue will make your time at home feel cozy and meaningful, then by all means buy it. (Nesting note: this is also known as "rationalization," but that is a counterproductive way of looking at the nesting process as well and should be ignored. Especially if you have credit cards.)

In any event, take your self-understanding and needs-assessment to a special place where you know you will find many beautiful things you can just barely afford. Find yourself standing in front of a lovely, hand-painted rug. Imagine it affixed to an empty wall in your apartment, and think, *Ah, if that were on my wall, I would feel warm and aesthetically pleased and possessed of good taste; I* need *that*. Buy the rug. Spot a long, narrow, hand-woven-and-hand-dyed cloth runner in shades of blue and beige and imagine it draped over a bare and bland coffee table in your living room. Think, *Ah, if that were on my coffee table, I would feel warm and aesthetically pleased and possessed of good taste; I* need *that*. Buy the runner. And so on.

Next, counter feelings of extravagance by purchasing something practical. Settle on white bookshelves at Conran's and feel pleased with your continued decisiveness. Nod earnestly when the saleswoman assures you that assembling said purchase will be "no problem" and that all you need is a screwdriver.

At this point, having spent a fair chunk of change on two pieces of cloth and one set of bookshelves, experience a stab of nesting remorse. Banish this unhealthy thought from your mind by thinking of women you know who have mastered the art of successful nesting. Think about how cozy and warm it can feel to sit in an apartment that's full of carefully placed *objets d'art* and collectibles and meaningful knickknacks. Consider what a simple and elusive pleasure it is to feel at home. Then think about how bland and empty your own apartment often feels, and contemplate the fact you've probably kept it that way because you've been waiting for someone to come along and rescue you from it. Decide that this is no way to live and resolve to undertake the next phase in the nesting process: chatchki shopping.

Buy vases. Buy pottery. Spend inordinate amounts of money on candlesticks and brightly colored candles to put in them. Stand in the line at Pier One Imports with $82 worth of candlesticks and experience nesting embarrassment. *Who buys $82 worth of candlesticks? Is this some kind of phallic obsession?* Banish unhealthy thoughts from your mind and proceed.

At this point, grow truly concerned about overspending and visit your mother, who just happens to live nearby. Inspect house of mother for furniture items that look underutilized or unneeded. Then sit in kitchen and adopt glum, pathetic look. Think of underutilized, unneeded blond-wood console table you saw sitting in back room. Look sad and say, *Gosh, I wish I had a console table for my apartment but they're so expensive!* Allow mother to donate console table to the nesting cause.

Go home. (Nesting note: this may involve spending 35 minutes stuffing table into Toyota, then lugging possessions, including 53 pounds of bookshelves, up five flights of stairs in 90-degree heat because at the very moment you entered your building, the elevator had an attack of nesting sabotage and stopped working.)

Now roll up your sleeves and spend Saturday night fully engaged in the nesting process.

Attempt to assemble bookshelves. Empty contents of Conran's box on living-room floor, then spend approximately 42 minutes blankly looking back and forth between assembly instructions and various parts, screws, nuts, bolts, and nails scattered on carpet. Read instructions: *Attach kickboard to wingnuts A1 through A4, keeping left hand firmly on screws B2 through B6 while nailing backboard to fixed shelf 3C with right foot.* Feel eyes glaze over. Begin to assemble sans instructions. Then realize you don't own a hammer; begin to nail pieces together with a rolling pin. Experience mounting feelings of nesting incompetence as very odd set of shelves begins to materialize. Say *Oooops* out loud a lot. *Oooops!* Shelves are upside down! *Oooops!* Nails are sticking out over there! *Oooops!* Where was that extra board supposed to go?

Sit on sofa. Feel inadequate, think morose thoughts: *I'm a loser. I'm incapable of creating a home. It's Saturday night and I'm here alone mangling bookshelves.* Contemplate bursting into tears, then banish unhealthy thoughts from your mind and understand that being mechanically inept does not mean you're a failure. Place completed bookshelves against wall where, lo! they don't look half bad. Fill with books, admire handiwork.

Spend next several hours in anal-retentive nesting frenzy. Slide console table against bare wall. Stand on table and pin hand-painted rug above it. Get down, observe rug. Get back up, move rug higher. Get down, observe. Get up, move it lower. Up, down, back, forth. Continue for a long period of time, wishing you were one of those people who had an innate sense of where to put things.

Do same thing with chatchkis and furniture. Place candlesticks about. Move various lamps and chairs. Sit. Observe. Get up, move everything again. Sit, observe, move. Wonder if all this is merely an elaborate ploy to avoid loneliness. Continue until you're exhausted, then go to bed.

Awake on Sunday and feel a familiar pang of anxiety at the thought of an unstructured day. As is your custom, begin to plot escape from the dread apartment, then get up, walk about, and realize that you actually feel okay in it. The new stuff makes it look warm and urban and rather cheerful; you can even imagine (wonder of wonders) spending a day there by yourself.

Consider again the concept of home. Decide that the nesting process has as much to do with the purchase of aesthetically pleasing *objets* as it does with elusive factors: a willingness to tolerate loneliness, to work at being happy in solitude. And with that thought, settle down with the *Times* crossword puzzle and allow yourself a moment of congratulation: you're a step closer to home.

BOSTON PHOENIX
DECEMBER 1994

OVERLOAD, POST 9/11

THE SENSE OF purposeless exhaustion set in around day four, Friday night, a fatigue that seemed both bone-deep and unjustified. Like me, most everyone I saw and spoke to that day was safe, insulated from the disaster, mere spectators: we hadn't lost loved ones, we'd only seen the devastation on TV and in pictures, we weren't involved in rescue efforts, and so our weariness felt out of proportion and strange. I walked my dog that afternoon; the people I ran into looked uniformly shell-shocked and felt uniformly guilty about it, as though we hadn't quite earned our despair. Fear and horror—the dominant sensations earlier in the week—had given way to a vague heavy-hearted despondency by then; the stories of individual tragedy were beginning, cruelly, to blur; even language had failed us, leaving most people I know with a single empty fall-back word, "stunned." *I'm stunned. I don't know what to do with myself, I'm just stunned.* I went home that night, watched TV in a teeth-clenched, blank-faced way, and then fell into the darkest sleep.

I am not used to harboring such a wide variety of conflicting emotions at one time. Usually, it's one feeling at a time, maybe two. Anxiety here, contentment there. A dash of melancholy on a bad day; a flash of joy on a good one. By Friday, and persisting well into this week, that simple synaptic system was all out of whack, consciousness on overload. This may be normal, but it's also deeply disorienting. The magnitude of the physical devastation; the fear about what it may unleash; the sense of sudden vulnerability; the reach of the grief, each life lost touching an incalculable number of other lives:

this is more than an ordinary brain can process, and so the mind is left to flitter from one sensation to another; it cannot land on just one, it cannot absorb them all.

Which is why the neurons seem to be firing from all directions. I feel enveloped in safety, insulated within my own little house, and also deeply jittery; a plane flies overhead and I freeze: What is it? Who's on it? Is it about to crash? I feel compelled to watch footage of the towers collapsing over and over and over and then compelled to look away, not sure what's voyeurism and what's an attempt to grasp the ungraspable. One emotion surges only to be supplanted by its opposite. A blind man tells a CNN reporter about how his guide dog, a yellow Labrador retriever with the most noble gaze, led him to safety down 87 flights of stairs, and the heart melts at the miracle, man and his brave attendant; moments later, an executive breaks down in sobs on camera, 700 of his employees unaccounted for, among them his own brother, and the heart tightens and sinks, a stab of pure sorrow. The most heartening pride at human kindness mixes with despair at blind human hatred, often in the same instant. A woman I run into tells me she started to weep without warning on a subway train in downtown Boston and that a total stranger, a man sitting beside her, took her hand and held it, simply and firmly, for the duration of the ride. She felt so touched by this display of compassion she cried even harder, but then, when she left the subway station, she saw fresh graffiti on a wall: NUKE ISLAM.

How to reconcile all of this? I, a woman who's never responded to an American flag with anything more stirring than benign indifference, feel deeply, surprisingly, wholly patriotic and also, perhaps less surprisingly, deeply skeptical, mistrustful that our political and military response will be anything but rash, costly, and short-sighted. I feel protective and defensive about the depth of hatred toward America, a mama bear guarding her cub, and I feel humbled, aware that we've played no small part in earning and fomenting that animosity, and I also feel ashamed, embarrassed by the self-constructed cocoon of ignorance and complacency I've been living in: until last week, I could not have spelled the name Osama bin Laden, let alone told you what degree of threat he and the networks linked to him represented.

Our culture thrives on black-and-white narratives, clearly defined emotions, easy endings, and so this thrust into complexity exhausts; too many feelings competing for head space, no happy ending in sight, no tacit belief that our minuscule attention spans will protect us this time, and little solace from our ordinary opiates, like movies and sports and computer solitaire. The people I talk to feel an odd, almost adolescent yearning for leadership, craving and mistrusting it in the same breath. Some of us feel compelled to reach out—give blood, light candles, sign petitions, anything!—and simultaneously compelled to retreat, edges of paranoia leaking in, talk of terrorists in the backyard. I feel catapulted between all these extremes: protected one minute and vulnerable the next, heartsick and then detached, connected and then estranged, so full of goodwill one moment I'd like to hug the guy at Starbucks who pours me my coffee, so irritable the next I'd like to slap the man who cuts in front of me while I'm trying to pour milk. Mostly I feel unmoored, some rock of permanence and safety having given way to shifting sands, the familiar now eerily unfamiliar. Sirens sound different, scary and consoling at the same time. Work feels irrelevant. Normalcy as yet undefined.

I suppose this is what people mean when they talk about being stunned—this gamut of feeling, which overwhelms the psychic system, leaves you feeling exhausted and powerless and unable to tease out one emotion from the next—and I think the response is both human and frightening; surely, it's one of terrorism's intended effects, to literally stun our morale, to blow up strength and will along with buildings, and the reaction is hard to counter. On Saturday, still feeling blank and enervated, I spent part of the afternoon at a gathering of people who met to talk about caring for a mutual friend, a man who's dying of cancer at the age of 49. The lens shifted suddenly, the unfathomably wide panorama of disaster yielding to a much more personal and individual close-up of tragedy, and it suggested something to me about the numbing effect of emotional overload, which can so easily mutate into a kind of hopeless despair. I did not particularly want to go to this meeting, I drove there feeling fragile and depressed, but I showed up anyway, and sat in a room with twenty other people, and faced a loss in a communal and reflective way. We talked about how we felt about watching our friend die, what we were scared of. We talked about practical things we could do: cooking meals, doing laundry, spending time with him.

Unlike the thousands of lives so hideously obliterated without warning, this man and the people who love him have an opportunity to approach death consciously and with foresight, to say things that need saying, to help one another without the mobilizing impetus of disaster. This, too, is exhausting work, but it's important work, its value immediate and tangible, and it reminded me that the line between feeling stunned and being passive can be very thin. I can give blood. I can send money to relief organizations, I can write letters and sign petitions. I can also be present and active in my own small world, which is a gift that cries out for recognition, even from this stunning roar of mixed emotion.

SALON
SEPTEMBER 2001

IN HERE

Reflections

LONGING FOR NORMALCY

I WOULD LIKE TO take Ordinary Joe lessons.

Can anybody out there help me?

I want to be a regular working stiff, a card-carrying member of Middle America, a nameless, faceless member of the teeming masses.

Do you know what I mean? Do you yearn for this, as well? If so, you probably understand that this is an elusive goal, more elusive than it sounds. It's about lying awake nights and wishing for a kind of simplicity that feels out of your reach most of the time. It's about longing for a humility of spirit, a perspective that brings your expectations down to manageable levels. It's about wanting to rest, about wanting to stop striving to be the things you're not and (big sigh of relief here) just be.

Lately, I find myself talking to friends a lot about my next life. "In my next life," I say, "I want to work in an optical shop." Sometimes the fantasy shifts—I want to be a bank teller, or manage a Store 24, or work on a ranch in Wyoming—but usually it's the optical shop. I'm drawn to the directness of it, the lack of mystery: all day long, steering clients into the chair, selecting frames, helping them to see in the most literal sense, instead of in the indirect, roundabout ways you struggle to help people see through a profession like writing. "There. How's that? Comfortable fit? Everything in focus? Great. Next!" Doesn't that sound satisfying? Doesn't it sound ordinary in the best sense? A simple, helpful life. Nothing too grandiose, nothing too complex. Just normal.

This goal—the normal life, the Ordinary Joe—has eluded me, I think, because I grew up thinking that normalcy was bad, that being ordinary was an unworthy goal. In part, this was the natural result of my environment, which was over-advantaged and rarified—when you're born and raised on the chic side of Cambridge, destined for an Ivy League education before you can even hold a spoon, and taught from a tiny age that what you do is at least as important as who you are, it's hard to set your sights on normal, ordinary ways of life. "Mom, Dad: I plan to graduate from college and manage a Store 24. Sound cool to you?" Instant coronaries, all around.

But I think the pull to be extraordinary, the sense that normalcy is not a valid option, goes deeper than that. I can trace some of it back to age seven or eight, when my father used to come into my room at night and ask me to draw pictures on a pad. He was a psychiatrist, an analyst, and this was a form of free association for children. "Just draw anything that comes to mind," he'd say, and I'd sit there in my bed with the pad on my lap, frozen. I didn't know what he was after at the time, but I could sense he was on an expedition, probing for something dark and complex, so I drew scary things: monsters, pictures of the dark. I have no idea if I was afraid of these things, but I thought the images would please him so I made them up. Those episodes have stuck with me, an early template for my experience of relationships: in his own awkward way, my father was singling me out as a special kid, seeing something original and complex in my mind, and trying to draw it out, and my response was to give him what I thought he wanted, to perform. That's a touching dynamic in its way, but also a complicated one for a child. Sitting there at seven or eight, it makes you wonder: isn't it enough just to be a kid? Can't I just be a regular, unremarkable kid?

What's troublesome is that I do exactly the same thing today, live with a chronic feeling of performance anxiety, as though I'm constantly taking a test: gotta stand out, gotta sparkle with insight and wit, gotta have the right answers, gotta be perfect and good and exemplary. I do it in work, having thrown myself into a profession where my work gets judged on a regular (weekly) basis. And I've done it countless times in relationships, throwing myself into involvements with men (surprise, surprise) just like my father, who set extraordinary standards and keep me in a state of constant vigilance, wondering if I'm good enough, smart enough, if my performance is up to par. Needless to say, there's not a very wide margin of error in a worldview like that: imperfection (in work, in love) makes me deeply uncomfortable, as though it reflects the most profound sort of failure on my part.

Not long ago, at a dinner party, I heard a woman with a background a lot like mine talk about becoming a professor. She thought the idea was to be brilliant and articulate and brimming with ideas, the kind of lecturer who knew everything and never ran out of things to say. Equipped with that perspective, she developed an incredibly hard and stiff teaching style, struggling to twist herself into this extraordinary version of a professor, and it took her many years to realize that it was not only okay but also considerably more effective to be a human being in her job, rather than an idealized model of one. "There is such joy in being ordinary," she said. "There is such relief in being able to be a fallible human being, with complicated feelings and flaws and imperfections." I sat there listening to her and nodded quietly: it sounded wonderful.

The alternative, after all, gets exhausting. When you're constantly striving for perfection, constantly measuring yourself against ideals, you lose access to a lot of simple feelings, a lot of humanity: you lose access to ease and joy and fun, to a sense that you're living in the present and that, for the moment at any rate, the present is good enough. You live your life with your teeth clenched, waiting—always waiting—to jump through the next hoop, pass the next hurdle, ace the next exam.

I thought about this the other night, oddly enough, during the two-hour season finale of Melrose Place, which I watched with my boyfriend and two of our friends, over pizza. It was the simplest sort of evening—four people passing a couple of hours together, hooting at Jo and Jake and Kimberly on TV, relaxing into the most basic elements of cameraderie: food and friendship and laughter. It was a nonevent, really, but at one point, I looked across the room at my friends, at these three people I geuninely love, and I had a sense, rare to people like me, of the deepest satisfaction, a sense of fit, as though everything I needed to be happy was right there in the room, available simply by looking and acknowledging. No struggle, no test to pass; just ordinary comfort and joy.

Isn't it enough just to be me? Can't I just be a regular, unremarkable woman? I've struggled with those questions my whole life, and for an instant that evening, the answers seemed to be quite simple: Yes.

Ordinary Joe lessons? Perhaps that was my first one.

BOSTON PHOENIX
JUNE 1995

ENDLESS (AND ENDLESS) SUMMER

THE LONGEST DAY of the year approaches—next week, June 21. For weeks to come, daylight will stretch out long into the evening: seven-thirty, eight o'clock, eight-thirty. We will leave our offices at the day's end and step into the long shadows of late afternoon, into that particular hot light of late June and July. A sense of lazy ease will hang in the air, subtle and low as the late-day sun. Lovers will walk after dinner; children will linger in front yards; summer sounds—the whirr of a lawn mower, the clang of an ice-cream truck—will echo in the distance. Another summer, another long, light stretch of sultry nights.

I hate it.

Oh, what a killjoy I am. What a mean and twisted thing, to hate the summer. But it's true—or, at least, it's true in certain respects. I look out the window on a warm summer day and I think, Feh: I wish it was raining. I watch those lovers stroll at night, hand in hand under the leafy arbors of summer streets, I watch those children romp across the fresh-cut grass, and I want to grab a semiautomatic weapon and pick 'em off. Bam! I long for howling winds and plummeting temperatures. I long for gray skies. I fantasize about wool. Irish sweaters. Knit scarves. Mittens.

I've been harboring this secret for a long time and I think it's time to own up: summer makes me nervous. Summer makes me sad. I am a sick human being.

Well, make that an anxious human being, a human instinctively drawn toward dark, protective places. Dark bars, for example. Or caves. I'm not particularly proud of this fact, and for this reason I like the concept of summer. I am drawn toward the idea of it: the sense of liberation that accompanies a long, gradual sunset; the freedom from bulky clothing and heavy boots; the ease and simplicity of moving from place to place, unencumbered by coats and snow shovels. I can understand why other people adore the summer, and I don't begrudge summer-lovers their affection at all. It's another item in my list of criteria for the next time around: in my next life, I'd truly like to be the kind of person who revels in the weather from late May to September, who feels her heart lighten and soar with the rising temperatures, who has what's known, appropriately enough, as a "sunny personality." But this time around? Sorry. It's not to be.

I suppose I'm feeling particularly summer-averse this year because we had one of those non-springs, one of those years that seemed to shoot straight from March to August, with barely a moment's respite in between. One of the coldest springs on record this year, with temperatures hovering around the 50-degree mark all through May. There wasn't much in the way of transition, not much time to prepare for the shift to real summer, and this makes me edgy somehow, resentful of the sudden change. A postal clerk commented on this to me a few weeks ago, when I stopped in on a damp, raw morning in mid-May to buy some stamps. She looked weary. "It's going to be one of those years," she said. "Cold and gray, cold and gray, and then—boom!—90 degrees and humid. Instant dog days." The prospect of this seemed to make her gloomy and, of course, I liked her immediately.

Me, I prefer interim weather. October weather. Temperatures warm enough to protect you from the discomfort of genuine cold but cool enough for boots, and layers. Cool enough for cotton sweaters and light jackets and heavy socks. That sense of light and liberation other people seem to experience in the heat feels oppressive to me: sticky and immobilizing. I feel stupid in the summer. I feel intellectually lazy and physically slow. I don't like to sweat.

But the real problem has to do with the larger cosmic matter of fitting in—or, more to the point, not fitting in—with the rest of the universe. It's no fun to hate the summer; you feel like an outsider, deficient on the capacity-for-joy scale. You wake up on a bright, hot, sunny morning, and you picture half the human population bounding off to the beach with their bright towels and coolers, and your heart sinks. Inside, you want to pull down the shades and crank the AC and this makes you feel guilty, a little ashamed. For years, I felt this most acutely in the first warming days of late spring, those days when every bud on every tree seemed to blossom at once—suddenly, green everywhere, and bursts of flowers and scents. This was back in my 20s, when I was anorexic and lonely and morbidly depressed nearly all the time, and all that growth seemed to add to my sadness, reinforcing the reasons behind it: everything blossoming but me. It was never any surprise to me that the national suicide rate took a sharp rise in April and May: I understood the phenomenon of spring depression all too well.

As I've gotten older (and happier), the warm-weather blues have abated considerably, but I still feel the tug of melancholy when the days stretch out like this, still feel that longing for the enveloping safety of cool, dark nights, of heavy blankets and coats, firelight instead of sunlight. It's a wish for retreat, really, a sense that summer is somehow too exposing. After all, undercurrents of sadness blend into cold, raw weather more effectively; they're easier to hide, both from the self and from the outside world. Gray feelings, gray skies: a more natural combination.

But such is the nature of cycles: cycles of season, cycles of feeling. Summer angst comes and goes. Like most of us, I will have my share of good days this summer: good, optimistic, lighthearted days, when my internal landscape matches or is more aligned with what's outside, when I can enjoy the feeling of sand beneath my feet and warm air against my skin, when it all feels right. And I will have bad days: days of resenting all that brightness and light, days of yearning for a dark cocoon, days when I see flowers wafting in the breeze and have to fight the urge to rip their smelly little heads off.

And when those days come along, I will cope. People like me, after all, have remedies, strategies to help us cope when the warm-weather melancholy sets in. We (I am convinced of this) are why God invented movie theaters.

Boston Phoenix
June 1995

COMING HOME

I'M HOME.

It's taken me 11 years to figure that out—or, to be exact, 11 years, one week, and three days. I moved to Boston, you see, on August 8, 1984, with no intention of carving out anything like a permanent life here. I figured I'd stay a year, two at the most. I figured Boston would be an interim city, a place to set down my bags until I moved on to some bigger, more exotic locale—New York, San Francisco, London. I figured I'd be transient, my sense of place fluid, my attachments focused on people and jobs rather than on locations.

And then, not long ago, I looked up one day and thought: Oh, my God. I have a life here. I'm not moving. I'm home.

A weird phenomenon, creating a sense of home, far less deliberate than I imagined it would be. The myth is that settling down is something you do in distinct stages, with specific goals and criteria, not unlike picking the right college or choosing a career: you plot it out, decide on a location, and, after lots of careful consideration, surround yourself with all the trappings of permanence—a house, a spouse, a couple of kids. In fact, the process seems far more haphazard to the people I know, far more random and unconscious. "There's a real passivity to the way I ended up here," says a New York–based acquaintance, a woman who moved to Manhattan from the Midwest nearly 15 years ago and simply never left, without consciously deciding to make the city her home. "I just gradually realized that my life is in New York now, that the chances of me picking up and relocating are slimmer and slimmer." That seems to be the way it works: you figure on one or two years in a new city and—presto!—you wake up one morning and realize that a full decade has passed, maybe more. You realize you've established roots, settled down in spite of yourself. You realize that leaving has ceased to be as simple or appealing an option as it once was.

My father used to say similar things about marriage, noting that that sort of commitment was something you did when you simply couldn't fathom doing anything else. "You rarely know that marriage is the right decision, with the kind of 100-percent certainty you may wish you had," he said. "You do it when it starts to feel like the only option." That may not be the most romantic perspective, but I think I know what he meant and I'd extend the argument to the process of creating a home: it's a gradual process, a little like standing on a seashore and letting the waves lap at you until they've dug your feet straight into the sand.

These days, I know dozens of people who've dug themselves into different homes in precisely that manner: my friend Jennifer went to college in Vermont, decided to stay there for a year after she graduated, and has been there ever since: same town, same job. My friend Sarah decided to spend the summer after she graduated from college in Wyoming: she never came back. My friend Sally met a guy in Rome during a semester abroad, went back to visit him the following summer, and is now entrenched there, living with the same man and their two small children. We've all just landed in these places, rather than sought them out, allowed our lives to build up around us rather than setting out to create them. Perhaps more than any other major life decision—choosing a spouse, say, or deciding to have children—finding a home appears to be something that happens to you, through the gradual and often only semiconscious accumulation of years and experiences.

I went to New York a few weeks ago on business and spent some time wandering around the city the way I always do when I'm away from home, scoping it out, fantasizing about where I'd live if I moved there, trying different neighborhoods on in my mind, the way you'd try on a new pair of shoes. Oh, I'd think, here's a nice little street . . . an ideal-looking townhouse . . . a lovely little roofdeck . . . I can see living here. . . . I've made this kind of mental move over the years to San Fransisco and Paris, to Philadelphia and Seattle and the north coast of California: there's a feeling of discovery to such fantasies, as though a part of you has been searching out a missing piece of a puzzle for a long time: Hah! Here it is! Here's a place I could call home. I felt that way in particular the first time I went to San Fransisco as an adult, an immediate, almost visceral sense of attachment, as though I'd found lost pieces of my soul carved into the hillsides.

For the most part, I think that sensation has to do with fantasy, with the wish, so deeply held among so many of us, that happiness comes from externals, that something outside of ourselves—a new job, a new relationship, a new place—will fill up whatever holes exist inside, provide a sense of completeness that we can't seem to generate on our own. The immediate attraction I felt to San Fransisco, for example, was pure projection: a beautiful city in which I could have a beautiful life, just by virtue of having the right address. I felt exactly the same way during a trip to Paris three years ago, a longing to live there and be a part of its elegance and grace, as though those qualities would simply rub off on me, a form of geographic osmosis. For me, the pulls to such cities have always had less to do with anything the new place might really offer than with what the old place—my own home—lacks.

Oddly enough, though, such pulls are diminishing. During this most recent trip to New York, I may have roamed around with my usual stable of fantasies, mentally plunking myself down into a funky new life in Greenwich Village or a sophisticated new existence on the Upper East Side, but I also had a more sanguine feeling, foreign to me in the past, a sense of truly belonging somewhere else. I walked around the Village and thought about my own little house in Cambridge, how carefully I've cultivated each room. I walked into different markets to do errands and thought about the little routines I've carved out at home: the convenience store where they know me well enough to reach for the right brand of cigarettes as soon as I walk in the door; the bakery where I pick up coffee and a scone every morning; the easy sense of familiarity I get out of such small rituals. For years now, I've been telling people I'm going to be wedded to Boston for the rest of my life because of the Charles River, where I scull four or five times a week. The Charles offers one of the longest, best stretches of flat water for rowing anywhere in the U.S., and my attachment to the sport rules out a move almost in and of itself. In fact, the Charles has emerged as one in a series of deep attachments, ties that have developed over the years so gradually I barely noticed how tightly bound I've become. My work is in Boston. So are my sister and brother, and my circle of true friends, as important to me now as family. So is my shrink, so is my history.

I may not have intended it, but like I said, I'm home.

BOSTON PHOENIX
AUGUST 1995

NOTHING TO WEAR

SPONTANEOUS WARDROBE Failure Syndrome (SWFS), a phenomenon in which every article of clothing a woman owns suddenly and seemingly inexplicably appears to her to be inappropriate, ill-fitting, unattractive, and "all wrong." Symptoms include anxiety; distress; periods of weeping; obsessive preoccupation with fashion magazines; frequent utterance of the phrase, delivered in a mournful wail, "I have nothing to wear." Causes are unclear. Prognosis: dire.

Alas, it's happened again. I stare into the closet: zippo. I open the bureau drawers: nada. I rifle through the shelves, the old suitcases where I keep stuff I can't quite bear to part with, even the laundry hamper: nothing. My wardrobe has spontaneously failed me; I have a major case of SWFS.

What is this? I haven't gained or lost any weight, so it's not a matter of physical fit. Nor is it a case of being out of step with current fashions, the stuff I wear being mainstream enough to make it from season to season without going hopelessly out of style. No, this is something deeper, something that seems to sneak up on a woman without warning every few years, usually on the heels of some other, more internal shift in outlook or style. Call it a garden-variety identity crisis. Call it a pain in the butt. Call it SWFS.

My friend Mary is going through the same thing, which means that she and I would be in for a long and grotesquely expensive shopping spree if we could only figure out what it was we wanted to look like. We talked about this the other night. I said, "I look into my closet and I think, 'Who wore this stuff?'" She said, "I know. I don't know what looks good on me anymore. I need a whole new . . . a whole new something."

Precisely. A whole new something. At the moment, my wardrobe feels like a whole old something, in that it seems to represent three or four worn-out versions of a person I used to be. Upstairs, in a closet I rarely open, hangs the Eighties me, summed up by a rack of power suits I wouldn't wear now if my life depended on it. Little skirts, big, unstructured jackets with shoulder pads the size of roasts. Very severe, very businesslike, and not just out of style here in 1996 but also out of synch with the way I feel inside. I wore those suits in my late 20s and early 30s, a time when I felt like a 12-year-old masquerading as an adult nearly all the time, and they were my disguises. They kind of give me the creeps these days, symbols of an uncomfortable time, an ill-formed sense of self.

Same with all that black. Racks and racks of black in those closets: black sweaters, black skirts, black blouses, little black dresses, about 75 pairs of black leggings. I never quite bought the line, delivered in ominous tones in the early '90s, that black was history, dated, out of style—black will always be in style—but all those dark and stormy outfits give me that same creepy feeling, reminding me of what a moron I've been about clothes over the years. I wore all that black because it was easy and nonthreatening, because I didn't know beans about color, and because, for a very long time, the idea of putting together an outfit consisting of more than one shade seemed more challenging than completing a Triathalon with a broken leg. Black reminds me of standing in clothing stores and staring dumbly at the racks: Uh . . . gee, I don't know . . . does it come in black?

Old personae, old insecurities, hangers draped with former lives. There are a dozen mini-skirts: my I-feel-totally-inadequate-but-at-least-I-have-good-legs phase. There are dozens of silk blouses, many of them unworn: my I-can't-dress-my-way-out-of-a-paper-bag-but-at-least-I-have-good-taste-in-fabric phase. There are numerous failed experiments in color (an inordinate number of them pink), assorted nods to recent fads (platform shoes), and God-only-knows how many catalogue-shopping disasters—sweaters that didn't fit, fabrics that turned out to be cheesy, colors that didn't bear any resemblance to the hue on the page.

And then there is the more current version of me, that one that seemed to stabilize for a few years there in the mid-'90s. Leggings, flat shoes, long shirts and big sweaters: my uniform for the last five years, and one that seemed to work quite comfortably until this latest bout of SWFS swept through and made everything seem hideous and wrong. What happened?

Well, several things happened. I quit my full-time job a year ago, and have been making the transition from Office Professional to Freelance Slob since then; suddenly all the stuff that looked fine in the workaday world—snappy little shoe-boots and long chenille sweaters—feels out of place and oddly inappropriate. Next, I got a dog, a phenomenon that totally transforms a woman's attitude toward her wardrobe, starting with the feet. Heels? Forget it. Shoes that look great but pinch even a little? No way. When you're out walking a dog two or three times a day, it's all Doc Martens, hiking boots, and sneakers, and that shift—from stylish shoes to comfortable shoes—echoes throughout the wardrobe, throws the previous look completely out of whack. I stand there in front of the closet with new priorities: what can I wear that will be comfortable working and walking the dog and still look halfway decent on the streets? Good-bye Ann Taylor; hello LL Bean.

But the real cause of my current wardrobe angst is deeper. I have a book coming out in the next few weeks, and I'm scheduled to do all the anxiety-provoking book-publicity things a writer sometimes has to do: readings, a tour, possibly some television. It's no coincidence that my clothing has spontaneously failed me at this precise moment, when my very private persona is about to become more public. A *Globe* reporter came to my house to interview me not long ago, and I agonized over what to wear: What to project? Who to be? What will people see when they look at me? I fell back on something utterly nondescript, from the leggings-and-sweaters days, but I've been aware since then of how closely tied up to identity the contents of a woman's closet can be. Who am I? How do the externals reflect what's going on inside? The fact that this book is a memoir—a deeply personal piece of writing that covers a lot of addictive, neurotic, self-destructive territory I'm not especially proud of—gives these questions even greater urgency. I want the look to communicate glowing mental health, to say: Healing; Together; I'm-Doing-Just-Fine-Thanks. It's probably no surprise that I watch TV these days with an eye toward models of self-assurance and poise: I want to look like Diane Sawyer or Jane Pauley; I want casual confidence and flair; I want to look well-put-together and grown up.

So I'll go shopping. I'll solve the problem, to the best of my ability, this time around. But I know my wardrobe will fail me again. It's inevitable, part of being female, part of the ongoing search for a sense of internal well-being that's solid and well-grounded enough to be visible externally. A friend, who's about to get divorced, says she spent the last seven years dressing as a married woman, and now she's trying to figure out how to look for this new phase of her life. She feels all uncertain inside, rocky and unsettled, and she's spending a small fortune on new clothes and makeup. It's all about fit, she says, matching the insides to the outsides, trying to get the two in synch. It's a lifelong process. It's why God invented Bloomingdale's.

Boston Phoenix
May 1996

EXERCISING OPTIONS

I'M SICK OF EXERCISING.

There, I've said it.

I'm sick of hot-weather workouts: sweat in the eyes; T-shirts soaked through; unquenchable thirsts. I'm sick of the planning that goes into exercising: when; where; how long; how to squeeze it in amidst everything else that needs doing. I'm sick of the pain: sore muscles, a persistent ache in my left hip, callouses. And above all, I'm sick of the emotional energy involved: the worrying (am I working out enough? hard enough? long enough) and the calculating (can I get away with not working out today? or tomorrow? or this week?) and the subtle contemplation of a never-ending, perhaps unanswerable question: am I burning all these calories because I *want* to—because it genuinely makes me feel good—or because I think I *should*, because at least on some occasions exercise answers some deeper need for a kind of self-punishment?

As we do with so many of the important activities in our lives—eating, drinking, working—most of us have an active, if not well-understood, relationship with exercise. Mine began rather late in life: I wasn't much into sports as a kid, never particularly liked the output of energy it took to run around and compete. It seemed a little silly to me, all that effort. In ninth grade, I belonged to the absolute worst softball team in my high school's history (we once lost a game by 127 to 3 and I swear I'm not making that up), and my dominant memory of the game has to do with the time I got hit in the nose by a line drive and ended up lying on the bathroom floor for 45 minutes with an unstoppable nosebleed, waiting for my mother to come pick me up. By 10th grade, I managed to bypass anything that required actual physical energy by becoming the manager of the girl's basketball team, a nice, passive post I held until I graduated. My college years were blissfully sedentary: I may have walked really fast to the cafeteria once or twice, but I didn't do so with the aim of working up a sweat and for the most part I didn't think about exercise, or give much thought to whether I should or shouldn't take it up.

Exercise for me (and no doubt for lots of women) accompanied concern about body image and weight, which blossomed into an obsession in my early 20s, the anorexic years. Fresh out of college, unanchored by academic rituals and responsibilities, and hell-bent on controlling *something* in what felt like a small, chaotic environment, I stopped eating and started jogging. A 10-minute run several times a week turned into a 20-minute run every other day, then a 30-minute run every day, and so on. At the height of my compulsivity, I weighed 83 pounds and was running six-mile road races, on an empty stomach, of course. The concept of carbo-loading seemed grotesque to me, and weak.

Those days (mercifully) are long gone, and my relationship with working out has become richer, more complex, less singularly self-destructive. Back then, the equation was simple, the relationship one-dimensional: exercise meant expending calories, the more the better and never mind how much it hurt. I hated jogging, actually, found it monotonous and painful, but I suspect that pain was the point, and enduring pain (both physical and psychological) was a prerequisite for feeding myself in any other way: I didn't feel I deserved to eat (or to relax, or to feel like a decent human being), couldn't allow myself such indulgences, unless I'd *earned* it somehow.

As anorexia lost its hold on me, so did compulsive exercising. In my mid-20s, around the time I began to get my relationship with food back on track, I discovered sculling, a difficult sport that gave me something to master besides the contours of my own body, and for the first time I realized that exercise could be something other than tedious and hard on the knees. I loved—and continue to love—the *feel* of sculling, the swoosh of it, the rhythm, the sounds of oars dipping into the water, popping out, sweeping back against the water. It's an aesthetically pleasing sport, physically demanding and yet meditative, and for the most part I've been grateful and enthusiastic about it for more than a decade.

And yet I sense it's time to rethink the relationship once again. The compulsive edge has lingered, particularly during times of stress. The summer my father died, four years ago, I rowed 1,000 miles: I rowed six or seven times a week, no matter what the conditions, often racking up seven or eight miles in a single outing. I went to France that summer for a week, came home, got off the plane at 2 p.m., and was on the river by 4. That was frantic exercise, an attempt to literally row away from my own feelings, and although I've not repeated the effort, I'm often aware of the same pulls and pressures, the same wish to muscle my way into some altered state, and an attendant struggle over the question of what's *enough*. How hard to work out? How often? How much pain is required in order to feel pleasure?

One day not long ago, a particularly hot, muggy, windy day in late August, I spent 50 minutes flailing around on the Charles River in my single scull, oars flapping against the chop, a large blister developing on my left hand, sweat running into my eyes and making them burn. I hated it. Two-and-a-half miles up the river, two-and-a-half miles back, and the whole way I kept thinking: Why do I *do* this?

I know myself well enough at this point to answer that question: That particular morning, I'd been feeling restless, edgy, a little lonely and depressed. For several days, I'd been eating too much, procrastinating too much, shying away from restorative things, like contact with friends, and sufficient sleep. Exercise at times like that *can* be a helpful thing, a way to jump-start myself into a more energetic mode, a path out of lethargy and the slothful sense of self that comes with it. But at other times, like that morning, it reverts back to its old self: a form of self-punishment, a way to literally beat myself up. I knew the water would be rough that day, the row unpleasant, the experience painful and lonely, and I did it anyway. That isn't a workout; it's an exercise in self-disgust, and I suppose that's the brand I'm tired of.

There is still nothing like a *good* row, when the water is flat and calm, the air cool, the conditions right for that particular combination of hard physical work and psychic reward. But I'd like my relationship with exercise to be less manic and less propelled by guilt, less forced. A rotten day? Don't row. A set of feelings that exercise won't resolve? Find another way to manage them.

For the last few Saturdays, I've been taking long, meandering hikes with a new friend and our dogs. We've tramped around the Fells, between Melrose and Winchester, and we've tramped around the woods in Lincoln, and I've discovered on these occasions a wonderful balance between physical exertion and social pleasure. We walk and we talk and we pause on occasion to sit and drink water and watch the dogs, tireless and ecstatic to be outdoors. I've come home from these walks feeling not only physically restored but also refreshed in other ways, connected and content and closer to the things that make me happy: my dog, good conversation, the quiet of the woods. I've tended to be the sort of person who believes that walking doesn't "count" as a form of exercise, that you're not really working out unless you hurt. But it occurs to me now, perhaps for the first time, that the heart is a muscle in many respects, and needs attending to beyond the gym.

BOSTON PHOENIX
SEPTEMBER 1996

I HATE MONEY

I AM ON THE phone with Paulette, my financial adviser and a woman I love dearly except for the times we actually have to discuss my finances.

Paulette and I are discussing a matter relating to my late mother's estate and I am trying very very hard to pay attention.

She says, "First you need the 1995 substitute form 1099 from Citibank, and then you need to find out the date of purchase and the purchase price of the treasury notes, and then you need to send me the year-end tax summary for the XTC–901-K form B on account number 108862, and then you need to check that against the downward flow of capital gains taxes on 1995 high-yield tax funds, and then . . ."

Paulette might as well be speaking in tongues. My eyes glaze over. I break into a fine sweat. And slowly but surely, I begin my long, downward spiral into monetary spaz mode.

Money.

I hate money. I hate dealing with it, thinking about it, managing it, planning for it, and accounting for it. On the other hand, I don't have too many problems spending it, which complicates matters considerably. Money brings out my worst, most regressive and immature side, transforms me from a comparatively competent 36-year-old woman into a whining, mewling child. *Paulette! Help me! Save me! Do it for me! Paulette! I don't even know how to add!*

To me, you see, money represents a final frontier of sorts, the last demarcation between the point in life when one is afforded a certain degree of irresponsibility in personal matters, and the point when one is not. To deal with money in a knowledgable, mature fashion is to move—finally and irrevocably, it seems—into that fearsome land inhabited by (gasp) real grown-ups. And a big part of me is just not ready for that. Bottom line: I can't even pronounce the word "fiduciary," let alone wrap my mind around what it might mean.

Of course, part of the reason I'm such a spaz about money is that I had so little of it for so long. My first job out of college, I made a whopping $9,000 a year, which is how I developed my first approach to money management: the highly developed and sophisticated use of complete and unwavering denial.

Bills? What bills? I don't see any bills. Who's Bill? Let's talk about something else.

A very handy technique. I never paid a bill until I got the really menacing, third-and-final, we-hate-you bill, the one that basically states that you're a delinquent and a very bad girl and unless you pay us right now we're going to hunt you down and kill you. When I finally did pay a bill, I did it quickly, my teeth clenched and gaze averted, and I never—ever—paid the full amount due. Throw them a bone, pay the minimum, and don't worry about interest on the balance due: it's too much and it's way too scary.

Actually, this was a humiliating state of affairs. Early on, money became the primary symbol of a rather gaping discrepancy between my economic realities and my expectations about adulthood. On side A of the gaping chasm: a big picture of the grown-up life, all sophisticated clothing and snappy car and expensive housewares and kitchen appliances. And on side B: a $150-a-week paycheck. Plastic became my bridge between the two, a long, sturdy, and (for a while, anyway) very reliable bridge: charge that cappuccino maker, charge those suede boots, charge that Mission-style dining room table and four matching chairs; open accounts at Bloomingdale's and Neiman-Marcus and Macy's. Interest rates at 12 percent? Eighteen? Twenty-one? Feh. Remember: denial is the key.

By 1988, I'd racked up $10,000 in credit card debt, a state of affairs I didn't get out of (I'm ashamed to admit this) until my grandmother died and I inherited enough to pay it off.

Since then, I've sworn off plastic: don't have credit cards, don't hold accounts at major department stores, and only use a debit card, so I can literally only spend what I have in my checking account. But for the most part, I'm still every bit as fearful and denial-oriented about money as I used to be. I never reconcile my checking account, for example. Never. Freaks me out, for reasons I don't quite understand. Instead, I use a rounding-off approach to account-balancing: if I've written a check for $51.68, I round it up to $52 when I enter it in my check register, and figure if I do this consistently, all those extra pennies will compensate for the buildup of assorted bank fees and errors in addition. Granted, this isn't a terribly exact approach, but it seems one step better than that employed by my friend Carla, who's such a spaz about finances that she actually closes her checking account every year and opens a new one at a different bank: she says this is the only way she can figure out how much money she really has.

Shortly after my last conversation with Paulette, the one about treasury notes and high-yield tax funds, a check arrived in the mail, representing the last little chunk of my mother's holdings. For the last three years, since my mom's death, Paulette has overseen this fund: it's been held in special account, available for my brother and sister and me to use for big, depressing expenses: legal fees relating to the estate, for example. When I read the letter that accompanied the check, I got a chill: it used jarring phrases like "final disbursement" and it underscored, at least implicitly, the fact of my mother's death, and it reminded me that my siblings and I are truly on our own now, with no reassuring, knowledgeable overseer—a mom, a hands-on account-managing financial adviser—to stand between us and potential disaster.

This is precisely what terrifies me about money: it's as easy to lose as it is to use and if you don't understand certain things about it—how it works, how to make it productive, how to keep it secure—it just sits there before you abstractly, a big, frightening blob with equal power to protect or devastate. I know my ignorance about money, willful and self-imposed though it may be, is what makes financal matters feel so scary, but I simply can't get myself to break through it. Paulette calls. She talks about investing in this company or that one, selling shares of X and picking up shares of Y. She talks about long-term gains and short-term risks and I nod into the phone and try to sound like an adult: *Okay; sounds good; let's do it.* In fact, I don't hear a word she says; the voices beckoning me back toward childhood and dependence are far too loud.

BOSTON PHOENIX
OCTOBER 1996

SATAN DEALS THE CARDS

JUST ONE. IT'S *okay—one won't hurt you. Just one.*

I hear that voice in my head, like Satan himself. I hear him coaxing, seducing, urging me on: just one, just one teensy little one; c'mon, it'll make you feel better.

I clench my teeth, steel myself, repeat the mantra of resistence: No. One leads to two; two leads to 14; you've never had "just one" in your whole life. Don't do it!

But Satan is strong. Satan is powerful. Against all reason and judgment, fully aware on some level of the havoc I'm about to wreak, I feel myself succumb. I know this is wrong, but I can't help it; the promise of oblivion is simply too alluring. So I take a deep breath, jump off the cliff. The relapse is upon me; I am about to be lost in . . . computer solitaire.

Argh!

What an insipid, insidious little vehicle for addiction. What a mindless, totally unredeeming activity. If you've just bought a new computer and you see a little file marked "Games" in the applications folder, trash it immediately. It probably means that solitaire (or one of its equally insipid cousins, such as mine sweeper) has been preprogrammed onto your system and this puts you in grave danger. Get sucked in and you'll lose whole chunks of your life to it, countless brain cells. Computer solitaire is like a disease and it's contagious: just about every computer user I know has it, plays it, loathes it because they can't stop once they've started. It's also the quickest route to ennui I've come across in a long while, one of the easiest ways to make your life feel utterly hollow and meaningless. Trust me: it's the devil in a new disguise.

Since last summer, when I discovered the benign-looking little solitaire icon on my Macintosh powerbook, I have played 2,825 games. I know this because my system, which is particularly sadistic, provides a little read-out at the end of each session informing you not only how many games you've played but also how many hours you've racked up (or, more aptly, wasted away) in the process. Ninety-six hours in my case. Ninety-six. That's four entire days. Twelve full workdays. A two-week vacation, lost in the abyss.

Sick, huh?

Actually, I've lost even more time than that. At one point, I copied the computer solitaire program from my powerbook and installed it on my main computer in my office. I'd be working on something, I'd get a little stuck or bored or tired, and I'd hear that satanic voice—Oh, play one game, just one—and I'd shrug and think: Why not?

It's just like drinking. One game leads to another, then another and another. The mind begins to rationalize. *Oh, just one more*. Or: *Oh, I'll just play until I win. Then I'll stop*. I don't know why this is, why it's so hard to stop once you've started, but there's something about the speed and tidiness of playing a card game without actual cards that's enormously seductive: click that mouse, watch those cards flip past, see that ace zip up to the top of the screen. The game requires virtually no physical effort, and absolutely nothing in the way of brain power; you just sit there in your chair with your hand on the mouse and zone out. Thirty-eight games later, your brain has gone completely numb and you've lost an entire day.

This is dangerous business, having computer solitaire on your primary work system, so about 1,500 games in, I did what any good addict might do: attempted a program of controlled solitaire usage. I copied the solitaire program onto a disk and deleted it from my main computer's hard drive. Then I put the disk on a high shelf, way on the other side of my office. That way, if the urge to play came upon me, I'd actually have to get up from my chair and go get the disk, a minor effort but one I figured would serve as an effective deterrent. It didn't, of course. I'd find myself coming up with random excuses to cross the room, get near that disk. I'd think: Oh, there's a pencil sharpener over there on that shelf—maybe I should sharpen a pencil. And then I'd meander over to the other side of the office, sharpen the pencil, grab the disk. Next, I started putting the disk in another room. Then I put it downstairs, in a kitchen cupboard. When I hit my 2,000th game, I took the damn disk and stuffed it deep in the garbage, resolving *never to play again*. And then I went to an AA meeting and talked about it. Lots of head nodding. Many expressions of sympathy.

❧

The addictive personality will latch onto anything, *anything* that provides distraction, oblivion, mental anesthesia. I use food as a drug, television as a drug, exercise as a drug, and it's probably no surprise that I'd be drawn to computer games for the same reason. It seduces you in the same way an obsession does, narrows the mind, puts you in one of those otherworldly psychic zones where large human concerns (fears, anxieties, longings) are obliterated, replaced by narrow, stupid concerns (red 10 on black jack, black seven on red eight). *Click, click, click. Click, click, click.* This is your mind on Eric's Solitaire Sampler.

The sorry thing about computer solitaire is that it offers all the mind-numbing properties of alcohol or drugs but none of the benefits. Sit there in your office clicking away at that mouse and you do not feel "euphoric." You do not feel funnier, or more attractive, or better able to connect with other human beings. Food tastes good; TV can entertain or amuse; exercise makes you feel stronger and more relaxed; drugs and alcohol can give you at least temporary access to feelings of intimacy and calm, even if the feelings are artificial. But solitaire? *Click, click, click. Click, click, click.* All you get is some temporary distraction and then the intellectual equivalent of a hangover: play too many games and you grow stupid; you start wandering around in a daze; friends call up and you can't say anything more engaging than, "Huh?" There is nothing redeeming about it.

But there is hope. These days, I consider myself a recovering solitaire addict. I still have a copy of the program on my powerbook, but I refuse to yield. I hear that satanic voice (just one, c'mon—just one) and straighten up in my chair and I resist. There is, you see, a solution, and I have found it.

In AA, there are a variety of slogans and clichés for the tools alcoholics use to stay sober: one day at a time; keep it simple; don't drink, go to meetings, ask for help. Me, I keep myself solitaire-free with an even simpler phrase, two words which have changed my life, given me access to a new world, a place of promise and hope and light. They are: computer scrabble.

Boston Phoenix
April 1998

TRANSFER STATION

A FRIEND (FEMALE) has suddenly fallen in love with her therapist (male) and, naturally, she is highly freaked out by this. Never mind that she grasps the concept of transference. Never mind that she knows this is not "love" in the boy-meets-girl sense, but, rather, love in the clinical sense, a classic phenomenon in which she has projected all her deepest fears and longings and hungers onto the blank screen of her psychotherapist. The feelings are real and she finds them agonizing, deeply unsettling.

She moans: "It's awful!"

I shake my head sympathetically.

She cries: "It's so embarrassing!"

I nod and reassure.

She wails: "Nothing like this has ever happened to me before!"

I beg to differ.

Sigmund Freud first developed his theories about transference between analyst and analysand in the late 1890s, but I suspect that if the good doctor had had to endure regular meetings with a dentist or a car mechanic or a Newbury Street hairdresser instead of his psychiatric patients, he would have hit upon the phenomenon a whole lot sooner. Transference is a daily occurrence, as natural to most humans as breathing. My friend may be experiencing a big, ground-breaking case of transference in the clinical sense, but all of us go through smaller, less visible forms of it all the time. Little projective moments. Isolated incidents that call forth our darkest fears and feelings, often with total strangers. Call them baby transferences, the stuff of everyday social intercourse.

Confused?

Consider:

I am halfway out the door, en route to a dental appointment I've been postponing for a year, and I am trembling with fear. Root canal? No. Oral surgery? Nope. I have merely scheduled an appointment with the dental hygienist for a routine cleaning, but my heart does not know this. In my heart, I am off to see the evil, punitive mother. And I believe what I feel, much as my friend believes she is in love with her therapist. I sit in the dental chair and cower. The hygienist begins to poke around in my mouth and I feel myself shrink: Uh-oh; she's onto me. I haven't flossed adequately. I haven't used my rubber tip. I've been a *bad girl;* she's *mad at me*.

The hygienist's name is Tiffany. She's about 22 years old, with big hair and blue eyeshadow. She looks about as scary as a Yorkshire terrier, but no matter. She says, "Got a lot of stain here; still smoking, eh?" and in that simple statement I hear an ocean of old associations. You have let me down. You are a disappointment. I am your mother, powerful and omniscient, and I know the truth about you: beneath that polished exterior, you are slothful and deeply lazy; you should be punished.

I want to weep.

In the process of renovating her kitchen, my friend Helen developed a full-blown case of transference with her contractor, a heavyset guy named Hank who became, mere hours into the project, her father: a remote, inaccessible figure whom she was desperate to please. Hank would amble into the kitchen and hitch up his jeans and say something perfectly benign—"Are you talking marble counters or butcher block?"—and Helen would begin stammering and stuttering like an 11-year-old, completely self-conscious and deferential. "Um . . . I don't know. Gee . . . I was thinking marble, but . . . what do *you* think?" Then she'd want to slap herself, she felt like such an idiot. She says, "He was—you know—Mr. Authority. All his opinions were going to be right and all my opinions were going to be wrong. It was Dad, standing there in the middle of my kitchen."

Another friend, Emily, is in the process of looking for her house; assisting her in the search is her mother, cleverly disguised as a real-estate salesperson. The realtor calls Emily to tell her about a listing and Emily says, "Oh, sounds great!" even if the place sounds terrible. She has gone to look at condos in neighborhoods she'd never investigate on her own, and she feels inordinately guilty every time she rejects a potential home. Crazy? Emily can't help it. The realtor stirs up some dark mother-inspired combination of guilt and need, and Emily feels desperate to stay on her good side. "I know it's nuts," Emily whispers, "but I really want this woman to like me. I feel like if she doesn't like me, if she doesn't see me as—you know—her *daughter*, she won't help me find a house."

So many interpersonal combinations; so many potential objects of transference. Car mechanics: dad. Lawyers and financial advisors: dad. Male physicians: dad. Female physicians: mom. Complete strangers can evoke this stuff: an age-old wish to please here; an ancient jealousy there; one's most deeply rooted feelings of being undervalued or inadequate or somehow lacking.

A few years ago, sitting in the waiting area of my hair salon, I watched my hairdresser finish up with a client, a young woman about my age. The two were engaged in some hilarious banter: they talked, they laughed, they seemed utterly at ease with one another, and I watched this with a combination of envy and despair. Clearly, she was the good client, the good daughter, the *good sister*, being valued and attended to by the adoring parent. Me? I sat in the waiting area and squirmed, certain that the hairdresser (dad with a nose ring) would find me drab and boring by contrast, that my small talk would never measure up to hers, that I would be exposed as the lesser being I felt myself to be as a child. Such agony! I watched some more. The client stepped off the styling chair and turned to look at her hair in the mirror. She cooed and enthused. She said, "You're a *genius*!" My heart sunk further. Not only was she better than me (prettier, perkier, more engaging, you name it), but they obviously had a long, rich history together, too—the happy family, creating years of happy hair—and I felt puny and unimportant waiting for my turn: the lowly little sister, the secondary relative about to be punished for her obvious inadequacy with a bad haircut. The client hugged the hairdresser. They exchanged air-kisses.

And then, just before he turned to summon me to the chair, he said to her, "God, it was *great* to meet you."

I nearly died.

So you see, my freaked-out friend, in love with her therapist, has it easy. I tell her the hairdresser story and she nods soberly. At least her shrink isn't wielding scissors.

BOSTON PHOENIX
FEBRUARY 1998

THE RAGE CAGE

LET'S DISCUSS ANGER, a brief case study.

A friend, we'll call him Bob, is in a common state of free-floating rage. The rage has both a specific object—it's directed at his brother, with whom he had a massive falling-out several years ago—and also a more general, core feel, as though it's been bubbling around inside him for much of his adult life.

Most of the time, Bob tends to deny this rage exists. He is not, by nature, a confrontational person and, like many humans, he is not particularly comfortable with angry feelings, so he does his best to steer clear of them. He rarely speaks to or about the brother, for example, and when you bring the subject up, he gamely tries to feign distance, detachment. "I'm not pissed at him," he says, sounding deeply pissed: stony and defensive. "What happened between us happened. It's history. I'm over it."

Clearly, he is not over it, but even when you get Bob to own up to his anger, he is at a loss as to what to do with it. He doesn't believe there'd be any value in expressing it, doesn't believe a yelling, screaming brawl with the brother would either alter their relationship or diminish his feelings. He is in the rage cage: unwilling to deal with the emotions directly, but also unable to let them go.

The rage cage is a very familiar place; scads of us live there. Not long ago, a woman I know talked to me at length about the buckets of rage she carries around toward her parents, a particularly nasty pair. This woman has been in therapy for many years. She has visited all the dark corners of her past, crawled around in the muck of childhood terror and disappointment, and still she cannot so much as speak to her mother on the phone without experiencing a spike in blood pressure, a pang of fury so ancient and fundamental it feels encoded in her DNA. "What do you do with rage?" she wondered aloud. "Do you lug it around with you your whole life, or at some point does it just go away?"

I wish I could answer her. Once upon a time, I suffered from the delusion that anger was a finite thing, the emotional equivalent of a natural resource, capable of being mined—and ultimately conquered—in therapy: if you found the right therapist, if you raged and stormed long enough and deeply enough, if you shed enough light on all those dark, angry corridors, you'd use it all up, expend your rage quota, walk out free. Anger transcended, serenity achieved. I still believe that therapy can help lessen anger, or at least temper the feeling with degrees of acceptance and forgiveness, but I've long ago let go of the idea that there's anything finite about it, let alone conquerable. You can (and many people do) deal with the primary sources of rage (parents, siblings), but unless you live in a cave, it's pretty hard to go through life without finding people who'll push your buttons from time to time. Anger, like love or need or affection, is part of the great complicated stew of human affairs, an ingredient that may feel toxic but can't be left out of the recipe entirely.

Of course, that little seed of wisdom isn't particularly useful: I'm no better at handling anger than the next guy. With the possible exception of jealousy, anger makes me more uncomfortable than any other human emotion, and, like my friend Bob, I usually go to great lengths to wall the feeling off. If someone infuriates me, it might take hours, maybe days, for me to even notice how angry I am. When rage does hit (or build up), my stock tools are deflection and indirection: I'll hiss at some stranger in the Star Market check-out line, or I'll slam doors in the privacy of my own home, or I'll engage in a bout of viscious, spiteful gossip. I'm much better at nursing grudges than I am at confronting people directly, and on the rare occasion when I do get really angry at someone, I get so violently uncomfortable that my whole body freaks out: I tremble, my voice shakes, I usually (gag) start to cry.

The trick, I think, is to pick your battles, to gauge the relative costs of expression and repression, for the costs can be high on both sides. A week or so ago, a friend asked me to walk her dog, a favor that sounds benign enough but actually infuriated me. Her reasons for asking annoyed me: her partner had the flu, which meant that she'd had to walk the dog twice the day before; she was also busy writing a paper for school, so taking the dog out twice for a second day felt unduly burdensome. I stood there while she told me this, and I thought: Wait a minute; I walk my dog twice a day *every* day, and I'm *always* on deadline, and this request feels both ludicrous and insulting to me. But instead of telling her to suck it up and walk her own dog, *I* sucked it up: picked the animal up at 6:30 a.m., dutifully trotted her around Fresh Pond, delivered her back to her owners, and walked around for the rest of the week feeling put-upon, taken advantage of, and—well, angry.

Should I have expressed that anger? Gotten my back up when she first made the request, and spared myself a week of private grumbing? As is often the case when I get pissed off, I'm really not sure. Expressing the feelings would have come with price tags, too, some obvious (she might have gotten angry at me in return) and some subtle (for good or ill, I might have compromised my well-honed image as helpful and accommodating). It seemed easier, in the end, not to ruffle any feathers, to indulge instead in a relatively short-lived bout of self-righteous indignation.

In more primary relationships, the costs and benefits seem a little clearer, although not necessarily any easier to act on. I think of how many times I've squelched anger at friends or family members, filed anger-provoking incidents away in a compartment in my heart labeled long-standing resentments. I think about the way those resentments fester inside, how they subtly infect relationships with mistrust and vague ill-will. I think about my friend Bob, who secretly worries that blowing up directly at his brother would detonate the relationship entirely but whose silence has eroded the bond in a quieter but no less devastating way. Unaddressed and unaired, his wounds have merely been sealed off but not healed.

Which is not to say that blowing up always works, that it inevitably leads to resolution or healing: sometimes getting really pissed off can make a bad situation worse, and I suppose it's important to pick your targets, as well as your battles: who can tolerate your rage and who can't? Who's willing and able to engage in a psychic brawl with you and who's not? Getting irate tends not to work—to be productive or beneficial to anyone—unless it involves two people who fundamentally trust each other, and who have a strong enough investment in the relationship to weather the painful patches. Oddly enough, the flip side of anger is often intimacy, which is probably what makes expressing it both so scary and, at times, so valuable.

So as creepy as the feeling is, I cast my vote for anger, for heated exchanges and tears and the gnashing of teeth. I might not be any good at it, but I believe it's a craft worth practicing.

Now, get off my back.

BOSTON PHOENIX
FEBRUARY 1999

THE FEMININE CRITIQUE

MY FRIEND JANE won't wear skirts because they expose her "bowling-champion calves."A colleague of hers says she can't wear shirts with collars because they make her "head and face look huge." Me, I have to pay special attention to the way I fix my hair in the morning: if it lacks the requisite amount of volume and falls too flat, I will be forced to leave the house with "seal head."

What is it with women and physical imperfections? Why must we exaggerate them so, blow them up into such epic proportions? Enormous rear ends, legs like tree trunks, noses described in such gargantuan terms you'd think we were talking about members of a different species. Necks, knees, shoulders, stomachs, thighs, eyes: no body part is too small or too insignificant to escape the feminine critique, and when we find a perceived imperfection, we hone in on it with our specially tailored girl microscope and magnify it straight off the charts.

"I hate the way my nose looks in photographs. It looks like a penis." The sister of a friend of mine said these exact words.

Excuse me? A penis? When women look at themselves, is there no sense of proportion?

No, there isn't.

I grew up believing that I had an absolutely enormous nose: a *huge* nose, practically as big as my whole head. I had bangs for a long time as a kid, and part of me always wanted to grow them down to my upper lip, so that they'd act as a built-in nose-shield, but I figured the nose would just poke through the fringe and make its size even more obvious. *Do* I have a huge nose? Not really: as noses go, it's fairly ordinary, possibly tending toward large. But no matter: when I was a kid, my brother and sister used to taunt me by telling me I had a big nose and that piece of information got lodged in my soul. Huge nose. Biggest nose you ever saw. It took nearly two decades and god knows how many therapeutic hours for me to even begin to see my nose in anything approaching realistic terms.

"I'm that way about my chin," my friend Susan says. "*Hate* my chin. Wish I could chop it off." She raises the offending chin so I can inspect it, turns her head to the right, then to the left. I see nothing: just a chin. "You can't see it?" Susan is certain I am lying. She juts the chin closer in my direction. "See? It's totally crooked. When I smile, it gets this little crook at the bottom. See it? Like a little flap?"

I am sorry: I see no little crook, no little flap, nothing wrong with it at all. But Susan is having none of this. "It's *hideous*," she says, her tone so final and unyielding I can say nothing more. Case closed.

Two pieces of female anatomy end up under that pesky girl microscope more than any others, of course: enormous butts and horrible hair.

"My butt looks huge." "I have a huge butt." "Does my butt look enormous in these jeans?" "I hate my butt." If I had a dollar for every time I heard those exact sentences, I'd never have to work another day. And hair? Well. Hair pouffs, and it frizzes, and it flips, and it juts out in any number of undesirable directions, and if it isn't up there misbehaving, it just hangs there like a limp rag. "I spend so much energy worrying about what my hair is doing it's a wonder I get any work done, ever." This from my friend Kate, who's never actually had a hair out of place her whole life. Kate also hails from the school of the Traveling Physical Imperfection: she isn't plagued by a lone anatomical enemy, like a penis-shaped nose or a crooked, flapping chin, but a series of smaller ones which crop up at odd times and preoccupy her on a rotating basis. "It's my legs one day, my rear end the next," she says. Then a pause. "But hair is more or less a constant." She sounds sad, saying that, but also resigned.

Of course, the fact that women are obsessed with their butts and their hair is hardly news, but what surprises me is the degree to which we denigrate these and other body parts, the utter conviction that what others may see as a tiny flaw, if at all, is in fact a physiological monstrosity, an abberation, a virtual mutation. *Bowling-champion calves?* Excuse me, but where does this come from?

I could take this opportunity to rant about the tyranny of fashion, about how media images of women undermine our collective self-esteem by offering up such consistently skewed and unattainable images of beauty. But I won't. I actually think that the way women describe their physical flaws is funny—in a ha-ha way, not an odd way—and, more to the point, I actually think it serves an important purpose.

When you listen carefully, it's not hard to see that we exaggerate our flaws in much the same way the media exaggerates perfection—we use potent words, like "hideous" and "loathesome," which are the direct opposite of words you read in fashion magazines, like "fabulous"and "lush." We also laugh: when I asked my friend Karen to describe her worst physical feature, she said, "Oh, definitely my upper arm flab. There's so much of it I sometimes think it could knock someone over in a high wind," and we both cracked up. I think we exaggerate in order to remind ourselves and each other, however unconsciously, how absurd all this attention to detail really is, how ridiculous our obsessions with appearance can be, and, at heart, how useless the ideals of beauty really are.

This isn't to say the feelings we harbor about our physical flaws, whether real or perceived, aren't genuine or that they don't hurt—believe me, it's no picnic to walk around as a 12-year-old convinced that you have a nose the size of an elephant's trunk. I also think the exaggeration can speak to deeper sources of pain: on days when I'm hyperconscious of my hair or my skin or my weight, I understand that the discomfort is really a more complex phenomenon, that it has to do with feeling unattractive (unworthy, flawed, bad) internally and not externally, and that I'm engaged in that particularly female wish, to make things right from the outside in. The logic: if only the hair or the skin were flawless, then the rest of me would be, too.

But exaggerating helps with this, too. By blowing our flaws out of proportion, we're able to defuse them a bit, to laugh both at ourselves and at the whole deeply exhausting cult of beauty.

I had coffee with my friend Karen recently, she of the dangerous upper arms. “How’s that flab?” I asked her.

She looked out the window, up at the sky. “Well, the air is calm,” she said. “No high winds. I think I’m safe today.” And we both giggled.

Boston Phoenix
October 1996

BARBIE DOES DEATH

REAL FANTASIES OF REAL GIRLS

June—wedding season—is in full swing, which means that the lifelong fantasies of countless young women are about to be realized.

Or does it?

The big walk down the aisle—white dress, flowing train, pretty bridesmaids all in a row—is allegedly something a girl starts dreaming about as soon as she's old enough to dream. The bridal industry certainly supports that sentiment (bridal mags are littered with words and phrases like "enchanted" and "fit for a princess"); so do popular portrayals of brides on TV (as Monica wailed to Ross on the season finale of "Friends," explaining his fianceé's perfectionism, "She's been dreaming about this day since she was *five years old*!"). Boys dream about heroism and strength (grand slams in the World Series); girls dream about beauty and romance (weddings). It's that simple.

For some of us, it may well be that simple. If women didn't harbor wedding fantasies, childhood or current, Mattel would stop selling bridal Barbies, the word "registration" would remain limited to the worlds of academe and vehicular transport, and no one would show up at the annual claw-and-scratch fest known as the Filene's bridal gown sale. But fantasy, as any good Freudian will tell you, is a complex phenomenon, and I suspect a good portion of that white-gown imagery has more to do with cultural fantasies about women (as virginal, family-oriented, limited in ambition) than it does with the hopes and fears a lot of us actually harbored in our younger days. Me, I never dreamed about the Big Event as a kid; can't remember entertaining the notion once. In an (admittedly unscientific) poll of 15 women friends and acquaintances, the wedding fantasy was shared by a scant two.

This may be generational: we came of age at a time when girls were just beginning to learn that they had options, that there were many possible doors open to them besides the one marked M for Matrimony. But the scarcity of wedding dreams may also say something about the nature of fantasy, too: about how doggedly our little psyches (at least some of them) were resisting that virginal image of women; about how far beyond the realm of beauty and romance our imaginations could take us.

The women I know fantasized about physical strength, intellectual prowess, escape. My unofficial poll turned up three would-be cowgirls; four superhero/crime-fighters; one Indian scout; three Olympic athletes; and five rock-and-roll singers. Janet, a painter who "never, ever" fantasized about the altar, dreamed about being a mathematician, vividly. In the fantasy, she'd wear a white lab coat and big tortoise-shell glasses, and she'd walk around holding a piece of chalk, and periodically she'd stop and write something imponderable on a blackboard, then stand back and study it. Barbie does math.

Pierce the soul of most well-behaved, good little girls and, nine times out of 10, you get a well-behaved, angry little girl who's been taught that it's unacceptable to express rage. And, of course, you get angry fantasies. Some women Dr. Freud might like to have lunch with:

A Murderous Fantasy, from Ellen, 35: "I recall a long period when I fantasized that my mother was trying to do away with me, and I also plotted elaborate fantasies about doing away with her, with the housekeeper, with my brothers."

A Murderous Fantasy with a Martyred Twist, from Hope, 38: "I had a lot of war fantasies, in which the Vietnam war extends to the U.S. and I'm the only one who manages to survive. Or Charles Manson breaks into our house and I somehow manage to crawl (stabbed and bloody) to get help to save my family (and then, of course, I die)."

An Apocolyptic Fantasy with a Martyred Twist, from Jan, 29: "I had a lot of nuclear war fantasies: the whole family in the basement, the bomb coming, me surprising everyone by being brave and stoic—giving my ration of food to my little sister, making moving speeches that make everyone rapt. And then, of course, I die first and the last thing I see is everyone huddled around me in a circle, weeping."

So Barbie does math, murder, and mayhem. These are women after my own heart. In my own version of the intellectual fantasy, I'd jet off to Stockholm to pick up my Nobel Prize, then return to glory (Barbie does Sweden); in my version of the death-and-martyrdom fantasy, I'd be dying of a terminal illness, lying bravely in my hospital bed surrounded by teary-eyed visitors, bestowing forgiveness on all the people who'd wronged me (Barbie does cancer).

A generation of morbid little girls with Zoloft in their futures? Not entirely. The most common theme (shared even among the murderous/apocalyptic set) involved moments of connection: the dream evening, in which some embodiment of male perfection (who tended to emerge as either a nameless, faceless lover or Paul McCartney) realizes how utterly unique you are, confesses his love, tells you he can't live without you, et cetera. Sexuality ranked high on the list, too, with six reports of time spent behind a closed bedroom door globbing on makeup, gazing into the mirror, putting socks in shirts for breasts, fantasizing about desire and desirability.

I don't mean to suggest that all girls who grow up dreaming about their wedding days end up in one camp, fixated on beauty and romance, while girls who don't give a hoot about the altar end up in another, fixated on sex and gore. No one holds to a single dream, and even the most die-hard romantic usually has a more complex and ambitious side. "I wanted both," says a onetime wanna-be bride named Annie. "I wanted the fairy-tale wedding with the horse-drawn carriage and after the ceremony I wanted to jet off to a remote village in Africa and save some exotic tribe."

What's interesting to me is the gap between the culturally supported fantasy and the real ones, the fact that so many dark and complicated threads are actually woven in with all that white organza. Whether common or twisted, the real-girl dreams we harbored are much richer than the bridal-girl variety; they're also much truer to the actual female experience. They are images of what we wanted for ourselves (to be strong, smart, and beautiful) and images of what we were (confused about our families, our anger and sexuality, our sense of the world as an unsafe place). They're about hidden ambitions and about longing for connection and the seeds of depression. They're about growing up female.

Granted, this is a lot of generalizing based on 15 opinions, but it seems to me it's time to do away with the wedding fantasy. Says Ellen, who along with plotting her family's demise entertained elaborate rock-and-roll fantasies: "Those wedding fantasies are nothing but elaborate stories where people are putting themselves at the center of a pageant, to be elevated in some faux-royalty event, and to think some girls might have these at the age of five sounds to me very sick indeed. Imagine having a mind that would build up that elaborate 'look at me, worship me' pageant. Ugh. Ick."

I agree. There is something rather dated and exhibitionistic about the wedding fantasy, and there's something rather sad about pinpointing that one day, early in a woman's life, as the peak experience of one's existence. So I say let's deep-six it. If there are any little girls in your life, do her a favor: buy her a toy guitar and a tiny set of amps. Equip her with a little white lab coat. Build her a teensy bomb shelter. Barbie does the real world.

BOSTON PHOENIX
JUNE 1998

BICEPS CHANGED MY LIFE

BEHOLD THE HUMAN arm, a limb of inherent beauty and paradox. Long, lean lines of bone—the ulna, the humerus—contrast with gentle swells of bicep and shoulder; grace of length contrasts with power of musculature; the motions of the arm are varied and fluid and contradictory: It can bend, stretch, flex, recoil, wave, lift, hug, power a punch. It can also tell a story.

My arms tell a story about transformation and victory, about the way internal shifts are sometimes made manifest on the human form. They are strong arms: I am a relatively petite person—five-foot four, light and small of frame—but I have been known to whop men in arm-wrestling contests, which pleases me deeply. Once, I actually bench-pressed my own weight, which made me feel Amazonian. A friend refers to me, only half in jest, as "La Brutita," The Little Brute. In the grand scheme of things, these may not sound like major triumphs, but they are to me. My arms embody a way of being in the world, a hard-won confidence and autonomy that's as personal as it is physcial. They are the one part of my body in which I have come to delight unequivocally.

Of course, that in itself is a statement of triumph, a woman's relationship with her body (and mine, historically, with my own) so often one of storm and battle and merciless self-scrutiny. Fifteen years ago, I didn't know a bicep from a tricep, I'd never even heard of lats, and my sense of physical self—arms included—was almost pathologically negative. Actually, it *was* pathologically negative. In my early 20s, I was young, confused, scared, and angry, and I did what a lot of young, confused, scared, and angry young women do, which was to develop an eating disorder—anorexia, in my case. This is an unfortunately effective technique, at least temporarily: feelings get whittled away along with flesh; the need to control something—anything—gets channeled into starving; the ability to deny appetite, to transcend the most elemental need for nourishment, provides a very seductive illusion of power. At my lowest weight—83 pounds—I was a waif, fragile as a wren, a mere line-drawing of a woman, but some deluded part of me felt supremely powerful and strong-willed, and I remember quite clearly how this twisted logic was reflected in my view of my arms. At night, I'd often lie in bed, one arm stretched out in front of me. I'd regard the limb—a skeletal appendage, veins visible beneath the skin, each bone distinct and pronounced, even the tiny finger bones—and the sight would fill me with dark pleasure, a perverse sensation of mastery.

That feeling, of course, was disembodied and false—it had to do with the shape of my body, not the state of my soul, and it was rooted in self-hatred rather than self-acceptance—and ultimately, the scrap of pride it gave me was about as sustaining as a saltine. And so, after much desperation and lots of therapy and many fits and starts, I began to eat again, and to crawl toward a more livable relationship with my own flesh and bones.

My arms were key to that effort, and I mean that quite literally. In 1985, I spent an exhilarating autumn on the Charles River, in Cambridge, Massachusetts, learning to scull. This is no small feat: maneuvering a single shell is like trying to stay upright on a giant knitting needle—a typical boat is 26 feet long and less than a foot wide; balance is either assisted or impeded by the oars, which measure about nine feet each. As sports go, it's like aquatic tightrope walking, requiring both enormous precision and guts, and I was terrible at it for years—flailed, teetered, nearly flipped the boat on every outing. But from the start, I was also determined to master the craft. The aesthetic beauty of rowing—the symmetry, the steady woosh of water against hull, the marriage of strength and grace—had captured me utterly, and I wandered around that first season like a teenager giddy with love, aware that I'd found something to master besides the shape of my own body, something that would transform me.

Which it did. I rowed and rowed. I rowed on stormy days and calm days, I struggled and hacked my way up and down the river. I developed patience, and then (more slowly) I developed confidence, and then (finally) I developed a bit of skill.

And along the way, I developed arms, strong and capable ones. Over time, my forearms grew firm and sinewy. My upper arms became toned, then defined. My shoulders grew round and strong. Rowing is actually considered a leg sport—a lot of the power of the stroke comes from the large muscles of thigh and butt—but the changes in my upper body were more visible to me, and in many ways more important, each sign of physical strength both correlating to and fueling a new sensation of internal strength. That first summer, I'd steal into the ladies' room at work and secretly flex my biceps in front of the mirror. Muscles! What a concept! The little thrill this gave me was utterly distinct from the thrill I'd once felt at my own emaciation, as different as self-care is from self-destruction, as giving is from withholding.

Like a lot of women, I've undertaken most of my efforts at physical transformation in the service of beauty and slenderness. Bad perms to make my straight hair wave, lotions and potions to smooth the complexion, stultifying exercise regimens (jogging, step aerobics) for weight control. Even anorexia, in its paradoxical and twisted way, owes some of its existence to this effort: it's a perversion of the ideals of beauty that surround us, a grotesque exaggeration that both capitulates to and protests against the mandate that women take up only a tiny bit of space in the world.

But my arms, strong and muscular, have been exempt from this paradigm, blessedly immune. This may be true for many women, arms offering a bit more wiggle room on the self-acceptance front than most of the female body. No one goes running to the plastic surgeon for tricep implants; you don't hear many of us standing around in locker rooms bemoaning our unsightly forearms or wailing about our elbows. Arms (at least so far) are among our least heavily scrutinized body parts, and also our least sexualized, which makes them a bit easier to love than, say, the hips or upper thighs.

But there's more at work here than simple relief from imagery. I got on the water early this morning, headed up the river under a cool and brilliant late-August sky, and lost myself in the rhythm of the boat, the sparkle of sun against the river's surface, the feel of blades moving through water. I felt strong and competent, the body doing what I'd taught it to do, and as I rowed along, I thought about arms, and about the relationship between power and beauty, and about the extent to which this sport has helped me reverse the standard equations about female shape and form. Most of the time, my arms are hidden from view, cloaked under sweaters or long sleeves; I don't show them off, or feel a need to. Instead, the satisfaction I take in them is entirely personal, which makes it particularly meaningful. Aesthetic pleasure that comes not from external imperatives about shape but from a passion and a set of skills; beauty from the inside out. This, I believe, is a definition of liberation; arms like wings.

DECEMBER 2000

THE MERRY RECLUSE

Solitude, Shyness, Loneliness

TIME ALONE

NAVIGATING THE LINE BETWEEN SOLITUDE AND ISOLATION

THE WHISPER BEGINS sometime around week two, maybe three.

First it observes: *You've been spending an awful lot of time alone lately, haven't you?*

Then it comments: *Kind of a relief, isn't it? Makes you feel pretty protected, pretty secure.*

Finally, it seduces: *More*, it says. *Let's prolong this soft, solitary state. The world out there is scary and full of risk, so let's stay in here, all alone, where it's safe.*

This is the voice of isolation, compelling and insidious.

I hear it a lot.

The phone rings. I hesitate before answering. Ugh, I think. It takes too much energy to talk to people. Let the machine get it.

A dinner engagement looms, a week away. I plot and scheme, even if part of me wants to go. What to do? Feign an illness? Claim unexpected house guests? How can I get out of this?

Another solitary evening stretches ahead, no social plans. I waver on the prospect, relief mixed with a vague sense of oppression. Can I bear another night of seclusion? Should I call a friend, make a plan? Four times out of five—four *nights* out of five—the voice of isolation wins: easier to stay in. Lonely, perhaps, but safer, much safer.

We tend to think of isolation as a product of geography and circumstance. The lonely widow, husband gone and children grown: she is isolated. The elderly and the infirm, physically unable to get out into the world: they are isolated. But isolation can also be, and often is, a state of mind, a need for retreat that dictates choices. I fall into it the way you fall into an abyss: a dark, involuntary tumble that gathers momentum, becomes nearly impossible to arrest. I choose to be alone and then, when I've made that choice 10 or 15 or 20 times in a row, I find I have no other choice.

Not long ago, an old friend came into town and, over coffee at my house, started using words like "luxury" and "relief" to describe my circumstances. I live alone, in a house where I have chosen every piece of furniture, hung every painting, placed every knicknack exactly where I want it. She looked about: what a luxury! She peered into my small, tidy office, where I work alone: no room in there for anyone but me, no one pulling on my sleeve during the workday, no one interrupting, dragging me into meetings or conferences. What a relief! This friend is married, employed full-time, mother of two young children; she literally cannot recall the last time she got to spend a night alone. Me, I can barely recall the last time I *couldn't* spend a night alone. "All that time to yourself," she mused. "What a pleasure it must be."

Well, yes and no. There *is* pleasure in the degree of solitude I enjoy. There is luxury and relief and there is enormous freedom. But I also know that she is confusing time out with time alone, time to rest with time to fill, solitude with isolation. The differences are vast. My friend sees an endless stream of serenity and calm, as though I spend my nonworking hours padding about the house with a smile on my face, baking bread, taking endless bubble baths. Me, I see something a little more worrisome, certainly more difficult: I spend this much time alone not because I always or necessarily enjoy it, but because I seem to *require* it.

Isolation—the impulse to isolate—is about fear and self-protection; it's about creating a cocoon, a place so seductively comfortable it becomes difficult to leave. It is not, strictly speaking, about solitude, although access to solitary time certainly comes in handy. But I can be isolated—can *feel* isolated—in a roomful of 25 people, at a party, in the middle of a week that's peppered with social obligations. The sensation has to do with flight, with distance, with a compulsion to erect barriers and hide behind them, lest others see how fearful I am beneath the surface, or how troubled. *Get me out of here.* That's the feeling. *I am uncomfortable. I need to be alone.*

Isolation is also insidious, in the same way depression is. It's a state of mind that creeps up like a weed, grabs hold of you and won't let go. You're alone for a time, simply solitary . . . and then you're isolated; you're contented . . . and then lonely; you believe you're in charge . . . and then you're stuck. The line between solitude and isolation is very fine and elusive, difficult to see because it exists in the mind.

My friend Grace is a solitary person who used to be isolated: this is to say that she spends a great deal of time alone but does so out of choice and out of a deep understanding of her own needs, rather than out of fear. Five years ago, 10 years ago, she hid in her home. She had friends, but most of her friendships were frenzied and complicated, and they left her feeling enervated, compromised, misunderstood. She'd meet this one for dinner, or that one, and then she'd come home and shut the door behind her with relief, her suspicions confirmed: Too hard! Too enraging, or disappointing, or wearying! So much easier to be alone! So she isolated: rarely answered her phone; accepted invitations only rarely and always with dread; pared down her world. And she worried: "I'd sit there on a Friday night, eating my nice chicken dinner and my salad and watching TV, and I'd think, 'Is this a life? Is this what I'm going to be doing for the next 40 years?'"

Today, at 46, Grace still spends a lot of Friday nights eating chicken dinners and watching TV but the worries have abated, largely because the fears that drove her into seclusion, the sense of being thin-skinned and unprotected, have eased as well. Grace has better, richer friendships than she once did. She has work that interests and sustains her. Thanks to a good therapist, she has a much higher degree of self-awareness, a clearer sense that she both requires and enjoys time alone, a better ability to make that time feel rewarding instead of empty. That's the difference between solitude and isolation: solitude is calm and serene, isolation is fearful; you bask in the one, wallow in the other.

And yet the differences are not always clear or neatly delineated; nor are the two states mutually exclusive. Solitude, as I experience it, is a slippery slope, a state that feels comforting at first but can metamorphose, often without warning or consciousness, into something far darker.

Not long ago, a bright Sunday in late July, I drove out to a piece of conservation land about 30 minutes away from where I live and went running with the dog, just the two of us. I'd been alone a lot over the preceding few weeks, the few humans I see with some regularity having gone on vacation or away on business simultaneously, and I was aware of a shift in my outlook, aware that the buildup of too many hours and days and activities spent in solitude were having a vaguely corrosive effect on my soul, making me a little nuts. That's how it tends to happen: you spend a little time alone—a few nights in a row, or a few uninterrupted workdays—and for a while you feel okay, comfortable and self-sufficient. And then something changes, an odd self-consciousness creeps in. You find yourself thinking in full sentences: Here I am, making dinner alone. Here I am, brushing my teeth alone. The solitary home begins to feel like a prison instead of a sanctuary; the idea of a social life begins to feel foreign and confusing, as though it's something you've simply forgotten how to do.

Solitude is like a protective older brother or an old and dear friend, someone you know well enough to share silence with. Solitude soothes, whispers pleasant messages: *Sit down, relax, take a little break from the fray; you deserve it.* Isolation is more like solitude's evil twin, or an abusive relative who arrives unannounced and starts berating you: *You can't handle it out there. You're ill-equipped, inferior,* different. *No wonder you spend so much time alone.* Or worse, it starts starts telling you lies, that seductive whisper: *You know,* it says, *you don't really* need *other people in your life. You're perfectly fine on your own.* This is the voice of fear disguised as self-sufficiency, the impulse to isolate masking as independence. Deep inside, I harbor the same anxieties that once so overwhelmed my friend Grace: a sense that the world out there is frightening and full of risk; a conviction that people will disappoint or hurt if I let them get too close; a deep aversion to vulnerability. These are very human fears, and very powerful ones, and when I spend too much time alone, their voices become louder and more resonant. *Stay alone. Stay inside, where it's safe.* These are the voices that lead me to turn down dinner invitations, that keep me from picking up the phone to call my friends, that trigger a slow downward spiral: solitude becomes loneliness; loneliness becomes despondency; despondency becomes inertia and despair. I look up; I am isolated.

I thought about this a lot as I was running: how quickly solitude can turn to isolation, how quickly that soothing sense of self-sufficiency can be replaced by the sense of estrangement, and how difficult it is to get back into the world once you've stepped away from it, as though you've entered some alien orbit and can't quite propel yourself back into the normal, human one. Solitude is about cultivating peace and quiet; isolation is about yielding to fear, and the more you yield to fear, the tighter its grip on you becomes. Spend too much time without people and the simplest social activities—meeting someone for coffee, going out to dinner—begin to seem monumental and scary and exhausting, the interpersonal equivalent of trying to swim to France.

So you retreat further, and you start to rationalize, to convince yourself you're perfectly fine on your own. Running along that day, I thought: *See? Here I am, bounding through the woods with my dog. A good and healthy activity, evidence of my happy self-reliance.* We ran and ran, endorphin city. Then we went for a leisurely stroll, wandered over to a pond. I threw sticks for the dog, smiled at her while she swam. Mood lifted, light returned. Heading back to my car, I thought: *I can do this. I can spend all this time alone and enjoy it.* And then I looked down at my hand and realized that somewhere along the line I'd lost my keys. This is what happens to me when I stray too far from the human orbit: my perspective gets skewed; I find myself feeling disoriented, wacked out, in my own way. I'd been holding my keys in my hand while I ran and in that state of zoned-out stupidity, that creeping despondency, I'd simply dropped them—car key, house keys, all my keys. There was no one to help me find them; I couldn't think of a single person who had an extra set; there I was, alone.

This image stuck with me for days: the joy of solitude and the despair of isolation.

In *The Last Gift of Time*, a collection of essays on life beyond the age of 60, writer Carolyn Heilbrun describes an ideal, which she has worked hard to realize in her own life: it is a state "with ample private space but with steady companionship." To Heilbrun, private space comes in the form of a small country house, companionship from family and a small corps of close friends. But reading her work, one senses that this combination—privacy tempered by camaraderie—extends beyond the physical and tangible, that cultivating it has been a largely emotional undertaking. Understanding that she needed that small country house and then finding it; finding, too, a sympathetic husband, and a close circle of friends, and work that engages both heart and soul—these are monumental undertakings, often lifelong searches, and Heilbrun was well into her 60s before she attained the right balance, the right blend of time alone and time among others.

Finding that blend is a deeply personal matter. How much time alone is enough? How much is too much? When does a state of safety and self-protection become a state of self-limitation? When, for you, does solitary bliss begin to sour, to mutate into isolated despair? Does it take a day? Ten days? A month? And when the impulse to shut the world out hits, what are the real motives? Are you taking time to heal or to hide?

I began yielding in earnest to the impulse to isolate about two years after I quit drinking, at a time when the emotions I'd so long blunted with alcohol—fears, old hurts and disappointments, feelings of sadness so old and inchoate I could barely identify their sources—returned in full force. It is no surprise to me that I began to hunker down in response, that the voices of isolation began to beckon so seductively. But I often come up confused about whether indulging the impulse is healthy or self-destructive. Is it okay to hide for a time, to ensconse myself in this safe space night after night? Or should I throw myself into the social world with more vigor? Is it possible to live a stunted social life without stunting other kinds of growth?

Being alone in all its varied forms—living alone, being single, spending time apart from one's spouse or family or friends—is a skill that requires practice. Solitude is hard work—it requires an impetus for self-care, an ability to soothe and amuse yourself. Cultivating a social life is hard work, too—it requires risk, an openness to vulnerability. It took Carolyn Hielbrun 60 years to master those twin arts. In her mid-40s, my friend Grace is getting there. After living alone for 20 years, she's able to hit a blend between privacy and companionship more often than not. Me, I've just begun the search.

New Woman Magazine
1997

SPEAKING OUT FOR SHYNESS

SO MY NEIGHBORS think I'm a bitch, snooty and cold. Two years ago, at a neighborhood pot-luck supper, they stood around in the host's patio, right behind my house, and talked about what a snob I was. *She never talks to anyone*, they said. *She acts so superior*.

I didn't hear any of this directly, of course, because I wasn't there. When the invitation arrived ("Come on over! Have fun! Get to know your neighbors!"), I told the organizers I had plans that night (a family thing, can't get out of it, so sorry), and then, on the night in question, I parked my car around the block, stole back to my house, and hid in the living room: lights out, curtains drawn tight.

A year or so later, I became friendly with the woman who lives next door to me, and she told me about the unflattering party chat.

I was aghast.

"They think I'm a snob? Superior? Can't they tell I'm just shy?"

She shrugged. "I guess a lot of people just don't get that. They read shyness as something else."

She paused, then added, "I think shy people are pretty confusing."

This conversation stuck with me for many months, plagued me like a mild but persistent itch. I have been shy my entire tongue-tied, self-conscious life. As a kid, my heart would pound every time a teacher called on me and I had to speak in front of the class. As a teenager, the mere presence of an attractive boy would obliterate my voice, send me into a state of mute terror; authority figures—college professors, therapists, my dad—could miniaturize me in a flash, simply by making eye contact. Today, I've outgrown—or at least learned to hide—some of the more obvious symptoms of shyness (the dry mouth, the sweaty palms), but I haven't outgrown the central feelings. Put me in a new social situation, ask me to walk into a cocktail party full of strangers, call on me to make a speech, and my first, most visceral reaction can be summed up in a word: ACK! The internal audiotape clicks on at high volume (*too scary; you won't have anything to say; people will judge you harshly*); the internal video shows me looking stiff and uncomfortable, an awkward grin plastered on my face; the gut impulse is to flee: find a way out, make up an excuse, park the car around the block and hide in the living room.

I'm hardly alone in this. In fact, if experts on the subject are correct, I have more and more company. The insulating, sometimes isolating effects of technology have created something of a safe haven for shy people, allowing us to avoid direct contact with colleagues, sales clerks, bank tellers, even friends. Conversational skills be damned—we can connect via Internet, e-mail, and ATM instead. And (not surprisingly) we seem to feel shyer as a result. In the last two decades, the number of people who describe themselves as chronically shy has increased from 40 percent of the general population to 50 percent. According to Philip Zimbardo, one of the nation's leading researchers on shyness, most of us (55 percent) report that we've considered ourselves to be shy at some point in our lives, or that we become shy in specific sitations (romantic and authority figures top the list of shyness-inducers); a scant 5 percent of Americans say they've never been shy at all.

The majority of shy folk tend to be like me—naturally inhibited, prone to imagining the worst when faced with new social situations, highly self-conscious—but increasing numbers appear to live on the extreme end of the shy scale. National surveys indicate that social phobia—shyness so pervasive and intractible it interferes with ordinary daily functioning—afflicts one out of every eight Americans at some point in their lives, making it the third most common psychiatric condition.

For most of my life, I've lived with shyness the way I've lived with, say, my hair, which is straight and fine and always has been. I might wish I had a thick, curly mane but the hair gods gave me this stuff instead; likewise, I might wish I were a confident, gregarious extrovert, but the gods of personality (a team, it appears, composed of geneticists, brain chemists, and environmentalists) decided to make me quiet and shy. Fact of life, case closed.

On some not-quite-conscious level, I've also expected others to accept that fact, to understand my shyness as a central, immutable part of who I am. If I'm the quiet one at the dinner party, I expect friends to understand it—cut her some slack; she's shy. If I'm not terribly forthcoming or demonstrative in a new relationship with a friend or lover, I expect the other party not to take it personally—give her some time; she'll warm up. I suppose this is why that conversation with the woman next door haunted me so: for nearly 40 years, I've seen my shyness as something that really only affects *me*—I'm the one who's uncomfortable here, I'm the one struggling with self-consciousness and anxiety, the less shy have it easy and should give me a break. But her statement—that shy people are confusing—raised some rather tricky questions about affect; about the particular kind of power a shy person wields, however unknowingly; about how shyness is experienced not just by shy people themselves but also by the people (shy or not) around them.

The shy often speak in code. My mother was a profoundly reserved person, shy to the core, and yet she had a subtle kind of warmth that the important people in her life learned to recognize. Her expressions of love were never obvious or direct (she didn't hug or coo or say "I love you"); instead, they were manifest in the quietest gestures and cues: a glimmer of eye contact here, a cup of tea there, a tone of voice that could communicate profound concern or pride if your receptors were properly tuned to receive the message. An outsider watching us interact might have described my mother as cold, withholding, detached, but her style seemed entirely normal to me. When I got old enough to spend the night at friends' houses, I always felt astonished by how demonstrative other mothers seemed to be, how they'd tuck their kids in, rub their backs or stroke their hair. Such behavior struck me as alien, even undignified, and although that interpretation may say something about how low my own expectations for affection came to be, it also suggests that I learned to decode my mother early on, to read between the lines of her reserve and tease out the warmth.

It's quite possible—actually, it's quite likely—that my own shyness is an inherited condition, passed on from my mother to me as directly as a physical trait, like fair skin or good teeth. Shyness appears to be among the most persistent and durable aspects of human personality, one with deep (and largely intractable) physiological roots. Social anxiety appears to run in families; the first signs of it can be detected even before birth (infants with fast fetal heart rates tend to be whiny and fidgety as kids, predisposed to anxiety and inhibition as adults); and if you're born with a shy personality (what Harvard psychiatrist Jerome Kagan calls a "behaviorally inhibited" temperament), you'll probably lug it around with you your whole life. Kagan, the grandfather of research on shyness, studied children who were classified as either inhibited or uninhibited at two, then retested the same kids at age seven and ages 12 to 14; more than 75 percent of the children initially assessed as shy turned into cautious, serious, and quiet seven-year-olds; the same behavior patterns were evident in adolescence.

Kagan theorized that a part of the brain called the amygdala, which triggers physiological fear reactions, might be activated more easily in the behaviorally inhibited kids. Other researchers have singled out the right frontal lobe as responsible (that's the part of the brain that seems to be involved in controlling negative emotions; shy kids appear to have higher right frontal lobe activity than bold kids). More often than not these days, the neurotransmitters serotonin and dopamine are considered as culprits: the naturally inhibited appear to have lower levels of both, possibly because of a single gene—the so-called shy gene—that creates either elevated or depressed amounts.

If personality is a marriage of nature and nurture—a product of what we're born with and what we're born into—then I suspect I inherited more than my mother's shy physiology: I also picked up her style of coping with inhibition, her reliance on code, and the expectation that others would be both willing and able to decipher me the same way I deciphered her.

Consider the parents of boyfriends, a category that's always ranked high on my list of shy-provoking personalities, always pushed the major fear buttons (fear of being judged badly, fear of failing to fit in, fear of being deemed an inadequate partner). I've tended to compensate for my discomfort and silence by acting the way I did as a shy kid at family gatherings, by reaching into my bag of good-girl tricks and expecting to be seen accordingly: I might not say a word during dinner, but I'll set the table, I'll leap up and clear the dishes when the meal is over, I'll work that smiling-shyly, eager-to-please affect for all it's worth. *See how helpful I am? How good-hearted and eager to please?*

Astonishingly, this hasn't always worked. In fact, it's almost never worked. Parents of boyfriends have typically found me aloof, standoffish, inscrutable. After a long weekend at his parents' house, a three-day family gathering in which I struggled to compensate for my mute discomfort by making beds, cooking breakfast, even chopping wood, one ex-boyfriend confessed that his mother thought I was downright rude.

The trouble with shyness—for both the shy and the people they interact with—is that it doesn't exist in a vacuum; it's but one ingredient in the larger stew of human personality, one element that's blended with—and often masked by—other qualities, which is part of the reason it's confusing: shyness might feel like the dominant and most motivating personality trait to the shy person herself, but it's not always so evident to outsiders. My friend Grace, for example, is deeply shy but also very warm and inquisitive: she's what's known as a "shy extrovert," which means that while she may feel tentative and fearful in new social situations, she covers it extremely well by exuding friendliness, asking questions, maintaining lots of eye contact. She's developed a front, in other words, that puts people at ease. Another friend, Beth, who is sweet and delicate, has a more classically shy affect: she blushes when uncomfortable, turns her gaze downward, comes across as bashful but genuinely *nice*. My shyness manifests very differently. Shyness aside, I'm also an essentially composed person, which is to say I've learned how to *appear* poised even when I don't *feel* poised; I've learned to shut down the tongue-tied, shaking, quaking part of my shyness and hide behind a rather calm facade. But shyness and composure are a complicated marriage: together, they create a certain blankness of affect, a stiffness that's easy to read as detachment. My friend Sandy—very sensitive, very shy, but physically imposing and rather brusque in affect—is similarly misread: people tend to find her aloof and scary, which drives her crazy. "The shyness is so obvious to me—why this scary interpretation?"

Interpretation, of course, is the key here, the gateway to confusion. Hidden behind that cloak of reserve, the shy person becomes a blank screen upon whom others project whatever fears or biases or self-perceptions they themselves bring to connections. If the person you're with worries (as many of us do) about being liked, your self-consciousness can look a lot like disdain; if he or she worries about measuring up or being charming, your discomfort or reserve may come across as boredom. Shyness flings the door to misunderstanding wide open; as a shy friend sums it up, "Silence is a Rorschach."

I moved into my house four years ago, and for a long time I doubt anyone took much notice of me, let alone projected much of anything onto my affect: I came and went, made next to no noise, lived a perfectly invisible shy life. A *quiet girl,* the neighbors might have said, *keeps to herself.* My reputation as the resident snob didn't seem to emerge until that neighborhood party, which took place shortly after my second book, *Drinking: A Love Story,* was published. The book had done well, spent some time on best seller lists, generated a lot of ink, and neighbors would occasionally see me walk in and out of my house that summer tailed by camera crews, which I found hugely embarrassing. If I saw anyone watching, I'd kind of grimace and look away. Internally, the sensations were quite clear to me: profound discomfort in the face of that kind of attention, paralyzing shyness. Externally, I guess all that stiff, embarrassed grimacing was read quite differently: my reserve, which might have seemed unremarkable or easy to ignore pre-book, became a blank screen for feelings about notoriety, professional adequacy, success; I came across not as self-conscious or insecure but as snooty and cold. The big-shot author who thinks she's better than the rest of us, who won't even deign to come to our supper.

And yet, I can't say I blame them. Familiar though it may be, I'm not much better at reading shyness, or tolerating it, than the average non-shy Joe. At a party not long ago, I found myself trapped in a conversation with someone even shyer than I am, a young woman writhing with social discomfort. I'd ask her a question—what do you do? where do you live?—and she'd grope for an answer, spit it out in as few words as possible (*Um . . . I'm still in school*), then look down at the floor, twist her hair around one finger, wait. I found talking to her agonizing, in part because her distress was so deeply familiar but in part because of something more complicated, an odd feeling of irritation, even resentment. I'm no stranger to awkward silences—I know them, dread them, hate them—but I'm not accustomed to being the one charged with filling them. And filling silence—whether by making idle chitchat or truly connecting—takes effort. A part of me wanted to shake this young woman by the shoulders and say, *Come on; I know how hard this is, I'm shy, too, but you gotta help me out here.*

The cold truth is, shy people can be tough to be with: however unintentionally, they force the people around them to pick up all the social slack, do all the grunt work that precedes connection. What this young woman didn't yet understand—what I am just coming to understand—is that although her shyness makes her feel inert and powerless, she is in fact equipped with plenty of power: simply by being in the room, she has a capacity to elicit feeling in others; as invisible or frightened as she feels, she has an effect. She also has a set of choices: she can either speak or remain mute, let others know who she is or shut down, take up some of the slack or leave the social rope entirely in someone else's hands.

I don't want to be hard on shy people. Indeed, I sometimes wish we lived in a culture that recognized and valued the heightened sensitivity that often accompanies shyness, that didn't so persistently reward more gregarious and assertive sorts. Nor do I want to suggest that shy people simply pull themselves up by their bootstraps, make more of an effort, *get over it*. It's hard to be shy, hard to feel controlled and crippled by excessive self-consciousness ("chronic emotional constipation," as a friend not-so-delicately puts it). The shy are painfully aware of this, painfully aware of how many doors our shyness closes, how much harder it makes the simplest things: walking into a party, speaking up at a meeting at work.

But I also think shyness has something to teach us about personal responsibility, about how we affect the people around us. Over the past summer, I took to walking my dog at lunchtime past the home of a retired couple in my neighborhood, a pair of avid gardeners named Helen and Frank. I resolved, each time I went by, to say something friendly and sweet, to try to dilute my superior-snob image with a good, old-fashioned dose of neighborliness. I'd comment on their roses, ask them a question about their cats, force my way through the awkward moments, chat about the weather. When I returned from a week in New Hampshire at the end of the summer, I brought them a blueberry pie. Gradually, they warmed up to me.

Not long ago, Frank knocked on my door and invited me over to their house for dinner, and in the long moment it took me to respond, I contemplated this business of affect and effect, of personal power and choice. I thought: Here's a chance to do the right thing, to come out from my shy cave and make an effort with my neighbors. I weighed the prospect of small talk, which I dread, against the prospect of connection, which I covet. I thought about how governed I've always been by social anxiety, how limiting it is to live with fear, how hard it is to change.

I took a deep breath.

I heard myself say, "Why, I'd *love* to. So nice of you to ask!"

And then, after we'd sealed the date and time, I bid Frank goodbye and shut the door. I felt brave and confident, fully aware that I'd done the noble thing, that I'd cast a vote for risk and sociability instead of fear and solitude, and that on the day in question (remember: change is hard! biology is destiny!) I'd come down with a horrible, debilitating case of the flu.

I did just that, or pretended to (*something awful going around, just hit me out of the blue!*). But I was really, really sweet about it.

SALON, 1999

THE MERRY RECLUSE

SOLITUDE IN THE CULTURE OF "WE"

NINE FORTY-FIVE P.M. I am standing in my kitchen preparing my very favorite meal, a zesty blend of wheat flakes, Muslix, and raisins that comforts me deeply. It is a Thursday, which means that *ER* is on in 15 minutes, and it is mid-May—sweeps month—which means that I am filled with anticpation: yes, a new episode. I feel serene. I am wearing torn leggings, a T-shirt, a bathrobe. The dog is in the living room, curled contentedly (and wordlessly) on the sofa; the phone machine is blinking with several messages, which I've dutifully screened and have no intention of answering until tomorrow. And a thought comes to me, a simple statement of fact that arrives in a fully formed sentence. I hear the words:

I am the Merry Recluse.

This, I must say, is a magical, transformative moment; it represents a kaleidoscopic shift of sorts, the kind of sudden internal restructuring that occurs when an established set of facts about the self spontaneously seem to shift, presenting themselves in a new order, a surprising new light. An old thought becomes a new thought; a prior definition takes on a twist, a new edge, a new meaning.

Listen to it again. *I am the Merry Recluse.* Doesn't that sound chipper and grand? Had you asked me to sum up my sense of place in the world a day before—an hour before, 10 minutes before—I would have offered something very different: *I am a single woman,* I might have said. *Age 38, a bit of a loner.* My voice might have had an apologetic edge, as though I were acknowledging the sad and spinsterish associations behind such words, and I might have shrugged a bit sheepishly, as if to say: *Ooops, sorry, this is all an accident; I was supposed to be married by now, I know this*. But in that instant, poised above my bowl of Wheaties, the psychic kaleidoscope turned a notch, the apology blurred, something new shifted into view, something that looked very much (dare I even say it?) like happiness.

~

Happy and alone, you say? Reclusive and *merry*? How oxymoronic! *Pas possible!* Alas, the concept is lost on so many.

A friend, recently divorced but involved with someone new, asked me a question over dinner not long ago: "So," she said, her expression concerned. "How does it feel not to be in a relationship?" I tried to ignore her tone, which was vaguely pitying, and pretended to be kidding when I answered by pointing at the dog: "But I *am* in a relationship," I said. "I have her." She laughed, a rather halfhearted and dismissive laugh, then resumed the line of questioning: Wasn't I lonely? she wanted to know. Didn't I find it hard to be responsible for all the household details—the cooking, the shopping, the errands and bills? Don't I worry about the future, about growing old alone, about whether or not I'll find someone?

I sat there and mused for a moment. The questions are difficult to respond to, not because the answers are complex (which they are) but because we live in a culture that puts such a high premium on romantic intimacy, that uses partnership as a measure of mental health and social normalcy. Answer affirmatively (yes, I get lonely; yes, solitude can be very stressful and worrisome), and you sound sorrowful, the slightly pathetic outsider; answer negatively (nope, I'm quite content, thank you very much) and you sound hermetic, incapable of following the accepted path to human happiness, pathologically disengaged somehow. In fact, 25 percent of the adult population lives alone today—that's almost double the number that lived alone 35 years ago—and although plenty of us may end up on our own for unhappy reasons (divorce, fear, geography, any number of quirks of fate and timing and circumstance), it seems both simplistic and erroneous to assume that solitude is an inherently sorry state, something you simply wouldn't choose if you had a better option.

I said as much to my friend. "Sure there are downsides," I said, "but I really like being alone." I ticked off a little list: the freedom to set my own hours, make my own rules, indulge my own tastes; the relief at not having to interact or negotiate or compromise with another human unless I choose to; the little burst of accomplishment I peridocally feel at being the architect of my own space, physical and psycic. "It's a choice," I said, "a style I'm comfortable with."

She listened, nodded soberly; I could tell she didn't believe a word.

Exchanges like this wouldn't bug me if they weren't so common. I often walk my dog in the morning with a friend named Wendy who's been in a relationship for the last 19 years and whose social calendar is packed so tight it makes me dizzy: a constant stream of parties and pot-luck suppers, movie and theater outings, vacations and visitors from out of town. Every Friday she asks me what I'm doing over the weekend and every Friday I demur: "Oh, not much," or, "The usual: just hanging." The truth is, I rarely make weekend plans, at least not social ones. My recipe for bliss on a Friday night consists of a *New York Times* crossword puzzle and a new episode of *Homicide*; Saturdays and Sundays are oriented around walks in the woods with the dog, human companion in tow some of the time but not always. This doesn't mean I'm a misanthrope: I have a small, carefully cultivated social life—a handful of treasured friends; a beloved sister; people whose presence and support mean the world to me—but Wendy can't quite make the distinction between a quiet life and an empty one, and she finds my style unsettling. A look of veiled discomfort comes over her face when I hem and haw about the weekend, as though she envisions 48 hours of disconnection and sadness, so sometimes I make stuff up to placate her: I tell her there are dinner plans, movies scheduled, a shopping trip with a girlfriend, and she always responds with a little heave of maternal relief, which I find mildly patronizing. "Oh, how *nice* for you!"

Me, I walk along and feel quietly defensive, a recluse in the Land of We.

That's quite the loaded word, *we*.

Not long ago, in the locker room of my gym, I eavesdropped as a woman held forth about her upcoming wedding. We're thinking about a honeymoon in Hawaii, she said. We're registering at Bloomingdale's. We're buying a new car. We're doing A, B, and C. We, we, *we*. I stood there, and I thought about how infrequently I use plural pronouns to describe the events of my life, and I felt a familiar stab of inadequacy, questions about priorities and social worth scratching at the subconscious. On the broad spectrum of solitude, I lean toward the extreme end: I work alone, as well as live alone, so I can pass an entire day without uttering so much as a "hello" to another human being. Sometimes a day's conversation consists of only five words, uttered at the local Starbucks: "Large coffee with milk, please." I also work out alone, and I grocery shop alone and I cook and eat and watch TV alone, and if you don't count the dog (I do; many don't), I sleep alone at night and wake up alone every morning. Much of the time I don't question this state of affairs—it just is—but I listened to this woman in the gym, and I spun out a vivid fantasy about her life (the best friend at the next StairMaster, the colleagues at the office, the fiancé at home, the 200 friends and family members at the wedding reception, the children two or three years hence), and I felt like an alien, a member of some mutant species getting dressed in the locker room before crawling back to her dark, solitary cave.

Why don't I want that? That's what comes up. Why do I find the fantasy—husband, family, kids—exhausting instead of alluring? *Is* there something wrong with me? Do I have a life?

In fact, that woman at the gym, poised as she is at the matrimonial brink, is not necessarily headed for a more "normal" life than the one I lead. For the first time, there are as many single-person households in the U.S. as there are married couples with children—25 percent of the population in each camp—but moments like that I understand that cultural standards and expectations haven't quite caught up with the numbers. Census figures be damned: if you choose to be alone, you're destined to spend a certain amount of time wondering why.

I suppose the why, at least for me, is internal, temperamental, as deeply personal as sexuality. Like most women, I grew up expecting to marry someday, expecting to have a family, expecting to want babies. And like some women (and men), I've found that the years have passed and passed and passed and those things simply haven't happened, as though some deeper yearning simply failed to kick in. Lots of life decisions are made that way: choices are revealed by default, answers arrived at far more passively than we might expect. I look up today and realize, with some surprise, that I've spent the bulk of my adult life alone—15 of the last 18 years. For much of that time—indeed, until my merry little epiphany in the kitchen—I've tended to see my solitary status as a transient state, a product of circumstance instead of a matter of style. In fact, I suspect I've lived this way for a reason, that the degree of solitude I've chosen feeds me in some way, that the fit—me with me—is right.

Considered in that light, the "why"—why spend so much time alone?—becomes a more interesting question: why *not*? I've always been drawn to solitude, felt a kind of luxurious relief in its self-generated pace and rhythms. I eat breakfast pretty much 'round the clock—muffins in the morning, scones for lunch, cereal at night—which may be odd but is also oddly satisfying, if only because the choice is my own. I am master of my own clutter, king of the television remote, author of every detail, large and quirky: the passenger seat of my car, uninhabited by humans most of the time, will always be a disaster area, repository of cassette tapes and empty coffee cups and errant dog toys; my alarm clock will always blast National Public Radio at precisely 6:02; my ashtrays (smoking permitted here constantly) will always be blessedly full and stinky. Solitude is breeding ground for idiosyncrasy, and I relish that about it, the way it liberates whim.

Of course, living alone can make you psycho, too. I often feel deranged in the supermarket, hunting down grazable foodstuffs that don't come in family-size packages, wishing I could buy grapes in bags of 10 so that the other 80 don't rot in the refrigerator, wondering if the check-out clerk has noticed my apparent obsession with wheat flakes. The lack of backup can overwhelm the solitary dweller, especially when you're confronted with life's more fearsome tasks (decoding assembly instructions, killing spiders); the lack of distraction, which alters your core relationship to physical space, can make you think you're nuts. The other night, I caught myself talking to a spoon, which had twice fallen off the counter and clattered onto the tile. "Hey!" I said. "Stop doing that!" And then I stood there and shook my head, aware of that tiny persistent question, the low-level mosquito whine inside: *Is this normal? Is it?*

For me, the most pressing challenge involves negotiating the line between solitude and isolation, which can be very thin indeed. Social skills are like muscles, subject to atrophy, and I find I have to be as careful about maintaining human contact as I am about maintaining physical health: drop below a certain level of contact with other humans, and the simplest social activities—meeting someone for coffee, going out to dinner—begin to seem monumental and scary and exhausting, the interpersonal equivalent of trying to swim to France. Solitude is often most comforting, most sustaining, when it's enjoyed in relation to other humans; fail to strike the right balance and life gets a little surreal: you start dreaming about TV characters as though they were real people; houseflies start to feel companionable; minor occasions that others find perfectly ordinary (the arrival of a house guest, an event requiring anything dressier than sweatpants) start to feel bizarre and unfathomable.

And yet I'd be hard pressed to leave this little world, singular and self-constructed as it is. I have lived in the Land of We; at times, I have pounded on the door for admission, frantic with worry and need. When the friend at dinner asked me how it felt not to be in a relationship, I remembered all too clearly what it was like to feel despair at the state, to regard my own company as scary and inferior. When I see that look of discomfort come over my friend Wendy as I talk about my unplanned weekends, I remember how horrifying I once found the concept of unstructured time, how much difficulty I've had simply sitting still, giving my own emotions room to surface. And when I hear people pepper their speech with the word "we," like that woman in the gym, I remember a lot of painful years spent struggling to define myself in relation to other people, as though my own existence didn't count unless it were attached to someone else's.

That night in my kitchen, fixing my Kellogg's feast, revelling in the order and quiet of my own home, felt like a gift, a victory of sorts, an awareness that some of those struggles have receded further into the past. I am shy by nature, a person who's always found something burdensome about human interaction and who probably always will, at least to some degree. Accordingly, I have always felt a deep relief in solitude, but I've not always been able to *bask* in it, to sit alone in a room without getting edgy, to feel that comfort and solace and validation are available outside the paradigm of a romance, to believe that my own resources—my own company, my own choices—can power me through the dark corridors of solitude and into the brightness.

I took my cereal bowl into the living room, settled down in front of the TV, and I thought, so merrily: *I'm home.*

SALON, 1998

B KNAPP
Knapp, Caroline,
The merry recluse :a
life in essays /

FAIRBURN-HOBGOOD PALMER

Atlanta-Fulton Public Library